LIKE REAL PEOPLE DO

E. L. Massey is a human. Probably. She lives in Austin, Texas, with her partner, the best dog in the world (an unbiased assessment), and a frankly excessive collection of books. She spends her holidays climbing mountains and writing fan fiction, occasionally at the same time.

Also in the Breakaway series

Like You've Nothing Left to Prove

LIKE REAL PEOPLE DO

A NOVEL

E. L. MASSEY

PAN

First published 2022 by NineStar Press
First published in India 2025 by Pan
an imprint of Pan Macmillan Publishing India Private Limited
707 Kailash Building
26 K. G. Marg, New Delhi 110001
www.panmacmillan.co.in

Pan Macmillan, The Smithson, 6 Briset Street, Farringdon, London EC1M 5NR
Associated companies throughout the world
www.panmacmillan.com

ISBN 978-93-6113-735-8

Content Warning: Depictions and discussion of epileptic seizures and social anxiety disorder.

1 3 5 7 9 8 6 4 2

Typeset in EB Garamond by R. Ajith Kumar, New Delhi
Printed and bound in India by Replika Press Pvt. Ltd.

FSC www.fsc.org
MIX
Paper | Supporting responsible forestry
FSC™ C016779

To the fan fiction writers: Past, present, and future.

1

THERE ARE ADMITTEDLY WORSE things in the world than having to walk two blocks on a Wednesday morning in July.

Eli knows from experience there are worse things in the world.

Like being diagnosed with epilepsy at sixteen.

Like having heat-induced seizures and living in *Texas*.

Objectively, he knows there are worse things, but right at this moment, he can't think of many because it's 6:00 a.m., and he isn't allowed to have caffeine because they've changed his medication again, and he's had to park in the visitor's garage because the only *two* handicap spaces at the north entrance of the Houston Hell Hounds official practice facility had been occupied by *one* parallel-parked Land Rover decidedly lacking handicap tags.

"Motherfucking hockey players," Eli says to the empty sidewalk.

So now he's running late because it'd taken him an extra ten minutes to find the visitors' lot, and he'd still needed to stop and let his dog pee before they entered the complex. Because being the disabled kid whose service dog pees in the rink on the first day of practice will guarantee he never has a collegiate social life to speak of. Not that he holds out particularly high hopes for that anyway.

The security guard at the door barely glances at his newly printed student ID before waving him to the left with a tired, "Rink Three, end of the hallway on your right."

She looks like she could use some coffee too.

"Right. Thanks." Eli shifts his backpack, sparing a last hateful glance at the Land Rover outside.

"Hey, do you happen to know whose car that is out front? License plate AP23?"

She lifts one eyebrow. "You mean Alexander Price?"

Because of course. Of course it was *Alexander Price*. Eli tries to avoid too much familiarity with the hockey world, but there are some things you just know if you spend enough time around ice, and one of those things is the name of the youngest current captain in the NHL, who is apparently just as much of a douche off the ice as tabloids would suggest.

Eli takes a steadying breath. "You know where I could find him?"

The security guard considers Eli's expression, then the dog at his feet, then the ill-parked vehicle outside. "I take it you don't want an autograph?"

"No."

She gives him an apologetic smile. "I don't think I can have his car towed, but I can file a complaint if you'd like."

"That would be great, thanks."

He starts to move forward again before pausing. "Do you know if Jeff Cooper is back from IR?" he asks. He doesn't make a habit of following hockey, but when he's potentially in the same building as a gold-medal-winning, world-junior-figure-skater-turned-NHL-player, he'd like to know.

"Yeah. As of this week, he's cleared to skate no-contact in practices." She grins. "He also parks in the players' lot like he's supposed to."

Eli would expect nothing less.

"They're in practice for another hour and a half," she adds. "But sometimes Cooper does the meet and greet afterward."

"Really?"

"Yeah, Rink Two." She nods to the right hallway. "Price will be there, too, but he almost never comes out afterward."

"Shocking."

The doors open behind him and an entirely too-awake girl wearing a hijab that matches her leggings waves at them both and hands over her student ID.

"Morning," she says, careful not to run over Hawk's tail with her rolling skate bag. "Your dog is beautiful."

"Thanks," Eli says. "Are you a freshman too?"

Which is a stupid question because he knows the rest of the figure skating team isn't supposed to start practice for another week. Obviously, she's there for freshman orientation just like he is.

"Yeah!" she says, apparently immune to his idiocy. "I'm Morgan. Just moved in last night. Thank god for coffee, right? I'm so nervous I didn't sleep at all."

"Right," he agrees wryly. "I'm Eli."

She gets her ID back from the security guard, and they start down the left hallway together.

"It's so cool the Hell Hounds share their facilities with the university," she says. "Did you know their practices are open to the public? I think I might go try to get an autograph or two later if we have time."

"Yeah," he says. "I might join you."

Practice is good. It's not a real practice since it's the first day, but Eli meets the coach and trainers, learns all the other freshmen's names, promptly forgets them, signs a bunch of paperwork, and spends a few minutes going over his medical information with the team doctor. Hawk keeps an unobtrusive down/stay on the first row of bleachers and watches, bored, as they warm up, do some drills, and then call it a day. No one asks about the dog or the scars, and Eli doesn't volunteer any information. It's strange to have that option. He's used to everyone knowing everything about him. The accident. The diagnosis. The dog. Hell, half of his hometown donated money to the GoFundMe for his initial treatment and got weekly updates on his recovery. He can't decide if it's a relief or a new form of stress to be surrounded by people who don't already know his story. Everyone knowing your business is annoying, but it also means no one asks questions.

After practice, Eli accompanies Morgan and another girl, who he's pretty sure is also named Morgan, to catch the last few minutes of the Hell Hounds' practice.

There are surprisingly few people in the stands: a haggard looking mother with a pair of toddler boys, a small group of college-aged girls who are probably also students, and a pair of old men.

Eli sits with the Morgans on the bleachers closest to the ice behind the far goal and crosses his arms. Hawk is a solid press of warmth against his leg; the Morgans are talking quietly about some Russian player who was traded to the team the previous year; and, surrounded by a soft buzz of conversation and the noise of sticks on ice, he suddenly remembers how tired he is.

He jerks when the buzzer goes off and players start to leave the rink. Once the ice is cleared and the Zamboni comes out, Eli follows the Morgans into the hallway outside where, according to the other spectators, the players will emerge to ... he doesn't know. Bask in the adoration of their fans? Sign hats? Take awkward selfies?

The players start to trickle out fifteen minutes later, and the Morgans try and fail to contain their excitement over the appearance of a man who doesn't look much older than them but is probably a solid foot taller. They take several pictures apiece with him, and he handles it with grace, laughing softly at their enthusiasm, his accent lilting and indistinct. *Russian*, Eli thinks, and then startles because Jeff Cooper has just exited the locker room.

Eli does what any other self-respecting teenage fan would in this situation and promptly loses his cool entirely.

"Hey!" he says, too loudly. "Jeff Cooper!"

Cooper adjusts his course and walks over. "Hi," he says, and *Jesus*, the man is even prettier in person.

"Hi," Eli parrots.

"Your dog is beautiful," Cooper says.

"*You're* beautiful," Eli answers because, hey, go big or go home, right?

One of the Morgans makes a choking noise behind him.

Cooper grins. "You know I'm married, right?"

"And to all appearances tragically heterosexual, yes."

"Tragically," Cooper agrees solemnly.

"Don't worry; I'm not actually hitting on you. Though it is on my bucket list to go on a date with a hockey player if you're interested." Eli wiggles his eyebrows.

Cooper's grin widens. "Are you trying to play the pity card right now?"

"That depends. Is it working? I mean, you do Make-A-Wish shit, right?" Eli gestures to Hawk, trying to look as feeble as possible. "Think of it as philanthropy."

Cooper outright laughs, and Eli is about to ask for a picture and let the guy go, but before he has a chance to say anything else, the Morgans let out an aborted in-tandem shriek, and behind Cooper, a voice yells, "HEY COOPS, are you—oh my god, a *dog*."

Eli glances up to find none other than Alexander Price leaning around the locker room door. He trips over himself to join them, graceless in a way that's strange after seeing him on the ice.

"What's a dog doing here?" Price asks, beaming at Hawk and completely ignoring the minor tumult his appearance has caused. "Coops, why aren't you petting him; look at this beautiful—"

Cooper throws out an arm, blocking Price from going down to his knees. "Reading comprehension, Alex."

It takes him a minute.

"Oh. Service dog. My bad, bro," Price says to Hawk. "Didn't mean to distract you. Er—" He glances up at Eli. "—him? Shit. I'm sorry. I'm not supposed to talk to him, am I? I read something about this, but I can't remember."

"No, you're not supposed to talk to her. But you're self-correcting, at least. Which is better than most folks," Eli allows.

"I really am sorry," Price says, and the earnestness is disconcerting. "That must get super annoying."

"Very," Eli agrees.

Price is biting his lip now, looking genuinely upset in a way that almost makes Eli forget that he's a massive illegally parked douchebag.

Cooper drops one arm around Price's shoulders, pulling him in as if he has a secret to share, and says, "This one is trying to guilt me into going on a date with him." He nods conspiratorially toward Eli. "Apparently it's on his bucket list to go on a date with a hockey player."

"I think 'guilt' is a strong word," Eli says.

A tentative grin returns to Price's face. "Playing the pity card? Really?"

Eli shrugs. "Hey, chronic medical conditions come with a lot of suck; I might as well embrace the occasional perks."

"You realize Coops is married, right?" Price says. "And like—all about monogamy."

"Yes."

"Also tragically heterosexual," Cooper adds.

"That too," Eli agrees.

Price laughs, startled and real in a way that's enough to make Eli take another look at him. Price considers Eli as well, his mouth still tipped up at one side, eyebrows furrowed.

"I'm not married," he says.

Eli squints at the non sequitur. "Okay?"

"So does it have to be Coops, or will any hockey player do? Because I'm a hockey player. And I like food."

Eli is probably gaping unattractively at him. The Morgans are completely silent.

"I don't—you want to take me on a date?"

"Sure, why not? I mean—I'd hate for you to drop dead tomorrow without fulfilling your bucket-list wish."

"Jesus, Alex," Cooper mutters.

"You," Eli says. "Alexander Price. Want to take me on a pity date."

"I—yes?"

Cooper makes a long-suffering noise. "All right, I'm going to let you kids figure this out. I'll see you later, Pricey."

"Yeah," Price says distractedly. "See you tonight."

Eli and Price stare at each other for a moment, and Eli realizes the magazines and billboards must airbrush Price's freckles out, which is a shame because they're pretty damn cute. Especially when he wrinkles his nose at the awkward silence between them.

"You're serious," Eli says finally.

"Yeah, why wouldn't I be?"

"Because you're *Alexander fucking Price*?"

Price runs a hand through his damp hair, which does nothing to dissuade the cowlick right above his left eyebrow.

"Why does everyone say my name like that?"

"Sorry, I just—It was a joke. I wasn't actually expecting to—You're really serious?"

"Yes."

"You know I'm gay, right?"

Price glances down at the rainbow patch on Hawk's vest, then back up to the off-the-shoulder shirt Eli's wearing. "Yeah, I kinda figured."

"And that ... doesn't bother you?"

"What the fuck—don't look at me like I'm going to steal your lunch money. I'm not a homophobe."

Which ... Eli thinks there are some Tweets that would contradict that, but he decides not to bring them up.

"Do you trust Coops?" Price asks, bouncing from the balls of his feet to his heels. There's a little line between his eyebrows, and he looks upset again.

"Cooper? Uh, I guess?"

"COOPS," Price yells. "TELL HIM I'M NOT A HOMOPHOBE!"

Eli covers his face with his hands.

Cooper appears in the doorway of the locker room again, looking fond, but exasperated. "Pricey isn't a homophobe." He raises his voice so everyone who is now watching can hear. "Just an idiot. I promise. Can I go home now?"

Eli waves him away with one hand, the other still covering his face.

Price laughs, more self-deprecating than anything else. "Ok, I admittedly didn't think that through. I hope you're okay with getting turned into a GIF because that's definitely ending up online."

"Oh god," Eli mutters.

"So. Lunch? I'm kinda starving."

"You want to go *now*?"

"Yes? Unless—I mean we could go some other time if you don't—Does it need to be a fancy dinner?"

"No! No, lunch now is fine. It's fine."

"Great. Do you have everything you need?"

"No." Eli jabs his thumb in the general direction of the other rink. "I left my stuff in the locker room."

"I'll grab my bag and meet you there. Rink Three, right?"

"Right," Eli says faintly.

Price flashes him a grin and disappears around the corner, at which point the Morgans converge upon him.

"That was Alexander Price," Morgan #1 says. "Alexander Price is taking you to lunch."

"What the hell," Morgan #2 says. "How is this your life?"

"I don't even know," Eli says.

Price meets him outside the locker room fifteen minutes later wearing mirrored sunglasses, a snapback, and a backpack that, combined, probably cost more than Eli's skates.

"Gotta say I'm a little insulted you thought I'd be a dick about the gay thing, but Coops got immediate trust," Price says, walking back toward the facility entrance. "I mean, Coops and I are in the same You Can Play video."

Eli resists the urge to roll his eyes. "Well, yeah, but you're the captain. I figured you had to. Everybody knows Cooper has a charity fund just for LGBTQ youth and was, like, completely extra for pride night last year."

"Okay, yeah, that's valid. But still. I'm a little hurt."

Eli can tell it's meant to be joking, but the words come out a little too honest.

"I'm not a dick," Price continues. "And if you—The thing on Twitter was a misunderstanding." He makes an annoyed noise in the back of his throat. "The point is, I'm not a dick," he repeats like it's important Eli believe him. "I promise."

"Right," Eli says, and then, because he's petty, "So the Land Rover parked across both handicap spaces outside ... "

Price stops in the middle of the hallway. "Oh, shit. I'm so sorry. I was running late, and no one ever parks there this early, which—That's not an excuse. I still shouldn't have done it. All right, I'm definitely a dick." He starts walking again, shoulders hunched. "I am. I'm such a dick."

"Just not a homophobic dick?" Eli says gently.

"Right."

They fall quiet as they pass the front desk, and the security guard watches them with unrestrained curiosity.

"I won't do it again," Price says, fishing his keys out of his pocket. "Swear to god. And I'll make a donation to—I dunno—something for disabled kids. As an apology. And buy you dessert after lunch."

"Jesus, Price," Eli says. "You weren't going to include dessert with lunch before? You have a 1.5 million-dollar annual salary. What kind of cheap date bullshit is that?"

Price gives him a soft, thankful smile.

"I would have. But now I'm taking you to the best frozen yogurt place in Houston. It's a secret. I haven't even taken Coops there."

"Well," Eli says, trying to ignore the facial expression of the eavesdropping security guard. "That sounds like a reasonable apology. Where are we going for lunch? I'll go get my car and meet you there."

"Oh, I thought we'd just take mine. Do you—is there something you need in yours?"

Eli looks pointedly at Hawk. "No, but I come with an eighty-pound fur factory with sharp nails, and you drive a car worth more than 100K."

"Pretty sure she can't do any more damage than Bells. Granted, Bells is only, like, six pounds. But she's full of fury and has a religious opposition to leather seats, apparently."

"I—Bells?" Eli asks, feeling a little lost.

Price frowns at him. "My cat."

"You have a cat?"

"Uh. Yes? Isobel Price? Like the Isobel Cup? She has her own Instagram. With over a million followers."

He seems genuinely insulted that Eli doesn't know this.

"Oh. Cool. What kind of cat?"

Price brightens. "She's a mix? I got her from the shelter, but I have pictures," he says. "You can look at them in the car. Come on; your dog—What's her name?"

"Hawk."

"Hawk can chill in the back seat. Let's go; I'm starving."

Eli allows Price to hold the door for him, laughing a little at the still-baffled security guard as he unclips Hawk's leash and tells her to get into the back seat. Moments later, Eli finds himself sitting in the passenger seat of Alex Price's car, scrolling through an album of cat pictures on Alex Price's phone while Alex Price drives them to lunch.

What even.

2

ELI DIDN'T HAVE A chance to cultivate an expectation of what lunch with a professional NHL player would be like.

He's pretty sure this isn't it though.

Price drives them to a storefront with an obscene amount of tie-dye and a sign font that is a little too close to Comic Sans for comfort. It's called The Pretty Bird Café, and Eli honestly isn't sure if this is supposed to be a joke or not. "Okay," Price says, seeing Eli's expression. "I know it looks a little wild, but this place makes the best salads in Houston, and I'm assuming your nutritionist gets just as excited about protein-fiber ratios as mine."

This is admittedly true.

"The best salads," Eli repeats, squinting at the café. There's *so much* tie-dye.

"I promise."

Price takes his silence as acquiescence and hops out of the car. He jogs over to open the passenger door before Eli can reach for it.

Price also holds open the cafe door, prompting all two dozen of the bells mounted above it to ring.

They choose a spot by the window, and once Hawk is tucked neatly under the table, Price hands him a menu.

"Just a heads up, some of the other guys come here for lunch pretty often too. So if Rushy or Kuzy or whoever shows up, feel free to ignore them."

"Rushy and Kuzy?"

Eli knew hockey players were all about the nicknames, but honestly.

"Oh, uh. Evan Rushmore and Dmitri Kuznetsov?"

Eli purses his lips. "I have no idea who those people are."

Price pauses in the middle of unwrapping his silverware from a paper napkin. "But you were at practice. You"—he gestures with his newly liberated fork—"have your whole hockey-player-bucket-list thing."

"I have a confession to make," Eli says.

Price brightens. "Oh, I love those. Hit me."

"It's not on my bucket list to go on a date with a hockey player. For the most part, I actively avoid hockey players."

"What? Why?"

"Self-preservation?"

Price looks lost.

Eli sighs. "Dude. I'm a gay mixed-race figure skater. I grew up in small-town Alabama. And I was stupid enough to come out when I was fourteen. I figured out pretty quick it was safest to avoid all sports teams. Granted, football was a more pressing everyday concern, but running into the hockey players at my home rink was never a particularly fun experience either."

"Oh." Price looks a little blindsided. A little hurt. Genuine in a way that surprises Eli. "Right," Price says. "That really sucks."

He takes a breath as if he's going to say something else, but a waitress skates over—on *actual roller skates*—to deliver water and take their order.

"Usual?" she asks Price.

"Yes, please," he says.

She tries to hand Eli a menu, but he waves her away.

"I'll have whatever he's having."

She nods and glides off.

"So," Price says, taking a sip of his water. "If you try to avoid hockey players, why were you at practice? And flirting with Coops?"

"Oh my god, I wasn't flirting with him. It was a joke. And he's not a hockey player—"

Price raises a disbelieving eyebrow.

"Okay, yes, asshole, he is *now*," Eli says. "But I grew up watching him figure skate. When I was ten, I memorized his entire gold-medal-winning world-junior routine. I could never do it clean, obviously, but still. I was so disappointed when he quit to focus on hockey in high school."

"He's a great hockey player," Price says. "The Hell Hounds are lucky to have him."

"Oh. No, I know. I have so much respect for him as an athlete. I just—" Eli runs a finger through the condensation on his glass. "His routines were really, really, beautiful."

Price chews on his bottom lip for a moment, thoughtful. "He still has figure skates. Sometimes he gets ice time on off-days and plays around a little. I caught him a few months back, and he let me watch for a while."

"I would literally kill a man to see that."

"Kill a man?" Price asks. "Really?"

"I mean—probably not a nice man. A shitty man?"

Price laughs as if Eli is joking. "I could ask him," he says. "Maybe. He probably wouldn't mind you watching as long as you didn't Snapchat it or something."

Eli doesn't get a chance to respond, which is probably good because, in the moment, he likely would have embarrassed himself.

"Incoming," Price says, sitting up a little straighter. "Sorry. Hazard of hanging out with me."

Eli doesn't understand at first until he notices two teenage girls making their way toward their table. Price thinks they're coming to ask for his autograph, but Eli doesn't think that's the case because he's intimately familiar with the look on the first girl's face.

"Hi," she says, glancing back and forth between them. "Can we pet your dog?"

Eli takes a moment to enjoy Price's perplexed expression. "Sorry," he says to the girls, trying not to laugh. "She's a service dog, and she's working, so you can't pet her. Thanks for asking though."

"Oh," the second girl says, ducking a little to look at Hawk under the table. "My bad, we couldn't see her vest from over there. Tell her she's doing a good job!"

"Will do."

The girls link arms and return to their table. Price still looks baffled.

"You're kind of used to being the center of attention, huh?" Eli says.

"I don't—does that happen to you all the time?"

"Sorry," Eli parrots. "Hazard of hanging out with me."

"Oh my god. Shut up. I can't help it if my face is on billboards all over this stupid city. I'm used to people recognizing me."

Eli grins. "I'll bet you five dollars that by the end of lunch more people will come to talk to me about Hawk than to get your autograph."

Price extends a hand. "I'll take that bet."

They shake. Slowly.

Price's hand is surprisingly large, considering he's on the small side for a hockey player.

Eli tries not to dwell on it.

He also tries not to dwell on the fact that one of Price's incisors is crooked, overlapping the tooth next to it, and for some reason, Eli finds this devastatingly cute.

"So, I'm assuming you're a student at HU?" Price asks.

"Freshman. Just moved in yesterday."

"Nice. Have you met your roommate yet? Rushy went to Boston for two years, and all he has is horror stories."

"No roommate. They gave me a single because of Hawk."

"Oh. That's ... cool?"

"I guess. I'm definitely glad I'll have my own space. But the whole forced socialization thing might have been handy."

Price tips his head to one side, bottom lip still tucked beneath his teeth. "Why? You don't seem shy."

This is suddenly not a conversation Eli wants to be having.

"No. But I'm from a small town. My closest current relationships are the result of forced long-term cohabitation." He circles his index finger around the rim of his glass. "I don't exactly know how to make friends."

"Oh. Yeah, I get that."

Eli finds that hard to believe. Price can probably tell.

Price bunches the paper wrapper for his straw between his thumb and forefinger, inhaling slowly, purposefully, the way Eli's therapist makes him breathe when they're talking about Serious Things that require Mindfulness. Eli wonders if Price has a therapist.

"I didn't have time to make friends as a kid," Price says, "since everything was all about hockey. So I only ever hung out with the kids on my teams, and I was so much better than most of them that they didn't really want to be my friends—and even if they *did*, it wasn't because they liked me; it was because they wanted to like, endear themselves to me so I'd pass to them more. And now ... I think my teammates are my friends? I mean, I know some of them are. But I'm also their captain, so—And all of them are older than me, and some are married and have kids and stuff, so."

Despite the confluence of sentence fragments, Eli does, actually, understand. "That sucks."

The words seem woefully trite.

"Sometimes, yeah."

They're both looking intently at their water glasses, and Eli is considering escaping to the bathroom for a minute because there are clearly some Emotions™ happening here, but then a little kid waves wildly through the window at them and, a moment later, comes crashing through the door.

His father, a bit more sedate, catches the jangling door behind him, looking resigned.

"Are you Alexander Price?" the kid asks, eyes wide.

Price laughs. "Yeah, buddy."

"See, Dad. I told you!"

"Sorry," the dad says. "There wasn't any catching him after he recognized you."

"No problem. You want an autograph?"

Price smirks at Eli. Eli rolls his eyes.

"Yes, please. Can you—Dad, do you still have my—?"

The dad pulls a small, relatively battered Hell Hounds hat from the backpack on his shoulder.

The kid grabs it and shoves it across the table toward Price. "I already got Kuznetsov to sign it. See? So you can sign next to him."

He points to a spiky Cyrillic signature, and Price obligingly signs his name beside it with a Sharpie he apparently produced from thin air.

Is that a thing? Eli wonders. Do celebrities just carry around Sharpies in their pockets? He feels like that would definitely be a laundry hazard. Then again, Alexander Price can probably afford to buy a new pair of jeans every few weeks.

The father thanks them, the boy immediately puts the hat on his head, and the waitress returns with two massive salads, loaded with chicken and avocado, as the pair return to the sidewalk outside.

Price shoves a forkful into his mouth immediately, making noises that are a little risqué.

"So," he says, mouth full and not at all endearing, "back to the whole making friends thing. I've heard there's a really great way to do that."

"Oh? Please. Share your wisdom."

"Hockey," he says solemnly.

"I'm not joining a hockey team."

"No! I mean hockey games. I could get you some tickets. And you could, like, invite some people on your floor in the dorm. Or, maybe those girls you were with this morning? They seemed cool."

"Oh. That's nice but, I'm not sure it's a good idea."

Price's face falls. "Too loud for Hawk?"

"No, I'm just not really a fan of crowds. Or places where I don't have an easy exit."

"Oh. Well, I could put you in a private box. You'd be farther from the ice but no crowds and a door right to the hallway. Would that work?"

Eli watches as Price shoves another too-big bite of food in his mouth.

"You're offering me and a bunch of hypothetical friends seats in a private box to try to help me build a social life?"

"Yes?"

"I think you're taking the philanthropy aspect of this outing a little too far."

"I'm not—"

"Hi!" a woman interrupts, waving long, manicured fingers at them. "Can I take a picture of your dog? He looks just like my Charlie. German Shepherds are just the best, aren't they?"

Price gives Eli a bewildered look.

Eli resists the urge to laugh. "Yeah, German Shepherds are the best. You can take a picture, sure. But don't distract her, please, she's working."

The woman makes an "ok" sign, winking, and drops onto her knees to get a better angle with her phone. Eli focuses on his salad and not how he now has a perfect view down the front of the woman's very low-cut shirt. When Eli glances at Price, he's surprised to find he is doing the same. When Price meets his eyes, Eli nods meaningfully toward the woman and holds up two fingers. He points to Price, mimes an autograph, and folds down one finger. Two to one. Eli is winning.

Price subtly flips him off.

When conversation resumes, they focus mostly on lighter topics: Houston, the new Hell Hounds facilities, cats—particularly Bells—and their mutual affection for the avocado.

The salad is, Eli has to admit, pretty damn good. And the frozen yogurt place they go to next is even better. It's tiny, tucked between neon-signed shops in a quieter part of town. Self-serve. A buffet bar of toppings. Colorful. Clean. It's entirely empty when they arrive.

"After-school rush won't hit for another hour," Price says as they sit down with their selections—Cake Batter with banana slices for Price, Vanilla topped with strawberries for Eli.

"We'll have to make sure to leave by 2:00 if we don't want to get mobbed," Price continues. "It already turns into a madhouse around then, but add in a professional NHL player and a dog—"

He doesn't have to finish.

Eli nods. "That's cool. I need to be back on campus for a meeting with my RA by three anyway. I've got to give him the down-low on me and Hawk for emergencies and stuff."

Price gestures with his spoon toward Hawk. "So am I allowed to ask about what you use her for, or is that not PC?"

Eli purses his lips and tries to be flippant. "My medical history is more of a third date conversation."

"Oh? Why's that?"

"Because. No one sticks around after that conversation, and I like to live in glorious denial for a short period beforehand."

It comes out more self-deprecating than he intended. Price looks thoughtful. "Does this count as one or two?

"Pardon?"

"This. Frozen yogurt. I mean, technically, it's a second location but the same day. So is this one date or two?"

"One," Eli says firmly. "If it's happening within the same three-hour period."

"You're the expert," Price says, which he's really, really not, but okay.

"So two dates to go then?" he continues.

"What?"

"We've got a roadie coming up, but then we're home for almost two weeks, and it's preseason, so. When does your semester start?"

"You want to do this again?" Eli asks.

Price stops idly twirling his spoon. "You don't?"

He does, Eli realizes. He really does. Because he actually *likes*

Alexander fucking Price. "I do. I just figured—pity dates are usually pretty singular."

"Oh. Well, it wasn't really a pity date. I just thought you were interesting. Still do."

He says it so completely without artifice that Eli is briefly winded.

"Oh," he says. "Cool. I mean—Yeah. My semester doesn't start for another week and a half, so whenever you've got time."

Price unlocks his phone and slides it across the table. "Give me your number, and we'll figure it out once I get back."

Eli stares dumbly at the phone for a moment. He puts his name and number in on autopilot.

A few seconds after handing it back to Price, his own phone vibrates with a text message. It's a thumbs-up emoji followed by two cats, fireworks, and an eggplant. Because Alexander Price is a ridiculous human being.

And he now has Alexander Price's phone number. Cody isn't going to believe this.

3

ELIJAH RODRIGUEZ MET CODY Edward Griggs the week after he turned nine.

Eli had been accepted into a figure skating team based out of Huntsville, and he really, really, wanted to join, but the twice-a-week forty-minute drive to his current rink was already difficult for his parents to manage. Huntsville was an hour away and practices were three times a week.

Cody Griggs was the solution to this problem.

Well, not Cody in particular, but the fact that Cody was already on the team and lived ten minutes from Eli, and once the coach contacted Cody's mother, she was more than willing to drive Eli too.

Cody was also nine, and he was, Eli thought, *annoyingly* American. The sort of tanned big-eyed kid that modeled for Gap and grinned toothily while holding fish in *Visit Alabama* infomercials. He was about as stereotypically Southern as apple pie and the big truck his mama drove, and Eli wanted to hate him on principle, except he couldn't because Cody was smart and funny and stupidly, ridiculously kind. They became best friends immediately.

Cody was the first person he came out to, twelve years old and curled up in the attic bedroom at Cody's house; night two of a weekend sleepover, wide awake from too much sugar and a scary movie they weren't supposed to watch.

"I think I have a crush on Andrew Murphy," he'd whispered, apropos of nothing. "I can't stop thinking about kissing him, but I'm pretty sure if I tried, he'd punch me in the face."

"If he did, I'd punch him right back," Cody had said, as if Andrew didn't weigh two of him and would have to duck if Cody wanted to get anywhere near his face.

"He has a weird-looking nose though," Cody continued. "You could do better."

"I like his nose."

"Well. There's no accounting for taste, I guess."

Things had devolved into a hushed and then a not-so-hushed pillow fight, and it wasn't until several minutes later, after Cody's mother had yelled at them to quiet down, that Eli asked, low and a little breathless, "We're—you're not mad, right?"

"What? No."

It was hard to read his facial expression in the darkness, but Eli's skin flushed with nervous energy at how quiet Cody was being.

"You can't tell anyone though, okay? Not yet."

"Okay."

A sour knot of anxiety settled in his stomach as the silence stretched between them. Because he'd been so sure Cody would be kind and bury him in a barrage of comforting, encouraging words. Cody hadn't responded *badly*, but he was also acting very strange and—

"Are you going to tell your parents?" Cody asked twenty minutes later when Eli had nearly worked himself up to the point of tears.

"Eventually? Maybe in a couple years. I don't know."

"You think they'll be mad?"

Eli took a breath, tried to steady his voice. "Not real mad, I don't think. My cousin brought her girlfriend to Christmas, and everyone was nice. Awkward. But nice. She and Dad got along. She plays soccer for her university, and they bonded over how much American football sucks or whatever."

"That is nice," Cody said quietly, still so out of character that Eli didn't know what to do.

A full minute later, Cody said, barely loud enough for Eli to hear, "I don't know if my family would be okay with it."

Eli closed his eyes, swallowing hard. "I won't tell them, okay? Just keep it a secret and everything will be fine. Unless—if you don't want to be friends anymore—"

He couldn't finish the sentence, and Cody suddenly had his arms wrapped around Eli's neck. He didn't realize he was crying until Cody used the cuff of his pajama shirt to wipe at Eli's face, hushing him with the same warm, gentle words Eli had heard Cody's mother use a dozen times after bad dreams and cruel kids and hard falls on the ice.

"No, no, no," Cody whispered, a little frantically. "No, I didn't mean you, I meant *me*. I meant *my* family—I don't think—Well, Mama might but—I don't know if I can tell them about *me*."

"You?"

"Me."

"Oh."

And then they were both crying, and it was all incredibly dramatic and embarrassing in a way only twelve-year-olds could be.

When Eli came out publicly two years later, his mother had a long talk with Cody's mom, and while she was a little quiet with him for a few weeks, she never refused to drive him to the rink or let him spend the night, and things returned to normal within a few months. No one told Cody's dad, and Cody stayed in the closet. Or the kitchen, more literally. If he wasn't skating, he was cooking. And since neither of them understood the concept of hobbies for enjoyment rather than competition, Eli started cooking, too, first his Mamá's and Abuela's recipes, then recipes from books and internet searches. The paltry amount of free time he and Cody spent playing video games quickly transformed into arguments over the cooking channel. This didn't help their already lacking social standing at school, but they were happy enough, and Cody's mother was all too willing to encourage them. Cody's father didn't complain because cooking often turned into grilling—a suitably manly occupation—and because 90 percent of the time, whatever they made was *good*.

Freshman year of high school, Cody quit figure skating.

He wasn't a huge kid or anything, but he was muscular and had had a growth spurt that summer, which made the figure skating coaches despair. He loved the ice, though, and within a week, he joined a hockey team at the same Huntsville rink. Their practices were, conveniently, within a half hour of each other, so Eli still rode with the Griggs three times a week and, despite his general dislike of hockey players, Eli grudgingly attended Cody's games and cheered loudly when he made opposing players look like lumbering idiots. Cody kept growing, but he stayed fast, faster than anyone else on the ice, and he had soft hands and even better reflexes, and he was fearless and confident in a way that made people—important people—quickly take notice. By senior year of high school, Cody was captain, and NCAA teams were scouting him. None of the schools offering Cody scholarships had offered Eli one, though, so Eli committed to the Houston University figure team while Cody packed his bags (and his smelly hockey pads; Eli would *not* miss riding in the car with those) for Princeton.

Their last night together in the attic was nearly as emotionally fraught as the night when Eli came out. It culminated in a badly thought-out and equally badly executed kiss that ended, at least, in laughter rather than tears.

"Never again," Cody said somberly.

"God no," Eli agreed. "Don't get me wrong; I love you. But no. Definitely not. No offense."

"Yeah," Cody agreed, somewhat wistfully. "You're way too skinny. I like big guys."

"Big, huh?" Eli said lecherously.

Cody went abruptly pink, muttered something about *muscles, you ingrate*, and well, that was that.

It's been a full forty-eight hours since he's last seen Cody, and Eli is secure enough to admit he is going through withdrawals. He can't remember a time when they'd gone more than a day without seeing each other, and now there are nearly two thousand miles between them.

He's unpacking when Cody finally FaceTimes him.

"Buen día, corazón."

"Hola, cariño," Cody says, clearly tired but beaming at him like the veritable ray of sunshine that he is. "Are you in your dorm? How was your first day of practice?"

Hawk's ears perk up at the sound of his voice.

"Yeah. My day was completely ridiculous. You have no idea. But tell me about yours first. Did you meet your—" He grimaces, intentionally dramatic. "*—teammates.*"

Cody laughs. "Yeah. They're great."

Eli carries his laptop from his desk to the still-unmade bed and lies on his stomach. He nearly falls off the bed reaching for his takeout box of food. "Any of them hot?" he asks, opening his plastic packet of cutlery.

Cody groans. "Only *all* of them. It's terrible."

"You poor thing. What a trial."

"Listen. Hockey asses are a thing, and they are glorious. Except when you have to share a locker room with them."

Eli snorts at Cody's expression. "Are there any out guys on the team?"

Cody purses his lips. "I don't think so? I can't figure out if Haney and Pauls are together or just ... close bros."

"The rituals are intricate," Eli agrees.

"And then there's Muzz. He dresses like my cousin Archie—"

"Way too much denim and American flag paraphernalia?"

"That's the one, but he also gave the frosh guys a lecture on intersectional feminism at dinner, and I'm pretty sure he kissed our goalie on the mouth after practice, but I'm *definitely* sure the goalie isn't gay." He shrugs. "Time will tell, I guess."

"Are you still planning to come out?"

"I think I may wait a few weeks. To make sure."

Eli must admit this is probably wise. "More important question," he says seriously. "Haney, Pauls, and Muzz? What the hell is with hockey players and their nicknames?"

Cody flips him off. "Why was your day ridiculous?"

"Well. After practice this morning, I went to watch the end of the Hell Hounds practice."

Cody gasps in faux shock. "You? Voluntarily spending time in the same rink as NHL players?" He shakes his head. "Twenty-four hours away from home and college has already changed you."

Eli rolls his eyes. "Anyway. I met Jeff Cooper."

"*No.* Is he as beautiful close up as we always thought?"

"Better. But listen. I went out for lunch with Alexander Price."

Cody just stares at him, so motionless that Eli thinks, for a moment, the video connection has frozen.

"What the actual fuck, Eli."

"Yeah, that was pretty much my reaction too."

"I don't—I'm going to need you to start from the beginning."

Eli does.

"So," Cody says, twenty minutes and a not insignificant amount of yelling later, "you're telling me Alexander Price bought you lunch, then dessert, offered you an entire private box worth of NHL tickets to help you make friends, and you now have his phone number and plans to meet again once he's back in town?"

Cody's voice goes progressively thinner and higher the further he gets into the sentence.

"Uh. Yeah, that about covers it."

"Only you, Eli. Do you think he's gay?"

Eli coughs on a bite of chicken. "No. He's the straightest straight dude to ever straight. And, you know, a professional hockey player. There's no way he's interested in me."

"I'm sorry; do you need me to list all the things that happened again today, or—"

Eli groans, flopping sideways and out of frame. "I think he's just lonely? He seemed kind of unhappy and I don't think he has many friends. Everyone on his team is older than him. I think he liked just being able to hang out with someone who didn't have any expectations, you know? And who wasn't infatuated with him."

Cody sobers. "I guess that would be tough. Being a captain so young. He's only, what, a year or two older than us?"

"Barely. He's not even twenty yet."

Cody quirks one eyebrow. "You googled him when you got home, didn't you?"

"Maybe."

"Definitely."

"Enough. Tell me more about your team."

Cody launches into a detailed breakdown of all the people he'd met that day, lingering for a while on the cheekbones of a defensemen and the piercing, dark eyes of their goalie.

"He was pretty weird with me," Cody says. "Or maybe he's just the strong, silent type with everyone. The intimidation factor was kinda offset by how hot he looks while brooding though. I dunno. I guess I've never known a normal goalie."

Cody goes all pensive for a moment, and Eli rests his cheek on his pillow, tipping the laptop screen so he stays in frame.

"Are you going to swoon?" Eli asks. "Should I leave you alone for a minute?"

"Says the boy who counted Alexander Price's freckles today."

"Fuck you. I didn't count his freckles. I just said I noticed them."

"Uh-huh." Cody yawns, and Eli glances at the clock, keeping in mind the time difference.

"You should go to bed," he says. "I'll call you tomorrow though, okay?"

"Okay. Goodnight, Elijah."

"Night, Cody."

He closes his laptop and gently redirects Hawk's nose, which is poking hopefully at his takeout box.

He hugs her for a moment, which she submits to with grace, and then reaches for his phone.

There are several message notifications—one from his mom, just checking in, and then nearly a dozen ... from Alexander Price.

Hey I'm at dinner with Coops, the first one says and then, in quick succession:

hes got private ice time at the igloo after free skate tonite 9-10.

mite bring his fig skates if u wanna join.

I'll b there too

this is Alex btw

Price

I can pick u up?

unless ur busy

just let me know

sorry for all the messages

"What the fuck," Eli whispers to Hawk.

He doesn't know how to respond.

YES seems a little too exuberant. Backspace.

Dude, yes

Backspace.

I might have time, let me check

Backspace.

He settles on, *Bro, seriously? That would be awesome!*

Alex responds with a thumbs-up emoji less than a minute later.

The typing ellipsis pops up, disappears, pops up again, and then:

Text me your address, I'll pick you up at 8:30.

Coops says bring your skates.

Eli rolls onto his back and stares at the splotchy particleboard ceiling, phone against his chest.

"What the fuck," he whispers again, a little more fervently.

Then he screencaps the entire conversation and sends it to Cody before lunging to his feet because he still hasn't unpacked the majority of his clothes, and he has less than two hours to figure out what the hell he's going to wear.

4

JEFF COOPER DOESN'T USUALLY feel particularly old. Twenty-three is still young for a hockey player, and he's only had one significant injury so far in his career. He knows guys in their thirties who take muscle relaxers like candy and do a series of convoluted stretches in order to hobble out of bed in the mornings, who visit the PT floor every day after practice and complain about their joints when it rains. Jeff can still stay up until 3:00 am, drink too much with the Russians, and recover in time for practice.

He's not old, okay?

But he's also been with the Houston Hell Hounds for less than a year, and already a good portion of the team, even those older than him, have started calling him "Mom." Because apparently, monitoring his budget, caring about personal hygiene, and checking the goddamn weather before he leaves the house makes him geriatric.

There's also Alex Price.

Jeff doesn't have any kids. He only just got married, and that was terrifying enough. He doesn't plan to procreate any time in the near future. But since the day eighteen-year-old NHL Captain Alexander Price called him to welcome him to the Hell Hounds—more soft-spoken and awkward than he ever expected—Jeff has had a deep and abiding affection for the kid. The kind that makes him want to fight people twice his size who so much as look at Alex funny. The kind that has resulted in Alex falling asleep on him everywhere from the team bus to airline seats to his own couch, where his wife stifles laughter over his internal struggle over whether it would be weird to pet Pricey's hair. Which—it's nice hair, okay? And the poor kid has a half-dozen cowlicks that make him look like a startled sunflower most of the time. It's adorable.

Jeff had a brief sexuality crisis shortly after these feelings started to manifest until he realized he didn't want to have sex with Alex, he just wanted to *protect* him. Which does not, in fact, make any sense. Regardless, Jeff loves Alex in the same way he anticipates he'll love his own children someday, and the fact that Alex is only four years younger than him doesn't really negate that.

So, no, Jeff doesn't usually feel old. But when he's sitting at the monstrosity of a kitchen island in Alex's ridiculous ultramodern penthouse apartment, drinking beer he brought with him and refuses to share—*there are laws for a reason, Alex, no*—while Alex quietly freaks out about whether he's texted a cute boy too many times, Jeff feels suddenly ancient.

"Should I apologize for all the messages, or does that make it worse because it's another message?" Alex murmurs, thumbing distractedly at his phone. "Oh god. What if he's an English major and he hates chat-speak? Why didn't I ask what his major was? That's such an obvious question. He's probably an English major. I should have typed everything out and used commas and shit."

"Alex—"

"He's probably just getting dinner, right? And left his phone in his dorm?"

"It's been less than ten minutes," Jeff says slowly, debating a brief abeyance of the no-alcohol rule; the kid could probably use a drink. "Don't start worrying until it's been ... an hour."

"Right. You're right. I'm being stupid."

Alex paces over to the couch where Bells is watching him with slitted eyes.

Bells and Jeff have an uneasy truce, which is better than most of the Hell Hounds can say. She doesn't tolerate most people other than Alex, but with Jeff, at least, she doesn't actively try to claw the shit out of his shins. Rushy is not so lucky.

"You said lunch went well," Jeff reminds him. "And he gave you his phone number. He wouldn't have done that if he didn't like you."

"I guess. But. Maybe he felt pressured? He hasn't had the best experience with hockey players, and he already thinks I'm a giant ableist douche bag. Which, to be fair, I kind of am? I just—didn't realize it."

"Ableist?"

Alex gestures vaguely toward his laptop. "I watched some YouTube videos when I got home."

"There are plenty of guys out there," Jeff says awkwardly. "Even if you never see him again, it's not as if it's the end of the world."

"That's not—" Alex sighs, finishing his circuit of the couch and returning to the island. "I don't want to date him. I mean—I would if I wasn't a fucking closeted neurotic NHL player. But I've never had any gay friends before. Well, except—but that wasn't really—"

He lets his head thunk down onto the granite counter, and Jeff gives up and shoves a beer toward him because, honestly, he is so out of his depth here.

"Don't get me wrong," Alex says. "You're great. And it's a huge relief to have someone on the team who knows. But I can't talk to you about, you know—" He raises his eyebrows. "—stuff. That I could with someone else who was into dudes. Or, at least, I'm pretty sure you wouldn't want me to."

"Oh god. No. You're right. I understand. Please don't talk to me about 'stuff.'"

Alex smirks a little. "Besides, I just—really like him. He's funny and sarcastic as hell. And he isn't a fan, but it doesn't seem like he hates me either."

Alex nearly drops his phone when it vibrates.

"Well?" Jeff asks because, dammit, he's invested now.

"He said yes! I should offer to pick him up, right?" Alex types something, then mutters about punctuation and backspaces, starting again.

A moment later, he says, "Yeah, there we go," and he finally palms the beer Jeff had proffered to him and takes a long drink.

"Jesus. No wonder I don't have any friends. This is stressful."

Jeff considers being affronted.

"Tell him to bring his skates," he says instead.

Alex frowns at him. "Why wouldn't he? We're going to the rink."

"We're professional hockey players, and it's my private rink time. From what you've told me, he probably thinks the invitation is just to watch."

"Oh. Right."

Alex sends another message and returns to the beer.

"I'm kind of bad at this, huh?" he says.

"Little bit," Jeff agrees.

Jeff Cooper met Alexander Price for the first time on the ice as an opponent. The Hell Hounds won 3–2 in overtime despite a dozen penalties, and Alex nearly took out Jeff's goalie making the game-winning shot. The second, third, fourth, and fifth time Jeff shared ice with Alex weren't much better.

And then Jeff was traded.

Jeff knew about as much as any other player in the league about Alexander Price: painfully young, cocky, first in the draft, soft hands, fast as hell, and the embodiment of dirty hockey. He'd also seen enough of Alex's off-ice behavior splashed across tabloids to know that the kid desperately needed his tweeting privileges revoked and a babysitter when he hit the clubs. But he was a superstar; his talent only upstaged by his ridiculous boy-next-door face and six-pack abs. He was given the *A* as a rookie, the *C* the following year. Jeff noted these things with passing interest until it was February, and Jeff's GM was on the phone, reeling off the canned trade script about how thankful the organization was for his years with the team, and they wished him all the best in

Houston. *Houston*. A less-than-ten-year-old franchise with no cups, a reputation for dirty play, and a teenage captain.

So it was with no little amount of resentment that he answered a Houston area code number on his phone only a few hours after he'd spoken to his own GM, knowing it was probably someone from his new home team.

"Uh. Hi," the other voice said. "Is this Jeff? Cooper."

"Yeah, this is Jeff."

"Right. Cool. This is Alex Price with the Houston Hell Hounds?"

The way he phrased it made it sound as if he wasn't sure.

"I just wanted to call and welcome you to the team," Price continued. "We're really excited to have you and think you're going to be a great fit for our organization."

That bit wasn't as unsure but sounded scripted.

"Oh. Yeah, thanks, man." Jeff tried to remember his media training. "I'm excited for the opportunity."

Things went awkwardly silent then, and Jeff was reminded, somewhat fondly, of phone conversations with his five-year-old niece.

He decided to throw the kid a bone because he was nice like that.

"God knows you need a winger who can tell his right from left, what even was that in the game against Tampa last week?"

Alex groaned. "Leave Bruno alone. It was his first game after being called up from the AHL, and he was so nervous it's a miracle he didn't pass out on the ice. The kid is doing his best."

Jeff resisted pointing out that Alex was, in fact, two years younger than "the kid" in question.

"Yeah, I feel you. It's too bad about Tervais's knee. And Lawrence's ankle. And Yevgini's shoulder. You've had a lot of injuries to contend with this year."

"Yeah."

Alex went quiet for a moment and Jeff realized maybe he shouldn't have brought that up.

"Mark isn't coming back," Alex said, kind of in a rush, and Jeff leaned his head back on the couch, closing his eyes against the emotion in Alex's voice. "They don't even know if—I mean—It sounds like he'll walk again, but ... "

"That sucks, man."

And it did. No one wanted to see a veteran go out with that sort of injury.

"He's great," Alex continued. "I'm sorry you won't get to play with him."

"I did, actually. Team USA three years back?"

Alex would have been fifteen then, Jeff realized. Jesus.

"I wasn't expecting to get picked," Jeff continued. "I'd just turned twenty, and I was more terrified than excited. They put us in the same room, and I latched onto him. He let me follow him around like a baby duckling the whole time and never gave me shit for it. I'll have to give him a call later. Good guy."

"Oh. Yeah. He's—I guess he's done the same thing for me. Helping me with captain stuff." There was a pause. Long enough that Jeff thought the connection might have been lost.

"I didn't want to be captain when they offered," Alex said finally. "He convinced me to accept."

Jeff had no idea how to respond.

"Sorry," Alex muttered. "You don't need to hear this. See? This is why I need help. I'm so bad at this stuff."

"Easy," Jeff said. "You're doing fine."

"I just really hoped—I thought he might have another year or two. I wanted to win a cup for him. With him. He put so much into the organization, turning the team into a real contender over the past few years, you know? He deserved a cup."

"You really think the Hell Hounds can get the cup in another year or two?" Jeff asked, admittedly a little disbelieving. "Honestly?"

"Yeah," Alex said, still quiet but confident for the first time in the entire phone conversation. "Yeah, I think we can."

And damn if Jeff wasn't suddenly, intensely, invested in making that happen.

Alex picked Jeff up from Houston airport a week later. He'd offered Jeff the use of his guest room until he could find a place and ship his stuff. Jeff had accepted because he'd spent enough of his life in hotel rooms already, and this way, he could get a better feel for his new captain. The phone call had been enough to disrupt the preconceived notion he'd held of who, exactly, Alex Price was, but there were still enough news stories and screen-capped, now-deleted tweets floating around the internet to leave him wary.

At the airport, Alex looked like a college student who'd gotten separated from his fraternity on spring break. He wore Bermuda shorts, Sperrys, a backwards snapback, and held an iced Starbucks drink.

"Hey!" he said brightly upon recognizing Jeff, not realizing until a moment too late that the hand he extended to shake was already occupied by his drink. He awkwardly fumbled the cup into his left hand and wiped his right palm on his shorts to get rid of condensation before offering it again, somewhat sheepishly, to Jeff. "Welcome to Houston."

Jeff tried really hard not to laugh at him and accepted the handshake.

Alex's guest bedroom was spare but clean and comfortable. Alex left him to his own devices until late afternoon when, fresh from a nap, Jeff argued amiably with him about dinner. They settled on Chinese and walked the three blocks together to pick it up.

They were nearly back to Alex's place when two guys—probably college students on spring break—stopped on the sidewalk in front of them to take a selfie backgrounded by the ornate gold doors of Alex's building. They waited patiently as the boys took a few pictures from different angles, and then the taller one ducked a bit, pressing a slow kiss to the other man's grinning mouth.

"Do you mind?" Alex snarled, completely out of character.

One of the men flinched.

The other jammed his phone into his pocket and squared up to Alex.

Jeff regretted all of his life choices.

"You got a problem?" the guy said.

"Yeah," Alex said, voice ugly. "Maybe suck face in front of someone else's building? I live here, fucking fa—"

And Jeff was done.

Conveniently, one of the residents was exiting the building. Jeff grabbed the back of Alex's shirt and dragged him inside before the door closed again, yelling an apology behind him.

"What the fuck?" he hissed, shoving Alex away from him in front of the elevator.

"Dammit," Alex muttered, rubbing the hand not holding their takeout bag over his face. "I didn't mean to say that."

They both noticed, at the same time, the girl in the lobby with her cell phone out, watching them closely. Their eyes met, and they went quiet, Alex biting his lip, Jeff digging his fingernails into his palms as they boarded the elevator.

Once the door closed to Alex's apartment, two eternally long minutes later, Alex threw his keys and the takeout onto the kitchen island, then leaned against it with both hands, head bowed between hunched shoulders.

"I didn't mean it," he repeated, subdued. "I don't say shit like that anymore."

Jeff took a breath. "Look man. I'm not going to tell you how to live your life, but if you're going to talk like that in the locker room, or on the ice, we're going to have a problem."

"I don't. I swear. I fucked up, okay?"

"It's just ... I work with a queer hockey camp during the summers back home. I know a lot of guys in the NHL don't realize how detrimental—"

"I'm not homophobic," Alex interrupted.

Jeff tried to remember some of the phrases from the most recent ally book his mom had sent him. "You're a figurehead, Alex. A lot of kids—a lot of players—look up to you. And ignorance is different from malice, but it's still really problematic if—"

"I'm not homophobic," Alex said louder, voice cracking. "I'm not. I'm *not*."

And the look on his face was—Oh.

Oh.

"Oh, kid," Jeff said.

"I'm not a kid," Alex whispered, probably automatically.

"You really, really are. Do you need to sit down? Come on, let's go sit down on the couch."

Alex sat down.

"So," Jeff said. "Not homophobic. Just really shitty coping mechanisms?"

"You can't tell anyone," Alex said, barely audible. "Jeff, you can't. Okay? Please."

"Of course not. Hey, breathe. I wouldn't. It's okay. Look at me. I've read a thousand books about this shit. I am 100 percent here for you, okay?"

"Okay." Alex didn't sound as if he believed him.

"Who knows?" Jeff asked gently.

"No one."

"You mean no one on the team?"

"No," Alex said, and at least his voice was a little closer to normal. "I mean no one, no one."

Jeff sat down too.

"Not even your parents?"

"There's only my mom. And no. She's—no."

"Jesus, Alex."

"You can't tell anyone," he repeated.

"I won't. Hey, come here. Can I hug you?"

Alex looked at him like he was certifiably insane. "I guess?"

"It'll help. Probably. The books say it helps."

"Well. If the books say it helps."

Jeff pulled Alex into an admittedly awkward side hug.

"How long do the books say we need to do this?" Alex asked, rigid under his arm.

"Shut up. At least ten minutes," he lied.

"Ten minutes?"

"Yeah, so get comfortable."

Alex did. Eventually. Slowly relaxing into Jeff's side.

"Can we at least watch some television or something?" Alex asked, trying to sound put out and failing miserably.

"No. We're going to sit here for another—" Jeff glanced at his watch. "—four minutes. And then we're going to eat food and talk about our feelings. And how you should probably get a therapist because I'm shit at talking about feelings."

"Fuck you."

"I know; I'm looking forward to it too."

5

ALEX TEXTS ELI AT 8:25 p.m. that he's outside the dorm.

By 8:28 p.m., when Eli exits the lobby doors, there are three people getting autographs from Alex.

"Eli! Hey!" Alex says, nodding since his hands are full. He takes a final selfie with someone, then waves them off so he can open the car back door for Hawk.

There's a fleece blanket spread across the seat, and a green water bottle with a collapsible bowl attached to it sits on the floorboard. They both look brand new.

Eli decides he'll deal with the feelings that gives him later.

The small group of undergrads watch from a few feet away as Alex proceeds to open the passenger door for Eli before returning to the driver's side.

"Sorry," Alex says sheepishly as he puts the car in gear. "I should have known better than to get out, but I wanted to unfold the blanket in the back for Hawk."

"No problem. Did you get that for her?"

"Yeah." Alex glances in the rearview mirror. "I think she likes it."

He appears delighted by this.

Eli takes a moment to appreciate the sunset outside and not stare at Alex Price's stupid freckled face and slightly crooked smile.

"Hey," Alex says urgently. "What's your major?"

"Uh, I'm not 100 percent sure. I'm undeclared right now."

"That's cool."

They merge onto the highway, and Eli realizes there's a distinct lack of music in the car. He can't decide if the silence is uncomfortable or not.

"So," Alex says eventually. "How was your day? Or, your afternoon, I guess."

"Good. Unpacked, FaceTimed with my best friend from back home." And then, because he can't help but brag on Cody a little: "He plays NCAA hockey. Or he will once the semester starts. He just moved into his dorm and met his team today."

Alex gives him a sideways glance. "I thought you said you avoided hockey players."

"Cody doesn't count. He did figure skating with me our whole lives. Switched to hockey in high school. He doesn't really act like your typical hockey player though. He cries at Humane Society commercials and has a lot of opinions about free-range versus cage-free versus pasture-raised chickens. Very nonthreatening. He just also happens to have the best scoring percentage in the Southern junior hockey league."

Alex whistles. "I like this kid already. Where does he go to school?"

"Princeton."

"Oh," Alex says. "Wow."

But Alex's voice has lost its brightness, his flat expression matching the suddenly impassive tone.

"It's a really good team, I think," Eli says, uncertain. "They scouted him and everything."

Alex is looking at him as if ... Eli doesn't even know. Like Alex isn't sure if Eli is messing with him or not.

He turns back to focus on the road, rubbing his chin with the hand not on the steering wheel.

"You really *don't* follow hockey, do you?" Alex says finally.

"No. No, I do not. What am I missing here?"

"James. Petrov." Alex says the name like there's a continent of feeling behind it. "He's the goalie at Princeton."

Eli tries to recall what Cody said about James. *Broody*, he remembers, *hot*. "Um. Okay?"

"Jesus," Alex says.

Eli is actually starting to get a little annoyed. "I'm sorry, but I really don't—Wait. Hold on."

He tries to think back to the articles he skimmed while googling Alex earlier that day. The name Petrov had been familiar when Cody said it, but he hadn't remembered until now—

"You played with him in juniors, right?"

"Yeah."

"What's he doing playing for a college team, then? Shouldn't he be sitting on a stupidly huge NHL contract like you?"

Alex makes a noise in the back of his throat. "How do you know we used to play together and not about why he's at Princeton?"

Eli doesn't have a way to answer that without embarrassing himself. He decides to go with honesty anyway. "I googled you when I got home today. There were articles about you in midget and juniors. Petrov was in a couple of them."

Alex coughs. Maybe it's supposed to be a laugh; Eli isn't sure. "You googled me?"

"Well, yeah. If you were a normal person, I would have Facebook-stalked you; if that makes you feel any better. I just—wanted to know who you were."

"You won't find that out from Google."

"Right. Sorry. That was a stupid thing to say."

Alex sighs, shifting his hands on the wheel. "No, it's okay. I probably would have done the same thing. It's just—James was my best friend. For years. He was supposed to go first in the draft—the first goalie in a *decade* to go first. I figured I'd be second or third. There was a lot of pressure on us but especially on James. Because of his family."

Eli knows he looks blank.

"Andrei Petrov?" Alex prompts. "Three-time Stanley Cup winner and two-time Olympic gold medalist? Hockey *legend*? And then his older brothers—Eric and Mark Petrov? They play for the Caps and the Bruins."

"Okay, yeah. I have heard of them. Guess I should have made that name connection."

"Anyway. We were both stressed before the draft. But James had anxiety, I guess. And depression? And he'd just started some new meds, which apparently can make things worse before—"

Alex swallows, starts again. "He disappeared. Two days into the combine. Like literally became a missing person. I went first in the draft because he wasn't there."

There's so much going on there that Eli doesn't even know how to begin to unpack it.

"It was a big deal," Alex continues, voice still flat. "Lots of news coverage when the crown prince of Russian hockey abdicates to a no-name American kid. He showed up again a few weeks after the draft, and his dad did a bunch of media appearances to smooth things over. He could have come back. Played overseas for a year or something—god knows the KHL was gunning for him—but he didn't. Said he wasn't ready. Decided to do the college thing."

"Is he—" Eli looks out the window; he doesn't think he can handle Alex's face right now. "Is he okay? The way Cody talked about him made it seem like he was"—well, happy would be a lie, but—"healthy?"

Alex's mouth goes thin and pinched. "I don't know. We don't talk anymore."

"Oh. That sucks."

"I get it. He probably has a lot of bad associations with me. Because of the circumstances. Not my fault."

"Sounds like you're still trying to convince yourself."

"My therapist thinks if I say it out loud enough, maybe I'll believe it or some shit."

"You have a therapist?"

"I'm a nineteen-year-old NHL captain for an expansion team in a league that collectively hates us. Of course I have a therapist."

"Makes sense. They can be useful though. Therapists."

"You have one?"

Eli opens his mouth. Then closes it again. "Medical history. Third date," he says somberly.

Alex laughs, which is what Eli was hoping for. "Right. Well, if you need a good one in town, I can give you a referral. She's Coops's too. He's the one that dragged me to her. Literally."

"I would have paid good money to see that."

"Eh. I wouldn't go by myself, and I wasn't handling things super well on my own. Things were—hard. My first year."

Eli remembers a picture of Alex's face on draft day, just turned eighteen, serious below a headline declaring him the savior of Houston hockey. Bolded quotes about the franchise putting their faith in his skills and leadership capabilities. Quotes from anonymous sources about whether he was mature enough to meet the expectations the franchise had of him. Eli imagines, in addition to that, the feeling of being chosen first only because the best was taken out of the running. He imagines what it would be like, knowing that his best friend had broken under the stress and expectations now afforded to him.

"Hard" is probably the understatement of the century.

"Are you okay? Now?" Eli asks.

"Oh. Yeah? For sure."

"Good."

"Yeah."

Alex blows out a breath, looking a little embarrassed. "So this is way more heavy than I anticipated. How did we even get on this topic?"

"Uh," Eli realizes it was definitely his fault. "You asked how my day was? And I bragged about my best friend. And then my complete lack of hockey knowledge sort of took things from there."

"Right."

They glance at each other with the same expression: eyebrows raised, lips tucked between their teeth, and simultaneously start laughing.

"So," Alex says, a little flushed. "This afternoon you FaceTimed with your NCAA hockey-playing best friend who happens to be on the same team as my ex-best friend. Anything else?"

"Um. I checked out the cafeteria? Food wasn't that bad. And as an athlete, my meal plan is awesome. What did you do this afternoon?"

"Nothing really. Just a nap and then Coops came over for dinner."

"Where you told him I had a massive crush on his figure skating?"

"Nah, just told him you were willing to kill someone for the privilege of seeing him skate again. He's very anti-murder, so."

"How decent of him."

They arrive at the complex after several more minutes of easy conversation, and Eli pulls his handicap hangtag from the front pocket of his backpack as they near the front of the building.

"You can park in the same spot you did this morning," Eli says because he's a petty asshole. "You know, legally, this time."

Alex's ears go red.

Eli hangs the tag from the rearview mirror with a grin.

"I really am sorry," Alex says.

"I know. But don't expect me to stop ragging you for it."

"Fair."

Alex takes off his hat and runs his fingers through his stupidly endearing hair before replacing it. "So. Are you ready for date number two?"

"Date number two?" Eli repeats. "This isn't a date."

Alex gives him a judgmental look. "Bro. I'm taking you to an ice-skating rink after hours. I picked you up. I opened the car door for you. This is like—shitty-Hallmark-movie levels of romantic. Of course it's a date."

"Okay, valid. It's still within the same day as the first date though. I don't know if that counts as a separate date."

"You said four hours was the cut-off. It's been four hours since I dropped you back at your car. In fact, it's been—" He consults his ridiculously gaudy watch. "—seven and a half hours."

"I did say that," Eli admits.

"So. Date number two."

"Date number two," he agrees. "But I expect you to buy me a snack from the vending machine."

Alex nods solemnly, extending his hand. "You drive a hard bargain."

Eli shakes it, equally serious. "Great. Now come open my door for me again."

Eli puts his skates on, sitting in a stall next to Alex Price in the official locker room of the Houston Hell Hounds practice facility, about to skate on the official Houston Hell Hounds practice ice with Alex Price and Jeff Cooper of the Houston Hell Hounds.

He struggles his way through this line of thought several times without it really computing.

Alex nudges Eli's elbow with his knee, and Eli fumbles his laces. He spares a quick annoyed sideways glance before starting over.

Alex looks sheepish. "You okay?"

"I'm about to voluntarily get on the ice with two professional hockey players; you're going to have to give me a minute," Eli murmurs.

"I thought Coops didn't count."

"I always count," Cooper says as he enters the locker room. He drops his bag into the stall three down from Alex's.

"You don't even know what we're talking about," Alex points out.

"No, I do not," Cooper agrees amicably. "Hey, Eli, right?"

"Yes," Eli says.

Jeff Cooper is talking to me. Jeff Cooper knows my name. I am about to skate with Jeff Cooper. Holy shit.

"You look like you're going to spontaneously combust," Cooper says. "Are you all right, kid?"

"Oh my god," Eli mutters, "can you let me live?"

"He's having a moment," Alex advises Cooper.

Cooper laughs and sits to put on his skates. There are two pairs in his bag, but he withdraws the figure skates—beautiful, barely worn Riedell boots—and Eli sighs a little.

"John Wilson Gold Seal blades?" he asks.

"Of course," Cooper says. "What else?"

"Only the best for Coops," Alex agrees wisely as if he has any idea what they're talking about.

Eli considers his well-worn—potentially overworn if he's being honest—Jackson boots and sighs again, resigned this time.

An NHL salary would be nice.

They make it onto the ice, dim-lit, freezing, and eerily quiet, a few minutes later, where Cooper and Alex immediately break into a game of tag that involves a lot of superfluous jumps on Cooper's part and a lot of swearing on Alex's as he tries to maneuver around him in hockey skates.

Eli does a few slower laps at the periphery, watching, and then stops at the glass to check on Hawk. She's content, comfortable on the blanket Alex bought for her, eyes following Eli's movements.

Alex pulls to an abrupt stop beside him in a shower of ice, cheeks pink, and only gets out the beginning of a "hey" before Jeff runs him into the boards a moment later.

"There's no checking in figure skating!" Alex yells, trying to shove him off, and the two devolve into a wrestling match that ends with Alex clutching Eli's leg and Cooper sitting on Alex's back, attempting to give Alex a mohawk.

Eli reminds himself that these men are professional athletes with more money than he can fathom and has to laugh. Maybe a little hysterically.

"So," Jeff says, still sitting on Alex, "I hear you memorized my World Juniors routine."

Eli throws Alex a betrayed look, which Alex does not see because he's facedown on the ice.

"I might have done that," Eli admits.

"You still remember it?"

"Uh."

"Because if you'll do it, I'll do it."

"I can't do it clean," Eli says.

Jeff snorts, flopping sideways as Alex rolls to dislodge him. "Neither can I anymore. Do whatever you can—skip the jumps if you want. I just want to see you skate."

"We don't have any music," Eli says, maybe a little desperately.

"I have the key to the sound box and the song on my phone."

"I haven't warmed up?"

"Guess you'd better get started, then."

He stands, brushing ice off the Under Armour leggings that make his ass look magnificent, and skates off, yelling something about leaving his phone in the locker room.

"I think I may pass out," Eli informs Alex, who is still lying spread-eagled on the ice.

Alex flaps his arms and legs a few times like he's making a snow angel.

"You're fine. We're not going to judge you."

"I'm judging you a little right now. What are you even doing?"

Alex sits up, absolutely covered in little flecks of ice, and sighs dramatically. "You know I've never made a snow angel before? Like—an actual one. In snow."

Eli raises an eyebrow at the non sequitur. "Okay?"

"I bet it's fun."

"It's cold," Eli says. "And half the time, you get snow down your pants and it melts and then everything is terrible."

"Stop talking," Alex says. "You're ruining it."

"Stop flirting and warm up," Jeff yells from the sound box.

Eli feels his face go hot, but Alex continues grinning at him as if everything is fine, as if this is normal. Eli shakes out his legs, deciding to take Jeff's advice before he does something stupid like run his fingers through Alex's ridiculous mussed hair. It's damp around the edges where the ice is starting to melt, which makes him look like he just got out of the shower or something, and that is not a train of thought Eli is going to follow.

Eli takes a couple laps: fast, then slow, then transitions to a few easier jumps, enjoying the untouched ice, finding his edges, warming up his muscles in the colder-than-usual air. He's glad Hawk has a blanket between her and the bleachers.

Just as he's starting to feel limber enough to attempt some harder tricks, Jeff yells, "Are you ready?" and the sound system cuts on with a crackle.

"Now?"

"Well, we don't have all night. You need to do your makeup or something first?"

"I hate you," Eli calls, moving to center ice.

"Don't play. You memorized my routine. You love me."

"Loved. Past tense. Crush is officially terminated."

"This is devastating news."

"I thought flirting wasn't allowed," Alex interrupts.

"All right, all right," Eli says, wiggling a little in place before going still. "I'm ready."

The music starts, loud in the silence, shocking like a plunge into cold water—and the moment the first beginning cello cords start, muscle memory takes over.

Eli knows the song as intimately as he does his own body. He's simultaneously eleven years old, full of the indomitable confidence only youth affords, and sixteen years old, in a hospital bed, eyes closed against the song playing in his headphones, uncertain if he'll ever skate again. He's seventeen and applying for colleges and bribing the Zamboni driver to give him another twenty minutes after practice because he's behind, dammit. And he's eighteen and skating Jeff Cooper's routine in front of Jeff Cooper hoping desperately he doesn't embarrass himself in a dark rink with echoing ceilings and low lights, and—it's surreal, is what it is.

He changes the first triple axel to a double and lands it, but he doesn't make the full rotation on the second and falls to a knee, adjusting the choreography a little to keep going. He finishes clean, otherwise, a little sloppy, not enough momentum on the flying spin, but he finishes, better than he anticipated, breathing hard, heartbeat loud in his ears as the final clash of music is followed by silence.

And then Alex starts clapping.

"The kid can skate!" Jeff yells from the booth with a whoop.

Eli bends at the waist to rest his hand on his knees, probably looking a little insane with how big he's smiling, but he can't help it. And then Alex skates into him, gentle but exuberant, and puts one hand on the back of his stillbowed neck, shaking him a little.

"That was *awesome*," Alex says.

"Way better than I could do it now," Jeff agrees, joining them at a more sedate pace. "Seriously, you're a little rough around the edges, but you're good. Really good."

"I used to be," he agrees, straightening. "I think it's your turn now."

Jeff balks. "After that? Are you kidding?"

"Hey," Alex says, "you promised."

Jeff sighs. "All right, but if I break an ankle, I'm telling management that you're a destructive influence."

"Is that something we should be concerned about?" Eli asks as he and Alex make their way to the sound booth.

"Nah, he knows his limits. He won't do anything that might jeopardize his play. He's just overly dramatic." Alex glances sideways at him, badly containing a smile. "I think it's a figure skater thing," he says seriously. "Very emotional, those types."

"Right, because hockey players aren't known for their theatrics at all," Eli agrees.

Alex's eyes go all crinkly with amusement as he ducks into the sound booth to start the music over. Eli moves to sit on the bench next to him, shoulder to shoulder, still breathing a little hard.

The music swells to life again, Jeff begins the opening choreography at center ice, and Alex leans into his space, head turned to speak directly into Eli's ear.

"Seriously though. I know nothing about that shit, but your skating is beautiful, man."

The words are earnest, Alex's breath warm against the sweat beginning to dry cold on Eli's neck. He shivers.

"Thanks," he says. "I haven't practiced it in a while; it was honestly a fluke I didn't fall more."

"Beautiful," Alex repeats firmly and then throws one arm over Eli's shoulder, chafing his palm against the goosebumps on the curve of his bicep.

Eli leans into him, just a little, eyes on Jeff as he settles into the first spin, still elegant despite his hockey bulk, and tries desperately to remember every second of the next four minutes.

6

ELI GOES HOME WITH the personal number of a second NHL player in his phone and the kind of memories that can't be paid for.

Memories like Jeff Cooper skating, mere feet in front of him, the routine that changed Eli's life.

Memories like *skating with* Jeff Cooper.

Memories like being kicked off the ice at 11:00 p.m. by a fond but harried Zamboni driver.

Memories like sharing a vending machine Snickers bar with Alex Price at midnight, giggling like they're getting away with something, sitting on the floor in a dark back hallway of the skating complex.

Memories like leaning out the open window of Alex's Land Rover, exhausted, eyes watering from the wind, grinning at the blur of nighttime Houston lights as Alex drives Eli home.

Alex texts him to make sure he gets into his dorm room safely, even though Alex just watched him walk inside the security door two minutes before.

What do you think is going to happen between the lobby and the third floor? Eli texts back. He waves from his window but isn't sure if Alex can see him from where his car is still idling at the curb.

It's 1:00 a.m., Alex answers. *Shit happens.*

Eli tells Alex to check in once he's home safe as well since, apparently, they're being ridiculous.

Alex does.

Jeff—and he is Jeff, now, in Eli's head, just like Alex is no longer "Price"—texts him a picture of Alex asleep on a plane the following morning. It's not flattering at all, but Eli finds it hopelessly endearing anyway.

You're a bad influence, Jeff captions it. *He always plays cards on morning flights, and now his routine will be off. If we lose tomorrow, it's your fault.*

It's a preseason game, Eli answers. *You'll survive. And whose idea was it to go skating last night anyway??*

He doesn't get an answer until several hours later:

Alex's

Which ... hmm.

He texts Alex the following night after the Hell Hounds' win against the Blues 1–0. Not that Eli checked or anything.

Go team. Do the thing. Win the points.

Did you watch?? Alex responds less than a minute later, though the game has only just finished.

Nope

Alex sends a range of distressed emojis.

I got an assist, Alex texts a while later when Eli still hasn't responded.

You want a gold star?

Yes plz.

The next morning, Eli wakes up to a FaceTime call from Jeff. Who is apparently sitting next to Alex on a plane that was supposed to have taken off thirty minutes ago.

"Alex is being a nuisance," Jeff says when Eli answers, sleep-bleary and grumpy. "Please distract him."

"Hi," Eli manages, squinting.

Alex fumbles Jeff's phone as it's passed to him, and Eli gets to look at the ceiling of the airplane for a minute until Alex retrieves the phone from the floor.

"Sorry," he says. "I told him not to call you."

"And I told you to quit complaining," Jeff says in the background. "As if it'd be better that they *didn't* fix the bathroom before we're airborne for four hours."

"I wasn't complaining that much," Alex says to Eli.

"He really was," Jeff says. "And now that he has a friend outside of the team, you better believe I'm going to take advantage of it. Keep him occupied for a bit, will you?"

Eli assumes Jeff is talking to him. "Okay?"

"I'm sorry," Alex says. "Honestly, I swear I'll shut up. You can go back to sleep."

"No, it's okay. My alarm goes off in—" He checks. "—sixteen minutes. So I can talk until then."

"Practice?" Alex asks.

"Mm-hmm. Need to take Hawk out and throw the ball for her first. And get some breakfast."

Hawk perks up, hearing her name, and wiggles her way to the head of the bed from where she was sprawled across Eli's feet.

"Oh, good morning, Hawk," Alex says.

Hawk shoves her nose in Eli's armpit and then sneezes.

"She says good morning back," Eli says dryly.

"Plans for the day?" Alex asks.

"Ugh. I don't know. Practice. Probably going to get some stuff for my dorm. And I need to find another kitchen to use because half the shit in this one is broken. I mean, the oven is being used for *storage* right now."

He presses his face into his pillow for a moment. "I may ask the Morgans at practice what theirs is like. Every dorm kitchen on campus can't be this terrible."

Jeff says something muffled off-screen, and Alex turns away to tell him that Eli and his best friend have a YouTube channel where they post cooking videos. Jeff wasn't there when they talked about that the night before the Hell Hounds left for their road trip—when they shared the two-dollar Snickers from the vending machine.

"Oh, cool. A vlog? What's it called?" Jeff asks, leaning into Alex's shoulder.

Eli can only see the edge of Jeff's eyebrow because Alex is holding the phone so close to his own face. The freckles are in full effect.

"I already asked," Alex says. "He wouldn't tell me."

"You can use my kitchen," Jeff says. "Jo can let you in. She works from home but has her own office upstairs, so she wouldn't be in your way."

"Oh, I couldn't—"

"My place is closer to your dorm," Alex interrupts. "Only four miles away. And the kitchen is really nice."

"How would you know?" Jeff asks. "Have you ever even turned on a stove burner?"

Alex flushes. "Well, I don't use my oven for storage, at least. And all the appliances are brand new. And there's ... a lot of counter space?"

"Alex does have a shit ton of counter space," Jeff allows.

"My doorman can let you in. His name is Dorian—I can text him and let him know you're coming." Alex pauses. "Bells will be there though. Will Hawk try to eat her?"

Eli blinks. "Uh. No? Hawk is great with cats. If I leave her vest on, she'll ignore her. If I take it off, she'll probably try to cuddle her."

Alex looks only a little relieved. "Okay. Well. Bells can be kind of ... "

"A bitch," Jeff supplies.

Alex wrinkles his nose.

"I'm not wrong," Jeff says.

"Not entirely," Alex admits. "So, uh. Watch your ankles. If you go."

"Are you serious? You'd let me just go cook in your kitchen? When you're not there?"

"Sure, why not?"

"Because you only just met me three days ago! And I could be some sort of deep-cover crazy journalist who will snoop through your stuff and write a damning exposé or something."

It's silent for a moment.

He's pretty sure Alex and Jeff—or Jeff's eyebrow, at least—are judging him.

"Are you a deep-cover crazy journalist planning to snoop through my stuff and write a damning exposé?" Alex asks.

"Do deep-cover hockey journalists even exist?" Jeff asks.

"No, I'm not," Eli says, exasperated, "but I wouldn't admit to it if I was!"

"How much sleep did you get last night?" Alex asks, and he has the audacity to actually look concerned.

"Oh my god," Eli mutters. "Fine. I'll go use your stupid kitchen tonight."

"Great! I'll text you the address and stuff, okay?"

"Mmkay."

"You look really tired. Do you want to go back to sleep for ten minutes before your alarm goes off?"

"Thought I was supposed to be sparing the team your theatrics," Eli reminds him, yawning.

Jeff sighs, overly loud. "I suppose I can shoulder the burden for a while longer."

"Okay. Nice talking to y'all," he says because, even half asleep, his mamá raised him to be polite. "Goodnight."

"Night," Alex agrees, grinning at him.

Alex has a nice smile. And face in general. And everything really.

Eli hangs up because he's staring, curls an arm around Hawk, and goes right back to sleep.

Isobel Price looks more like a ferret than a cat—like a long, fluffy white tube sock with ears. She has a narrow face and wide-set gray-green eyes and a very insistent meow.

He stands just inside the door, apprehensive as she approaches him, then sits a few feet away, studying first him, then Hawk.

Hawk's nose twitches excitedly, but she otherwise keeps her heel.

After several more seconds of consideration, Bells jumps onto the island, tucks herself into a little loaf, and blinks slowly at him.

Eli takes that as tacit approval of their presence and moves farther inside. He kicks off his shoes and removes Hawk's vest. He tells her to lie down out of the way and then takes a moment to just stare out the window.

Alex's place is ridiculous, which Eli expected, considering he's a single NHL superstar living in Houston, but Eli was wholly unprepared for the view out of Alex's penthouse floor-to-ceiling windows.

The whole of downtown is laid out before him, a lit-up canvas that fades to shades of dark blue against the backdrop of the nearly set sun.

It's quite possibly one of the most beautiful things Eli has ever seen.

He whistles to himself, then moves to lean against the island.

"This is a little unhygienic, you know," he tells Bells.

"I'll need to use this area for prep in a minute. Do you think you could relocate?"

She blinks at him.

"Or not. That's fine. Maybe I'll just use this side over here; it's big enough for both of us, huh?"

He takes his laptop and portable light out of his backpack, sets them up on the opposite counter, and then stands in the middle of the kitchen, hands on hips, and takes in his surroundings.

The place is shockingly neat, simply but elegantly decorated in shades of gray and white. There's a Hell Hounds sweatshirt on the couch and running shoes by the front door. There are two closed doors on either side of the living area, which he assumes are bedrooms.

"Well," he says to Bells, who is still watching him sleepily but has yet to show any of the malice he expected. "Shall we get started?"

She appears to approve.

He unloads his canvas bag of ingredients and starts searching through cabinets. He figured Alex would have the basics, and he's right, though nearly all of them still have their Williams Sonoma sticky tags on the bottom. He sighs a little at the injustice of it all and gets to work.

Two hours later, he sits at the bar facing the Houston skyline, eating probably the best chicken ragout he's ever made. He edits footage while listening to the vinyl version of *Badlands* because, of course, Alex is the kind of pretentious bastard to have a record player.

Eli refuses to think it sounds better on vinyl. (But it does. It totally does.)

He texts Alex a picture of his bowl and asks if he wants some boxed up and put in the freezer for when he gets back. Alex sends back several heart-eyes emojis—which Eli takes as a yes—and then Alex asks if Bells is behaving herself.

She seems pretty apprehensive about Hawk, but I topped off her water and shared some chicken with her, so I think we're friends now, Eli answers.

It takes Alex several minutes to answer.

She didn't get rude with you though?

Nope. Perfect lady.

Huh. Cool. Got to head out for warmups. I'll ttyl.

Eli moves to find some Tupperware but backtracks when his phone buzzes with another text from Alex.

u know since ur at my place and I have NHL netwrk u should watch the game.

I'll consider it, Eli answers.

He gets a praying-hands emoji and a winky face back.

Eli rolls his eyes and takes a detour into the living room to stop the record player and turn on the TV instead.

It's not like he'll watch the whole thing, but playing it in the background while he finishes editing wouldn't hurt.

Three hours later, Eli leaves Alex's condo with a sore throat from yelling at the refs.

Good game, he texts Alex. *That was some bullshit calling though. Is your ankle okay?*

He doesn't get a response until after he's home and in bed.

Tell me about it. Just bruised. Scratched next game though. Maybe two.

That sucks.

Yeah.

Eli takes a picture of Hawk, sleeping upside down, her little bottom teeth and edge of a pink tongue showing, and sends it to Alex because he doesn't know what else to do.

Alex sends back a laughing emoji. *Thanks.*

Hawk says goodnight.

Goodnight Hawk.

I say goodnight too.

Goodnight Eli.

Goodnight, Alex.

Eli's phone rings in the middle of what he is certain is an important REM cycle. He fumbles for it in the sheets for a moment, squints at the caller ID, and answers.

"Oh my god, Cody, it's five in the morning."

"Elijah."

There is a continent of feeling in the way Cody says his name.

Eli is instantly awake.

"What? What's happened? Are you okay?"

"No, I'm fine, it's just—You're on TMZ."

"I'm *what*?"

"Someone recognized Alex's cat in the video you posted last night. And I guess Alex has done interviews with SportsCenter in his kitchen before, and someone made a post with screenshots on Tumblr? And it just kind of blew up. Not, like, big-big, but hockey-big. Our channel has over *forty thousand* subscribers now."

"Fuck. *Fuck*, I need to call Alex. Do—are they saying he's gay?"

"No? I mean, some of the posts on Tumblr are, sure. But not the hockey blogs and stuff so far. Mostly, those are just speculation about who you are and how you have access to his place while he's on a roadie."

"Oh. That's not bad. What are people saying?"

"It's ... not very nice."

"Cody."

Cody exhales. "So that asshole Ron Barrowman who runs the blog *Thin Ice*? He said you were probably the pet sitter or housekeeper or something and took advantage of Alex being out of town."

"That's not so bad. I mean. A little racist, maybe."

Cody sighs again. "Barrowman also wrote that Alex probably didn't know you were gay, and if he had, he wouldn't have let you into his home. He made some jokes too. About what else you might have done in Alex's house while he was away."

"Oh." Eli takes a breath. "Well. That's still better than—I mean ... La vida es así ... "

"Elijah."

"It is! People thinking I'm some sort of pervy fan is better than—"

His phone buzzes with an incoming call, and his stomach goes sour.

"Hey, Cody? Alex is calling. I've gotta go."

"No, yeah, go."

He hangs up on Cody and closes his eyes as the call transfers to Alex.

"I'm so sorry," he says.

"Hey, I—" Alex cuts off. "What?"

"Cody just called me about TMZ and *Thin Ice*. I didn't—"

"Shit. You read Barrowman's post?"

"No? Cody was just telling me about it."

"Don't read it," Alex says darkly. "My agent is threatening him right now, trying to get it taken down."

"I'm sorry," Eli repeats, and he knows that his voice is going funny, but he can't help it. "I'm so, so sorry. I didn't even think—"

"Why are you apologizing? I'm calling to apologize to *you*. The stuff they're saying is bullshit, and I never would have suggested you use my kitchen if I'd known this would happen."

Alex sounds so honestly, genuinely angry on his behalf that Eli is uncertain how to respond.

"Oh."

"So. Yeah. I'm sorry. I'm about to make some tweets. I just wanted to warn you. I guess Cody beat me to it though."

"Yeah. Apparently, our channel has a ton more followers now though."

Alex makes a considering noise. "Are people talking shit in the comments?"

"I haven't looked."

They both go quiet.

"So," Eli says, just to make sure, "you're not mad at me?"

"What the fuck? No. Why would I be mad at you?"

"It's pretty clear on our channel that both Cody and I are gay. People could make assumptions."

Alex makes a dismissive noise. "Go check my Twitter. Tell me if you want me to say anything else."

Eli squints against the brightness of his phone, thumbing open the Twitter app and searching for Alex's handle.

APrice23 retweeted a link to Barrowman's article with the added comment: His name is Eli not "teenage twink." He had permission to use my kitchen because he's my friend. If you had those you'd understand.

APrice23 tweeted: My friend Eli is an awesome cook and if you're going to be a dick about his sexuality you aren't allowed to sit with us (or eat his chicken ragout).

This tweet is accompanied by the picture Eli sent Alex the night before.

APrice23 tweeted: Also if you see a brown guy in my kitchen and your first thought is that the help must be overstepping their bounds you're racist as hell and can kindly fuck right off.

"The last one might be a little heavy-handed," Eli says.

"Hey, I said 'kindly.'"

"Well. Your publicist probably isn't going to like it," he murmurs.

"Probably not. But do you?"

"Yeah," Eli says, grinning a little into the fabric of his pillow. "I do. Thanks."

"Good. Hey, I know it's super early for you. Go back to sleep, okay? We can deal with this more when it's actually light outside."

"Okay."

"Cool. I'll call you back once we're in Detroit. Probably around 11:30 a.m. your time; that work?"

"Mm-hmm."

"Hey, Eli?"

"Yeah?"

"You realize I have access to your YouTube channel now."

"Oh, no."

"Jeff and I are going to watch all your videos on the plane. Would you rather I send running commentary or save all my thoughts for date number three?"

Eli hangs up on him.

Alex sends him an emoji blowing a kiss.

Eli groans and goes back to sleep.

7

IT DOESN'T OCCUR TO Eli until half past eight, fifteen minutes into his blessed cup of coffee (the first he's been allowed in a week, how did he even *live*?), that he and Alex are not the only ones impacted by the whole kitchen debacle. Cody has also been outed to his team.

He nearly spills his coffee in his haste to get to his phone.

"Hola, cariño," Cody answers. "How you doing?"

"I'm so sorry," Eli says. "It didn't even occur to me until just now that you were effectively outed by extension with this whole thing. Are you okay? Is your team being cool?"

"Oh," Cody pauses for a moment, murmuring something in the background. "No, they've been great. I'm with them now. At the house."

"The house?"

"The house. It's—" He cuts off, then says lowly, "Don't touch that. It's not ready," before addressing Eli again. "Anyway, it's a house where some of the hockey team lives and throws their parties."

"You're using a kitchen in a frat house? To make food? Food you plan to *eat*?"

"Fuck off. It's better than the dorm kitchen—something I'd think you would understand."

"Valid."

"Anyway, I actually spent the night here because they had a party yesterday. Muzz is the one who saw the news first. He likes to take his iPad to the roof and check all the gossip blogs while doing yoga in the morning. It's a thing."

"A beautiful thing!" someone yells distantly in the background.

"Yoga?" Eli says, a little baffled. He can't picture a hockey player doing yoga.

"Well. He does it naked. I'm not sure how much of it is about the yoga and how much of it is about doing a lot of downward dog poses facing the rugby house."

"Oh god."

"The rivalry is real. And their windows face us."

"I see."

"Yeah."

"So Muzz woke you up?" Eli prompts.

"Right, and said a lot of supportive things and brought me downstairs and a couple of the other guys were up and they were all really chill. I don't think it was a surprise to anyone, honestly. They're more excited about the food aspect than anything else. Now that they know I can make brownies and shit—"

"You're making brownies right now, aren't you?"

"Yes, but Haney isn't going to get any if he doesn't SIT DOWN AND STOP PLAYING WITH THE MIXER."

Eli snorts. "Mixer? You decide to not buy books this semester?"

"God no, it just sort of appeared? About an hour ago. Black KitchenAid. The one that I've mentioned, oh, a thousand times on the channel. I have my suspicions it was Muzz because it seems like the supportive shit he'd pull, but most of the boys have a stupid amount of money, so who knows. I'm not about to look a gift horse in the—*Luke Takahashi*, if you touch that cream cheese one more time, *I swear to god*—"

Eli grins, leaning back against the wall, and Hawk nudges his thigh with her nose: a gentle request for pets.

He obliges because he knows if he ignores her, the requests will get less gentle.

"So you're good," he says to Cody. Just to be sure.

"I am. Thanks for checking though."

"I'm sorry it didn't occur to me sooner."

"Don't even worry about it. You had bigger things on your mind. I saw Price's tweets. It doesn't seem like he's mad."

"He's not. He was calling because he was worried about me. I think his agent is trying to get the Barrowman blog post taken down. He said he'd call back later once they land in Detroit."

"Good," Cody says approvingly. "Don't read the post."

"Wasn't planning on it."

"So what are you going to do with your Saturday?"

"I'm not sure. I may go back to Alex's place again tonight. Might as well get a buffer of videos done while I have the time and the space."

"You're still going to use his kitchen?"

Eli shrugs, realizes Cody can't see that, and makes a "why not" noise. "Damage is already done. Might as well. Besides," he sighs. "It's a really, really, nice kitchen."

"I know," Cody says dryly. "I've seen the video. Along with a couple hundred thousand other people. And counting. My videos are hardly going to compete now."

"Yeah, yeah. What about you? Plans for the day? Besides brownies?"

"Covering up a murder," Cody says, intentionally loud. "I think there's a kiln big enough to fit a body in the art building."

"Damn," someone says in the background, sounding impressed. "Better watch out, Haney."

Cody sighs into the phone. "I swear, it's worse than cooking at Mawmaw's with all the baby cousins around."

There's a racket in the background—several shouting voices and a slammed door—and it takes a minute before Cody speaks again.

"Sorry, the rest of the team just got here. I should probably go before—Muzz, don't you dare—"

The call ends, and Eli smiles into his coffee mug.

Cody sounds ... happy. Not just happy though. Confident. Something Eli had honestly been very afraid Cody wouldn't ever be while playing hockey at a collegiate level. Eli's so grateful to Cody's team, so relieved that they have been kind when many teams would have become vicious.

He finishes his coffee, collects Hawk's leash, and shoves on his shoes. He needs something to distract himself, or he's going to go find that stupid blog post.

"You want to go for a walk?" he asks.

Completely unsurprisingly, she does.

Over the next four days, Alex's agent reigns victorious, the worst blog posts are taken down or retracted, and the internet appears to forget about Eli.

Eli makes three more videos, stuffs Alex's freezer full of hockey-diet-friendly Tupperware meals, and works his way through a quarter of Alex's record collection. There's a lot of Hozier. Bells now greets him with a chirp and a disdainful look at Hawk. She still has yet to let him pet her, but she also hasn't tried to eviscerate him, so he figures that's fine.

Alex calls him the night the team returns to Houston, and at first, Eli can't understand him because he's clearly talking with a mouthful of food.

"What?" he says for the third time.

Alex makes an exasperated noise and hangs up on him.

Less than thirty seconds later it rings again.

"Hello?"

"Eli," Alex says. "This is the best damn thing I have ever tasted. I can't even—how did you make *turkey* chili taste this good?"

"Oh, are you eating the chili I left in the freezer? Thank you?"

"I will pay you to make this for me every week. I'm not even kidding. Holy shit."

There's a clink of cutlery and a low moan on the other side of the phone, and Eli tries not to dwell on exactly how indecent Alex sounds while eating food he's made.

"Well. If you keep letting me use your kitchen, I can definitely do that."

Alex mumbles something around his mouthful.

"What?"

"Groceries," he says. "You make me food, and I'll buy all your groceries—whatever you need for you and for me. I'll give you a card. Or Venmo you. Whatever."

"Oh, you don't—" But he does, actually. Eli only has so much disposable income, and routinely feeding a hockey player would be no small addition to the budget.

"Don't even," Alex interrupts. "I'm paying for it. Holy shit this is good. Hey, what's in the blue containers?"

"Oh, that's chicken stuffed eggplant with quinoa and tahini."

"I haven't seen that video," Alex says, sounding affronted.

"I haven't posted it yet. I made a buffer since I had the time and knew I wouldn't be bothering you if I went over."

"Oh. Okay. Well, you won't be bothering me even if I'm here, so you can come over whenever. Hey, are you free tomorrow night?"

"To come cook?"

"No, for date number three."

"Oh." Eli had forgotten about the catalyst for this whole thing. "Sure. What do you want to do?"

"It's a surprise. I'll pick you up at 5:30, cool?"

"5:30? That's early."

"I have an early bedtime."

"No you don't."

"Eli, can I pick you up at 5:30?"

"I guess?"

"Good. See you then."

Alex hangs up, and Eli remains baffled.

Alex arrives at 5:23 the following day, blanket on the back seats for Hawk, an extra Gatorade in the cupholder.

He looks tanner than Eli remembers, his freckles stark over the bridge of his nose.

"Hey!"

His enthusiasm is contagious.

"Hey," Eli parrots. "How was your trip?"

"You talked to me every day; you know exactly how my trip was. Three wins, one loss. A bruised ankle and a very pissed off Kuzy."

Eli realizes Alex's rose-gold aviators match his massive white-marble-faced watch and smiles despite himself.

Eli tries to determine when he started finding Alex's horrible bro fashion endearing. That's probably not a good sign. "So where are we going?"

"Surprise," Alex reminds him, pulling out of the parking lot. "Buckle your seatbelt."

Fifteen minutes later, Alex puts the car in park and gestures expansively at the building in front of them. Eli is lost. "Goodwill?" he asks incredulously. "You're taking me to Goodwill? That's the illustrious third date?"

"Oh, no," Alex says seriously. "This is the pre-date. The tailgate of the date, if you will. The Official Date Pregame."

"Right. So. We're pregaming our date at Goodwill?"

"Exactly."

"I'm lost."

"Before we go to dinner, we have to pick out outfits for our date. Here."

Eli just looks at Alex.

"We'll set a cost maximum of ... twenty dollars? Yeah. Twenty dollars each."

"So I just have to pick some clothes, change, and then we go? Is this some sort of weird thing rich people do?"

"Oh, no," Alex's serious expression finally breaks. "No, no. I will pick your outfit. You will pick mine. The more ridiculous the better. And then we will go out to eat at a very nice restaurant and pretend everything is completely normal and we are wearing normal outfits that we intentionally chose to leave the house in."

"Oh my god," Eli says, suddenly understanding. "There are going to be so many pictures."

"So many," Alex agrees somberly.

"What will TMZ say?"

"I'm looking forward to finding out."

It takes them forty-five minutes and a not insignificant amount of laughter to pick out their clothes for the evening. Alex ends up wearing high-waisted metallic parachute pants straight out of the '80s with a pale-pink shirt and wide-lapeled floral blazer. Eli is wearing a three-piece suit, each piece a different type of plaid, and a turquoise trilby. They clash horribly, and it is magnificent.

They leave wearing their purchases, much to the bemusement of the cashier, and they're not able to keep straight faces while the hostess at the five-star steakhouse tries and fails to not stare while seating them.

They giggle through ordering appetizers and drinks, their waitress impressively impassive as she repeats back their requests, and then grin at each other while other patrons try to surreptitiously take pictures of them.

"This is kind of nice," Alex says, taking a sip of his wine. "I don't think any of them are taking pictures of me because I'm Alexander Price."

"The blazer is so terrible, no one's even noticed your face."

"Or Hawk," Alex points out.

"We should do this all the time," Eli agrees.

They've only just ordered their main course when Hawk sits up under the table and paws at Eli's knee.

Eli closes his eyes—too slow to be a blink—and exhales.

Hawk nudges him again, insistently, and Eli sets aside his napkin and moves to slide out of the booth.

"Okay, I hear you," Eli says.

Hawk swats at Eli's knee again, whining.

"What's wrong?" Alex says.

Apparently, his face is doing a thing. "I'm about to have a seizure. I can't—I'll explain after, okay? But I have to go. It'll be probably fifteen minutes, maybe more."

"What the fuck? Go where? Are you—" Alex looks from Hawk, clearly agitated, back up to Eli's face.

Alex takes a breath. "What do you need me to do?"

And that—Eli is pretty sure that is Alex's Captain Voice. Which is something he'll need to revisit later. "Nothing. Just wait here. Hawk knows how to take care of me. I'll be back, okay? Just don't leave. Please."

"Okay."

He finds their waitress in the hall by the kitchen. "Hi," he says, making sure he has her full attention. "I have a seizure disorder, and my service dog just alerted me that I'm about to have one. Is there a back room where I can lie down for a few minutes? It's no big deal, and I'll be fine. I'd just rather not hang out in the bathroom if I can help it."

"Oh," she says, a little wide-eyed. "Yeah, we have a break room; will that work?"

"Perfect."

Hawk head-butts his knee, and Eli winces, gesturing for her to lead the way.

The break room is standard. A table with mismatched chairs, a microwave, sink, and refrigerator. There's a couch along the back wall.

The waitress tucks her hair behind one ear. "Is this okay, or—?"

He shifts his backpack on his shoulder. "This is perfect, thanks. If anything bad happens, the dog will bark to get someone's attention. But that's never happened before. This is normal for us. We'll be out in ten or fifteen minutes."

"All right. I'll put a note on the door not to disturb you. Is there—are you sure you don't need anything?"

"Nope. We're good."

She leaves the room with a last concerned glance from him to Hawk and then closes the door.

Eli lets out his breath, then sets his backpack, jacket, and the stupid turquoise trilby on the couch. There's a compact travel blanket in the front pocket of his bag that he lays out on the floor. He then pulls up the emergency contact screen with his medical information on his phone and puts that on the floor as well.

Hawk whines.

"I know, baby girl. Give me a second."

He lies down, holds up one arm so Hawk can press herself along his ribcage, and takes a deep breath, focusing on the weight of Hawk's head on his chest.

It hasn't gotten any less uncomfortable, asking for accommodations, but doing it dressed head to toe in plaid definitely ups the embarrassment factor.

He exhales, closes his eyes, and waits.

He doesn't know how long it's been when he opens his eyes again, which remains disconcerting no matter how many times he does this. Hawk is mostly on top of him, licking his ear, and as the fuzziness fades and he starts to feel like a person again, he takes stock of himself and—

He sits up, pushing Hawk off him roughly enough that he'll feel bad about it later.

Fuck.

Fuck.

He takes a moment to breathe and not punch the couch or something. Because it isn't the couch's fault that he's just pissed the stupid plaid pants he's wearing. That's why the travel blanket is waterproof. That's why he carries an extra pair of leggings and gallon zipper bags in his backpack all the time.

But preparation doesn't negate that he's going to walk back out into the restaurant where Alex Price is waiting, and it's going to be immediately obvious what has just happened.

He briefly considers just ... not leaving the room.

Briefly.

"Sorry," he tells Hawk, who is watching him a little sadly.

He gives her ears an apology scritch and then goes about changing. He shoves his boxers, the blanket, and the plaid pants into plastic bags and then shoves those bags with more violence than is strictly necessary into the bottom of his backpack. After a moment of thought, he crumples the trilby and pushes it into the backpack as well.

He considers how he feels—slight headache, a little tired and off-balance, but no worse for wear—then examines his reflection in the mirror next to the sink. With just the plaid vest and leggings, he almost looks normal, at least.

The scar that cups his ear, trailing down the line of his throat, seems particularly stark in the fluorescent lighting. He rubs it with his thumb for moment, stalling, and then turns around, takes a fortifying breath, opens the door, and walks purposefully back to the table.

Alex is hunched over, spinning his phone anxiously, and immediately jerks upright when Eli rounds the corner.

"Are you okay? What did—Dude, are you wearing different pants?"

Comprehension dawns, and Alex goes quiet.

"Can we go?" Eli asks.

Alex snaps his fingers at the waitress, which is super rude and they'll need to talk about that later, but—

"Hey," Alex says to the girl. "Can you get me the check? We have to leave."

She nods, and Alex half stands, digging in his pocket. He leans forward and hands his keys to Eli. "You want to go hang out in the car? I'll finish up here and meet you there in a minute."

"Okay."

"You all right to go by yourself?"

"Yeah."

"Okay."

There's a little worried pinch between Alex's eyebrows, and Eli hates it.

He goes to wait in the car.

When Alex joins him a few minutes later, it's with three takeout boxes in his hands.

"Our food was just coming out, so I had them box it for us, and I didn't know if you'd want bread or not, so I had them throw a couple rolls in as well."

"Okay."

Alex passes the boxes over, then runs a hand through his poor, wild, hair.

He takes a breath, opens his mouth, closes it again with a scowl, and starts the car.

It's quiet until they're on the highway.

"So," Alex says, "do you want me to just take you home? Or maybe we could go back to my place?"

"What? Why?"

"To ... eat?" Alex looks genuinely confused.

"I'm—" Eli feels a little lost. "I need a shower."

"I have one of those. And clothes you could borrow. Or we could go to your place. I just figured you wouldn't want the circus it could cause if I went up to your room with you. Or I could just drop you off if you want to call it a day."

"Alex," Eli interrupts. "Your place is fine. But maybe we can stop by my dorm first? So I can, uh, put my clothes in the washing machine?"

"I have a washer too," Alex points out. "Top of the line. It even has Wi-Fi connectivity."

"It does not."

"It does too! The app lets me know when it's done. And I can check and see how much time is left whenever I want. It has Flex Wash too."

"What the hell is Flex Wash?"

"No idea. It sounds impressive, though, right? I should probably read the manual."

Eli laughs, but it's a strained little thing. "You sure you want my clothes in your fancy-ass washer?"

Alex makes a judgmental noise. "Dude. I am a hockey player. We are disgusting human beings. Bodily fluids do not bother me."

"All right."

"Hey," Alex says, "seriously."

"Okay."

When they get to Alex's place, Alex lets the valet park his car, and everyone stares as they walk into the lobby.

Alex's ears are beet-red by the time they get to the elevator. "This was just your super sneaky way to get out of wearing that awful outfit, wasn't it?" He whisper-shouts at Eli. "Did you see their faces? I'm over here, still looking like a moron, but you look relatively normal. And where the hell is your hat?"

Eli can't help but laugh, which is probably Alex's intention.

"Backpack," he says. "Might be a little crushed."

"I'll just have to get you another one."

"Please don't." Alex grins at him.

Eli smiles, more than a little helplessly, back at him. "Have you used any of the groceries I left? The butter or—"

"No. I've just been eating what's in the freezer. And protein shakes. Why?"

"Because. Third date. It's easier to talk about medical histories if you have cookies to eat afterward."

"Oh yeah?"

"Speaking from experience."

"You know that's not why—" Alex licks his lips, eyebrows pinched as he holds the elevator door so Eli and Hawk can enter first. "You don't have to tell me if you don't want to."

Eli shrugs. "You should know the basics anyway. If we're going to keep hanging out."

"Well, we are, so."

"Okay then," Eli says.

"Okay then," Alex agrees.

8

ALEX IS A PROFESSIONAL hockey player. More than that, he's a comparatively small professional hockey player. He's 5 feet 10 inches and 180 pounds, and he's widely hated by a good percentage of the NHL. He gets hit a lot. Mostly by people who are bigger than him, some of them a lot bigger—honestly, what are they *feeding* the Russians these days?—which is a pretty constant source of stress.

But nothing in his nearly twenty years of life has ever been quite as nerve-racking as sitting uselessly at a five-star restaurant in parachute pants and a floral blazer while his—while Eli—is off in some back room having a goddamn seizure.

A *seizure*.

Which—Eli had seemed so calm about it. But seizures are a big deal. Seizures are scary.

Seizures kill people.

He calls Jeff because he doesn't know what else to do.

"Hey, kid, why are you calling me in the middle of your date? That's rude as hell."

"Eli is having a seizure," Alex says because tact has never been his strong suit. "And I'm freaking out."

"What the fuck? Why are you calling me? Call an ambulance."

"No—that's not. It's normal? For him? Hawk started whining and shit, and then he was like, 'oh hey, I'm gonna go have a seizure now, no big deal, see you later,' and then he just left to some back room, and I—*Fuck*. Should I be telling you this? Am I, like, violating his privacy? Jeff. I'm freaking out."

"You are a little bit. Deep breath, okay?"

"Okay."

Jeff pauses for a minute. "That wasn't a deep breath. That wasn't even *a* breath. Work with me, Alex."

"Oh. Right."

Alex breathes.

"Okay, good. So. Eli probably has epilepsy or something. If Hawk is trained to detect seizures this is normal for them and you're making a big deal out of nothing."

"Seizures are a big deal," Alex says, probably louder than is necessary. He hunches over the table a little and takes another breath. "What do I do?"

"What did he tell you to do?"

"To wait here. For him to get back."

"Then that's what you do."

"What about after? Do I take him home? Or, like, the hospital?"

"I don't know," Jeff says patiently. "You should probably ask him when he gets back."

"Right."

"But make it clear that you're cool with this. You are, right?"

The question sounds a little like a threat.

"So cool," Alex says faintly.

"Good. Make it clear that if he wants to go home, he can, but you still want to spend more time with him tonight. Maybe offer to take him to your place. But don't be insulted if he just wants to call it a night either."

"Okay. Yeah."

"Listen, I'm at the movie theater with Jo. Do you want me to stay on the phone with you until he's back, or are you good?"

"I'm good. Yeah. Sorry for freaking out. Get back to your wife."

"Sure?"

"Yeah."

"Let me know how it goes. And if you need anything else, okay?"

"Okay. Thanks. Bye."

Alex hangs up and spins his phone mindlessly on the table.

He presses the home button and sighs. It's only been five minutes.

When they get to Alex's apartment, Alex shows Eli how to work the washing machine, ushers him into the master bathroom, shoves a towel into Eli's hands, and tries to explain his ridiculous shower. There are six different wallmounted nozzles as well as a rain-emulating thing in the ceiling, and the hot and cold adjustment handles, as aesthetically pleasing as they are, don't make much logical sense.

It's a bit much. He'll admit that.

He leaves Eli, who is definitely judging him, but at least doing it quietly, in the already steam-filled bathroom and goes to pick out a pair of shorts and the softest T-shirt he can find. Because, well, he wants Eli to be comfortable. He might intentionally pick a shirt that's a little big on him because he knows it will look even bigger on Eli, and the idea of that is ... compelling. He agonizes a little over whether he should give him underwear, too, and throws in a pair of black boxer briefs that he got from a Diesel photoshoot a few months back. They shrank in the wash, so they'll probably fit Eli perfectly, which he will not continue to think about.

Alex knocks on the bathroom door, opens it a few inches to put the clothes on the floor inside, and returns to the kitchen to transfer their boxed food to plates.

Bells joins him on the countertop and unashamedly begs for attention.

"You need to be extra nice to Eli today, okay?" Alex says, running his knuckles down the curve of her arched spine. "He's had a seizure. Which is bad. And we like him, so we need him to feel welcome and safe and shit, all right?"

Bells appears to agree, but he gives her a little bit of fat from the edge of his steak just to make sure she's in a good mood.

He brings their plates and utensils into the living room because sitting on the couch will be more comfortable than the bar stools. It had seemed as if Eli's balance was a little off, so bar stools probably aren't a good idea anyway.

Then, out of things to do, Alex sits on the couch, adjusts the silverware a little on the coffee table, and waits.

He's not good at waiting.

He turns on the TV to SportsCenter, then immediately turns it off because he doesn't want it to seem as if he's avoiding talking to Eli or something. But Eli isn't even in the room, so he turns it back on, absorbs absolutely nothing for several minutes, and turns it off again the minute he hears the bathroom door open.

Hawk precedes Eli and makes herself at home on the rug under the window. Eli moves into the living room, and Alex—Alex did not adequately prepare himself for this. For Eli with damp ringlet hair and a flush to his dark skin from the heat of Alex's ridiculous shower.

He looks so soft and unassuming that it feels like a personal attack.

"Your shower is ridiculous," Eli says.

He sits down next to Alex and he smells like Alex's shampoo.

It somehow smells a whole hell of a lot better on Eli.

"It is," Alex agrees.

"I want to marry it though. Can that be part of our deal? I cook you food in exchange for shower privileges?"

Alex swallows. "Yes."

Eli purses his lips, studying Alex, and Alex suddenly wonders if he looks awkward, clutching the TV remote in one hand, sitting a careful distance between the middle of the sofa and the edge, trying to leave enough space for Eli to sit without it looking like he's trying to avoid touching him or something. He doesn't even know.

He tries to be less awkward without actually changing anything about his position, and from the look on Eli's face, fails miserably.

"Are you okay?" Eli asks.

Alex lets out a breath through his nose. "I'm fine. I'm just—are *you* okay? Because maybe this is normal for you, and I don't want to make a big deal out of it, but I was scared out of my mind waiting for you to come back at the restaurant, and now I'm trying to be cool because I don't want you to feel weird, but I don't know—"

"Hey," Eli says, "whoa."

And that's—that's Eli's hand on his knee.

"Sorry," Alex says, slumping a little.

He scoops Bells up from the back of the couch and repositions her in his lap so he'll stop squeezing the remote and won't try to do something stupid like hold Eli's hand instead.

Eli looks like he's trying not to smile too widely at him.

"Thank you," Eli says, squeezing his knee a little.

"For what?"

"You were worried about me."

"Um, yeah?"

"That's—nice."

"Okay?"

"It is! And you handled things well. Except for being rude to the waitress. I mean. Snapping your fingers at her? Really?"

"I didn't—Okay, yeah, I did do that. I, uh, left her a big tip?"

"That helps."

Bells repositions herself in such a way that she can butt her head against Eli's wrist. He lets go of Alex's knee to pet her.

"Hey, sweet thing," he murmurs, soft and a little reverent, "finally decided we're friends?" and Alex cannot handle this.

"So," Alex says, maybe a little desperately. "Food?"

"Food," Eli agrees.

They eat in companionable silence, watching with amusement as Hawk slowly scooches her way across the floor, a little army-crawl at a time, until she's curled between their feet with a hopeful expression. She doesn't beg but makes it very clear she's available and amenable to sharing if they are. Alex is sorely tempted but doesn't know if feeding her people food is allowed or not.

"So," Eli says eventually, leaning forward to put his plate on the coffee table. "Two years ago, I was in a really bad car accident. I was hospitalized for several months. Had a couple surgeries. Broken ribs, ruptured spleen, traumatic brain injury."

"Fuck," Alex says.

"Yeah. It sucked. I'm good now, mostly, but the TBI has some pretty shitty lasting effects. Like balance issues and memory problems, or like minor aphasia when I get really stressed."

"Like seizures?" Alex asks.

"And like seizures," Eli agrees.

"Are they—will they ever stop or—?"

"Maybe. Probably not. Doctors aren't sure. Brains are pretty weird and kind of unpredictable, I've learned. And mine is still healing."

"What causes your seizures?"

"Also unsure. I usually have one or two a month, completely unprovoked, but if I'm really emotional or stressed or overheated, that can prompt one too. That's why I have the handicap parking tag—because something as minor as walking two blocks in Houston heat could induce one."

"Fuck," Alex says again. "I'm sorry. I'm *so* sorry."

"Hey, no, that's not—I wasn't trying to make you feel bad again. I know you weren't being malicious or anything."

"Still. I shouldn't have—"

"Yes, I know. But we've moved on, okay?"

"Okay." Alex considers going and drowning himself in his stupid shower because he is the literal worst, and Eli is being way too nice to him.

"Anyway," Eli says, "I got Hawk once I was out of the hospital. Between her and my medication, it's not so bad."

Alex reaches down to pet Hawk without thinking, then jerks back his hand. "Sorry, is it okay to—"

"Oh, yeah, totally. When the vest is off, she's just a dog. She'll still alert for me as long as she's not distracted, but she's free game for petting, absolutely."

Alex doesn't have to be told twice.

Bells isn't particularly pleased by this development and retreats to her former position on the back of the couch, closer to Eli than Alex.

Alex rolls his eyes at her and smooths the fur over Hawk's eyebrows with his thumbs. He tries to tell her telepathically that she's a very good dog and he's happy Eli has her. She blinks knowingly at him.

"So," Alex says. "How does that work, with the skating? If heat is a problem. Doesn't any kind of physical activity put you at risk?"

"Sort of? There's a threshold, and I'm getting better at telling where it is. And figure skating is one of the best possible sports I could be part of, honestly. It's a lot easier to cool down in an ice rink and stave off getting overheated, to begin with, than it is on, like ... a football field or something." His lopsided grin fades a bit. "I wasn't able to skate for almost a year initially. Between the balance issues and the surgery recovery and stuff ... " He pushes one palm gently against his belly.

Alex has to resist the urge to cover it with his own hand, to pull up Eli's shirt and get to the skin underneath it so he can—what, he doesn't know—make sure Eli is all right now? How would Alex even tell?

"That's why I'm behind," Eli says. "Why I'm here. I had a spot to compete at Worlds when I was sixteen, but the accident happened two months before, and now—I still haven't managed to get back to the competitive level I was at then. Might not ever."

Alex can't imagine that: Losing skating. Losing hockey. Losing ... his identity. It's one of his worst fears, one of the few things that gives him nightmares. What if he gets hurt? What if he's not good enough? What if he can't live the only future he's spent the entirety of his past preparing for?

"I'm sorry," Alex says, and it seems woefully inadequate.

Eli shrugs. "I'm still recovering. Still improving. I'm not giving up yet."

"Good."

It's quiet for a moment, and Alex gives Hawk one final pet before leaning back into the couch. "Can I ask, like, what happens? When you have a seizure."

"Oh. Well, there are a lot of different kinds obviously."

Alex raises a self-deprecating eyebrow.

"Or," Eli corrects himself, "I guess not obviously for most people. The kind I get are called tonic-clonic, which is basically where I lose consciousness for a minute or two and have muscle contractions. It's pretty scary to watch, but it doesn't hurt or anything as long as I'm ready for it."

"Tonic-clonic," Alex repeats.

"Hawk usually lets me know about ten minutes before I have one. Then I get somewhere safe, lie down, and she makes sure I don't hurt myself while I'm out of it. A minute or so after I wake up again, I'm usually good to go, sometimes with a headache. I don't usually—" He grimaces and starts again. "They're usually not as bad as today."

Alex bites his lip. "Is that something to be concerned about?"

"No. Not unless I have several bad ones in a row."

"Okay."

The washing machine beeps, and Eli goes to switch his clothes into the dryer. Hawk stays with Alex, but she lifts her head to keep Eli in her sight, craning her neck a little when he turns the corner.

"He'll be right back," Alex says.

She is not reassured.

When Eli returns a minute later, he settles on the couch closer to Alex than he was before. "Any other questions?"

"What do I do?" Alex asks. "If this happens again."

Eli shrugs. "Mostly, what you did today. Wait for me. Take me home if I want. Maybe skip the slight panicking. But that was my fault. It wasn't fair to spring that on you."

"Okay. What are they called again? The kind of seizures you have?"

"Tonic-clonic."

Alex repeats that several times to himself. He'll need to google it after Eli leaves.

"So we're cool?" Eli asks.

Alex blinks at him. "Yes? I mean, yeah. Of course."

"Cool. So ... " Eli claps his hands together, looking pleased if a little embarrassed. "Medical history portion of date three is over. You ready for cookies? Or do you have something to contribute to tonight's heart-to-heart? Any personal revelations? Deep dark secrets to share?"

And Alex—

He doesn't mean to. Not really. Because Eli is clearly joking and not actually expecting him to answer, but he can't help it.

He just.

Says it.

"I'm gay."

9

ELI HAS NEVER BEEN punched before. It's something he's pretty proud of, considering he grew up gay and Black and speaking Spanish in rural Alabama but this—

Eli imagines this is a little like what it would feel like.

Not in the face, but maybe in the chest. Right down the center. Where there's a knotted line of scar tissue that he rubs with shea butter every night.

Eli swallows, standing. "If that's supposed to be a joke, it's not very funny."

And Alex. Alex looks devastated. "It's not. I'm—I am. I swear."

Eli sits back down.

"Fuck," Alex says. "I'm sorry. I wasn't going to tell you until later, but you just bared your soul to me or whatever, and I felt like I needed to, uh, reciprocate? And then you said—And I know you were joking, but I'd imagined a thousand different ways I could tell you, but not once was I afraid you'd take it badly, you know? Which is new. For me. So I guess I jumped the gun a little. And you can't tell anyone. Unless you wanted to tell Cody, I guess, but *he* definitely couldn't tell anyone. I don't even know what I'm—"

Eli realizes he's not the only one in something of a panic spiral. "Alex," he interrupts. "Alex. Hey."

"Yes. Hi."

"Hi. Take a deep breath, maybe?"

Alex takes a deep breath.

Eli does too for good measure. “Sorry, I’m just going to need a minute.”

“That’s fine,” Alex says, subdued.

Eli closes his eyes because he is doing this all wrong, but he really does need a minute because *Alexander fucking Price*, number one draft pick, youngest captain in the NHL, and last year’s league point leader—yes, okay, Eli has been paying closer attention to that kind of shit lately—has just come out to him.

“You do realize,” Eli says, a few moments later, eyes still closed, “how ridiculous it is that we’ve been on three dates, and the fact that you’re gay is a revelation.”

“Uh. Yeah,” Alex agrees tentatively. “That did cross my mind.”

“So,” Eli straightens. “Were you—were those actual dates? I thought—” He takes a breath. “I thought you were just being nice to me. Like, oh, big sports star, charmed by the sarcastic kid with the service dog. And then you realized you actually liked hanging out with me because of my stunning personality or whatever. And that’s fine, but—”

“I don’t know,” Alex interrupts, voice a little too loud, a little thready.

“How can you *not know*?”

Alex gestures wordlessly, making an uncertain noise in the back of his throat. “I knew you didn’t think they were real, but I just—I liked you, and I wanted to be your friend, and the whole ‘three dates’ thing was an opportunity to spend more time with you.”

He runs a hand through his hair. “And I’ve never been on a date before. And I liked the idea. Of that. With you. Even though I knew it wasn’t real.”

Eli leans back against the couch and closes his eyes again because that makes things easier. He opens them and sits right back up.

“What do you mean, you’ve never been on a date before?”

Alex lifts one shoulder. “I haven’t. I’ve known since I was twelve I was gay, and by then, I also knew I was probably going to end up playing professional hockey, and there aren’t any out NHL players.”

"So you've *never* been in a relationship?"

The idea of twelve-year-old Alex quietly accepting he would never get a normal romantic adolescence makes something in Eli's chest clench. Possibly because it's a little too familiar.

Alex worries his bottom lip between his teeth. "Once. Sort of. In juniors. We were both players, though, both headed for the draft. So we had to keep it a secret. And I don't—I don't know if we actually were."

"If you actually were what?"

"In a relationship. Together. I thought we were, but he—"

Alex pauses.

The pause turns into silence.

He shrugs, clearly not sure how to finish, and Eli has never felt so compelled to hug someone.

"That sucks," Eli says. "I mean. That's terrible."

Alex shrugs again. "After I was drafted by the Hell Hounds, I went out to clubs a couple times. Uh. Gay clubs. Just for hookups. But then one time, someone recognized me, and I decided it wasn't worth it. Especially when the Hell Hounds gave me the captaincy. It was just too risky to go out anymore. It would jeopardize the whole team if someone went to the media."

Eli doesn't even know how to respond to that.

"So. What?" he says after a couple minutes. "You're just going to stay in the closet until you retire?"

Alex laughs without humor. "That's the plan."

"That's a terrible plan. You won't retire for like—"

"Hopefully another decade. Maybe two if I'm lucky."

"And you'll just be alone. Until you're forty or an injury forces you out sooner? Hockey can't be worth that."

"Look, I don't expect you to understand."

"Shit. I'm sorry. I mean. I really, *really* don't understand, but that's your choice. I shouldn't—judge you. For that. Sorry."

They both fall silent.

"Have you?" Alex asks after a moment.

"Have I what?"

"Ever been in a relationship?"

Eli snorts inelegantly. "No."

Alex appears genuinely surprised by this information.

"But you're out."

"Yeah, and up until two weeks ago, I was living in a tiny town in Alabama. Cody is literally the only other gay person I've ever met in real life." Eli startles. "Well. Until you, I guess."

"Oh. Right. And you never—with Cody?"

"God no. We kissed each other the night before we both left for college."

Whatever face he makes must indicate exactly how uninterested Eli is in recreating the experience because Alex laughs.

"Not good?"

"I dunno. The kiss itself was okay, I guess? Not that I have any comparative data. But Cody is more like a brother than anything else. Besides, he's not out to his family, and I don't think I could do that. Be someone's secret."

"Oh."

"I, uh, I'm going to join the GSA, though, I think. The first meeting of the semester is next week. So. Maybe I'll meet someone there."

"GSA?" Alex asks.

"Gay Straight Alliance."

Alex nods, mouth a little pinched. "Well. Let me know if you need any date ideas. I've done research."

Eli thinks Alex is trying to be funny, but the delivery isn't quite right.

He wants to ask the initial question again—or maybe amend it: did you *want* them to be real dates? But even if the answer is yes, he won't go back into the closet. And Alex can't come out.

"So," Eli says and then stalls.

"So," Alex agrees.

"Just ... to make sure I'm clear. You still want to hang out?"

It feels embarrassingly trite, phrasing it like that.

"Yes," Alex says. "Please."

"Okay. Well. Good."

Eli curls his bare toes into the shag of Alex's rug, uncertain how to proceed. "Do you want to make some cookies now?"

"Also yes."

"All right, then," Eli says, standing to collect their empty plates. "Go wash your hands, and we'll get started."

"I just washed my hands before we ate."

"And then you petted both Bells and Hawk."

Alex stretches and stands to follow him. "If I'm just watching, I don't need clean hands anyway."

"If you want to eat any of the cookies, you're not just watching."

Alex grins a little crookedly at the ice in Eli's tone. "Why don't I go wash my hands?"

"Good plan."

Eli expects things will be weird after that night. They make cookies and eat too many and stay up later than they should, and things are fine. But after Alex has dropped him off at his dorm, Eli doesn't know what to expect. Because there's definitely something there, he thinks. Something between them. And the knowledge that nothing will happen doesn't particularly dampen his interest in spending time with Alex, but he doesn't know if it's mutual or not. And, well, he thinks things will be weird.

They aren't.

He thinks maybe they'll stop talking as much once the semester begins and regular season games start.

They don't.

Alex sends him sporadic texts throughout the day, Jeff sends pictures of Alex sleeping in increasingly contorted and unattractive positions, and Eli gets used to FaceTiming Alex whenever the Hell Hounds are on the road—layovers, busloadings, etc. because apparently, he really is a significant annoyance when forced to sit still in one place for an extended amount of time.

Eli uses Alex's kitchen at least once a week, filming for the YouTube channel but also making sure Alex has healthy meals in the freezer for dinner every night he's home. Sometimes Alex is there, sometimes he isn't. Sometimes Jeff is there too.

Eli also has the email of the Hell Hounds' nutritionist, Sonja, now.

By October, he and Alex have cultivated a solid friendship through insults, social media, private ice time, food, and violently discordant opinions on reality TV. They have a routine. It's comfortable.

And then, in October, Alex goes down in overtime in a dumpster fire of a game against the Stars.

It's a blatantly vicious cross-check by Pavel that ends with Alex helmet-less and facedown on the ice, trying to get his knees under him and failing. He has to be carried off between Kuznetsov and the team doctor, a swarm of trainers blocking the camera's view of his bowed head.

Pavel gets five minutes in the box, and Eli packs an overnight bag.

He knows he can't go to the arena, but he also knows Alex will fight tooth and nail to go home unless a hospital stay is absolutely required.

So Eli goes to the grocery store, and then he goes to Alex's apartment.

Jeff calls him as he's chopping tomatoes.

"Hey, kid," he says tiredly. "Were you watching the game?"

"Yeah, is he okay?"

"He'll be fine. His neck is a little jacked up, and he's got a minor concussion. Couple weeks off, maybe more. But he'll be fine. We're going to be here for another hour or so, but they're letting him go home tonight if you—"

"I'm already at his place."

Jeff laughs softly, maybe a little fondly. "All right. I'll text you when we're on our way."

Eli finishes the casserole, sets the timer on the oven, puts on a Hozier record, and opens his history textbook.

Two hours later, when he's dozing on the couch, there's a commotion in the hallway. After a longer-than-usual pause, the door opens.

Hawk sits up.

Bells streaks across the kitchen to perch on the refrigerator and yowl at the intruders.

Dmitri Kuznetsov enters first with Alex's bag and what looks like several prescription bottles and paperwork.

"Oh," he says, seeing Eli, and breaks into a smile. "Hi."

Kuznetsov shouldn't really be handsome. His nose is too big for his face, his mouth too wide. But between his pretty brown eyes, straight—probably fake—teeth, and generally ridiculous height, Eli finds himself grinning a little helplessly back at the man.

"Hi," Eli says.

Kuznetsov points at him with one gigantic finger. "You! You're little YouTube cook. You talk to Pricey on the plane so he's not annoying everyone. You skate like Jeff—but best now."

"Okay," Jeff intercedes from the doorway, hovering behind a slow-moving Alex. "Eli *figure* skates better than me now, not, like, skates better than me in general."

"It's what I mean," Kuznetsov says consolingly. "English is hard."

"Bullshit," Jeff mutters.

"Eli?" Alex says, clearly a little drugged, as Jeff herds him toward the couch. "What are you doing here?"

"I thought you might like some company tonight after that hit. I even got the recipe for Cody's Mawmaw's get-well-soon casserole and tweaked it a little so Sonja doesn't kill me. It's in the oven."

"I'm injured," Alex says grumpily, "not sick."

"You better be appreciative of my efforts, or I'll be making a *funeral* casserole, Mr. Price."

Kuznetsov laughs, delighted. "You can't kill Pricey," he says somberly. "I'm need good center, and he's best."

"Well, you better tell him to mind his manners, then."

"You mind," Kuznetsov repeats to Alex. "Be good. Let Eli take care."

"Ugh," Alex says. "You guys are the worst."

"Best," Kuznetsov argues amiably, setting Alex's various accouterments on the counter. "See you tomorrow?"

"Yeah, man."

"Bye little cook," he says. "Nice to meet you."

"It's Eli," Eli says.

"Dmitri," Kuznetsov answers. "Or Kuzy."

"Kuzy? Is every hockey nickname just slapping an *Y* on a piece of someone's last name? Hockey players are idiots."

"Yes," Kuznetsov—Kuzy—agrees.

Eli laughs a little. "Okay, nice to meet you, Kuzy."

The Russian leaves, and Eli returns his attention to Alex. He's wearing a mostly unzipped hoodie over melting ice packs saran-wrapped around his shoulders and neck, and he looks so exhausted Eli thinks he might fall asleep at any moment.

"Can you eat? Are you hungry?"

"Yeah," Jeff answers for him. "He probably should try, at least. He hasn't had anything since before the game."

Eli moves to get the plate of casserole from the still-warm oven. He brings it to Alex on a bed tray he found in the cabinet by the cat food and sets it over his lap.

Eli watches as he takes a bite, arm moving gingerly, not moving his neck at all, and jumps when Jeff nudges him with an elbow.

"I was going to stay the night with him, but if you've got that—" Jeff nods to Eli's backpack and duffel bag leaning against the entryway wall. "—I'll just come back first thing tomorrow. Is that your plan?"

"Yeah. I mean. I can. If that's okay. I brought my stuff, just in case."

"When's your first class tomorrow?"

"Not until 11:00."

"No practice?"

"Not on Thursdays. I have an optional ballet class at 9:00, but I've yet to miss one this semester, so it's fine if I don't go."

"You do ballet?" Alex interrupts. He's holding his fork halfway to his mouth and looks like maybe his brain has just short-circuited.

"Yeah? Not at a superhigh level or anything, but it's good for figure skaters. I go to a class through the dance school two times a week on the mornings we don't have skate."

Alex makes a pained noise. "That's cool," he says weakly.

"Alex loves ballet," Jeff says. "He went to *The Nutcracker* four times in three different cities last year."

"I hate you," Alex says.

Eli is charmed.

"Anyway," Jeff continues, "I'll come back around 10:00 tomorrow so you have time to go back and get ready for class, cool?"

"Works for me."

"All right." Jeff bends to give Alex a gentle, smacking kiss on the top of his head and then retreats. "There's a list of his meds and when he can take them here." He proffers a folded packet of papers. "He can't sleep for another three hours. But after that, he can stay asleep as long as he wants, so you don't need to wake him up through the night or anything. Any blurred vision, nausea, forgetfulness—you know the drill probably—call his neurologist. Her number is also here."

Eli takes the papers from Jeff. "Okay. Anything else?"

"Uh. No screen time for forty-eight hours, and he has to sleep on his back."

Alex makes a despairing noise.

"Which he's going to be a giant baby about."

"No kidding."

"Anyway, let me know if you need anything."

"Will do."

Jeff leaves, and Eli returns the paperwork to the counter, turns off the kitchen lights, dims the living room lights, and then joins Alex on the couch.

"Hey," he says, settling slowly, careful not to jostle him.

"Hey."

"So that was a pretty terrible hit."

"Yeah."

"Probably a dumb question, but are you okay?"

"I don't know."

Eli wishes he hadn't dimmed the lights quite so much. He can't really tell what Alex's face is doing under the soft watercolor bleed of neon from the window.

"It was scary," Alex says. "I couldn't get up. I was trying, but I just—couldn't. That's never happened before."

"Yeah. It's scary when your body won't listen to your brain. Feels kinda like you're trapped."

Alex meets his eyes. "Exactly."

"Better now? Or are you still processing?"

"Still processing, I think."

"That's allowed."

Alex pushes a little at the tray, and Eli moves it off his lap and onto the coffee table. He hasn't even eaten half of the casserole slice, but Eli figures that's better than nothing. "Do you want some water?" he asks. "Maybe some Gatorade?"

"No. I already drank two at the hospital."

"All right. Can I get you anything else?"

"No. Just. Can you—"

He reaches toward Eli without turning his head, finds Eli's forearm and trails his fingers down to circle his wrist, calluses rough against the thin skin beneath Eli's palms.

He pulls, just a little, and Eli goes.

Eli settles in the cup of space between Alex's arm and his ribcage, leaning against Alex carefully, in increments, unsure of how much of his weight Alex can take without it becoming uncomfortable. Alex's outside forearm moves to circle his waist, pulling him closer, hand spread against his abdomen, and then they go still, pressed together in the semidarkness, the damp of melting ice and silence between them.

Alex exhales. "Thank you."

"Whatever you need," Eli says and then pauses, realizing he means it. "Don't fall asleep. Not yet."

"Talk to me, then."

"About what?"

"Anything."

"Well." Eli considers for a moment. "I've got some serious beef with my history professor's lecture from Monday."

Alex laughs, and Eli can feel it under his ear. "Is this the ancient civilizations class? With the old white dude?"

"Yup."

"Tell me about it," Alex says.

10

ELI MANAGES TO COMPLAIN about his history professor for nearly an hour, which is impressive considering he really doesn't have that much beef with him. But it's easy to exaggerate, and he keeps Alex giggling and awake which was the goal. Well. Awake was the goal. The giggling is a definite bonus though. Because Alex wrinkles his nose when he laughs, and Eli has a newly discovered thing for adorably scrunched-up freckled noses.

"I mean," Eli says, voice a little rough, "I am learning from his lectures. I just feel like he takes every opportunity to ignore or blatantly excise any mention of non-heterosexual relationships that any prominent historical figures had—even the widely accepted ones."

Alex makes an encouraging noise.

"It's just," Eli continues, "why can't we talk about the fact that King James had a boyfriend, and his love language was promoting him? Or that Alexander the Great was probably bisexual. Why is this professor so afraid of the historical gays, you know?"

"Who wouldn't be afraid of Alexander the Great?" Alex says sleepily. "He's one of the most merciless conquerors in history."

"Okay, that's a fair point, but definitely not what I meant, as I'm sure you're aware." Eli pauses. "Wait. You know who Alexander the Great is?"

Alex opens his eyes, shifting a little so he can frown at Eli. "I read."

"I know."

"We spend a lot of time on buses and planes, and history is interesting, okay?"

And Alex ... Alex seems genuinely upset. It's hard to take him seriously since his hair is a mess, and his eyes are all pupil and bleary from the meds, but Eli manages a placating, "Okay, sorry. I know you're not some dumb hockey robot."

"Good."

It goes quiet for several long seconds.

"I've always liked history," Alex says a minute later—a little hesitant, awkward after the extended silence. "When I was younger, I usually didn't have anyone to talk to on roadies. So I got in the habit of picking up historical novels and biographies and stuff. So. It's a habit now."

Which—That's actually incredibly sweet. And more than a little sad.

Eli doesn't know how to respond to that, but he doesn't have to because Bells gets up from where she's been sitting on the coffee table and stalks purposefully over to where Hawk is lying at their feet, jumps lightly onto her back, and settles in a little cat-loaf between her shoulder and bent elbow.

Hawk looks baffled.

As do Alex and Eli.

Hawk picks up her head and sniffs gently in Bells's direction, which gets her a bat on the nose and a quiet hiss.

Hawk drops her chin back onto her feet, bemused, watching Bells out of the corner of her eye.

After a few minutes, when Bells's sleepy blinks have turned into actual napping, Hawk slowly relocates her nose so it lies lengthwise against, and just barely touching, Bells's side.

She glances up at Alex and Eli, looking pleased with herself.

"I don't think it counts if Bells is asleep," Eli says. Hawk doesn't seem overly bothered by this.

Alex sighs, a strange expression on his face, and then winces.

"New ice packs?" Eli asks.

"Yeah, probably."

Eli unwraps him as gently as possible, noticing the goosebumps and chill of his skin beneath the hoodie.

"Cold?" he asks inanely.

Alex huffs out a laugh. "Yeah."

"Do you think a warm bath would help instead? With Epsom salts? And then you can ice again after?"

That's one of the things Eli most misses from home, aside from Cody. Epsom salt baths were a near-daily part of his required recovery and, until he'd moved into the dorms with only shower stalls—he'd still had at least one bath a week. He wonders if he and Alex are at a point in their friendship where he can ask to come borrow his bathtub. If they're not already, he thinks they probably will be after tonight.

Alex makes a grumpy noise that is weirdly adorable. "That would be nice, but I don't think I can lean back in a bath right now. I'm not supposed to be anything but upright or flat on my back."

"Oh, right. Sorry."

Eli stands in the kitchen, hands full of mostly-melted ice packs, and doesn't know what to do. At least that eliminates the emotional trial of helping Alex get in the bath—something that would likely be fraught with badly suppressed arousal and a fair amount of guilt.

"A hot shower would be nice though," Alex says slowly. "I didn't get a chance after the game, so I feel pretty disgusting. I'll need help though.

"Oh."

"Coops can help me tomorrow. It's not a big deal if you're not comfortable—"

"No, it's—" completely, horribly, unfair. "I don't mind. That's fine. I'm just afraid I'll hurt you."

And, hey, maybe that will help with the arousal if he's terrified the whole time of breaking the top-scoring center in the NHL.

"I trust you," Alex says quietly, and Eli has to turn and drop the ice packs in the sink before he says something stupid in response.

There isn't anything sexually fraught about helping Alex shower. Because Alex is in pain, and Eli isn't a sadist. The only thing Eli feels while slowly getting Alex settled on the bench in the stupidly complicated shower is an aching second-hand discomfort and a relatively desperate, fruitless, desire to take Alex's pain himself somehow. Because Eli is used to being in pain, he has a lot of practice, and, granted, Alex probably does too because he's a hockey player, but—well. He doesn't know where he's going with that. He wishes, nonetheless.

And then Alex makes him adjust the water temperature sixteen times and complains about the method Eli uses to shampoo his hair. When he does it the way Alex wants, Alex complains about soap in his eyes, which is why Eli had done it the first way to begin with. By the time the whole showering ordeal is over, the only thing Eli feels is frustration.

"I'm sorry," Alex says, naked and bedraggled, sitting stiffly on the teak bench next to the tub while Eli finds him some clothes. "I know I'm terrible when I'm injured, and you're being really nice, and I'm treating you like shit even though you should be home studying or—fuck, I don't even know what time it is—sleeping, probably, instead of here dealing with me. I'm sorry."

"I'm not going to say it's okay, because it's not. But I understand you're in a lot of pain right now," Eli says diplomatically.

"Yeah," Alex murmurs, and he's so damn pitiful Eli forgives him entirely.

"Here," Eli says, kneeling with a pair of Alex's boxers and judiciously ignoring how it puts his face at dick-level. "One foot at a time, okay? Don't look down if it hurts to. I'll just—right foot first—good—and now—nice."

He slides the boxers up over Alex's knees, then helps him stand, pulls them the rest of the way, and smooths his thumbs over the elastic band to flatten it.

Alex's skin is warm from the shower. Warm and tan and surprisingly hairless and—nope. Refocus.

"You want to bother with anything else or is this good?" Eli asks.

"This is fine."

He sways a little, and Eli wraps a steadying arm around him.

"Okay, bed then."

Alex is miserable—or, even more miserable—by the time they get him lying flat on his back in bed.

His hair is in the awkward phase between wet and dry and has gone fluffy and wild. Eli is pretty sure he would hate it if he knew. Alex seems to constantly be at war with his hair.

"Ice packs?" Eli asks.

Alex makes a noise that could mean anything.

"Right. Well, I need to go put the others back in the freezer anyway, so I'll grab a few new ones while I'm there. Anything else you need?"

Alex makes a noise that is probably negative.

Eli resists the urge to roll his eyes.

He tucks new ice packs around Alex's shoulders, tidies up the kitchen, packs his books back in his bag, and then feeds Hawk and Bells.

By the time he's back upstairs and changed into his pajamas, the alarm on his phone says Alex only has to stay awake for a few more minutes.

He informs Alex of this quietly, setting a glass of water on the bedside table.

"Umph," Alex responds.

"You can also take another painkiller now if you want."

"Please," Alex says.

Eli helps him sit up enough to swallow the pill, then deals with Alex's various forlorn exclamations over how he's entirely incapable of sleeping on his back, so it doesn't even matter that he doesn't have to stay awake much longer, and he hurts so much he definitely won't be able to sleep.

"Eli," Alex says with mock solemnity. "I think I may be dying."

"You're not cute," Eli says, even though he is. Very cute.

Possibly the cutest.

"No," Alex agrees a little mournfully. "Not right now. Bells is the cute one. And she's too busy cuddling with your dog to care that I'm dying."

Eli has to laugh. And then, because he can't help himself, he smooths a hand over Alex's ridiculous hair. "Seriously, do you need anything else?"

Alex's exaggerated grimace fades. "No. I'm okay. Thank you."

"Okay, well ... " He doesn't really want to leave, but there's no reason to stay, either, not unless—

"Can you stay with me? You said I still have a few minutes, right?"

"Oh. Of course. Should I—?" Eli nods toward the bed.

"Yeah. Plenty of room."

That's not entirely true. Alex's bed is a queen, which means, with Alex arranged in the center, it's impossible for them not to touch when Eli stretches out carefully beside him. He reaches to turn off the lamp, and then the only light is that from the windows—the Houston skyline, lit up like a marquee.

"What's your real bucket list?" Alex says, apropos of nothing.

"What?"

"Well, you said that going on a date with a hockey player wasn't really on your bucket list. What *is*?"

"Oh." Eli hasn't thought all that much about it. "All sorts of things, I guess. I'd like to travel. There's only a couple bioluminescent bays left in the world, and it would be cool to see them. And I'd want to get married and have kids."

"That's big stuff," Alex says. "What about little things?"

"Little things." Eli thinks. "I'd want a pair of—well, basically, the pair of skates Jeff has. And the entire Glossier skincare line. And ... " He laughs softly.

"What?"

"Cody and I had this joke, when we started our YouTube channel, that if we ever got famous and started generating income through ads, the first thing we'd do is buy a pair of Louboutins. So a pair of those, I guess."

"Louboutins?" Alex repeats. "What's a Louboutin?"

"Jesus, Alex. They're shoes. Really beautiful shoes. Cody and I wear the same size, so we agreed that sharing a pair of obscenely expensive ones would make it, I dunno, acceptable, or something."

"What's so great about these shoes?"

"They're Louboutins," he repeats a little helplessly. "It's stupid. It's not like we're ever going to make that kind of money anyway."

Alex is frowning seriously at him. "How much are they?"

"Like a thousand dollars. It's ridiculous."

Eli is suddenly uncomfortably aware that this is not a large sum of money for Alex.

"Huh," Alex says. "I don't think any of the shoes my stylist found even cost that much. What do they look like? Show me a picture."

"You're not supposed to have any screen time for forty-eight hours," Eli reminds him.

"Oh my god," Alex groans. "You're worse than Coops. Two seconds. That's all I'm asking."

Eli decides it's not a battle worth fighting and pulls his phone out of his pocket. It's easy enough to find a picture of The Shoes: black platform pumps. Red soles. Gold interior stitching.

He sighs a little as he hands the phone over.

Alex laughs incredulously. "You want a pair of *women's* shoes? Why?"

And the tone—the inflection—mimics so closely the derision he's come to expect from the kinds of people who like to hurt him that Eli's stomach immediately goes sour. Because it hadn't even occurred to him that Alex might—But he's a hockey player. A closeted hockey player. And he probably—

"Fuck," Alex says, and Eli doesn't know what his face is doing, but it's not anything good, judging by Alex's expression. "That was really shitty of me. There's nothing wrong with that. I was just expecting, like, fancy high-tops or something."

"It's fine," Eli says, taking back the phone. "I told you it was stupid."

And it is, but the hollow feeling in his chest hasn't gone away. Because he doesn't know Alex that well, and this is just a gentle reminder that he needs to stay cautious.

"Hey. Eli."

Eli licks his lips and glances back up at Alex. "What?"

"My therapist says your first response to something isn't really your response. It's society's response—or the way you've been trained to respond from your environment? But your second response, after you've had a minute to think about, you know, how you really feel, that's the one that matters."

Eli isn't sure where he's going with this. "Okay?"

"So. Can I give you my second response?"

"Yes?"

Alex laboriously holds his hand out, and it takes a moment for Eli to understand that he wants to see the picture again. He sighs but gives the phone back to Alex.

"You're still not supposed to have screen time," he says, knowing it will have absolutely zero effect.

Alex studies the phone with furrowed brows, the same way he looks at hockey plays or a pair of near-identical pictures of Bells when he has to pick just one to post to Instagram.

"I like the red bottoms," Alex says seriously. "They're, um ... really nice. Could you walk in these though? What if you twisted your ankle and couldn't skate?"

Eli is overcome with fondness for a moment.

He clears his throat. "I've practiced. Cody and I can do the entire 'Single Ladies' dance in heels so—"

"Jesus," Alex says, eyes wide. "Really?" He seems genuinely impressed.

"Yeah."

Alex looks back at the phone again, a new, sharper edge to his admittedly still drug-addled expression. "Where would you wear them?"

"At home. Cleaning. Cooking. Whatever. I wouldn't wear them out to class or something."

"Cooking," Alex repeats. And Alex's face is—Eli isn't sure what Alex's face is doing. "Cooking here? In my kitchen?"

"Alex, I'm not actually getting a pair of Louboutins."

Alex looks like he's about to argue, but the alarm on Eli's phone goes off, startling them both, and Eli retrieves it to turn it off.

"You should probably try to sleep now," he says, hoping to head off whatever weird direction the previous conversation had been going in.

Alex agrees, a little grudgingly, and Eli realizes his fingers have returned to Alex's hair and are ... well, petting him. A little.

The realization is embarrassing, but clearly Alex doesn't mind as his eyes are closed and he's leaning into Eli's hand. Eli is suddenly, intensely, reminded of Bells and has to take a moment to compose himself.

Within fifteen minutes, Alex is dead to the world, breathing slowly, the pained wrinkle between his eyebrows smoothed away, and Eli is sleepy enough to consider staying. Alex is warm and solid beside him, and Alex wouldn't mind, he doesn't think; he might even like it, if Eli stayed.

He could stay. If he wanted.

And that's the problem.

Eli carefully rolls off the bed and retreats to the guest room.

He doesn't stay because he wants to just a little too badly.

11

IT STARTS WITH AN Instagram post.

Jeff's Instagram post, surprisingly.

It's not his fault. Jeff wouldn't even *have* Instagram if the Hell Hound's PR department hadn't been insistent that "responsible" players—*which really did not help with the "mom" comments, could you please lower your voice, Jessica*—have a strong social media presence. He'd created one because it seemed simple enough to post behind-the-scenes shots from practices, selfies with fans, and pictures of his wife with adoring commentary.

He's boring. He knows. It's fine.

As a result, he doesn't have all that many followers, so it's something of a shock when he gets done with practice and finds his phone struggling to accommodate the thousands of notifications he's received. It takes him an embarrassing amount of time to figure out what's going on.

He'd posted a set of three pictures shortly after arriving at the igloo—all taken early that morning when he'd arrived to relieve Eli of Alex-duty. The first picture was a selfie with Eli in the kitchen in which Eli looked harried but fond as he tried unsuccessfully to scowl at the camera. He was brandishing a spatula and being generally adorable.

The second was a close-up of a breakfast plate—migas accompanied by cut fruit.

The third was Eli and Alex on the couch, backlit by the sunrise out the floor-to-ceiling windows behind them. Alex had a smear of sauce across his cheek and was sticking out his tongue at Eli, who held a plate in his lap and a fork suspended in midair between them. Eli's head was thrown back, laughing, the profile of his face, the curve of the narrow column of his throat, a sharp contrast against the watery pastel light of the city behind them.

It was an awesome picture, Jeff thought. He'd used a filter and everything.

It seemed the internet agreed.

He'd captioned the photoset:

Things we already knew:

I am not a good sous chef

@AP23 is a terrible patient

I would kill a man for @elijahrr as long as he keeps cooking for me.

He then tagged it:

#breakfastofchampions #migas #yeschef.

A good portion of the Hell Hounds on Instagram had liked it, if not commented something about feeling left out. Eli's friend Cody had commented with a link to a video how-to on migas from nearly two years before, suggesting the complainers make their own. Most of the comments, however, were about Eli.

who is @elijahrr and what do I have to do to get him to cook for me?

Where can I get an @elijahrr???

Or, overwhelmingly, the third picture in the set.

Okay but that last pic is disgustingly sweet. I need to go punch a wall now or something to reclaim my masculinity.

I'm having an emotion about that third picture.

Oh my god, is @elijahrr feeding @AP23 in the last picture?? I cannot handle the cute.

Jeff turns off his phone, feeling a little overwhelmed, then immediately turns it back on to call the team's PR lady. He doesn't think he's done anything wrong, but he's learned over the years that it's always best to check.

She gives him the verbal equivalent of a pat on the head and tells him to keep up the good work. He sighs and leaves the facility, trying to figure out how to disable Instagram notifications.

He still hasn't figured it out by the time he gets back to Alex's place because there are too many screens and buttons to contend with, and technology is the devil, and maybe he is just as old and crotchety as his teammates think he is.

Alex is exactly where Jeff left him, sitting awkwardly upright on the couch, scowling fiercely at the black TV.

"I've never been this bored in my life," he complains before Jeff is even fully in the door.

"Hey, Alex," Jeff says amicably. "Practice was good, thanks. My slapshot is really improving, and PT said my ankle probably won't need surgery next summer."

Alex sighs. "Sorry. I'm grumpy."

"Yes, you are. I'm amazed Eli was still willing to cook you breakfast this morning. Either he's a saint or you're less of a dick to him than the rest of us, in which case: rude."

"No," Alex says. "I was definitely a dick to him too. I apologized though."

"Apologized with words?"

"Yes," Alex says, aggrieved. "Used the phrase 'I'm sorry' and everything."

Jeff pretends to wipe a tear from his eye. "I'm proud of you," he says seriously. "This is a big step."

"What do you know about Louboutins?" Alex asks, and it takes Jeff a moment to adjust to the conversational whiplash.

"Uh. You mean the brand?"

"I mean the shoes. The, uh, high heels."

"Oh. Well, they're expensive as hell and, apparently, the shit if you're into that sort of thing? Jo has a pair. You have to send them to a special place to get the red bottoms repainted every now and then. It's ridiculous. Worth it though."

"Why?"

"Why's it worth it?"

"Yeah."

"She adores them, for one thing. Also, her legs look amazing in them. And her ass. And I can't think of a single time that she's worn them where I haven't gotten laid at the end of the night, so."

"Positive association?" Alex says dryly.

"Definitely. Why the sudden interest in couture footwear?"

"Where do you buy them? Can I just order a pair online?"

Jeff leaves his bag on the counter and moves into the living room to make sure Alex knows Jeff is frowning at him. "You realize not answering the question just makes me more suspicious, right? Is this your way of telling me you have a thing for female-coded footwear? Because I love and support you and all that, but your ankles are worth several million dollars, and no offense, you really don't have the coordination to walk in heels. We could find you some nice flats though. Strappy sandals? At least until the off-season."

"Oh my god, they're not for *me*," Alex says. "Not," he hastily adds, "that there would be anything wrong with that. If they were."

"Okay," Jeff says slowly.

They stare at each other for several seconds.

Alex sighs. "Eli wants some."

"And there we go."

"He's always wanted a pair."

"I should have guessed."

"Him and Cody both."

"Why didn't I guess? It seems obvious now."

"Jeff."

"Hmm?"

"Is that weird? If I buy them for him?"

"Yeah, probably. I mean—those are definitely Sex Shoes, and you two aren't having sex, so."

"They are not *sex* shoes."

Jeff makes a derisive noise. "You know what they look like, right? Picture Eli wearing them with one of those little pairs of shorts he likes and tell me those are Very Platonic Gift for Your Bro shoes."

"He said he'd cook in them," Alex blurts out, ears pink.

Jeff has no idea what that has to do with anything, but clearly Alex is embarrassed about whatever it is in his head that's prompted the admission. "Okay?"

"So. I have been, uh, picturing that."

"Oh," Jeff says. "*Oh, kid*. I thought you said you weren't—"

"I'm not. I can't. I just—" Alex exhales as if it hurts. "I want to."

"This is bigger than shoes," Jeff points out.

"Yeah."

"You really like him."

"Yeah," Alex repeats.

"I mean, I don't know if it helps, but I'm pretty sure the feeling is mutual."

"It doesn't."

Jeff sits on the couch next to Alex, careful not to jostle him.

"It's not fair," Alex says quietly.

"No, it's not."

"He won't date someone in the closet."

Jeff leans against him, just a little, to make his presence tangible. "You can't resent him for that."

"I know. And I don't. I just—I can't—" Alex closes his eyes. "I can't."

"That's okay too," Jeff says. "But if you ever wanted to ... If you ever decide to just say 'fuck it' and come out and screw the consequences, you know I'd be behind you 100 percent. Most of the team would."

Alex laughs without humor. "Can you imagine the shit show? The media would be terrible, yeah. But the other teams—it'd be a miracle if I survived a month after coming out." Alex's voice dips, wavers a bit before leveling off again. "So many of them already hate me. I can't imagine it being worse than it is already, but *it would be*."

Jeff wants so badly to hug him but can't.

"It's not fair," Alex repeats, and Jeff's chest aches.

It starts with an Instagram post. But the Snapchat escalates things. Well. The TikTok really.

The TikTok of the Snapchat.

Damn kids and their social media, Jeff thinks.

The TikTok is Kuzy's fault. It's two screencaps of Snapchat messages from Eli. The first is a photo of various food ingredients spread out across Alex's island countertop, some with Russian packaging, captioned *guess what I'm making??*

The second photo is of Bells sitting on top of, and mostly obscuring, a handwritten recipe for pelmeni. The caption for that one is a simple winking emoji.

Kuzy sets the screencaps to a terrible techno Russian song with smiling emojis, three Russian flags, and the caption: *Eli best*.

Three hours later, he posts a video that Jeff had taken of Kuzy holding a laughing, protesting Eli bridal-style. Kuzy is pressing an exaggerated kiss to Eli's temple while Eli tries to fend him off with an oven mitt. He captions it: *Eli's pelmeni 2nd place only for Mama's.*

The internet decides this is even cuter than the picture of Alex and Eli.

Apparently, the size difference between them is particularly adorable. Or something. Jeff doesn't know. The point is: people care. And as a result, Hell Hounds PR cares.

They're not even done with dessert—the video has barely been posted for thirty minutes—when Jeff's phone rings.

"It's Jessica," he says, and Kuzy and Alex both wince. It's ingrained at this point really. A trained response.

Because usually the only time Jessica calls you is when you've done something wrong.

"Get it over with," Kuzy says bracingly.

Jeff sighs and answers. "Hello?"

"Jeff," Jessica says. "Are you at Alex's place with Dmitri right now?"

"Um. Yes?"

"I assumed you were the one to take the picture. Is your new friend Elijah still there?"

"Yes."

"Good. May I speak to him?"

"Sure?"

Jeff hands the phone to a confused Eli. "It's Jessica. Hell Hounds PR."

Eli's eyebrows arch. "Hello, Jessica from Hell Hounds PR," he says, a little sharper than usual, his accent a little more pronounced. "How can I help you?"

His tone immediately mellows. "Oh. Well, thank you."

He leans one elbow on the table, listening, then cups a hand over his mouth, hiding an embarrassed smile. "It's no imposition. They're good boys."

Jeff isn't sure how he feels about being referred to as a "good boy" by an eighteen-year-old.

"I can't speak for them," Eli says after a moment, "but I'd be interested. I'd have to check with Cody, of course, but I'm pretty sure he'd be fine with it. Whether the boys are willing or not ... "

Alex meets Jeff's eyes across the table, brow furrowed, and Jeff shrugs at him.

"That's too kind of you. Yes. I can give you my cell phone number, if that—oh, great."

Eli lists off his number, says "thank you" another half dozen times, and then hangs up. He hands the phone back to Jeff, looking a little dazed. "They'd like to come film a behind-the-scenes bit for the Hell Hounds social media. Like some shots of me cooking here. And they'd like it if y'all helped me. She said they would post a short segment to their various sites, but I could have all the original footage and edit my own full-length how-to for our channel."

"Yes!" Kuzy says.

"Sure," Alex says, a little more subdued. "They'll need to wait a week or so if they want me to actually do anything though."

Eli beams at them both. Alex and Kuzy turn to Jeff expectantly.

"This is going to be embarrassing," he says. "But yeah, I'm down."

Eli takes turns hugging them all—Alex, very, very, gently—and then retreats to the guest bedroom to call Cody.

Kuzy happily returns to his dessert—some creamy custard thing (also Russian)—but Alex is looking at the closed bedroom door with a serious little pinch between his eyebrows.

"How you doing?" Jeff asks. "You haven't iced in a few hours."

"I'm okay," Alex says. "Maybe in a little bit. How did Jessica know he was here?"

"Oh. Kuzy posted some things on TikTok."

Alex wrinkles his nose. "Can I see? And what the hell did you do with my phone?"

"It's in hiding," Jeff says. "For your own good. You're still not supposed to have screen time, remember?"

"Yes," Alex says through gritted teeth, "I fucking remember."

Jeff decides a quick look at social media won't hurt him, and then, in the interest of full discretion, shows him the Instagram post from that morning as well.

Alex, much like the internet, lingers on the third photo. "This is a good picture," he says quietly. "I didn't even realize you took it."

"Sorry," Jeff says because Alex is making a face that looks hurt, maybe.

"No. You don't need to apologize. It's just. A good picture."

"Yeah. I, uh, took some others too. If you want to see them." He opens his photo reel and hands the phone back, not sure if it makes things better or worse as Alex scrolls through the pictures. He pauses on the second-to-last one, like Jeff knew he would. Like Jeff had himself.

In it, Eli is holding Alex's chin in one hand. The other hand had just wiped the smear of sauce off Alex's cheek, and Eli is in the process of licking his thumb clean, still smiling slightly, attention wholly on Alex.

And Alex.

Alex is looking at Eli as if he is the most beautiful thing he's ever seen. The expression of naked admiration on his face is—well, it certainly isn't something Jeff would post on Instagram.

Alex hands the phone back. "I didn't know I looked at him like that."

"You do," Jeff says inanely.

"Thanks." Alex's tone is dry.

"It's not that bad?" Jeff tries.

Alex doesn't even dignify that with a response.

Eli emerges from the guest bedroom, giddy after talking with Cody, and immediately gets to work cleaning the kitchen and sorting the dishes into the dishwasher, moving with excited energy that appears to rub off on Kuzy, who stands to help him.

Jeff gets Alex settled on the couch with more ice packs and agrees to turn on the sound for the Redwings-Pens game provided they don't turn on the actual television screen.

Kuzy leaves shortly afterward with a stack of Tupperware containers and a prolonged hug from Eli, and Jeff pretends not to notice that Alex's expression goes a bit murderous for the duration of the hug.

"Eli," Alex says seriously once the door has closed behind Kuzy, "I'm kind of cold; can you come sit with me?"

And Eli, because he's either oblivious or very good at faking artifice, immediately settles himself against Alex's side.

Jeff suppresses the urge to roll his eyes at the superior look Alex gives him. As if he's somehow won a competition for Eli's affections against a straight man who is no longer even present.

By the end of the first period of the game, Eli is nodding off against Alex's shoulder, his entire body curled toward Alex, knees resting on his thigh, face tucked neatly into the curve of his neck. Alex has his left arm wrapped around Eli's back, and his fingers absently play with the hem of his shirt, knuckles occasionally brushing skin.

By the end of the second period, Alex is asleep too, head tipped back against the couch, hand curled proprietarily around Eli's hip.

Jeff knows he probably shouldn't.

But he takes another picture anyway.

12

THEY FILM THE SEGMENT four days later when Alex is no longer moving so gingerly. Kuzy has acquired a black eye from a fight the night before, which he bears with unapologetic levity as Eli despairs over him. It's just a single-camera guy and Jessica, who consults briefly with Eli before setting up. Eli decides to treat it like any other video blog. He tells the camera their recipe for the day—a new iteration of Alex's favorite chili, with bison rather than turkey—then takes great pleasure in bossing the others around.

Kuzy takes it upon himself to "introduce" them all once they're set to their individual tasks.

"I'm pretty sure that's not necessary," Eli says, turning on the stove burner.

"It's important," Kuzy argues. "Guest stars need introduce. And cooking people don't know hockey people, maybe. Hockey people don't know you."

"He has a point," Jeff agrees.

Eli makes no more protests and starts sautéing some diced onion. He's learned to pick his battles.

"Okay," Kuzy begins again, gesturing toward Eli with the chives he's supposed to be cutting. "This is Eli. Tiny YouTube chef. Best figure skater. More best than Jeff."

"Oh my god," Jeff says, aggrieved. "Is that really a necessary part of his introduction? I'm a hockey player now. A *professional* hockey player. I'm not supposed to be good at figure skating anymore."

Kuzy widens his eyes, feigning contrition.

"You figure skate?" Jessica says.

Eli has a feeling she already knows this, but he plays along. "Yeah. I'm on the HU team."

"And he can do Jeff's old gold-medal routine almost perfect," Alex says proudly. "Jumps and all."

Which isn't strictly accurate, but Jessica looks genuinely surprised at that. "Really? You memorized Jeff's World Juniors routine?"

"Oh," Eli says. "Yes? But I can't do it perfectly."

"He skates it really well," Jeff interrupts him. "Give him a month or so of concentrated practice, and he could probably do it flawless."

"You've seen him do it?" Jessica asks Jeff.

"Yeah. Sometimes he comes with Pricey and me to skate when I have private rink time."

Jessica looks delighted by this information.

Eli has a feeling Jeff is going to get a request to film his private rink time in the near future.

"Anyway," Eli says, a little desperately, adjusting the heat on the stove. "Kuzy? Introductions?"

"Yes," Kuzy agrees, gesturing to Alex with his knife this time. "This is Alex Price, but team calls Pricey. Hell Hounds hockey captain. Best center. Hurt little bit now, but good soon. Team miss."

Alex's ears go pink.

"And this," Kuzy continues, pointing to Jeff, "this is Jeff Cooper. Team calls Coops. Is left-wing player. Very fast but needs work on slapshot. More power."

"Hey," Jeff says.

"And me!" Kuzy continues quickly. "I'm Dmitri Kuznetsov. Team name Kuzy. But Eli calls me 'Sweet Potato' because I'm most favorite."

"I do not," Eli says.

"You do!"

"I called you that once, and I was kidding."

"Kidding?" Kuzy says, hurt.

"It's not nice of you to play with Kuzy's feelings," Alex says somberly. "It's hard for him to understand sarcasm in English."

"It's true," Kuzy agrees.

Eli rolls his eyes. "You, Mr. Price, are a joke."

Alex grins. "Well, if I'm a joke, you're a whole standup routine."

"It might behoove you to remember that I have a scalding pan in my hand," Eli says.

"Ohh, 'behoove,' huh? Breaking out the big college words."

"Yes. Because unlike *some* people, I went to college instead of making a career in *losing* braincells."

"Children," Jeff says. "I only coach one week of mite camp every summer for a reason. Can we not?"

"Is good practice, Coops," Kuzy says wisely. "For when Jo wants to make baby with you. Maybe takes a long time, though, for want. Because of face."

"I mean," Alex says, "to be fair, she married that face. So she knew what she was getting into."

"Oh my god," Jeff says. "I am the only hockey player in this kitchen with all his original teeth. Do not try to start a who's-the-ugliest contest because it will not end well for either of you."

Eli blinks, whipping his head around to study Alex. "Really? You have fake teeth?"

Alex taps his upper lip. "Two middle ones are both implants."

"No kidding." Eli hitches his hip against the counter. "What happened?"

"I have video!" Kuzy says, dropping the chives and wiping his hands off on his apron before retrieving his phone. "Very pretty play. Lots of blood."

Eli gives Kuzy a bit of side-eye for the description, and Jeff sighs.

"It was admittedly a nice play," he says. "Stupid. But nice."

"I made the goal," Alex says defensively as if that's what matters. Which, Eli supposes, for Alex, probably is what matters.

Kuzy hands over his phone with YouTube open and the clip already playing.

Eli abandons his pan and leans in close to watch.

Alex has the puck and is streaking down the ice. There's an *A* on his jersey rather than a *C*, so it must be during his first season with the Hell Hounds. He passes to a teammate to evade a defenseman, then is fed the puck right back and goes down on one knee to shoot. It's deflected by the goalie, and Alex nearly dives to recover it in a desperate onehanded shot made while he's in the process of falling. It miraculously connects, popping the puck right over the left shoulder of the goalie. At Alex's lunge, however, several players all converge in front of the goal, and in the chaos, as Alex tumbles onto the ice, he gets a hard-swung stick to the mouth.

Kuzy is right.

There's a lot of blood.

Eli winces through the slow-motion replay, then hides his face in Kuzy's bicep when the camera zooms in first on the red patch of ice beneath Alex's bowed head, and then on the stained towel clutched to his mouth as he's helped off the ice.

Eli pushes around Kuzy's bulk to gain access to the present-day Alex, who looks sheepish where he leans against the island.

Eli doesn't say anything, but he reaches automatically for Alex's face.

Alex goes pink under his scrutiny. "I'm fine. It was over a year ago."

"And it was just your teeth?" Eli asks, turning his head first one way, then the other.

"Just my teeth. And a busted lip. I was good as new a week later. And," he says as though he can't resist, "that was the game-winning shot. So."

"Hockey players are stupid," Eli says.

"Yes," Kuzy agrees.

"Hey," Jeff says, aggrieved. "What am I supposed to do with this cabbage?"

The video is an unmitigated success. It becomes the most-shared piece of media from the Hell Hounds Facebook page within twenty-four hours, and the collection of stills they post on Instagram are equally popular. Between the constant sarcastic banter, Jeff's long-suffering expressions, à la *The Office*, the general ineptness of the hockey players in the kitchen, and how delicious the chili they make looks (the combined delighted moans during taste-testing at the end were also a hit in some circles), the Hell Hounds get the positive attention they wanted, and Eli and Cody's channel nears 60,000 followers.

The reaction on Tumblr is a little different.

Despite the Hell Hounds not having an official Tumblr page, the video, along with several photosets and GIFs, all immediately go viral, where the chief discussion in comments and tags is who, exactly, is banging whom. General consensus is that Jeff is the Beleaguered Straight One, but otherwise, Tumblr is pretty divided on whether Eli and Alex are together or Kuzy and Eli. A few enterprising individuals make a solid case that they're very happily polyamorous.

There is also an impressive influx of fan fiction in the Hell Hounds tag.

Eli doesn't read any of it. Yet. He's sorely tempted to at least skim a few of the Eli-Alex ones because of their teaser blurbs. That would just make things worse, he thinks.

The week after the video is published, Eli gets a call from Cody as he's leaving practice. Which is strange because they already have a FaceTime date planned for that night.

"Buen día, corazón," Eli says, a little distractedly. Since the regular season started, the Hell Hounds have moved their practices to 11:00 a.m., and every other week or so, Eli will stay in the icehouse and do homework in the hour interim between his own practice so he can watch. Or heckle, as the case may be. He checks his backpack to see if he has his stats textbook.

"Hey," Cody says, and he sounds—off.

"Hey," Eli repeats. And then he waits.

"So," Cody says. "James."

Eli stops digging through his bag. "Are you okay?"

"What? No, oh no, he didn't do anything *bad*; he, um ... "

Cody makes a noise that, despite years of knowing him, Eli has no idea how to interpret.

"Since your videos have been getting so much attention," Cody continues, "I've been—not jealous!—okay, a little bit jealous. Because yours have so many more views than mine now. And I know that's petty as hell, but it still bothered me. Uh. Bothers me. I guess."

"Oh," Eli says, feeling sucker punched. That hadn't even occurred to him. Why hadn't that occurred to him? He's a terrible friend. "I'm so sorry, Cody. I had no idea. What do you want me to do?"

"No, hey," Cody says, and it sounds like he's smiling, at least. "Honestly, I'm so happy for you, and the traffic is good for the channel. We're making actual ad revenue now. But listen. I was in a bit of a funk yesterday night, and James found me on the roof feeling sorry for myself."

"Were you drunk?"

"I may have been the slightest bit drunk."

"And you were on the *roof*?"

"Do not start with me, Elijah. The point is that in a moment of extreme weakness, I may have cried a bit on James Petrov about my—well—*feelings* about the situation."

"Oh my god. I can't even imagine. And?"

"James volunteered to be in my next video? He said we could do the same thing you did with the Hell Hounds, except with a couple of the boys here. He thinks his name would be enough to generate some interest. But I figured I'd better ask you first. And maybe get the number of the Hell Hounds PR person to ask them. I don't want to cause any problems."

Eli is honestly a little shocked. "That's really cool of James. You realize he hasn't done any kind of media since before the draft. Like. *Any* kind of media. And he rarely shows up in his dad or brother's posts. He doesn't even have a Twitter."

"I know." Cody's voice has gone quiet and thoughtful. "He's been different recently. Nicer, I mean. I don't know. There's moments now when—"

"What?"

"When I think we might be friends. He'd only be willing to suggest the video thing if he thought we were friends, right?" Cody sounds more than a little pleased about this. Worryingly so.

Eli decides not to mention it. "Yeah, for sure. That's great."

"Anyway." And now Cody sounds embarrassed.

"Well, let me get Jessica's number from one of the guys and call her. I'm pretty sure the more publicity the better. I can't imagine she'd have a problem with it. Besides, it's your channel too."

"True," Cody agrees, laughing. "Thanks for understanding."

"Of course. You still want to FaceTime tonight?"

"Sure do. Oh shit, it just occurred to me what time it is for you. I didn't interrupt your practice, did I?"

"No, you're good. I was just packing up to head over to the rink."

"Watching the boys practice again today?"

"It's Alex's first day back. No contact, but still. We made dinner together last night to celebrate. For being so terrible at chopping vegetables, I've found he's very dependable with measuring and mixing ingredients. Excellent whisking form."

"Eli," Cody says, still laughing a little, "you realize falling for a closeted professional hockey player is just as bad as falling for a straight boy."

Eli doesn't laugh. "Yeah, I know."

13

ALEX MISSES ELI.

It's stupid because Eli hasn't gone anywhere. He still comes over at least once a week and shows up intermittently to practices and sends daily texts and Snapchats to Alex, as well as what feels like half the team at this point. But it's still not the same as having Eli in his home. Playing his records. Dancing in his kitchen. Sleeping across the hall.

He only stayed for three nights, but it was enough that now, two weeks later, Alex still knows exactly what he's missing.

And his chest hurts with overwhelming affection and resignation and other emotions he doesn't even have names for.

He doesn't know what to do about it.

He buries his face in Bells's soft belly fur, risking her wrath, and dedicates the first fifteen minutes of his Saturday morning to feeling sorry for himself. Half because he's hungover from the team's game-winning celebration the night before, half because he's pretty sure he's in love, and it's terrible.

"It would be nice if Hawk lived here too, huh?" he asks Bells.

She bats his ear with one paw but keeps her claws sheathed, so he takes that as affirmation.

"Maybe next year?" he says, getting fur in his mouth. "I know Eli doesn't want to stay in a dorm, but his scholarship only covers on-campus housing. Do you think he'd want to move in with us? I know he really likes the kitchen. And there's a dog park right around the corner for Hawk. I could reserve him a parking garage spot by the elevator. Should probably get on the waiting list for one now though."

Bells, it seems, has had enough.

With a sigh, Alex watches her escape to the opposite end of the bed. "It would be weird to ask him now, huh?"

It's hard to believe they only met three months ago. Bells is judging him.

He decides to go make breakfast, and by "make breakfast," he means defrost a stack of Eli's blueberry protein pancakes and continue to feel sorry for himself because the pancakes are amazing, but they would be so much better if they'd been made fresh. By Eli. In his kitchen right now.

Twenty minutes later, Alex has ordered a pair of Louboutins to be delivered to Eli's dorm by express mail later that day. And he's booked Eli a flight to visit Cody over Thanksgiving break because he knows Eli can't afford to go home, and Cody can't go back either because he has a game the day before Thanksgiving. Eli really misses Cody, so seeing him would make Eli happy. Apparently, Alex doesn't know how to handle emotions, and he's a dumpster fire of a human being. He starts shopping for new skates in Eli's size, too, but stops himself because he's probably already progressed into unacceptably creepy territory.

Come take my laptop away from me, he texts Jeff and then decides to go back to sleep and deal with the world later.

When Alex wakes up again, it's to his phone ringing (maybe it's been ringing for a while? The world is still fuzzy) and his bedroom door opening, which is a weird confluence of events.

He doesn't answer the phone in favor of squinting at the intruder.

It's Jeff, looking amused.

Which makes sense because only Jeff and Eli have a key to his place.

"Hey kid," Jeff says. "You might want to answer your phone."

When it starts ringing again a second later, Alex does. "Muh?" he manages.

"*Mr. Price*," Eli says, well, shouts really. "Do you mind explaining to me why I have two airplane tickets in my inbox?"

"Um. So you can go visit Cody? You said he had to stay over the break since he has a game. And you couldn't go home. And you wished you could see him play."

"Yes. Yes, I did say all of those things, but that doesn't tell me why I have airline tickets that *I did not buy*."

"I bought them?"

"I gathered that, thank you." He doesn't sound very thankful.

Alex's head hurts. "I'm sorry?"

Eli mutters something in Spanish, and Alex is still confused but is now also a little turned on. He knew angry Russian did it for him, but it seems he needs to add judgmental Spanish to his list of kinks as well.

He groans a little and decides maybe he should pay attention to what Eli is hissing at him through the phone.

"—not like I don't appreciate it because, holy shit, it will be so good to see Cody. But you can't just *do* things like that without asking!"

"I'm sorry," Alex repeats. "You were so great while I was hurt, even though I was a dick, and you're one of my best friends now. And, like, if Coops wanted to go visit a friend, he'd just buy a ticket himself because he's loaded, which makes it hard to do things for Coops. But you're not, uh, loaded, which means I can do things for you. And I want to. Because you do things for me."

Eli is quiet for a moment. "That ... is weirdly sweet."

Alex exhales in relief. Then winces. "Also, uh, your last class gets out at 3:00 today, right?"

"Yes."

"Will you be back at your dorm between 4:00 and 5:00? You should be getting a package then. You'll have to sign for it."

"Alex."

"It's not a big deal!"

Except it is. Especially if Eli thinks the plane tickets are too much.

Jesus. What was he thinking? He should have at least spread them out a little. Plane tickets for Thanksgiving. Shoes for Christmas. But he wants to give Eli *skates* for Christmas.

"Alex," Eli says, voice sharp. "I don't know what's going on with you right now, but I don't need some sort of charity if that's what's happening here."

"It's not charity! It's nothing! I didn't even get you a first-class ticket!"

He seriously considered it. And he did make sure it was a bulkhead seat so Hawk would have plenty of room. Eli doesn't need to know that though.

"These tickets are four hundred dollars!" Eli shouts. "That's not 'nothing'! It's something!"

"I was just having a lot of feelings this morning!" Alex yells back. "And I have way too much money. Can you *please* just let me do nice things for you?!"

Eli is silent for several seconds.

"Fine."

"Fine."

"I'm coming over to make you dinner tonight," Eli snaps.

"Great," Alex mutters back. "Just make sure it's after 5:00 so you can sign for the package."

"Fine."

"Fine."

They hang up on each other at the same time, and Alex childishly throws his phone to the foot of the bed.

"That went well," Jeff says.

It doesn't occur to Alex to warn Jessica because he doesn't anticipate it will be a big deal. After a run with Jeff and a late lunch with Kuzy, he's cleaning the kitchen counters, guard down, when he gets a call from Jessica.

"Hey, what's up?"

There's a distinctive, judgmental pause.

"Are you and Elijah dating?"

"What?" He sets down the counter spray. "No."

"Then do you want to explain to me why you bought someone who is *not* your boyfriend *nine-hundred-dollar* sex shoes?"

"Oh my god, they are not *sex* shoes—and how do you even know about that? He probably doesn't even have them yet."

"They really are. And he does. Because he's just posted a picture of them on Instagram, and the internet is already collectively losing its mind."

"I—hold on."

Alex puts her on speaker so he can open the Instagram app.

Sure enough, the top photograph on his feed is a picture of the shoes, newly unpackaged and arranged artfully on top of the gilded box they came in.

Eli has captioned the picture:

When you're friends with @AP23 you must submit yourself to ridiculous gifts as thanks for common decency.

#excessive #louboutins #heisaterriblepatienttho

Alex doesn't see what the big deal is.

"I don't see what the big deal is."

"Alex," Jessica says patiently. "This is not the kind of gift a heterosexual guy gives to his male friend. Would you ever buy Jeff shoes like this?"

"Yes? If he asked for a pair. Look. I just wanted to do something nice for Eli because he took care of me the first couple days when I was injured. And he cooks for me all the time. And just—I knew they'd make him happy."

"Oh my god," Jessica says faintly. "I can't even be mad at you when you're so stupidly earnest."

"Thank you?"

She sighs. "Listen; up until now this thing with Eli has been great publicity for you. It humanizes you; makes people forget about your past ... exploits. And since Dmitri and Jeff seem just as close to him, no one was talking or making assumptions. The narrative was progressive without being polarizing. Straight Hockey Players Cool with Gay Friend. But we might have to do some damage control now."

"They're just a pair of shoes," he says, still baffled.

"And that's the line you'll stick to. Unless you want to come out."

"No. I'm not—" He chokes a little on the denial because he hasn't had to say the words in so long that he's gotten a little too comfortable with the truth.

"I'm not gay," he says, voice rough. "Eli is just a friend."

"Also the line you'll stick to, then. You have a video interview with *V Magazine* the day after tomorrow. Considering the timing, they'll likely ask you about this. If you don't think you can handle it, we can postpone."

"No," Alex says, breathless. "It's fine. Do people really think—?"

Jessica sighs again. "This isn't a disaster, Alex. But little things like this can quickly add up. You need to be careful."

He swallows, and it hurts his throat.

"If—" She pauses and then starts again. "Just so you know, if there *were* a gay or bisexual player on the team, the organization would back them 100 percent. PR already has an assortment of mock-up press releases and game plans in the event that a player is forcefully outed or intentionally decides to come out. It wouldn't be easy by any means. But it wouldn't be the end of the world either."

Alex knows he should probably say something but can't seem to make words work.

"Alex?" Jessica says, sounding concerned.

He hangs up because he can't breathe.

He tries to call for Bells, but the room tips sideways, and he has to lean against the island for support. He slowly slides to the floor, back pressed against the paneled wood. His breath is harsh and discordant in his ears.

Eli finds him that way some indeterminable amount of time later.

He comes in yelling but stops almost immediately when he sees Alex on the floor. "What the fuck—Alex, are you—? Hey. *Hey.*"

Alex tries to tell him he's fine even though that's demonstrably untrue.

"Shit," Eli says. "So, I think you're having a panic attack. Is it cool if Hawk and I help? Can I touch you?"

Alex manages a nod, and Eli unclips Hawk's lead, murmuring something to her. A moment later, there's a heavy weight across his lap, a sharp elbow pressed to his upper thigh, and a large warm mass of dog leans back against his chest. He tucks his face into her neck because it seems like the thing to do.

Eli slides onto the ground next to him. "Hey, can you try to breathe with me?"

Alex nods.

It takes several minutes, but eventually, his breathing slows to something like normal, and the top of his head feels solid again.

Eli, still pressed shoulder to shoulder with him, gives him a little nudge. "How you doing?"

"Better," he admits, straightening.

Hawk tips her face up to lick his chin.

He smiles despite himself.

"So," Eli says conversationally. "I didn't know you have panic attacks."

"It's been a while," Alex says, exhausted. "I had a bad stretch where I used to get them all the time, but it's been months since I've had one."

"You want to go lie down in the bedroom for a little bit?" Eli asks.

"You coming with me?" Alex answers because he's shameless.

"Sure," Eli says quietly. "We can even give Hawk special permission to join us on the bed if you want."

"Yeah, okay."

They move to the bedroom—where Bells has been asleep the entire time—rude—and Alex sheds his jeans without thinking.

Eli doesn't seem bothered, though, and follows him onto the bed, still fully clothed.

Well. "Fully" might be arguable; the tiny shorts he's wearing don't leave much to the imagination.

Alex fumbles for a moment, one hand blind in the drawer of his nightstand, until he manages to find the remote for the window blinds. He presses the button to close them, and the room goes slowly dark, leaving him feeling vulnerable and unsettled.

He watches as Eli curls into a half-moon facing him, then pulls the duvet up to cover them both. Hawk settles, warm and solid, at the foot of the bed. Bells moves from the chair by the window, stretching, and repositions herself in a spherical lump beside Alex's head.

Eli watches him, quiet, maybe a little worried.

"Sorry," Alex whispers because the dark makes him feel like he should. "I know you were probably looking forward to yelling at me when you got here, and I ruined it."

"Ah, yes," Eli says. "I'm sure that was your conniving plan all along. You want to tell me what happened? I can save the yelling for later. Or—do you want to call your therapist?"

"No. I see her the day after tomorrow anyway. Could you call Jessica back for me though?"

It's embarrassing to ask, but he's so tired.

"Sure. What were you talking about?"

"The picture you posted on Instagram. Of the shoes. She called to tell me I have to be careful. Because giving you a gift like that causes speculation."

Eli narrows his eyes. "Speculation about *your* sexuality? You didn't buy the shoes for yourself." He sits up for a moment to extract his phone from his pocket. "I have notes turned off; I haven't even looked at it since I posted it. Hold on."

Eli scrolls through the comments for a moment and then bites his lip. "I mean. There aren't many mean ones, but most of the comments are about what a 'gay' gift it is. That could just be in reference to me, but—I'm sorry. I didn't even think about how it would look. I can take it down? Except that probably wouldn't help at this point. Shit," he exhales, turning off his phone and then flipping it over as if that will give him additional distance from its content.

"I just keep making things worse for you."

Eli goes quiet for a moment, bottom lip tucked tightly between his teeth. "Maybe," he says haltingly, "I shouldn't spend so much time with—"

And Alex can't even let him finish that sentence because no. Because once again, Eli is upset and feels responsible for something that isn't even his fault, when he hasn't done anything wrong. It's completely unfair, and the fact that Eli is talking about spending even less time with Alex to protect him and his fucking 'image' or whatever is—

"No," Alex interrupts. "No, you know what? This is bullshit."

"What?"

"I shouldn't have to not give you certain gifts because of some fucked up unwritten heteronormative rules about what men are and aren't allowed to do for their male friends. I should be trying to change the way people think, not just blindly following the shitty system that exists."

Eli blinks at him. "Alex. That's admirable. But it's not your responsibility to try to challenge the system. Just like it's not your responsibility to come out just because you're gay and have a platform. You have to do what's best for you and—"

"What's best for me is not having to overthink every single thing I or my friends post on Instagram. Or remembering to police the way I act, or—The whole point of the You Can Play videos Jeff and I do is that even if you don't fit into the stereotypical profile of a hockey player, you can still play, and you can still play well. I may not be ready to come out, but the least I can do is not be a massive hypocrite by intentionally fitting myself into a mold while telling kids they shouldn't have to."

He feels a little breathless again, but this time in a good way.

Eli is smiling at him. "Okay," he says.

"Okay?"

"Yeah. Okay. I agree with you. Also, points for using 'heteronormative.'"

"That would be Jeff's influence," Alex admits. "Here, can you hand me my phone?"

Eli does and a few moments later, Alex tells him to check Twitter.

Alex has posted two screencaps from Eli's Instagram—one of the post itself, another of some of the comments. He's captioned it:

Can't a bro buy his bro a pair of Louboutins?

#fuckyourheteronormativebullshit #treatyobro

Jeff has already liked it. As Eli's looking at it, Kuzy, then two more Hell Hounds like it, then Cody, and then it's too hard to keep up.

Alex's phone rings a moment later.

He answers without looking and is entirely unsurprised to hear Jessica on the other line.

"I really wish you would consult with me before you do things like this," she says, more fondly than aggrieved. "Though I will admit, it's an approach I hadn't considered."

"Uh. Okay."

"I guess if anyone can pull off cavalier, hypermasculine security, it's you."

"Thank you?"

Jessica doesn't say anything for a short stretch, and he can hear her typing in the background.

"Alex," she says finally. "Are you okay? I was a little worried after our conversation earlier."

He swallows. "I'm fine." And then, because he's feeling reckless. "Eli is here with me now."

"I see."

"Yeah."

"Well, I'll let you get back to ... Eli. But, Alex, please do keep in mind what I said earlier."

"Okay."

"I'll see you on Wednesday."

"Okay, thanks. Bye."

He drops the phone onto the mattress between him and Eli and closes his eyes.

"You all right?" Eli asks, bumping his knuckles against Alex's.

Alex catches Eli's wrist before he can retreat, turns Eli's hand so he can press his thumb gently to the center of his palm. He traces the lines there—the indentations he can feel but not see. He slides their fingers together, and they mesh like a habit.

He's being selfish, he knows that, but he's also so tired, and he just wants—

"I'm good," he says belatedly, opening his eyes.

Eli looks ... confused, maybe. Or sad. But he doesn't pull his hand away.

"Okay," he says. "Good."

14

V MAGAZINE DOES ASK Alex about the shoes.

It's supposed to be a puff piece in an online series about the average everyday life of celebrity Texas athletes. The reporter spends the first fifteen minutes on questions about his actual everyday life first, which is longer than Alex anticipated.

"So," the guy says, his smile both too wide and too white. "As I'm sure you're aware, you were responsible for the hashtag *#treatyobro* trending on Twitter yesterday. You want to talk about what prompted your tweet?"

A copy of said tweet is projected on the screen behind them.

Alex glances at it briefly before responding.

"I bought my friend Eli some shoes as a thank-you for taking care of me when I was injured a few weeks back. The tweet was in response to an Instagram post Eli made with a picture of the shoes—you can see it there. I thought a lot of the comments on his post were messed up, and I just wanted to call people out, I guess."

"Well," the interviewer says, still grinning broadly. "I think buying Louboutins for your 'bro'"—and he's totally using verbal quotes the way he says it, *gross*—"is a little different than buying, say, a pair of Jordans."

"Yeah," Alex says, intentionally missing the point. "They're a lot more expensive, for sure. But I don't think you understand how terrible I am to be around when I'm hurt. Jordans would not have been enough for the shit he put up with. Not to mention that he cleaned Bells's litter box for *four days*."

The interviewer laughs as though they're sharing a joke.

Which they're not.

Alex doesn't laugh.

"So," the guy says a little awkwardly. "Buying them for him didn't make you uncomfortable?"

"No? Why would it?"

"Because they're women's shoes?"

"They're Eli's shoes," Alex says with studied blankness. "I bought them for Eli. And he's a man. So, I think they're men's shoes, in this case."

The reporter doesn't seem to know what to do with this.

"Look," Alex says. "I don't get what the big deal is. I'm grateful for Eli's friendship and his help, and I knew they'd make him happy. I bought Coops a watch for his birthday over the summer that was worth four times as much. With, like, diamonds and shit. He put it all over his Instagram then, and nobody cared."

"You don't think that's different?" the reporter asks, his smile getting a little pinched.

"No," Alex lies, thinking about Eli dancing in his kitchen the night before: the arch of his feet in the shoes, the distinct cut of his calf muscles, the twist of his narrow hips grinding to a low bass beat, the glow of the Houston skyline behind him.

"Not at all."

It doesn't end with the interview.

If anything, it gets bigger.

Tumblr collectively decides that maybe Alex is no longer a "problematic fav." Tumblr also collectively appears to think this is due to Jeff's influence.

They're not wrong.

Eli has nearly as many followers on Instagram as Alex. The YouTube channel is making real money on ads.

The day after Alex's interview, when the Hell Hounds have just won a hard-fought home game and the postgame interviews are winding down, Jeff is asked about his addition to the *#treatyobro* phenomenon: a picture of him and Rushy getting pedicures earlier that day.

"Playing hockey is really rough on your feet," Jeff says. "And goalies are on their feet the whole game. Some of the guys have started taking turns treating Rushy to a foot massage and a pedicure every two weeks or so. Just to show our appreciation, you know? His girlfriend sent us a thank-you box of cookies after the first time too. The kid is brilliant at hockey but not so much at hygiene. His feet were pretty fu—uh—jacked up before we intervened."

"HEY," Rushy yells from his locker a few feet away.

"Don't even," Rushy's former roommate, Mugs, says. "You straight-up shanked me with your jagged-ass toenails the first time we ever played video games together."

"That was an accident!" Rushy whines. "The couch was too small. I didn't mean to kick you."

"That makes it worse! And I didn't even say anything about the *smell*—"

"Anyway," Jeff says.

"So you agree with Price, then?" the reporter asks, clearly trying to contain his amusement. "That we should reexamine assumptions about what behaviors are and are not socially acceptable between male friends?"

"For sure, I agree," Jeff says. "Where do you think Alex learned the word 'heteronormative'?"

The man laughs. "And your thoughts about some of the unkind comments left on your friend Elijah's Instagram post?"

"Dude," Jeff says. "Eli can do the entire "Single Ladies" dance in five-inch heels. I've seen it. That's not laughable or embarrassing or an affront to his masculinity. That's a feat of athleticism. And potentially the work of dark magic."

He sobers a little. "Seriously though. I think it's stupid to say that men can't give certain gifts to other men because they're too 'feminine' or too 'gay.' Not to mention how problematic it is to imply that 'feminine' or 'gay' are somehow bad things."

"I think this is the most progressive conversation I've ever had in a locker room," the reporter says.

"Good," Jeff answers, and winks.

Tumblr really loves Jeff.

As does most of the internet at large.

He becomes a reaction GIF. He becomes a meme. People who don't even like sports know who Jeff Cooper—woke hockey player extraordinaire—is.

The *#treatyobro* hashtag starts trending again shortly afterward, this time with an influx of all sorts of different athletes posting pictures on Twitter and Instagram. A lot of them are in the same vein as Jeff's—pedicures and spa days. But there's a range: An NFL player wearing plastic gloves while dying the bleached tips of his teammate's dreadlocks bright pink; another NFL player looking delighted as he opens a monthly tea subscription box; two NBA players surprising a rookie with a new suit; an MLB player and his Newfoundland puppy gifting his relieved-looking roommate a Pet Hair Edition Roomba; a rugby player, a bit shiny in the eyes, holding a tiny kitten with a bow around its neck.

One that goes largely without much attention, however, is posted by one of the Princeton hockey players. Alex would have missed it if not for Eli retweeting it. It's a picture of Cody standing in the kitchen at the hockey house, pink-faced and beaming. Spread across the counter is an assortment of mixing bowls and measuring cups, all in the same matte-black of Cody's mixer. Several players are clustered around him, looking proud of themselves, but what catches Alex's eye is James.

James is in the background, practically out-of-frame. He's not acting like the others—flexing, hugging, or hamming it up for the camera. He's just sort of awkwardly standing there, hands in his pockets, present but not participating. He's wearing sweats and an old T-shirt from juniors, the same shirt he used to sleep in on roadies when he and Alex shared a room. Alex remembers exactly how soft the fabric is. The way it smells.

In the picture, James is looking at Cody. And he's smiling.

Eli has to leave town for his first big competition the week before Thanksgiving break. It's in Los Angeles—the fall regional something or other—and it coincides with a long weekend when the Hell Hounds will be on the road as well. It's not like Alex could have seen him during that time anyway, but for some reason, Alex has a minor crisis about it.

"Hey," Jeff says as Alex paces in the weight room the day before they're supposed to leave. "I think you're being a little dramatic."

"I just—What if something happens? I know Hawk will be with him, but what if he has a seizure?"

"The coach, who is familiar with his condition, will take care of things. He's going to be fine."

But Alex doesn't *know* that. And he realizes he wouldn't be able to ensure it, even if he somehow managed to go. But Eli won't be in the normal places that Alex associates as safe: Eli's dorm. The rink. Campus. Alex's home. With Alex. It's a problem for his brain.

Alex knows he has issues with anxiety.

He knows he has issues with protective instincts. He knows he has issues with control.

But knowing these things doesn't negate that he's more nervous about Eli's impending trip than he is about his own away games. Because even aside from medical concerns, what if someone is mean to Eli? What if people make fun of his scars or say something rude about Hawk?

"Are you friendly with anyone on the Kings?" Alex asks casually.

Jeff sighs. "Bud. You are not allowed to ask random professional hockey players to go attend Eli's competition as some sort of weird protective proxy for you. He'll be gone for three days and back in Houston before we are. You need to chill."

Jeff is right.

He needs to chill.

"I should probably call Anika for an extra session, huh?" Alex says.

"Probably," Jeff agrees, racking his weights. "Props for suggesting it yourself though. Can you imagine having this conversation a year ago? If I so much as said the word 'therapy' you probably would have thrown a kettlebell at me."

Alex snorts, swapping places with Jeff on the bench. "We wouldn't be having this conversation a year ago because I would still be freaking the fuck out about liking dick, and I definitely wouldn't be friends with a gay guy."

"Valid," Jeff says, glancing at the door automatically. "Can you imagine saying that sentence out loud in the weight room a year ago?"

Alex winces, also glancing at the door. "I should be more careful. Hanging out with you and Eli makes me forget, sometimes."

"Only if you want to," Jeff says with studied disinterest. "If you wanted to come out, you know I'd fight anyone who came after you on the ice. Might spend all my time in the box and end up traded, but I'd do it. If you wanted to."

For the first time, Alex doesn't immediately dismiss the suggestion.

"So," Jeff says a few minutes later, when they've moved to the stationary bikes. "Did you see that video Cody posted last night?"

He did not. He'd spent the evening interfering with the filming of Eli's new video by "accidentally" walking into the frame in his most lurid pair of boxers, making faces at Eli from behind the camera, and helping Bells moonwalk across the counter top while Eli's back was turned at the stove.

And then Eli had tried to teach him how to play chess because, apparently, it was inexcusable that he'd never learned.

There was a lot of laughter. It was a nice night.

Especially because Alex convinced Eli to stay in the guest room since it was late, and he could just head to campus from there the next morning.

So Alex got to eat pancakes with a rumpled, sleepbleary, pre-coffee Eli before meeting Jeff at the gym.

It was a nice morning too.

Alex refocuses on Jeff, who looks a little too knowing about where his head just went.

"Well," Alex says. "How was it?"

"Honestly? Pretty hilarious. Similar dynamic as our video in terms of banter. That Muzz guy Eli has told us about is a riot, the captain is chill, and the two D-men are just as codependent as you'd expect. But, uh ... it was definitely the James and Cody show. They play off each other really well."

Alex waits for that to hurt.

It doesn't.

Jeff is looking at him with a degree of caution, which is probably fair since he's the only person, aside from Alex's therapist, who knows about his history with James.

"I'm okay," Alex says. "Maybe I won't be after I watch it, but—" He shrugs.

"Good. One more set?"

Alex agrees.

They go to the Pretty Bird Cafe for lunch, and then Alex drives home and stares at the YouTube front page for a solid ten minutes, absently petting Bells in his lap, before finally going to Eli and Cody's channel.

He clicks on the new video link before he can talk himself out of it.

Jeff is right. The towering D-man pair is endearing in the way big, earnest people are, finishing each other's sentences and trying to do delicate work with hands that are simply too large. Muzz is a comedic star in his own right with snappy one-liners and occasional rants about consumerism and The Patriarchy. If the internet loves Jeff, they'll really like Muzz. James and Cody steal the show though. The chemistry between them is undeniable.

They're opposites in the most complimentary way—James, overly serious, brows pinched as he tries to measure the exact amount of paprika the recipe calls for, while Cody teases him gently and nudges his elbow so the teaspoon runs a little over into the bowl. James, soft-spoken and measured movements; Cody, darting around, loud and laughing. Even their voices are oddly suited, the drawl of Cody's long, southern consonants and James's slightly accented Russian vowels seamlessly meshing as they chirp at each other, familiar and fond.

It does hurt, after all.

Just not in the way Alex expected.

He's not in love with James anymore. The realization is its own sort of relief. But he still misses him. Misses the only childhood friend he's had. The only person he'd trusted until he met Jeff. The past is a powerful force, though, because Alex did love James once. Loved him in the way young, lonely people love—too fast and with too much of themselves, and Alex remembers. And remembering hurts.

He considers James's face on the computer screen, paused mid-laugh, head ducked, eyes on Cody, and then closes his laptop, exhausted.

He doesn't feel the same way about Eli as he did about James.

Loving James was terrifying. It was danger and shame and the constant anxiety of discovery or abandonment. What he feels for Eli is still scary. But a different kind. A kind that might be worth it.

He and James were bad for each other. Something it took him nearly four months of therapy to realize and another two to say out loud. The problem is he thinks he and Eli could be good for each other. Really good. Under different circumstances. In a different life.

Or maybe, if he was just a little braver, in this one.

15

ELI WINS SECOND. A silver medal.

He has near-flawless performances all weekend, and the final round is the best he's ever completed before, and he honestly feels a little bit like an imposter because he's not usually this good.

He's also kind of euphoric though.

He nearly trips, leaving the ice with his medal. He folds himself around Hawk, waiting with his coach, and then calls Alex before it occurs to him there are other people he should probably call first. Like Cody.

Like his *mother*.

"Eli," Alex answers on the second ring, sounding more out of breath than Eli is. "Are you okay?"

"I got second," Eli says, gasps really. "Silver. I'm—I got second."

"Oh my god, that's—" Alex says, then yells, "GUYS!" And it occurs to Eli that Alex has probably just finished playing his game against the Wild. "GUYS, ELI GOT SECOND PLACE."

"FUCK YEAH," someone yells, and, oh, apparently, he's now on speakerphone.

"Eli!" Kuzy says, followed by something incomprehensible in Russian, then, "Knew you could do. Best figure skater."

"I mean," Eli says. "Not best. Best would be first place, but—"

"No," Kuzy says. "Best."

"Good job, kid," Jeff interrupts. "And thanks to you, we won our game, so—"

There are a couple indistinct shouts in the background.

"What?"

"Nothing!" Alex yells, followed by the sound of ... hockey players being children, probably.

"Alex told us we had to win in regulation because if it went into overtime, he might miss your call," Jeff says. "He was on fire tonight. Very motivated."

"Oh, really?"

"Two goals and an assist. And Rushy got a shutout."

"Congratulations!" Eli says, grinning. His calf starts to cramp, and he stands, realizing he should be taking off his skates. "Okay, I've got to go. I just got off the ice and still need to change and do my cooldown."

There's a brief scuffle, and then Alex's voice, louder than the background noise, saying, "Hey, wait!"

"What's up?"

"Hold on, I'm—"

The locker room noise fades, and Alex's line goes echoy. Like maybe he's in a hallway somewhere.

"Sorry. Anyway. I'm happy for you." Alex's voice is rough. Warm and proud and—Eli closes his eyes.

"Thanks. I honestly shouldn't have scored so well my last run. It was a fluke."

"*No,*" Alex argues as if Eli has just suggested something terrible. "It was you. You've been working your ass off. You spend hours at the rink every day, even when you don't have practice. You deserve this."

"Thanks," Eli repeats, a little overwhelmed at the vehemence in Alex's voice.

"So," Alex continues, a little softer, "I know you need to cool off, but can you call me later? When you're back at the hotel?"

"Sure."

"Okay. Be thinking about what you want to do to celebrate when we get back to Houston."

Eli looks heavenward, then moves to sit on the closest bench and starts taking off his skates. "We aren't doing anything to celebrate because you already got me Louboutins and tickets to go see Cody next week, and you will *not* be getting me *anything else* for a very long time."

The line goes suspiciously silent.

"Alex," Eli says warningly.

"It's not really even for you," Alex argues. "It's for me. For my kitchen."

Eli is pretty sure he knows what it is because he mentioned in passing how happy he was that one of the Princeton boys had bought Cody a mixer. Alex had gotten a considering look on his face, which Eli is starting to recognize as dangerous.

Alex is worse than Eli's grandmother on a shopping trip to Walmart. You can't so much as look at a package of socks or it'll end up in the cart.

"Alexander Maxwell Price," Eli says.

"Aw, don't full-name me," Alex whines.

Eli's coach taps him on the shoulder, and Eli sighs. "I have to go, but we're talking about this later."

"Fine."

"Fine."

Eli arrives back in Houston to a small unruly group of professional hockey players waiting at the airport baggage claim with ridiculous, and in some cases hardly legible, handmade signs. When he comes into view at the top of the stairs, they start screaming so loudly that Hawk is momentarily a little scared, and a security guard drifts closer to investigate the situation.

Eli's team finds this charming.

Eli considers killing Alex.

Kuzy gets to Eli first because he's the biggest, and Eli finds himself being picked up and swung around like some sort of Hallmark movie heroine.

Kuzy plants a smacking kiss on his forehead before setting him down and letting Alex wrap him in a hug.

Eli folds into him gladly, even though Alex is covered in glitter and his sign is probably the gaudiest thing Eli has ever seen. It says, in wobbly gold lettering, "Eli: #2 on the ice, #1 in our hearts."

It's so awful he kind of loves it.

Alex smells good, and the flannel shirt he's wearing is soft and well-worn over the firmness of his chest, and—

Eli squeezes him a little harder than is necessary and then tells himself firmly to let go because bros don't tuck their faces into their bros necks and then just hang on for extended periods of time.

Alex doesn't seem to want to let go of him either though. So there's that.

Jeff manages to get a hug in, too, before Alex slings a proprietary arm around Eli's shoulders.

Alex has already gotten permission from Eli's coach to take Eli home from the airport, so he waves goodbye to the Morgans. He joins the boys for a celebratory dinner for which Kuzy and Alex physically fight over paying the bill. Kuzy wins by sitting on Alex. Alex is a sore loser.

Two hours later, he's on Alex's couch, wedged between Alex and Jeff, trying to finish his psychology homework, while Kuzy and Rushy are locked in an epic video-game battle. The others went home already, and once Alex notices Eli nodding off on his shoulder, he sends everyone else packing as well.

"What, Eli doesn't have to leave?" Jeff asks, feigning offense.

"Only silver medal winners get to stay," Alex answers.

"I have silver medal," Kuzy says. "Olympics."

"I have two gold ones," Jeff adds.

"Oh my god, go away," Alex says and more or less pushes them out the door.

Eli yawns. "I should probably go too. We have practice tomorrow morning, and I still have to finish reading this article."

"Or you could stay, and I'll drive you to practice tomorrow. We could get lunch after, and then I could take you to campus for your stats class at one."

"Pretty Bird for lunch?"

"Of course."

"All right, sold."

He watches Alex load the dishwasher for a moment, thinking vaguely about helping him clean up the minor mess the boys made, but returns his attention to his laptop. He really does need to get through this, and he's so tired.

An indeterminable amount of time later, when he's on the last page of the article, Eli glances up at the sound of Hawk's ID tag clinking against ceramic. She has her own set of bowls now, on the opposite side of the island from Bells's. Alex is rolling up the top of the bag of dog food he keeps at the bottom of the pantry.

He says something quietly to Hawk as he puts it away, then reaches for the bag of Bells's food next, and Eli has to close his eyes against the domesticity of it.

This isn't normal, he thinks tiredly.

In addition to Hawk's food and favorite brand of treats in the pantry, there's also Eli's favorite brand of horchata in the refrigerator. And in the pantry, there's pumpkin granola that Alex thinks is too sweet, and wasabi flavored peanuts that he thinks are too spicy, and kale chips that he won't even try. And the cabinets are slowly filling up with roasting pans and Corning Ware bowls and pretty sets of measuring spoons that Eli never sees Alex buy, but they just sort of appear. And in the guest bathroom, he has a toothbrush and toothpaste and hair products that stay there. Permanently. On the counter and in the shower, and they aren't even travel-sized. Which is important, for some reason. And—

And—

Alex turns out the kitchen light, then vaults over the back of the couch to settle, horizontally, with his feet against the far arm rest and his head on Eli's thigh. He squirms, making discontented noises, until Eli moves his free hand to Alex's hair.

And then there's this.

They've been straight-up cuddling for weeks now. At some point, they're going to have to talk about this ... *thing* that is between them. But Eli sure as hell isn't going to be the one to broach the conversation because then it might *stop*.

Alex squints at the laptop screen, oblivious to Eli's existential crisis. "What's this?"

"Psychology article. Homework."

"Mm." Alex closes his eyes. "What's it about?"

Eli drags his fingers through Alex's hair because it's hard not to. He's not wearing any gel for once, which means his cowlicks are in full force, and Alex is rumpled and kind of sleepy and—Well.

"It's by this guy named Arthur Aron. It's called 'The Experimental Generation of Interpersonal Closeness,' and it's actually pretty interesting. Basically, he paired strangers up, and they asked one another a series of questions that got more and more personal, and then they had a period of sustained eye contact afterward."

Alex makes an encouraging noise.

"And there was a second group of strangers who were paired up and just left to have small talk. The pairs that did the questions and the eye contact all reported feelings of significantly more closeness with their partner afterward, compared to the small talk ones. A couple of the question pairs even fell in love and got married."

Alex opens his eyes. "Huh. That is interesting. What are some of the questions?"

Eli scrolls back up in the article. Then laughs softly.

"Like—would you want to be famous? In what way?"

Alex smothers a laugh of his own in Eli's thigh. "Yeah. Guess my answer to that one is obvious."

Eli considers letting it go but, "Do you though?"

"Do I what?"

"Did you want to be famous? If you could change things, would you?"

Alex doesn't answer immediately, which is a bit of a surprise.

"I don't think so," he says, rolling a little so he can see Eli's face. "I don't really like it. It puts limitations on me that—" His forehead creases, and Eli presses his finger to the line there before he can stop himself.

"Hockey is worth it though," Alex finishes after the silence has begun to stretch uncomfortably. His voice is quiet and a little rough, and he clears his throat before repeating, louder, "Hockey is worth it."

It sounds like maybe he isn't sure.

"What about you?" Alex asks, avoiding Eli's eyes.

"Would you want to be famous?"

Eli lifts one shoulder. "Well, yeah. Olympic gold medalist. I know that's not going to happen. I'm too far behind. But if you gave me the choice? Hell yeah. I could retire young and start my own skate school and live off, like, social media sponsors and shit."

"Hmm. What's another question?"

"If you were able to live to the age of ninety and retain either the mind or body of a thirty-year-old for the last sixty years of your life, which would you want?"

"Body," Alex says promptly. "I would never have to retire."

"Not if you have dementia or CTE."

"I'll read and do Sudoku to keep my mind sharp. And I've only had one concussion in my career so far; I'd be fine. What about you? You'd take a thirty-year-old mind?"

"Definitely. And I'd eat well and exercise to stay physically fit."

"That's fair," Alex muses. "This is kind of fun. Another one?"

"Before making a telephone call, do you ever rehearse what you are going to say? Why?"

"Oh, damn. Yeah. Every time."

"Really?"

"Yes," Alex says, a little despairingly. "It's the worst thing about being captain. They make me call all the new recruits and trades to welcome them to the team. I don't even like ordering takeout. Calling guys that just lost their team and are about to uproot their lives? It's awful."

"But why?" Eli asks, genuinely baffled. "I mean, I get the trade phone calls, but normal phone calls? To friends? Or your internet company about your bill or something?"

"Because. If I have a chance to think about things and write them down, it's less likely I'll say something stupid or embarrassing. Real time, I can't guarantee that. Same reason I hate video interviews."

"Huh." Eli knows Alex isn't the unflappable, cavalier asshole the media purports him to be and, admittedly, the persona he seems to market. But this is surprising. He scratches his nails lightly across Alex's scalp. "Good to know."

"So, you don't?" Alex asks. "Practice phone calls before you make them?"

"Nope."

"You're ordering Spinelly's next time we want pizza, then."

"Spinelly's?"

"Little Italian place a few blocks away. They don't do orders online, so I just never get delivery from them."

"Yeah," Eli agrees, and he did not need to know more things about Alex that make him endearing. "Sure, Spinelly's. Whenever you want."

"Cool. Another one?"

Eli yawns, and Alex sits up.

"Never mind, you're tired. You want to go to bed?"

He does, but he also desperately wants to know Alex's answers to some of the more personal questions. "Yeah, but I need to shower, and that'll wake me back up for a while."

"So," Alex says, "meet in my bedroom in ten? We'll hit a few more until you're tired again?"

"Done."

Alex stands, his hair an absolute riot, and stretches before he heads in the direction of his bedroom, absently scratching his stomach.

Dios, dame fuerzas, Eli thinks.

16

FIFTEEN MINUTES LATER, IN boxers and an oversized raglan Hell Hounds shirt with Alex's name and number on it—the shirt just mysteriously appeared in his skate bag one day—Eli heads to the kitchen for a glass of water, sock feet soundless on the concrete floor.

When he moves toward Alex's bedroom, he pauses.

Because Alex is talking to Hawk.

She'd left the bathroom when Eli did, but rather than following him to the kitchen, sought out Alex for attention.

Eli leans against the doorframe, watching as Alex, kneeling with his back to the hallway, smooths his thumbs over Hawk's brow bone, fingers curled in the thick fur beneath her jaw.

"—and I'm working on it. It's just—You do a really good job, you know that?" Alex is murmuring. "You take such good care of Eli, and I probably would have been freaking out a lot more if you hadn't been with him. So. Thank you. For that." He presses a kiss between her little furry eyebrows, sitting back on his heels. "You're such a good girl."

The fondness Eli feels for Alex in that moment—rumpled, barefooted Alex, knelt on the floor and thanking his dog—it's almost stifling.

Eli knocks his glass against the doorframe and moves to sit on the bed, pretending he doesn't notice the red flush on Alex's neck when he joins him a moment later.

"So," Eli says because he doesn't do emotions well, and there are a lot of them happening right now. "Um—questions?"

"Yeah."

Alex closes the shade and pats the foot of bed, letting Hawk up to cuddle with Bells. They're best friends now. Eli also has emotions he's ignoring about that.

"Okay, questions." Eli sets his water on the nightstand and pulls his laptop over between them. "Uh—when was the last time you sang to yourself? To other people?"

"The locker room after practice this morning was the last time I sang to other people. By myself? Probably yesterday night in the shower. You?"

"Oh. I don't sing."

"Ever?"

"Ever. And you should be thankful."

Alex grins. "I'm going to get you to sing one day. It's on my bucket list now."

"Yeah, good luck with that," Eli says, and Alex looks like he's ready to settle into an argument, so he quickly adds, "If you could wake up tomorrow having gained any one quality or ability, what would it be? That's easy for me—the ability to pull off a quadruple salchow."

Alex rolls onto his side to face Eli, tucking a pillow under his head. "Is that a spinny thing?"

"Yes," Eli says dryly. "It's a 'spinny' thing."

Alex thinks for several more seconds. "I guess I'd like to be fluent in Russian, probably? Kuzy doesn't have anyone on the team to talk with, and I think that'd make him happy. He gets homesick a lot."

Eli wants to punch Alex a little. Because Alex is just so—he's—

Moving to the bedroom was a bad idea because now they're tucked close in a pocket of dark, warm, intimate space, and Alex's hair is a mess, and he's being selfless and kind, and Eli can't help but want to touch him: the curl of hair falling on his forehead, the mostly healed abrasion at the curve of his jaw from a collision on the ice three days before.

Eli clears his throat and asks the next question.

They work from the more general questions to the personal, answers coming slower.

If you were going to become a close friend with your partner, please share what would be important for him or her to know.

"I have a shit ton of medical issues," Eli says. "I'm a perfectionist, I'm introverted so I don't like to go out a lot, and I need my space sometimes."

"I have anxiety and OCD," Alex says. "I'm also a perfectionist. And I'm impulsive and quick-tempered. I have bad habits, and I'm kind of an asshole, but I'm trying to be better."

Tell your partner what you like about them; be honest.

"I think—the effortless confidence you have on the ice is really beautiful," Eli says. "I'm really impressed with how dedicated you are to your own hockey but also, like, the team as a whole, helping the rookies after practice and stuff. And I love how you are with Bells. And Hawk. And the way you care about other people. The fact that you'd want to know Russian for Kuzy. And, um. Your freckles. I guess."

"My freckles? Really?"

"Yeah."

"Well, you—" Alex says, "you're really strong, and fast, and your skating is beautiful, obviously, but in general, you're just so much more of a person than your, uh, body. That sounds stupid—shut up, don't laugh at me—but you're also really smart. And funny. And I love that you have really serious opinions about history and literature, and you'll get all worked up talking about them. And I like how confident you are. And your cooking! And the way you talk about cooking. Like it's art, or something. And I like your hands, I guess."

"My hands?" "

They're nice."

Eli doesn't know how much time has passed, but it's late—his eyes heavy, breath slow—when he asks, squinting at the laptop propped on the pillows above them, "What is your most terrible memory?"

Eli sighs. "Mine is probably the first time I woke up after the accident. Well, the first time I stayed awake for more than a few minutes. When they told me all the damage. And that I'd be lucky to walk again. My whole life—the plan I had, just—" He exhales. "I can't even explain to you the feeling."

Alex bumps his knuckles against Eli's shoulder.

"You?"

Alex doesn't say anything, and Eli shifts from his back to his side to face him.

"Hey, you okay?"

"Yeah," Alex says, but it looks like he's lying. His face is pale in the shadowed bleed of city lights through the curtains. His jaw is tight. "I'm just trying to figure out how to say it."

"You don't have to."

"No. I should. It would probably be good for me. Only Coops and Anika know, and I've never told anyone sober before."

Eli blinks. "You went to see your therapist drunk?"

"Look, I'm not in counseling because I handle personal issues well."

"Point."

Alex takes a studied breath. "You know—about James?"

It takes Eli a moment to readjust. "Petrov? Cody's goalie?"

"Yeah. You know how he went missing?"

"During the combine?"

"Yeah."

Alex takes a second purposeful breath. "He was my best friend. My only friend, at that point. We'd been rooming together for the combine. And it was—"

Alex breathes again. Five seconds in. Seven seconds out.

"I was the one that found his note. And it wasn't exactly clear. Probably because he wasn't in a clear frame of mind, I guess. But I thought at first—" Another breath.

"I thought he was dead. Or going to kill himself, maybe. And he didn't, obviously. But I didn't know that for another month until he turned back up again."

"Fuck."

"I knew he was struggling, and I left him alone. I knew he'd been having issues with his new meds, and I knew he was having a bad night. I *knew*. And I went out anyway. Because we'd had a fight, and I was mad at him, and I didn't—"

Alex drags in another breath, but doesn't quite make it to five seconds before he's exhaling again, too fast, and Eli pushes himself forward into Alex's space, tucking his head under Alex's chin, looping an arm around his waist.

Alex's free hand settles like a habit between Eli's shoulder blades, fingers curled into the fabric of his shirt, probably right where "Price" is written across his back.

"It's not your fault," Eli says, the words smudged against Alex's collarbone. "It's not your fault, and James is okay now. He's happy and healthy, and you're happy and healthy. And that's—I can't even imagine how horrible that was, but think about how much you've both changed since then. You know that, right? That neither of you are the people you were then? You've been working so hard with Anika. And James—James is part of a team that respects and appreciates him, and he eats homemade cooking at least once a week. You're both doing so well now."

Alex pulls Eli closer with a hurt noise, barely audible from the back of his throat. Eli doesn't know if he's helping or not at this point, but he holds still, consciously measuring his breathing—hoping Alex will mimic it.

They stay like that for several minutes until Alex's heartbeat under Eli's ear has slowed to something like normal, and Alex starts to trace his fingers over the 23 on Eli's back.

It's late, and they're both exhausted, physically and emotionally, and Eli is so warm and comfortable pressed against Alex that he just can't make himself move. Even though he should.

The silence stretches between them, and Eli is nearly asleep when Alex whispers, "What's the next question?"

Eli shifts, putting some space between them, not much, not enough to throw off Alex's arm, just enough to leave them face-to-face. He doesn't look at the laptop because he already knows which question he wants answered the most. And it's not fair for him to ask it, for either of them, but he does anyway, says it softly into the pocket of recycled air between their mouths.

"If you were to die tonight, what would you regret not having told someone? Why haven't you told them yet?"

Alex stays silent, just looking at him in a way that makes Eli's chest feel like it's cracked open.

"Eli," he says finally.

And that's—he doesn't know what that means.

Alex moves his hand slowly up the pebbled line of Eli's vertebrae, calluses catching on the soft knit of his T-shirt. He cups the back of Eli's neck and presses his thumb gently to the rift of scar tissue that hugs the curve of his skull. Alex's eyes are dark and serious, and his mouth is so close, but he looks so sad, and Eli can't—

"I'm sorry," Eli says. "That wasn't fair."

Alex exhales, pulling Eli against him, tucking his face back into his neck where it belongs.

Except it doesn't; it just feels like it does. Which is its own kind of unfairness.

"We should go to sleep," Alex says.

They should. And Eli should go to the guest bedroom, but he doesn't. Worse, he sneaks one hand up the back of Alex's shirt. Just a little. Just a few inches. To rest his palm in the warm dip of Alex's spine.

He knows he can't have this, but pretending for a while isn't going to make things any worse than they already are.

On Wednesday morning, Kuzy takes Elijah to the airport because Alex has a photoshoot with Under Armour that he can't reschedule. Alex is pretty pissed about this, but Eli isn't too bothered because Kuzy picks him up early and takes him to a tiny Russian cafe that Eli finds entirely charming. He was a little nervous, initially, for it to be just the two of them. While Kuzy has always seemed incredibly kind, he is also very big and very Russian and very straight, and Eli is ... none of those things.

He really shouldn't have worried.

"Think you can make?" Kuzy asks, gesturing with a fork to their plates.

Eli hopes he can figure it out because the food is delicious, a cross between a crepe and a pancake, topped with strawberries and pale-pink sauce that is lightly sweet but not overwhelming.

"I can definitely try," Eli says.

"I'm miss Mama's cooking. Maybe I get her, um"—he gestures for a moment—"cooking plays?" he says a little helplessly.

"'Cooking plays'," Eli repeats. "Oh, you mean recipes?"

"Yes. Recipes."

Could he be more adorable? Cooking plays, honestly.

"Maybe I get her recipes? For you?" Kuzy looks so shyly hopeful that Eli wants to hug him.

"Of course," Eli says, "I'd love that. If she's willing to share them, sure."

"Okay, I'm ask. Oh, question. Internet question."

Eli takes a sip of coffee and waits as Kuzy gets out his phone.

"This Tumblr you talk about is confusing for me. All the hashtags?"

"Yeah, right there with you," Eli says. "A lot of people on Tumblr use the tagging system as extra commentary rather than organization. It's not like Twitter or Instagram."

Kuzy makes a noise of agreement. "Okay, yes. On picture of me—on video of me—lots people tag this. You know what is mean?" He hands his phone across the table, and Eli takes it.

There's a picture of Kuzy in a celly, one knee bent, mouth wide open in a jubilant yell. It's tagged: *#Kuznetsov #a good giant #body by Maytag*.

Eli coughs on a laugh and sets his coffee down. "You mean the 'body by Maytag' one?"

"Yes. I'm not understand. Is making fun?"

"Oh, no. It's—so Maytag is an appliance company. They're known for making refrigerators and stuff. So they're basically calling you a refrigerator."

Kuzy continues to frown at him.

"Okay, that sounds like a bad thing, but it's not. They're just saying they think you're big and strong. Sort of like why they called you a 'good giant'."

Kuzy's expression clears. "Oh. Okay. And—go down—" Eli scrolls down.

"There. What is 'softbro' mean?" For a minute, Eli doesn't get it.

Someone has posted a collection of GIFs all featuring Kuzy. There are a few on ice: one where he's stooped over, a glove held between his teeth, fixing Rushy's helmet strap; one where he's hugging Jeff in a celly; one where he's looking innocent while the ref points at him. There are others off the ice: when he's got post-game fluffy hair and a big grin, talking to reporters; when he's holding Alex on his shoulders in the locker room while Alex tries to dislodge a soccer ball stuck in the rafters with a hockey stick; when he's wearing Ray-Bans and drinking a frappuccino as he exits the team bus. The last several are all from the recent charity calendar shoot, where Kuzy is holding an armful of puppies and looking delighted.

The post is tagged: *#a soft bro*.

"Oh," Eli says. "It's a good thing too. So. You know how 'bro' is used to describe a person who is buff and plays sports and wears a certain type of clothing?"

"Yes." Kuzy says. "Alex."

Eli grins. "Right. Well, a 'soft bro' is a bro who looks like a bro, but is also really sweet and gentle and extra loveable.

"Oh. And they say is me?" Kuzy asks, delighted.

"Yep."

"I am soft bro."

"Yeah, you are."

They spend most of breakfast talking about social media and the most prevalent Tumblr tags for various Hell Hounds players. Rushy is pretty universally "sweet goalie prince," while Alex is anything from "captain pretty eyes" to "dumpster-fire child" depending on the poster. Coops is "woke bro" or "husband goals." The rookies all get "this boy" and "my son" interchangeably with the occasional "Beautiful Cinnamon Roll Too Good for This World, Too Pure" that it takes nearly five minutes for Eli to try to explain. They giggle to themselves over a Tumblr dedicated to pictures of Hell Hounds in the sin bin and then argue amicably over who should pay for breakfast. Eli doesn't put up much of a fight. He knows how much money Kuzy makes.

"We do breakfast again?" Kuzy asks when they're back in the car and heading to the airport.

"Yeah?" Eli says. "For sure."

"Good. You, uh, nervous, maybe? Sometimes. About touch me. Good now, but—" He gestures a little. "—when we first meet, no."

"Oh."

He hadn't thought it was obvious—that he'd been more careful around Kuzy, initially, than he was with Alex and Jeff. He'd fallen back on his Guy Interaction Protocol from home: as long as the other boys initiated physical contact, they couldn't get mad at him for being "creepy" or whatever the fuck they—

"You okay?" Kuzy asks.

Eli sighs. "Yeah. Sorry. At home, people weren't super great about the gay thing. So I got in the habit of never touching guys unless they touched me first. Just to make sure I didn't make anyone uncomfortable or mad."

Kuzy brakes a little too hard at a stoplight. "You're think I'm get mad? If you touch me? I'm hug you all the time. Is friends. Uh. Friendly?"

"Yeah, friendly," Eli agrees. "And no, not really. It's stupid. Like I said. Bad habit."

"But—" Kuzy thinks for a moment. "But you're—not nervous. With Coops. With Pricey."

"Oh. Well, I knew Jeff would be cool because of the fundraisers and camps and stuff with You Can Play. And Alex—"

Eli stalls there. Because he can't very well say that Alex is gay too.

"Alex loves you," Kuzy says easily. "So touch okay."

"What? *No*. No. Alex doesn't—"

"I'm not stupid," Kuzy says, "just because English bad. Very smart in Russian. Not need smart, though, to see Alex loves you. And"—it's almost an afterthought—"you love Alex."

Eli feels like he might be having a heart attack. Hawk, in the back seat, whines.

Kuzy glances at her, then Eli, and frowns. "Hey. It's okay. It's secret, I know."

Eli doesn't say anything. Can't think of what to say.

Kuzy continues to frown at him, then shifts his hands on the steering wheel, clearing his throat. "At home, in Russia, when I'm little kid—no father, Mama work always, home late, always. So, after school, I'm go, uh, house by house?"

"Next door?" Eli supplies faintly.

"Yes. After school, I'm go next door. Two men live next door. Old men. Funny. They listen to the radio and yell. Not angry yell, just—loud. Happy. They take good care for me and always have food for me and little things for play—toys ... " He says a word in Russian, shrugs, and moves on. "They help with school. Help buy hockey gear. Good men. People say they're ... family, but not brothers?"

"Cousins?"

"Yes, cousins. But they're not cousins. I'm see, sometimes, they hold hands in the house, on the couch—where no window. Touch hip. Touch neck. Soft. Like normal thing. Sleep in the same room. I'm not see kiss, ever, but I know what love looks like when it have to be secret."

Eli feels like he might cry.

"I think it's bad," Kuzy continues gently, "not fair. But I'm not—it's secret. I promise. Don't worry."

"That's not—" Eli swallows around the hotness in his throat. "There isn't anything to tell. I wish there was," he admits, because why not? "But there *isn't*."

Kuzy makes a disbelieving noise. "You think you have feels—"

"Feelings," Eli corrects. "The internet is ruining you."

"You think you have *feelings*," Kuzy repeats, rolling his eyes, "but not Alex?"

"I don't know how Alex feels. But he wouldn't—there's no way he'd risk his career even if he was interested in me. So I just have to get over this crush."

"Hard to 'get over' when Alex texts you always, touch you always, buy you pretty shoes and airplane for visit friend."

"Yeah," Eli sighs. "Tell me about it."

Kuzy glances at him, eyebrows pinched and unhappy. "Sorry." He reaches to pat Eli awkwardly on the back. "Not fair."

"Not your fault. But thanks. I, uh, really appreciate you telling me that story."

Kuzy squeezes his shoulder.

When they get to the airport, he comes around to the passenger side to help Eli with his bags.

Once everything is unloaded on the curb, Eli stands on his tiptoes and, without a moment of hesitation, hugs him very, very tightly.

17

CODY MEETS ELI AT the baggage claim, and Eli tackles him.

Legitimately tackles him.

They end up sprawled on what is undoubtedly a disgusting floor with Hawk jumping excitedly around them, trying to lick Cody's face. Which Eli probably shouldn't allow since her vest is still on, but he's lost all sense of decorum, and it seems only fair that Hawk gets a temporary pass as well.

It's cold, colder than Eli was prepared for, but Cody is dressed even less appropriately for the weather in shorts and a hoodie and flipflops and *god, he's such a bro*. But he looks happy. Comfortable with himself in a way he never seemed at home. It makes Eli want to hug him. So he does.

Cody talks at him nonstop while they wait for Eli's checked bag, and then he leads Eli to the parking garage, where he unlocks a very large, very new, very shiny black pickup truck.

Eli whistles. "Nice truck. You get a sugar daddy and not tell me?"

"Oh, it's James's. I was going to borrow Muzz's car, but it's a coupe, and James thought there'd be more room for Hawk if I took his truck instead."

"Did he."

"I don't know what you're trying to infer with that tone, Elijah, but if you want cookies ... "

"You'll make me whatever kind I want regardless. Don't play. You missed me."

"I did. So much."

Cody looks like he might get a little teary, which Eli cannot handle after the morning he's had, so he punches him lightly on the shoulder and moves to get Hawk settled in the back seat.

"Now," Cody says once they've started driving. "The boys are really excited to meet you, and I've told them to take it easy, but they'll probably still overwhelm you a little. Don't worry though. They're big and loud, but they're all sweethearts."

"You realize I spend time with professional hockey players on a near-daily basis now. I think I can handle an NCAA team."

"Sure you can," Cody says placatingly. "Just wanted to warn you."

Cody's concern is sweet, Eli thinks, but at this point, completely unnecessary.

It's only a twenty-minute drive, and Eli had planned to let Cody talk for most of it (Lord knows the boy can talk). But Cody asks him a couple innocent questions about Alex, and the next thing he knows, he's ranting about his unfair eyes and how his weird fixation on internet quizzes should not be cute.

"Internet quizzes?" Cody prompts.

"YES. And not even the normal ones. Weird ones. Like 'Could you live through the Oregon Trail?' and 'What would your Victorian minstrel name be?' And his teammates send him links to more and more obscure ones all the time because they all know he'll take them because for some reason he will just have to find out what sort of *breakfast cereal* he would be. It's so stupid."

He says "stupid" with a degree of fondness that is a little embarrassing.

Cody is judging him quietly, bottom lip tucked between his teeth.

"Yes, thank you," Eli says. "I'm gone on him; I'm aware. But you don't have any place to talk. The last three recipes you've made were traditional Russian dishes."

Unlike Alex, whose blushes tend to manifest in his ears and the back of his neck, Cody's flush dapples the sides of his cheeks.

"There are two Russians on my team."

"And you have a giant crush on *one* of them. What was it you were telling me the other day? About falling in love with hockey players? Hi, Mr. Pot, I'm Kettle."

Cody sighs. "Fine. I have a problem."

Eli reaches over the center console and laces their fingers together. It's a little strange because the only person he's held hands with recently is Alex. Cody has calluses in a lot of the same places as Alex, but his hands are strangely unfamiliar after nearly four months apart.

"We make terrible life choices," Eli points out.

"So terrible," Cody agrees.

"It would be a lot easier if we could just be in love with each other."

"Yeah, no. I'm not kissing you again," Cody says.

It turns out that Eli is not, in fact, prepared for Cody's team.

Unlike Alex's teammates, Cody's make no attempt at either suppressing their exuberance, nor impressing him.

Five minutes after meeting the residents of the hockey house, he's seen Pauls entirely naked, discussed the fact that Muzz is probably going to be on academic suspension after he took a midterm while hungover that morning (but at least it won't be graded until after the next game, bro!), and he knows that Haney, blessedly not naked, apparently has a suspicious rash.

Eventually, Cody ushers him into the kitchen and away from the madness of the living room, laughing a little at his facial expression.

"I did warn you," he says.

"You did," Eli agrees.

Hawk leans against his leg but doesn't make it a secret that she'd rather return to the couch where three different people had been petting her a few minutes before.

Eli sits on one of the mismatched chairs at the wobbly, heavily scarred kitchen table. "Any plans for tonight?" he asks.

"Nah, Cap said no parties until after the game Friday. We talked about how to handle that for you, and we think we have a plan."

Eli narrows his eyes. "Okay?'

"It won't be, like, super crazy, since a lot of people went home for the break today, but even a chill kegger is probably going to be too much for Hawk. James said maybe you could keep her in his bedroom upstairs where it's quiet, and you could run up and check in with her every so often? Or escape if you get overwhelmed."

That might work.

"Hell Hounds game is starting!" someone yells from the living room.

"We're watching the Hell Hounds game?"

"I figured you'd want to."

"They don't mind?"

Cody gives him an unimpressed look.

"We're hockey players. If there's a game on, we're usually watching it. And the only other teams playing tonight are the—"

"Sabres and the Canucks," Eli supplies absently, pulling his phone out of his pocket. He realizes he never turned off airplane mode, does so now, and his phone lights up with notifications.

Cody has gone quiet, and Eli glances back up at him.

"What?"

"It's just so weird. You knowing things about hockey."

"Proximity."

"Fair."

They move back into the living room where Hawk happily returns to the couch to be smothered in affection.

They're singing the national anthem on the television, so Eli returns his attention to the notifications on his phone. He's missed several texts from Jeff and a series of snaps from Kuzy. He reads Jeff's texts first:

Just a heads-up, you were papped at the airport. Kuzy thinks it's a riot, but you probably want to call Alex tonight if you're still awake after the game.

Also, Jessica says it's no big deal, so don't worry. But yeah. Call Alex. Please.

Frowning, Eli opens his snaps from Kuzy.

The first one is a screenshot of a headline on gossip website surrounded by emoji hearts:

Gay Romance Between Russian Hockey Star and Teenaged YouTube Personality?

The second is another screenshot—this time of several thumbnail pictures of Kuzy dropping Eli off at the airport.

To be fair, Eli thinks with a sigh, the hug does look ... incriminating.

He also gets why the internet likes to ship them because the pictures really emphasize their size difference. And the way Kuzy has his shoulders all hunched and his head ducked like he's trying to envelop Eli entirely is ... well, it's pretty damn cute, honestly.

The third snap is of Kuzy's grinning face, aviators on, and baseball cap turned sideways.

I'm soft boyfriend now, the caption says, accompanied by a winking emoji.

Eli coughs on the bite of sandwich in his mouth, then waves a concerned Cody away, trying to swallow and laugh at the same time.

He checks his Instagram, TikTok, and Twitter, all of which have an influx of people inquiring if he's dating Dmitri Kuznetsov, then taps back over to his texts.

Where he pauses.

Because Alex hasn't sent him anything since right before he boarded the plane that morning. Which would be odd, but not really strange, if not for the fact that Alex always texts him before a game. An hour and forty-five minutes before. Always.

Hey, Eli types, *I hope everything is okay. I made it to Princeton, and we've got the game turned on. Kick some Blackhawk ass for me. FaceTime tonight?*

The game starts, and Eli tucks his phone back in his pocket, still frowning.

If hockey players are anything, they're predictable—especially Alex when it comes to his pregame rituals.

"Hey," Cody says, leaning against him. "Everything okay?"

"I dunno. Probably. Alex stuff."

James, sitting on the floor, glances sharply at him, then just as quickly redirects his attention to the TV.

Where the Blackhawks have just scored less than a minute into regulation.

Shit. Eli thinks.

The Blackhawks slaughter the Hell Hounds.

The game ends 6–1 with Alex in the box for the third time that night, the highest number of penalty minutes he's taken in a game all season.

He's been playing overly aggressively, and for a brief, terrifying moment, Eli thinks he may fight someone after words are exchanged at a faceoff. Alex, for all the penalties he takes, has never actually fought anyone in his NHL career. Something is clearly wrong.

Pauls offers Cody and Eli his room for the night since he's staying with his girlfriend, and, cold as it is, neither of them wants to trudge across campus to the dorms in the dark with Eli's luggage.

They get ready for bed, subdued, not talking through the brushing of teeth and washing of faces, then fit themselves together in the twin bed, piling an extra two blankets—loaned from James with a gentle chirp about Alabama blood—on top of them.

"Is something wrong with Alex?" Cody whispers.

"Yeah. I don't know what though. He was fine yesterday night. I asked him to FaceTime me after the game, so—"

"Oh, for sure. Don't worry about waking me up."

"Okay."

Eli stares at his phone, plugged in and resting innocuously on the nightstand, and waits for it to ring.

It doesn't.

When he wakes up the following morning—the gray light coming in the window telling him it's still far too early—there aren't any missed calls. And no new text messages.

He carefully extracts himself from Cody's clinging limbs and tucks his phone into his hoodie pocket before shivering his way down the stairs.

He's pleased to find that, while meager, the refrigerator's contents are enough to work with, and after ten minutes and half a cup of coffee, he has several pieces of French toast slowly cooking in a well-buttered pan.

Which is when James comes in the front door.

He's wearing leggings, a thermal turtleneck with reflective stripes, and running shoes.

His face is flushed with cold or exertion or both.

"Oh," James says. "Uh. Good morning."

"Morning," Eli says and then hands him a glass from the cabinet because the man is clearly thirsty.

James fills it up in the sink, drains it, and sets it on the counter, hands on his hips, still breathing hard. "Couldn't sleep?" he asks.

Eli shrugs. "I take it you're awake at 5:00 a.m. on purpose?"

"Oh. Not really. I was just—thinking. And decided to go for a run. Do you want some help?"

"It's almost done. But thanks. Want to share?" James moves to fill up his glass with water again. "No thanks. I'll make a protein shake in a minute."

He takes his time drinking the second glass, and Eli has to fight not to stare at him because the man is, admittedly, quite attractive. Particularly in Lycra.

"So," James says carefully. "I know it's not any of my business, but I've been watching your videos, and Cody has shown me some of your Instagram posts, and it seems like—" He licks his lips, ducking his head a little, and yeah, Eli can see exactly why Cody is so infatuated with this giant, handsome, awkward turtle of a man.

"Alex seems happy," James says finally, as if it takes significant effort. "Well. Not last night. He was angry about something last night. But I mean, in the videos, when he's with you. He usually seems happy. And I was wondering, um, if he is. Happy."

Eli doesn't know how to respond. He moves to the refrigerator to put away the eggs, stalling for time. Because he doesn't know what Alex would want him to do, here. Doesn't know what he can share without—

"I know what I did to him wasn't fair," James says lowly, words bumping into one another. "And I know you probably don't like me very much because of it. But I had to cut him off so I could figure out—but it still wasn't right. He was nearly as messed up as I was at that point, and without him, I, at least, still had a support system. Alex didn't. He lost his boyfriend and his best friend all at once, and I really regret doing that to him."

Eli doesn't drop the eggs but it's a near thing.

He closes the refrigerator door slowly.

James considers his expression and then leans back against the counter, looking a little struck.

"He didn't tell you."

"He told me about his ex. And about you. But not. No. Maybe I should have guessed with the things he *has* told me but—"

James exhales. "Shit. I'm sorry."

"It's okay. I mean, he probably wanted to tell me but didn't want to, like, violate your privacy or whatever. I just—Wow. Is that why—? No. Sorry. That's a completely invasive question. I'm going to need a minute."

James laughs a little. "I don't mind if Alex tells you"—he gestures a little awkwardly between them—"uh, everything. I thought he already had. But I probably shouldn't say anything else. It's not just my story."

"No, that's totally fair. Do you mind if I ask if anyone else on the team here knows?"

"Knows what? About me and Alex?"

"Knows that you're gay."

"Oh. I'm bi? Actually. And no. I'm still considering the NHL when I graduate, and I don't know if I could handle that. Being the first. Especially with my family and if I want to play for Russia in the Olympics one day. And the team is great, I trust them all, but the more people who know ... "

"Yeah. I understand. There's only one, well, I guess two people on Alex's team who know about him."

"He has you though," James says softly, maybe a little pensively.

"Yeah," Eli says. "But we're not, like, together, if that's what you're thinking."

"Oh."

James looks even more surprised by this.

"I think," Eli says, picking up the whisk so he has something to do with his hands, "that maybe we could be. In different circumstances. But Alex has said pretty clearly that he isn't willing to risk his career by dating. Or even hooking up. So."

James crosses his arms, his face doing something complicated. "So. He's just going to be alone."

"Until he retires, yeah."

James closes his eyes.

"He's good though," Eli says, moving to flip the bread in the pan. "I mean, better, definitely. He's been in therapy. And he is happy, most of the time."

"Good," James says. "Do you think he'd want to talk to me? I meant to get back in touch once I was in a better headspace. But then so much time had passed, and I didn't know how. Or even if he'd want me to."

Eli has to think about that for a minute. "I think he misses you. But I think talking to you would be difficult for him. At least at first."

He glances at his phone. "I also think contacting him *now* would be a bad idea."

James huffs out a laugh. "Yeah. I was watching the game last night too."

Eli plates the four pieces of completed French toast, twists closed the bread and puts the bowl of leftover egg mixture in the refrigerator for later.

"You sure you don't want one of these?" Eli asks, moving past James to the table.

James eyes the plate with a familiar, longing expression, and Eli grins.

"Maybe just one piece," James says, and then, a moment later, "Cody keeps powdered sugar next to the microwave if you want to put some on top."

"I think we'd better," Eli agrees seriously.

18

ELI GETS A TEXT from Jeff while he and Cody are getting post-lunch Boba Teas at the campus coffee shop. They're closing early for Thanksgiving, and he and Cody just barely make it in time.

Jeff's text reads: *Alex is home alone right now and having a lot of Feelings. Can you do us all a favor and call him?* Eli is kind of pissed at Alex by this point, but once they return to the house and he sheds his various winter layers, he takes his phone upstairs and calls anyway.

Alex answers on the third ring. "Hi," he says, sounding suitably cowed.

"Hi," Eli agrees.

"I'm sorry," Alex says.

"Can you tell me what happened? Because I'm lost."

"I don't know. Those pictures—"

"Oh my god," Eli says. "Are you kidding me? Kuzy isn't gay."

"I know."

"And even if he was, and we were, like, romantically involved, you wouldn't get to be angry about that."

"I know."

"Because *you're not my boyfriend*!"

"I *know*," Alex says, and his voice goes high and tight. "I'm sorry. I'm just. I'm not in the best place right now. Brain wise. And the pictures didn't help. I realize I'm being stupid, okay? I'm sorry."

Alex sounds so miserable that Eli can't sustain his frustration.

"Okay," Eli says, absently petting Hawk's head. "You want to talk about it?"

Alex makes a derisive noise.

"Mm. Rephrase," Eli says. "Should we talk about it?"

"Probably."

"Ready when you are."

Alex sighs. "I was already anxious and, like ... not uncomfortable, but—You're with James. Right now. And thinking about you spending time with James has made me think about before. And it's not bad or anything. It's just weird. So I'm working through that. And then with the pictures of you and Kuzy ... I was, uh, jealous. I guess."

"Of *Kuzy*?" Eli says, still baffled.

"Because it *didn't matter* to him," Alex says, voice raw.

"When he saw the article, he thought it was funny. He wasn't scared or immediately on the phone talking damage control with Jessica. Because he's straight, and he doesn't have anything to hide. It's—it was *funny* to him."

"Oh." *Oh, Alex.*

"And I know that's not your fault, and I shouldn't have ignored you. I just needed time to sort out my head, and I knew if I talked to you, I'd probably say something stupid, so."

"Okay."

"Okay?"

"Yeah. I mean, next time, I'd like a text letting me know what's going on. So I know you're not hurt or something. Or mad at me."

"I can do that."

"Good."

They both just breathe for a minute.

"Is your shoulder okay?" Eli asks.

Alex makes a confused noise.

"Second period. Eklund ran you into the boards pretty hard. Looked like you were favoring your right arm most of the third period."

Alex doesn't answer, and Eli, still feeling off-center, wonders if he's said something wrong.

"Alex?"

"Sorry. No. I mean, yes, my shoulder is okay. It was only a pinched nerve. I'm surprised you noticed. I thought I was hiding it."

"Oh. Well. I know you."

It comes out a little more honest than intended.

"Yeah," Alex agrees softly.

They both clear their throats, then laugh at their simultaneous awkwardness, and Eli suddenly misses Alex so much he's not sure what to do with himself. He can't just say it. He doesn't do things like that, but—

"I miss you," Alex says, and Eli has to take a moment.

Maybe a couple of moments. "Hey," Alex says, "you still there?"

"Yeah, sorry. I, uh, miss you too."

It's stilted, but Alex sounds pleased anyway when he says, "I'm picking you up at the airport on Saturday afternoon."

"Does that mean I should prepare myself for a small cheering section and too much glitter again?"

"No," Alex says. "Just me."

"Oh. Okay."

"How's Cody?" Alex asks.

"Good. Really good. He's happy here, and the boys are all—well. They're hockey players—" Alex laughs. "—but they're great. We're doing Thanksgiving dinner with them tonight, and I'm looking forward to watching them all play tomorrow. What are you doing tonight?"

"Just takeout with Kuzy. Everybody else has plans with family."

He doesn't sound upset about it, but Eli suddenly wishes he'd brought Alex with him. So he could wrap him in a scarf and feed him turkey and not have to miss him, even though it's barely been forty-eight hours since he last saw Alex's stupid crooked smile.

"I wish you were here," Eli says. If Alex can make an effort, he can too.

"That would probably be a disaster," Alex answers.

And oh. Right.

"I had an interesting conversation with James this morning," Eli says. "He thought that I knew. About you. Y'all. Being together."

Alex doesn't answer immediately, but Eli is pretty sure he just needs time, so he waits.

"What did he say?" Alex asks, quiet and a little thready.

"Nothing much, just, he was apologizing, I think? He said he knew what he did to you was messed up because you weren't in a very good place then either. And James still had a support system without you, but you lost both your best friend and your boyfriend when he disappeared and then cut you off."

Alex makes a noise that makes Eli's chest ache. "He said that?"

"I mean, I'm paraphrasing, but yeah. He feels bad, I think."

"No," Alex says, insistent. "I mean. He called me his boyfriend?"

"Yes?"

"Fuck. Okay."

Eli gives him another minute.

"Okay," Alex says again. "That's—good to know. What, uh—what else did you talk about?"

"Not much. Once he realized I didn't know about your history, he didn't want to say anything else. Though he did say you could tell me."

"I wanted to." Alex says. "But I felt guilty enough that I'd told Jeff when I got really drunk, one time last year. But—" He takes a breath. "I do. Want to tell you. Whenever you're back."

"Okay," Eli agrees. "James also wants to get back in touch with you but wasn't sure if you'd be okay with it. I said you might need time but would probably like that."

"Yeah. If you want to give him my number before you leave, that would be okay."

"All right."

Alex is quiet, and Eli isn't sure if it's a good kind or a bad kind of silence.

"Hey," he says. "Are you all right?"

Alex breathes. "I think so? I mean. I'm going to go call Anika the minute I hang up with you but, yeah. I think I'm good."

"Good. Well. You go call Anika. I have a turkey to cook."

"Okay. Can we FaceTime tomorrow night after the game?"

"Yeah. Absolutely. Just let me know when."

"Thanks. Say hi to Cody for me."

"Will do. Bye, Alex."

"Bye, Eli."

It's possibly the best Thanksgiving dinner Eli has ever had.

Between him and Cody and Muzz's MasterCard they manage a turkey, dressing, salad, cornbread, fried okra, and a vegetable casserole that is more comprised of cheese than vegetables in the hopes that the boys will actually eat it. There are also brownies and three different pies.

After dinner, they take turns getting third and fourth servings of dessert, drink terrible cheap beer, and complain about how full they are. Hawk, exhausted from all the excitement, is asleep on James's bed upstairs.

Eli is two beers in, considering going upstairs to join her, when Muzz slings an arm around his shoulders and ducks to nuzzle into his neck a little.

"I like you," he says in an indiscreet whisper. "You kept Cody sane through the tribulations of southern youth, so I appreciate you for that." He takes a drag on his joint, leaning his head against Eli's shoulder. "You're also, like, very, very pretty, my dude. I hope you're aware."

"Um," Eli says, laughing a little. "Thanks?"

"I gotta say. You are quite possibly the most beautiful specimen of a man I have ever seen."

There's a chorus of offended "Hey!"s from the other assembled men in the room.

"Don't get me wrong, bros," Muzz says, stepping away from Eli's side. "You're all killing it. I mean, Haney's got the cheekbones, and Luis—that jawline. Codes has the whole all-American-boy thing going on, and James—well—" James neatly sidesteps the slap that Muzz aims for his ass. "But Eli. Bro. Brother. Brethren. Your whole look is just so—"

"If you say 'exotic,' I will punch you."

"I would NEVER," Muzz says, aghast. "Parks would murder me from a continent away. Oh, man. Parks would love to photograph you. With your—neck and collarbones and shit. You should come back next semester. Actually, no. Don't. You're too pretty."

"Who's Parks? Eli asks, bemused.

"One of the sports photographers from the art department," Cody says.

"Is *he* gay?"

"They," Muzz interrupts, "do not believe in the bullshit heteronormative social constraints of gender or sexuality. And I salute them." He does, with beer still in hand. Then sighs. "I'm gonna go send them an email."

"You do that," Cody agrees and says aside to Eli, "They're doing a semester abroad right now. I think Muzz is a little in love with them."

"A lot in love with them," James corrects.

Their conversation devolves into a discussion of the kegger they plan to throw the following night and who will probably attend. The general consensus is most of the swim team since they had a meet, and both men and women's soccer teams since a good portion of them are from out of the country.

"Wait," Eli says. "I thought you hated the soccer team?"

"Oh, no," Cody corrects. "We're good with the soccer team. It's the rugby team we have a problem with."

"FUUUUCK THE RUGBY TEAM," everyone choruses—Muzz, upstairs, a few seconds behind everyone else.

Eli drinks to that because he feels like he ought to.

"Hey," James says, sharing a look with Eli. "Why don't you put on some music, Cody. You can try to teach us more TikTok dances."

"Ugh. No, sir," Cody says from where he's sprawled on the couch, a red solo cup balanced on his sternum. "I am way too full to dance."

"You sure?" Eli says.

"So sure."

Eli gestures for James to hand him his backpack, then squishes onto the couch between the arm rest and Cody's head.

Eli withdraws the Louboutin box from his bag and swaps it for the cup resting on Cody's chest. "You really sure?"

"Oh my god," Cody says.

"Oh my god." Haney half sits up from where he's lying on the floor. "Luis!" he yells toward the kitchen. "He brought the shoes! You owe me twenty dollars!"

"You brought the shoes," Cody says, eyes wide. "Why didn't you tell me?"

"Surprise?"

Cody sits up and removes them from the box slowly, touching the stiletto heels with reverent fingers.

"Yes," he says, a little breathless. "I think you're right." Eli and Cody do the "Single Ladies" dance together because, obviously, but then Eli lets Cody have his fun as the center of attention, taking turns dancing with the other boys and generally enjoying the hell out of himself.

Eli gets himself a third slice of pumpkin pie and leans against the kitchen doorjamb to eat it, watching as Cody, now wearing a pair of tiny shorts with his oversized knit sweater, grinds to "Partition" with Muzz on top of the coffee table.

His calf muscles look fantastic, Eli thinks absently. All of him does. Clearly an NCAA training regimen has added even more muscle to his frame, which is both evident and compelling as he moves—his body spangled with red and green from newly erected Christmas lights around the windows. Eli wonders, briefly, if this is what Alex would look like dancing: a golden-haired icon of confidence—a fierce brightness in a dark room.

He notices James watching Cody from the other side of the couch, eyes hooded, leaning against the wall next to the stairwell.

Eli pushes off the doorframe, makes his way across the room, and stops, right next to him. He leans a little farther into James's space than he probably would have without the two beers in his system.

He takes his time licking the tines of his fork clean. "You have a type, Mr. Petrov."

James ducks his head, sheepish, but doesn't take his eyes off Cody. "Yeah," he says quietly. "I guess I do."

19

THE DAY AFTER THANKSGIVING, the Hell Hounds tally another loss, this time against the Sharks. It's a frustrating battle against injuries—a slash to Jordie's hand that broke two fingers, a sprained ankle for Jeff, a collision that resulted in a concussion for one of the rookies—and a confluence of bad calls. It comes down to a shootout, and Rushy blames himself for the loss. Alex spends the first five minutes after the game trying to convince Rushy that drowning himself in the San Jose locker room shower is not the best course of action.

Kuzy takes Alex's place after a while, a wide hand on Rushy's hunched back, and Alex returns to his own stall to pull off his jersey. It's half over his head, snagged on his chest protector, when he hears the new trade, Justin Matthews—dubbed Matts by the team—swearing about the ref's shitty calls.

Fucking cocksucker.

Alex doesn't even flinch.

He's used to it. Hell, he's said the same thing, and worse, countless times up until the previous year, but Jeff goes still beside him, midconversation.

"It's okay," Alex mutters, still tangled in his jersey. Either Jeff doesn't hear him or elects to ignore him.

Probably the latter.

"Hey, Matts," Jeff says casually. "You like getting your dick sucked?"

Matts pauses in his diatribe. "Uh. Yeah?" he says, laughing a little uncomfortably.

"I'm assuming you don't mind if a girl does it, right?"

Matts half stands. "The fuck are you—"

"I mean—you wouldn't call her a cocksucker. Not like it's an insult. You still respect her and shit?"

"'Course I wouldn't. I don't know what your problem is, but—"

"So it isn't the actual cock sucking you have a problem with, then. It's the idea of a man doing it."

"What? *No.* You know I didn't mean it like that."

"How did you mean it, then?"

Matts glances around the locker room, obviously looking for support, but doesn't get any. At best, people are watching, at worst—Kuzy, Rushy—they're glaring.

"It was a joke," he says.

"Nah," Jeff says and goes back to stripping out of his pads. "It was an insult. One that doesn't have any place coming out of your mouth. I tell kids every summer that being gay doesn't prevent them from playing professional hockey. That it's a much more accepting sport, now. That locker rooms aren't the shitty, homophobic places they used to be. Don't make me a liar, man."

Matts swallows but doesn't say anything.

"It's not a big deal," Jeff continues more gently. "You probably didn't realize how problematic it was before. But now you do. Cool?"

"Yeah, man."

"Good."

"So," Jeff turns his attention back to Alex. "You were saying?"

The noise level ratchets right back up again, and Alex lets out the breath he hadn't realized he was holding as he finishes stripping down. He leans into Jeff's space for a moment before heading for the showers.

"Thanks," he murmurs.

Jeff punches him in the shoulder.

They don't get back to the hotel until nearly 10:00 p.m. Rushy is still with Kuzy, probably drinking too much at the bar downstairs, but they don't have another game for four days, so Alex is pretending he has no idea what they're up to.

After a second shower, Alex pulls a hoodie on over his boxers and T-shirt and wanders his way to the pool on the roof outside. There's no one there and his legs are a little chilly in the breeze. He sits on one of the chaise lounges and stares up at the stars for a few minutes, trying not to be too melodramatic and ultimately failing.

He gets out his phone and pulls up the last conversation he had with Eli. There have been two subsequent messages from Eli since Alex sent his usual pregame text, one railing against a call at the end of the third period, which makes Alex smile, and a sad-faced emoji at the end of game.

Hey he types. *u awake? I'm still down to FT if u are.*

His phone rings with an incoming video call less than a minute later, and he leans back, the night already feeling slightly less dire, as he swipes to accept.

Eli grins at him, hair a mess and what looks to be the remains of glittery face paint smeared around his temples, but Alex—

Alex's stomach goes sour.

"Are you in James's bed?" he asks. And he can barely get the words out. Because he knows those sheets. He knows the comforter around Eli's shoulders. He knows them intimately. They're the same sheets James has had since he started billeting at fifteen—when his host mother dragged him to the store and bought four different packages of the same bed-in-a-bag because she knew his terrible teenage laundry quirks, but she also knew James was a creature of habit. Alex wonders if James still switches sheets every Thursday like he used to, if any of the sets have worn out at the corners yet, if James still lets a month go by before he actually washes his massive pile of laundry.

"Yeah," Eli says, oblivious to the fact that Alex's hands have gone clammy, and his heart is beating like he's just finished a double shift on the power play.

"James let Cody and me have his room for the night. He's staying with Muzz. Look, Hawk says hi."

He shifts the phone so Alex can see Hawk at the foot of the bed. He can also clearly see that Eli is alone in the room.

"Hi," Alex says weakly.

"I'm the only one upstairs," Eli continues, words blurred at the edges from alcohol or fatigue or both. "I got a little overwhelmed and decided to call it a night an hour or so ago. I listened to the end of the game. Sucks."

"Yeah," Alex agrees, still trying to get his breath back. "How was Princeton's game? Google said they won."

"They did! Cody didn't get to play much—just a couple minutes. But he got an assist."

Eli sighs, repositioning his phone so it's propped against the pillow, and then pulls James's comforter more closely around his body. "All the boys did really well. And James's tending is—Well, he could be in the NHL right now. Obviously."

"Yeah."

There's a distant crash followed by excited yelling in the background, and Eli glances toward the closed door behind him, grinning. Alex's chest gets tight. In a better way than before.

"I've never been to a party like this before," Eli says, "because I didn't want to gamble with leaving Hawk. It's fun. Being—" He gestures vaguely. "—young. Stupid. I mean, I wouldn't want to all the time. But."

Alex curls on his side, wishing he'd thought to put on pants. Who knew California could get so cold at night? "So you're having fun?" he asks.

"Yeah. So much. Thanks for the tickets. Oh, and Cody says thanks for the shoes. He's wearing them right now; said he's going to—" Eli yawns, and it's cute as hell. "—get as much time with them as he can before I get full custody again."

Alex frowns. "Should we get him his own pair?"

Eli's face screws up for a moment, and then—then Eli is laughing at him.

"What?"

It's not really laughing, it's giggling, and Alex wonders how much, exactly, Eli has had to drink.

"Seriously, *what*?"

"Nothing," Eli says. "You're just so good." His smile dims a little. "It's not fair."

"I'm ... sorry?"

"No, that's not—" Eli makes an irritated noise, pressing his palms to his eyes, then drags both hands through his hair. "Never mind."

The giggles come back while Alex tries to figure out how to respond to that. "Oh my god," he says, a little exasperated but smiling despite himself. "What now?"

"I think Cody will have his own Louboutins by Christmas anyway," Eli says, tone conspiratorial. "James awkwardly asked me where to buy a pair about an hour ago when Cody was dancing with some soccer player. James was practically salivating but also, like, ready to go defend Cody's honor if the guy got too handsy. You should have seen his face." Eli dissolves into laughter again, and Alex isn't sure what his feelings are doing.

"Oh, shit," Eli says abruptly. "I'm sorry. I wasn't thinking. Are you okay?"

He leans closer to the phone, eyes bleary but concerned, and Alex wants to touch him so badly he sits up so he has something to do with his hands.

"I'm fine," he says, and it's true. "I haven't been in love with James for a long time."

"Okay." It doesn't look like Eli believes him. "I'm sorry," he repeats, subdued.

Alex shifts position with a shiver, tucking one arm ineffectively around his body. "Eli," he says.

"Hmm?"

"When you first called me a minute ago, I almost had a heart attack."

"What? Why?"

"I recognized James's sheets. And you were drunk and in his bed, and I know it was stupid, but my first thought—"

"What? *No*."

"But." Alex takes a studied breath. "If it was true. If you *had* slept with him. I wouldn't have been jealous of you," Alex says slowly, trying to make sure Eli understands. "I would have been jealous of *James*."

Eli doesn't say anything, and Alex closes his eyes because he doesn't want to see Eli's expression. Because this isn't a conversation they should be having when Eli is drunk and Alex is three thousand miles away. It isn't a conversation they should be having *at all*—

"Alex."

"Hmm?"

"I'm not sober enough to do this right now."

He sounds sad, which makes Alex feel even worse.

"I know. I'm sorry. That wasn't fair."

"Well," Eli muses. "I guess we're even now, then."

Alex has a sudden visceral memory of Eli in his bed, asking him what he'd most regret not telling someone and—

"Yeah," Alex says wryly. "Guess so."

"Wait," Eli says. "How long has James had these sheets?"

Alex laughs a little helplessly. "Juniors."

"*What?*"

And then they're both laughing, and it's not exactly a relief, but Alex is able to breathe a little easier.

Eli squints at him. "Are you shivering?"

Alex makes a studied effort to stop. "No."

"Alexander. Go inside right now. The last thing we need is you getting sick."

"Fine. You should go to sleep."

"Okay."

"Drink some water first though."

"Okay."

"I'll see you at the airport tomorrow."

"Okay. Goodnight, Alex."

"Goodnight, Eli."

Alex sits next to Jeff on the plane for the flight home early the next morning.

"You look terrible," Jeff tells him pleasantly. "You want to call Eli and flirt for a few minutes to cheer yourself up?"

"It's 5:00 a.m.," Alex grouses. "Even with the time difference, he would kill me."

He thinks, a little anxiously, about the degree of slur in Eli's speech the night before and says more to himself than Jeff, "I hope he's not hungover today."

Jeff makes a disgusted noise.

"Also," Alex says, lowering his voice, "I don't flirt with him. There's no flirting."

Jeff wordlessly opens his photo reel and hands over his phone.

Alex gets three pictures in and flushes. "How do you keep taking these without me noticing?"

"Flirting," Jeff repeats.

"Yeah," Alex admits, continuing to scroll. "Maybe a little."

"You're picking him up at the airport tonight, right?"

"Mm-hmm."

"You want company?"

Alex tries to figure out a nice way to say *no*, and Jeff laughs.

"Never mind," he says. "I can tell when I'm not wanted."

Alex hands back Jeff's phone and pulls out his own. Eli will probably wake up before they touch down in Houston, so he composes a basic "good morning" text and follows it with a *see you tonight!!*

“Do you think two exclamation marks are excessive?” he asks.

“Oh, yeah,” Jeff says. “He’ll for sure know you’re in love with him now.”

Alex shoves an elbow into Jeff’s side. “I don’t know why I’m friends with you.”

“Because no one else will put up with your shit.”

“True,” Alex admits, and it feels a little too honest for comfort.

Jeff slings an arm around him. “I have a gift for you.”

“Okay?”

“Permission to sleep on my shoulder for the duration of this flight.”

“How is that different from any other flight?”

“I have another gift for you.”

“Okay.”

“An invitation to shut the hell up.”

“Thanks,” Alex says seriously. “I hate it.” He leans his temple against Jeff anyway.

Jeff grumbles something about ungrateful children but doesn’t push him away.

20

SOMETIMES ALEX WANTS ELI so badly it's like resisting a physical confrontation. Like a fight on the ice in the third period of a playoff game. Like someone has a hand in his jersey and is dragging him forward and he knows it's going to end in a fist to the face, gloves off and bloody, but there's nothing he can do to stop it, just maybe delay it a little. Because it's going to fucking hurt when it's over.

It's all Alex can do not to kiss him when Eli comes down the arrivals staircase. Instead, he hugs him. Well. It's a little excessive for a hug. "Picks him up and shoves his face in his sternum" might be a little more accurate but—

"Alexander Price, you put me down right now."

"What," Alex says, grinning up at him, arms tight around Eli's hips. "Kuzy can do it, but I can't?"

"I'm not afraid that Kuzy is going to drop me."

"EXCUSE YOU?"

Eli laughs, stealing Alex's hat and settling it, backwards, on his own head.

Alex puts him down so he can take it back. He'd left the house in a hurry, and his hair is a mess.

That's when he notices the man with a camera.

He's standing just to the side of the first rental car kiosk, all the way on the other side of the baggage claim atrium. The telephoto lens on his camera tells Alex that his presence there isn't an accident.

"What?" Eli asks but notices where Alex is looking before he can respond.

Eli takes a deliberate step away from him, expression shuttering, and Alex is abruptly furious.

He slings an arm around Eli's shoulders. "Ignore him," he says, pulling Eli tightly to his side. "Let's go get your bags."

Eli glances up at him, uncertain, but doesn't pull away. "Okay."

The pictures are on the internet before they even get back to Alex's place.

Alex knows this because his phone starts ringing as they're waiting to pull into the parking garage.

"It was half an hour ago," Alex answers in lieu of a greeting.

Jessica's silence is judgmental. How, he isn't sure. But it definitely is.

"Kuzy did the same exact thing, and he didn't get in trouble," Alex interjects before she has a chance to say anything. "I should be allowed to hug my—Eli, without people freaking out about my goddamn sexuality."

He realizes he's whining. It's fine.

"First, you're not 'in trouble.' If you want to pick up your friend at the airport—literally," she says, sotto voce, "that's your prerogative. I'm just here to talk to you about public reception and potentially mitigating speculation."

"So?" Alex says. Well, sighs really.

He wedges the phone between his ear and shoulder so he can roll down the car window and scan his fob for the garage gate.

"So Eli's pictures with Dmitri last week were actually helpful. Obviously, it's early, but the journalist who published the pictures, and most comments so far, seems to think you're intentionally messing with the press at this point. It also helped that you looked right at the camera before you put your arm around his shoulder."

"Oh ... kay?"

"Of course, there are those who speculate you've employed Dmitri's help in covering up the fact that you're in a relationship with Eli, but we can deal with that."

Alex rolls his window back up. "Why do they think it's me hiding a relationship and not Kuzy?"

Eli, quiet until then in the passenger seat, sucks in a breath.

Jessica doesn't respond for a moment.

"What?" Alex says.

"You've never had a girlfriend," Jessica says. "You've never even been seen spending one-on-one time with a woman. Never been caught on a walk of shame. And, for all your ill-advised exploits your rookie year, you've never been photographed in a compromising position with a woman. Ever. Do you know how unusual it is that I've not once had photographs of you groping some girl in a club come across my desk? Which—don't get me wrong—I'm very happy about, but people who have been paying attention to your past are all too happy to point out that you have zero history with dating, or even hooking up with the opposite gender. Dmitri, on the other hand ... "

Alex sighs.

Kuzy is a serial monogamist. He loves quickly, and wholly, and documents the minutia of his affection across various social media platforms until the relationships end. There's no question that Kuzy loves women.

"There's also—" She pauses, and Alex doesn't like the sound of that at all. "There's also James Petrov."

Alex wrenches the steering wheel a little too sharply as he's turning the corner and flails for a moment, dropping the phone as he tries not to sideswipe a Mercedes.

He curses while Eli leans over the center console to retrieve it.

"Hey. Sorry. Dropped my phone. What about James?"

Eli stills beside him.

"No one has published anything yet, but I did a little digging myself. Just to cover our bases. You two weren't exactly subtle, in juniors. It's like I said before—little things add up. And if someone ever decides to compile all the little pictures and interviews and Instagram posts ... it might be compelling enough for people to take notice, is all I'm saying. Which is why you need to be careful. Provided—"

"Provided I don't want to come out," Alex says. It occurs to him he's never actually confirmed to Jessica that he's gay. But then, she always has been very good at her job.

"Yes," Jessica agrees.

"Right."

Alex pulls into his parking space and leans on the steering wheel for a minute. "Okay. Thanks. Keep me posted, I guess? I just got home."

"I'm assuming Eli is with you?"

"Yeah."

"Good. Go enjoy your evening. We can talk more later." Alex hangs up but doesn't move.

"Should I ask?" Eli says.

"It's not a big deal," Alex says, turning off the car. "Jessica was warning me there's speculation. That we're—you and me—are together, and Kuzy is, like, trying to help throw people off."

"Oh."

"Apparently my history doesn't really help things."

"History?"

"I've never had a girlfriend. And all the old media from juniors with me and James is a little damning, I guess."

He takes off his hat and scrubs a hand through his hair before replacing it. "I've never been good at hiding how I feel."

"That's ... not a bad thing," Eli says. "Normally."

"Yeah," Alex agrees. "Normally. Come on."

Alex pauses as he's pulling Eli's suitcase out of the back hatch. "Oh. Are you staying tonight? I didn't even ask if you wanted to come here; I just assumed. Do you want to go back to your dorm? I can take you now. Or maybe after we've eaten?"

Eli reaches for the side handle on the bag and helps Alex pull it all the way out. "I was planning to stay here tonight, if that's okay."

"Oh. Good. Cool. Yes."

They're quiet on the way up to Alex's apartment, elbows bumping in the elevator.

Once inside, Eli takes off Hawk's vest, and Alex immediately drops into a crouch to say hi. She locates her braided rope toy under the couch, and they roll around the kitchen floor while Eli goes to shower the airplane off his skin.

Eventually, Alex's arms get tired of playing tug-o-war, and he lies on the rug, faceup, letting Hawk use him as a pillow while she chews triumphantly on her rope—the knotted end occasionally whacking Alex in the face. Bells watches judgmentally from the couch. He loves it.

Eli, barefooted, damp, and smiling, finds them there a few minutes later.

He's wearing Alex's clothes. The T-shirt is one he's had for years, over-washed and soft, the collar separated in places. Alex has to close his eyes for a minute.

"Hawk missed you," Eli says, sitting next to Alex's head.

"I missed her too." He shifts Hawk off his chest and onto the floor so he can sit up. "Are you hungry?"

"Not really. Just tired. It was a good visit, but it was also ... a lot."

Eli's phone buzzes on the counter, and he stands to retrieve it, huffing out a laugh as he returns. He sits closer this time, cross-legged, one bare knee touching Alex's hip. His skin is still flushed from the hot water. He smells like Alex's soap, and Alex can't decide if he loves it or hates it.

"I'm sorry," Eli says, looking at his phone.

Alex takes a moment to refocus. "Hmm?"

"Kuzy just sent me some screencaps of gossip articles, pretending to be jealous."

"Jealous about what?"

"About how you and I have some sort of epic hidden romance. I know this is what you were trying to avoid, but it's also—" He shrugs a little helplessly.

"It's also what?"

"It's nice. That people think, you know. That."

"What?"

"That someone would want me. That someone like *you* would want me."

The look on Eli's face—a little embarrassed, a little pleased—makes Alex feel like he's just been punched in the stomach.

And suddenly he's angry.

"I need you to do me a favor and never say anything like that ever again," he says.

Eli laughs, but it's self-deprecating. And Alex just can't handle it anymore.

It's not graceful.

There's a dog in between them, and Eli's mouth is half-open because he's about to say something else, but Alex just—

Kisses him.

In an awkward half lunge with one hand braced on the floor and the other moving to turn Eli's face into his, and it's—

It's not graceful. But it is good.

At least until Eli shoves him away.

"What are you *doing*?" he says, standing with none of his usual grace.

Alex stands, too, because it seems like the thing to do.

"I don't know," he admits. And it occurs to him now how horribly, horribly stupid that was. "I'm sorry. Fuck. I'm sorry. But your *face*."

"My face? What does that even—" Eli paces into the kitchen and leans both hands on the island, and Alex follows because of course he does.

"You drive me crazy," Alex says. "All the time. And then you say things like—And it's stupid. Because you're"—he gestures wordlessly, unable to describe everything that makes Eli so—"you're you. And that's ... the best thing. Anyone would be lucky to have you. *I* would be lucky to have you. Not, like, the other way around."

"*What*?" Eli says.

"What *what*?" Alex answers.

Hawk, baffled and a little concerned, sits up to watch them.

"You can't say you'd be 'lucky to have me' when you don't want me. That's bullshit, Alex."

"I don't—what are you talking about? Of course I do."

"No," Eli says. "No, you don't. Because you said—you said you weren't willing to risk your career, and you wouldn't date anyone until you were retired."

"Yeah, but I'd only known you for like a week at that point. How was I supposed to know that you'd—that you're—"

"That I'm what?"

"*That you'd be worth it*! Maybe. I don't know. And what about *you*? You said you wouldn't be okay with dating someone who wasn't out."

"Okay," Eli says, sounding a little winded. "That's—I could say the same thing."

"Say the same thing as what?"

"*That maybe you'd be worth it*," Eli shouts.

"Well, *fuck*," Alex says.

"Yeah."

Eli exhales, sliding down the side of the island to sit with his back braced against it. After a moment of consideration, Alex joins him, pressed shoulder to shoulder, breathing unsteadily.

Hawk happily moves to drape herself across their laps, and they both reach out to pet her automatically.

Neither of them says anything for several seconds.

"So what if we ... tried," Eli says, attention on his fingers sifting through Hawk's fur.

Alex opens his mouth and closes it again. "I'm going to need more than that."

"We could try. Being together. I guess."

"But you don't—"

"You don't either, but—"

"Yeah."

This isn't actually a conversation, Alex thinks a little hysterically. "We'd just—keep it a secret? And ... see?"

"Yeah."

"Are you sure you're okay with that?" Alex asks.

"Yes."

"You shouldn't have to be anyone's secret."

"You shouldn't have to *keep* me a secret, but the world sucks. So."

There's this feeling of rising ... euphoria, maybe? It's hot in the back of Alex's throat, like maybe this can happen; maybe he does get to have this after all.

But he tries to push it down, at least momentarily, in favor of rational thought. "What if we're a disaster? Apart from Jeff, you're my best friend, and I don't want to fuck that up."

Eli leans into him a little, thinking. "We'll just agree not to let things get weird. If it doesn't work, we'll be awkward for a couple weeks, and then everything will go back to normal."

"Just like that?"

"Just like that."

Alex breathes for a moment. Because things not working isn't his biggest concern. And he could leave it. He doesn't have to talk about it now. But he should. Because he learned the hard way that letting someone in doesn't mean they'll stay.

"And what if it's great?" he asks.

"Then that's ... good?"

"No. I mean, what if we're perfect together, and shit's, like, real. And nobody knows."

Eli bites his lip.

He doesn't say anything for several seconds, which is a comfort; it means he's really thinking about it.

"I'm not sure I could do that indefinitely," Eli says finally. "Waiting until you retired, or whatever. I think I would get mad. Resent you. If I tried. So I'd have to know there was an end point. Even if the timeline was years and not months."

"How many years?"

"Alex. We haven't even—"

"No," he says, insistent. "I'm not starting something if it's just going to fall apart because of—"

"Three," Eli interrupts. "Three years, max. By the time I graduate."

"Okay," Alex says.

"Okay?"

"Yeah. If things work." He rubs his palms down Hawk's spine, trying to get his hands to stop shaking. "I think I could be ready by then. I'm not now. But I could be, eventually. For a good reason."

"I'm a good reason?"

"Best one I've found."

"Holy shit. That was smooth."

Alex laughs, which was probably Eli's goal. "Thanks."

Eli loops his arm through Alex's, resting his head against Alex's shoulder, and drags the knuckles of his opposite hand up and down the soft skin of Alex's inner bicep. "I'm assuming you need a minute?"

And Alex does. Because this is big. This is huge. And the happiness in his gut is tempered by warranted fear.

"Do you need to call Anika?" Eli asks.

Alex's first reaction is anger. That shouldn't even be a question. It's not fair that he lives in a world where getting something he wants—something he wants *so badly*—also necessitates a talk with a goddamn therapist. His second reaction, though, is overwhelming affection. Eli is probably freaking out just as much as he is right now, but Eli is still trying to take care of him and that's ... good.

"No. I'll call her tomorrow. Thanks though."

"Yeah. Sure." Eli clears his throat. "So. We've been very mature and rational about this whole thing, I think."

"Yeah?"

"Which is great. But could we maybe not? For a minute?"

Alex doesn't understand. "I don't understand."

"Well, all this talking about the future and stuff is, uh, healthy. But—" Eli licks his lips, then bites them, then makes an embarrassed noise.

Oh.

Alex grins. "You want to make out like a couple of teenagers for a while?"

Eli grins back at him. "Yes, please."

"I'd be okay with that," Alex says magnanimously.

Eli leans over to snag Hawk's rope toy and tosses it into the living room. The moment she scrambles after it, skidding a little on the concrete floor, Eli climbs into Alex's newly vacated lap.

Alex's hands settle automatically at Eli's waist, palms cupping the lean swell of his hips, thumbs pressed to the sharp jut of his hipbones, nails dragging, lightly, against the warm skin just beneath the hem of his shirt. His hands move without him really telling them to—up the taut muscle of Eli's sides, fingers settling briefly in the trenches of his ribs as Eli inhales sharply.

There's so much of him that Alex wants to touch, and he *can* because it's allowed now and—

Eli reaches for Alex's face, laughing, and Alex remembers, a little belatedly, that he's supposed to be kissing him.

"Hi," Alex says.

"Hi," Eli agrees.

21

ELI WAKES UP TO Hawk's insistent nose in his face.

This isn't particularly unusual.

What *is* unusual is that he's being aggressively spooned by one Alexander Price. Alex's left arm is tucked tightly around Eli's ribcage, and Eli gets caught up for a moment, staring down at the little white scar on Alex's first knuckle, the subtle map of veins embossed on the back of his hand, the fine blond hair on his forearm, pale and bright in the watercolor light of early morning sun.

There's something revelatory about Alex's sleep-slack fingers—still curled in an approximation of a fist in the fabric of Eli's shirt.

Hawk makes a disgruntled noise, and Eli sighs, extricating himself from Alex's various clinging limbs. He steals Alex's hoodie and keys from the counter and squints his way down the elevator and out to the dog relief area.

He's still mostly asleep when they get back to the apartment a few minutes later, and he makes it as far as opening the guest bedroom door, resisting the urge to climb back into bed with Alex before realizing he doesn't have to resist anymore.

And holy shit.

That is the best feeling.

"Hey," Alex murmurs as Eli squirms his way under the sheets again. "Hawk?"

"Yeah."

"Time is it?"

"Six."

Alex makes grabby hands toward him, and Eli tucks himself back against Alex's chest, face-to-face this time.

"Hey," Alex says again, blinking slowly at him. "You're here."

"Uh. Yeah?"

"Good. You should always be here."

And then he's tugging Eli into a sleepy, off-center kiss, which is cute right up until Alex pulls away a moment later and whispers in his ear, "Your breath is rank."

Eli shoves Alex's face away. "Yours ain't so great either."

"Oh, it ain't?"

"Shut up. At least I brushed my teeth last night unlike someone."

"Don't be like that," Alex grouses. "The southern-y thing you do when you're mad is adorable, though, just so you know."

"'Southern-y' isn't a word."

"Oh, and 'ain't' is?"

Eli hits Alex with a pillow.

The ensuing pillow fight is short-lived because Hawk gets involved, and then they're sneezing and picking feathers out of each other's hair, and Alex bemoans the passive-aggressive note he knows the maid will leave him while Eli drags him for having a maid at all.

They brush their teeth, and Eli puts a record on, and they make pancakes together. Or more accurately, Eli makes pancakes, and Alex drapes himself over Eli's back, making commentary on his flipping technique and pressing occasional minty kisses to the nape of his neck.

Alex's eyes are puffy and there are pillow creases on his cheek and his hair is an absolute mess, and it shouldn't be a big deal because Eli has spent plenty of mornings with Alex before. But never this close. Never this real. So it is kind of a big deal, after all.

Eli takes a deep breath and tries to focus. "So." He pours batter out of the bowl and into the skillet. "Can you take me by my dorm first to drop off my suitcase before we go to the rink? I don't want to deal with hauling it around all day."

"Or you can just leave it here," Alex says into his shoulder.

Eli shifts his weight from one foot to the other, and Alex sways with him. "I can leave some things." He isn't sure how to say it. But he needs to. "I wasn't planning on coming back here after class today."

Alex straightens, pulling away from him. "Right. Of course."

"Hey. Wait." Eli catches Alex's wrist in the hand not occupied with a spatula and tugs him back. He rubs his thumb against the knob of Alex's wrist bone because it seems appropriately conciliatory. "Remember when we were doing the questions thing? From my psychology homework?"

"Yeah?"

"I told you then that one of the things you'd need to know if we were going to have a close relationship is that I need space sometimes, especially after I've been around a lot of people for an extended period of time."

"You're all peopled out?"

"I am *so* peopled out. I'm also behind on my homework. And after last night ... I just need some processing time."

"Right. Okay. So. You haven't changed your mind?"

"No. God, no."

"How much, uh, time do you think you'll need? Should I—will it bother you if I text you, or ... ?"

"No, please, text me. And probably just a day or so."

"Okay." Alex reels Eli in closer again, tentatively at first, then a little more confidently when Eli goes willingly. He links his fingers behind Eli's lower back, still swaying a little to the music. "So. Obviously you can say no, and I won't be, like, mad or anything. But do you maybe want to go to the game on Wednesday? Coops is out with his ankle, so you could sit with him and Jo in a private box."

Eli rests his hands on Alex's chest, trying not to smear batter from the spatula on his shirt. "Yeah. That would be great. I've been wanting to go to a game in person for a while now."

"Really?"

"Yeah."

"Cool." Alex takes a steadying breath. A Mindful Breath, Eli thinks. "It would be important to me," Alex says slowly, "if you went."

"Then I'll be there."

Alex grins, the big, honest, crinkly-eyed smile the media never gets, and leans down to press a chaste kiss to Eli's mouth.

It doesn't stay chaste long.

Eli isn't sure what happens. One second, he's chasing Alex's mouth for a quick second kiss, and then he's sitting on the counter with Alex's hips between his splayed thighs, ankles hooked behind Alex's waist, fingers knotted in his hair. The spatula is ... somewhere, and one of Alex's hands has pushed up the leg of Eli's boxers, palming the curve of his ass and—

And Eli gathers enough presence of mind to push Alex away, breathing hard.

Alex looks a weird combination of sheepish and turned on, and Eli just—can't. He slides off the counter and then nearly to the floor because his balance is a little off.

Alex steadies him, going from flushed arousal to concern in .03 seconds. "You good?"

"Yeah." Eli glances at the stove and winces. "Pancakes aren't though."

He bins the pan's blackened contents, finds the spatula on the floor—licked clean by an unrepentant Hawk—and sets about starting the process over while Alex hovers anxiously behind him, no longer touching, but a warm, distracting, presence that makes him want to abandon breakfast all together and just drag him back into the bedroom and—

Eli takes a breath and pours a new round of batter into the pan.

He turns to face Alex and licks his bottom lip, which feels a little tender and puffy and probably looks that way, too, judging by the way Alex is staring at his mouth.

"So," Eli says. "Uh. The talking thing? We should probably do that. About—" He gestures between them. It seems saying "sex" in the early morning light of Alexander Price's kitchen is beyond him, despite the fact that they were just grinding against each other a few minutes before. It's fine. He's a teenager and hasn't reached full maturity yet or whatever.

"We should talk about sex?" Alex asks. Clearly that extra year makes a difference.

"Yes?"

"Okay." Alex moves a little closer, pulling Eli flush against him again, and then looks down at him expectantly and Eli regrets all of his life choices.

"Maybe you could start?" Eli says.

"Uh," Alex says, a little bemused. "I'm in favor? Of the sex."

Eli coughs on a laugh, exhaling, and lets his forehead fall forward to rest against Alex's collarbone. He smells good. "Noted."

"Are you also in favor of the sex?" Alex asks.

"I'm not opposed?"

Alex smirks, hitching one thigh a little where it's pressed against Eli's dick, and yes, okay, it's pretty obvious he's not *opposed*, but—

"Hey." Alex takes a step back, not letting go of him but putting an inch or so of space between them, a little pinch between his eyebrows. "Are you okay?"

"Yes. Jesus. I'm so happy right now, you don't even know."

"I might," Alex mutters, and Eli has to kiss him. "But?"

Alex asks.

"But I've never done this before. The relationship stuff or the—" He waves a hand.

"Sex stuff," Alex supplies helpfully.

"Right. Just ... any of it. Everything in the last twenty-four hours has been a first for me, and the fact that it's with *you* is ... "

"You're thinking 'Alexander fucking Price' in your head right now, aren't you?" Alex sounds a little resigned.

"I might be."

"But it's just *me*."

"I know. You're not the problem. Well, you are, a little bit. Because I don't want to fuck this up. But the circumstances are, uh ... "

Alex winces, and Eli cups his hands around the back of Alex's neck.

"It's not your fault," Eli says. "But this is all really overwhelming. And back home when you like someone, you go on a couple of dates and hold hands and sneak kisses, and then one day you leave a movie early so you can make out in the back of a pickup before your parents expect you home and then—My point is, there's a process. And usually, you go through that process with multiple people before you find a person that's important. But I didn't get to do any of that, before. And now I'm here, and I'm sleeping in your bed with you, and I don't have a curfew, and it's just—"

"Overwhelming," Alex repeats.

"Yeah. And the whole professional NHL player, keeping things a secret aspect doesn't really help."

"That's fair. So. We'll take things slow, then?"

"Please. I mean, this—what we've been doing is fine, just ... Nothing more until I've, like, acclimated. If you don't mind."

"Okay."

They stand there for a moment, holding on to each other, and Alex purses his lips. "While we're on the topic of serious shit ... "

"Oh my god. More talking?" It comes out a little whinier than Eli means it to, but Alex seems endeared rather than annoyed, so it's okay.

"Yes," Alex says. "More talking. Anika will be so happy she'll let me choose something from the treasure box."

"Your therapist has a treasure box?"

"Yours doesn't?"

"If he does, he probably only offers it as a reward for *children*."

Alex sticks out his tongue, which really doesn't do him any favors in terms of proving maturity. "Anyway," he says, hiking up Eli's shirt a little so he can sneak his thumb under the fabric. He pets the skin over Eli's hip bone absently, like he doesn't even realize he's doing it. "I think we should talk about what we mean when we say we're going to keep this a secret. Are we telling people close to us, or—?"

"Oh. The only person I'd want to tell is Cody."

"Of course. Yeah. I'd like to tell Jeff. I also want to tell Kuzy about, you know, me in general. I think I'm ready, and seeing how cool he's been with you has been encouraging."

Eli bites his lip, and Alex narrows his eyes.

"What?

"Uh. I'm pretty sure Kuzy already knows? About you. He told me at breakfast last week that you—that he could tell we were interested in each other. I told him I was into you, but I wasn't sure if you, like, reciprocated. He was really cool about it. That was the reason for the airport hug."

"Oh." Alex takes a steading breath. "Okay. I want to tell Kuzy and Jeff then. Jeff will probably figure it out fast anyway." He pauses, thumb stilling against Eli's hip.

"What?"

"Do you want to see?" Alex asks, and he's got a look on his face that can only mean trouble.

"See what?"

"How long it takes Jeff to figure it out."

Eli grins. "Definitely."

Alex ducks to kiss him again.

... And then again.

And then—

Eli is pretty sure he's the instigator of the third kiss, maybe the fourth one, too, and it's not until Alex is lifting him back up onto the counter that he remembers—

"Oh, shit, the pancakes."

Eli takes a two-hour nap after class, plays fetch with Hawk, eats at the dining hall with the Morgans, and then, feeling suitably well-rested and somewhat human again, he FaceTimes Cody.

It's nearly 10:00 p.m. Cody's time, and he's clearly fresh from the shower when he answers the call, all damp and rumpled and pink from the steam. He's wearing an unfamiliar sweater that looks too big for him. And he's ... in James's room.

"Why are you in James's room?" Eli asks.

"Hola, cariño," Cody says blithely. "It was so good to see you this weekend. How was your first day back?"

"Yes, yes. Hello, hi, why are you in James's room?"

Cody sighs like he's a lost cause. "My dorm lost power from the ice storm today. James is letting me stay here for the night."

"Where is James sleeping?"

"With Muzz. He's got a bunk bed in his room."

The screen is pixelated, but Cody looks a little disappointed.

"Ah."

"Hopefully class will be canceled tomorrow though. There's supposed to be over a foot of snow tonight."

"I miss you," Eli says because apparently all this talking about feelings has made him a little less emotionally stunted.

Cody's face goes all crumply, and Eli wishes he could take it back.

"I do too. I'd forgotten how much I missed having you around in person and now I've remembered and it's like ... a fresh wound, you know?"

"Yeah."

They both stare at each other, getting progressively shinier around the eyes until Hawk climbs up onto the bed and sidles her way forward so her head is in Eli's lap. He moves the laptop a little farther away so she doesn't knock it off the edge of the bed on accident.

"So," Eli says. "I wanted to tell you something."

"Oh?"

"But you can't tell anyone else. And I do mean anyone."

"Okay."

Cody gets up, leaving the screen for a moment, and Eli can hear him shouldering the door to James's room closed. It doesn't fit in the sagging frame anymore, and there's a distinctive screech against the wood floor when he finally gets it in place.

"Okay," Cody repeats, jumping back onto the bed. "Hit me."

"Well," Eli says, and he can't help it, he's already grinning like a maniac. Because here's a sentence he never in his wildest dreams thought he would get to say:

"I'm dating Alexander Price."

Cody doesn't say anything for several seconds.

"Are you serious?"

"I am so serious."

Cody screams. Just. Straight up. Screams. "Fuck you. No. That's—seriously?"

"Seriously."

"Oh my god. Eli. I'm so happy for you. But how—" Cody glances away from the screen when someone knocks on the door.

"Codes?" It sounds like Muzz. "You okay, bro?"

"Fine!" Cody yells back. "I'm just talking to Eli, and he had some good news. But everything's fine!"

"Okay," Muzz answers. "Hi, Eli! Hi, Hawk! Congratulations on the good news!"

Eli kisses Hawk's head, laughing, as Cody returns his attention to the screen.

"Tell me," he demands.

"Well. Yesterday Alex picked me up at the airport—"

"*Yeah*, he did," Cody interrupts.

Eli rolls his eyes. "And we sort of ended up yelling at each other but then talking about things? And we decided we would try. Being together."

"He's not going to come out though, right?"

"No, not right now. But he said he would. If things go well."

Cody sucks in a breath. "You believe him?" And that's the question, isn't it?

"Yeah," Eli says softly. "I do."

"All right, then," Cody agrees, positively beaming at him. "Only you, Eli. An NHL star." His smile dims a little. "So. Not to be downer. But you know I've got your back, right? However all of this turns out?"

"Yeah, of course."

"Good." Cody considers him for a minute. "You look exhausted. Did you sleep last night? Or were you ... *busy*."

Cody does lecherous a little too well.

"Excuse you, we are taking things slow," Eli says primly.

Cody makes a judgmental noise. "Why? He's not exactly my type, but I do have eyes. I've seen the photosets on Tumblr. His ass is a national treasure."

Eli's not about to argue with that.

"Everything is really new. And it's a lot. To deal with," Eli says, and Cody sobers.

"No, I know."

"I did, uh, touch it though?"

"The Price Booty?"

"We're not calling it that, but yes."

"Verdict?"

"Very firm. A-plus work."

"And on the eighth day," Cody intones, eerily similar to the pastor at Cody's church back home, "the Lord made hockey asses. And Eli felt one. And it was good."

"Hallelujah," Eli agrees.

22

ON WEDNESDAY, ELI GOES straight from class to Alex's apartment.

Alex isn't there—it's an early game, so he's already deep in his pregame rituals at the arena, but it allows Eli to take his time sorting through Alex's closet for something to wear. He realized that morning that every single piece of Hell Hounds–related clothing Alex has given him, or snuck into his skate bag, or left in the guest closet, or—The point is that all of the shirts and jerseys and sweaters have Alex's name and number on them, and while Eli may *want* to explicitly flaunt his loyalties, it's probably not a good idea, considering recent media speculation.

Eli eventually borrows one of Alex's Hell Hounds hoodies and waits in the lobby for Jeff and his wife Jo to pick them up. He sits in the back seat of Jo's car with Hawk, apologizing about the dog hair because that's his life, while Jeff complains about never walking again, even though he's in a boot and walking fine.

Jo does that thing where she meets Eli's eyes in the rearview mirror, and they commiserate for a moment about what a giant baby the professional hockey player in the passenger seat is.

Eli likes Jo. He already knows from Jeff that she's a twenty-seven-year-old doctoral student in biology, currently working on her dissertation. Jeff has repeatedly said that she's far too smart for him, and he's lucky he conned her into marrying him with his good looks and charm.

By the time they get to their seats, Eli's also learned that Jo grew up in California, nearly became a professional skateboarder before going with academia instead, and usually drives a motorcycle when not chauffeuring her injured husband, a disabled kid, and a service dog around.

"She's a lot cooler than you," Eli tells Jeff when they get to the stadium.

"She is," Jeff agrees.

"I married him for his dimples and money," Jo says.

"Fair," Eli says. And then adds, "His ass isn't half bad either," because he's been thinking a lot about butts recently and apparently lacks a filter.

"True. Dimples, money, and ass," Jo amends.

Jeff looks smug.

The box is comparatively quiet, there's a bathroom less than a hundred feet from the door, and Eli is feeling pretty good as he settles in. He gets Hawk tucked next to his seat, then leans a little toward Jo as she continues to tell him about the new bike she has her eye on.

Judging by the look on Jeff's face, it's going to be her Christmas present.

By the time warmups are over, Eli's gotten the rundown on Jo's dissertation, knows more about Mexican free-tailed bats than a good portion of the US population, and has also heard the story of Jeff and Jo's bizarre courtship.

"I'd never seen a hockey game in my life, but Jeff was playing for the Stars when I was doing graduate coursework in Dallas. I ran into this guy in a bar one night in Dallas and—"

"She was so drunk," Jeff notes.

"I was a little drunk," she admits. "And I mentioned the connection between bats and tequila."

"She talked for twenty minutes about how vital long-nosed bat migration patterns are for the distribution and diversification of agave plants—which tequila is derived from—and how the decline in their species is affecting the alcohol industry. And although she was wasted, she was super eloquent and used a shit ton of words I didn't understand. It was adorable."

"He immediately fell in love with my wit and bat-savvy," she continues.

"I did."

"And we went out on our first date the next night."

"By summer, I was so in love with her I voluntarily spent two straight weeks in Mexico with her, knee-deep in guano, with no electricity half the time, and no idea what the hell was happening because everyone was speaking Spanish."

"Qué triste," Eli murmurs.

Jo laughs. "It wasn't that bad."

"Well, yeah," Jeff says. "You get excited about guano, and you speak Spanish. You had a blast."

"I do not get excited about—"

"And what about the drug cartel!"

"The drug cartel?" Eli asks.

"It wasn't a big deal," Jo says.

"We nearly died."

"We did not."

"I'm sorry," Eli repeats. "The drug cartel?"

"One of the caves housing a colony she was researching was being used by smugglers to hide their cocaine stash or whatever," Jeff says.

"We don't know that," Jo mutters, aggrieved.

"So, what, the angry men with guns were protecting a stash of *jellybeans* in their top-secret cave?"

"Once they understood we were scientists, they let us go, and no one got hurt," Jo says to Eli. Her tone implies that her husband is being ridiculous. "They understood the importance of bats in the propagation cycle of agave plants. They appreciated the work we were doing."

"Yes. Thank god for environmentally conscious drug lords," Jeff says.

Jo rolls her eyes. "Anyway, luckily I was finished with the bulk of my research in Mexico by the time he was traded. So when he asked me to marry him and head for Houston, I said yes. I mean, I still have to travel quite a bit for ongoing research and to meet with my committee members, but his ridiculous paycheck facilitates that, so living here isn't a huge imposition."

"Don't let her lie to you," Jeff says, "She complains all the time about the quality of the caves near Houston. She has strong opinions about caves. Almost as strong as her opinions about guano. She's a cave person."

"That joke never gets old, dear," Jo says flatly.

"I know."

Jeff smooshes a kiss against her temple, and she swats him away.

Eli is charmed.

The game starts, and they fall mostly quiet. The Hell Hounds are playing the Kings, and while they've been doing really well this season, Eli is pretty confident the Hell Hounds will win.

When Alex takes the face-off against a man who towers over him and wins it, Eli is, quite literally, on the edge of his seat. It's nothing like watching at home, on his laptop or Alex's couch, where there's this sense of separation—as though it's not really happening because it's on a screen. Here, he holds his breath through each of Alex's shifts and winces every time someone tries to run him into the boards. He screams encouragement when Kuzy retaliates for a dirty hit and jumps out of his seat at a particularly pretty save by Rushy.

Jo spends most of the game laughing at him.

Jeff spends most of the game muttering under his breath and leaning back and forth in his seat like he can telekinetically influence the puck.

The Hell Hounds win 3–2 in overtime: Kuzy with an assist by Alex, Rads with an assist by Matts, and Alex unassisted.

There's this brief moment immediately following the puck's slick slide beneath the goalie's descending left leg, when Alex's arms go up before the goal horn has even sounded. He turns, momentum carrying him back around the boards—and he points directly to the box where Eli is sitting.

It's too far away. Eli can't see Alex's face, wouldn't even be able to tell that the small figure on the ice so far below is Alex without the name and number emblazoned on his jersey. But for a three-second stretch of interminable time, it feels like Alex is looking right at him.

Everyone piles on Alex a moment later before they take turns knocking helmets with Rushy who blocked thirty-six shots and generally kicked ass. And then they're leaving the ice, and Eli's face, a little open-mouthed and dumb-looking, is on the jumbotron. Jo throws an arm around his shoulder and waves, and then Jeff lounges across both of their laps, so he's in view of the camera as well before the screen changes to show a group of blonde women who all look eerily similar, cheering in the stands.

"Those are some of the WAGs—wives and girlfriends," Jeff says, his head still mostly in Eli's lap. "Jo hates that she looks so much like them."

"I'd dye my hair brown on principle except it'd be all wrong with my skin tone."

"Your hair is beautiful," Eli says loyally, because it is.

Jo's hair is this nice honey-gold color, thick and wavy, with a blunt edge just below her shoulders.

"Once Kicks graduates, you'll get a little diversity," Jeff says.

"Kicks?" Eli asks.

"Rushy's girlfriend. She's playing NCAA hockey at Stanford right now. She's Japanese-American."

Eli whistles. "Stanford?"

"I know," Jeff says. "How he managed that, no one knows. He doesn't even have dimples."

"Still a nice ass," Eli and Jo say simultaneously, and Jeff rolls his eyes.

Jeff shifts to his feet awkwardly, then offers his hand to Jo, intentionally flashing his dimples at her. "Want to drop by the locker room?" he asks Eli. "Alex would probably like that."

"Are you sure it's okay?"

"Yeah, definitely. Come on."

"I'll go get the car and wait for you outside the player's exit," Jo says, kissing Jeff absently.

They take a special elevator with a bored-looking attendant down to the locker room level of the stadium, where the various people they pass, both press and staff, look like they have Very Important Things to do. After a few minutes of walking the wide cinderblock hallway, Eli can hear music.

"Star of the game picks music," Jeff says fondly.

Eli listens to Halsey declare that she's heading straight for the castle, and laughs.

"Alex?"

"Definitely Alex."

Jeff shoulders open the door, and Eli has to take a moment because A. the locker room is ridiculously large and expensive looking, B. the smell is pretty terrible, but C. there are a lot of attractive, naked, or nearly naked men ambling around, and one of them is probably Alex.

His awkward pause just inside the door isn't noticed. Most of the guys immediately converge upon Jeff, patting his back with a degree of roughness that seems counterintuitive to recovery from an injury.

When Jeff turns to introduce Eli, he's more or less prepared with a nervous smile, carefully keeping his eyes at shoulders-or-above height.

"Guys, this is Eli," Jeff says, simultaneously taking a step back and pushing Eli forward.

"And Hawk!" Rushy yells from his stall. He's stripped to the waist but still has his goalie pads on his legs. The dichotomy is kind of hilarious.

"And Hawk," Eli agrees. "Hi, Rushy."

Rushy blows him a kiss, then glances back toward the door as if he's afraid he'll get in trouble.

Eli doesn't know what that's about, but if there's one thing he's learned about hockey in the last few months, it's that goalies are weird.

He gets several handshakes and jarring shoulder-slaps as he meets various people he's interacted with on Twitter or Instagram but yet to meet in real life.

"Eli!" A very tall, very blond man—kid?—says. "I'm Asher. I private messaged you about the picnic? It totally worked, man. My girlfriend thought it was the sweetest thing and totally forgot she was mad at me."

"I'm tell you Eli's best," Kuzy yells, coming out of the shower area.

Kuzy is in the process of tucking a towel around his waist, and he's all wet and—listen. Eli has no designs on Kuzy. But the man is jacked.

"Nice to meet you, Asher," Eli says. "I'm glad she liked it."

"For sure. I'm already planning our anniversary dinner. I'm going to make the mango salsa fish thing you did last year and then the key lime bars from a couple weeks back."

Asher seems genuinely excited about the prospect.

"Do you know a wine that would go with that? Becca likes wine, but I'm—"

"Stupid rookie baby?" Kuzy says helpfully.

"Eli's underage," Jeff points out.

"So am I?" Asher says, confused.

"Baby," Kuzy says again.

"Get a nice sauvignon blanc or pinot grigio," an older man says. He's got laugh lines, gray at his temples, and warm brown eyes that make Eli want to trust him. "I can help you pick it out if you want."

Asher looks delighted and a little frightened. "That would be really great, Rads, thanks."

He sidles away, and the older man takes his place, extending a hand.

"I'm Derek. Radulouff. Nice to meet you, kid. It's about time; Alex won't shut up about you."

Eli isn't sure how to respond to that. "It's nice to meet you too."

The handshake is firm but not unkind, and Derek crosses his arms afterward to look down at Hawk, who's a little uncertain in the new, loud environment but holding her heel at Eli's ankle.

"Good looking German shepherd. Working line?"

"Yessir," Eli says because Derek seems like someone you're supposed to *sir*. "She's from a Czech line. Bred in the US though."

"She's beautiful. Good nerves, too, with all this—" He waves a hand to encompass the general madness of the locker room. "My wife has a German import boy."

"That's awesome." Eli is about to ask if he has a picture since 99 percent of people who bring up their dogs in conversation will happily provide one, but before he's able to, Alex pushes his way into the locker room, still in all his gear and a backwards snapback, and the minute he sees Eli, he breaks into a giant grin.

Derek makes an amused noise and, with a pat to Eli's shoulder, heads off to the showers.

"Eli!" Alex says.

"And Jeff," Jeff says beside him, long-suffering.

"And Jeff," Alex allows.

Jeff and Alex fist bump, then tap each other's chests with their fists, and then Alex is in front of Eli, flushed pink with exertion, grinning crookedly, and for a moment, all Eli can think about is the way Alex lifted him up onto the counter two days before, the way Alex's hips felt between his thighs.

"Hi," Alex says.

"Hi," Eli agrees.

He steals Alex's hat; he needs to do *something*, and that's suitably flirtatious without being damning.

"You played pretty good," Eli says, settling the hat on his own head.

"Pretty good? I was the star of the game. If I'd had the forethought to punch someone, I would have gotten a Gordie Howe."

"Rushy still got the first interview," Jeff points out.

"No comment," Rushy says.

"Star of the game," Alex repeats. "And I'm pretty sure my interview was longer."

He walks over to his stall, pulling off his jersey and sits down with a sigh, bulky padded legs stretched out in front of him. He takes off his chest protector next, and by the time he's stripped down to his Under Armour, Eli is biting his bottom lip. Alex's hair after a game is—it's delightful really. Eli understands why the minute Alex's helmet comes off, he's usually jamming on a hat. There's no way any reporter would take him seriously if he did post-game interviews like this.

There are little damp ringlets of half-formed curls stuck to his forehead, but a good portion of his hair is in that awkward stage between wet and dry—fluffy and completely at the will of his cowlicks.

"Your hair is ridiculous," Eli says.

"Your face is ridiculous," Alex retorts.

Eli ignores him, reaching to run his fingers through the hair in question. It's sweaty and gross, but the action is worth the soft expression he gets in response.

"I kind of love it," Eli says.

Alex opens his mouth and then closes it again. His ears go a little pink.

Eli realizes Rushy is watching them, and he musses Alex's hair roughly before shoving at Alex's forehead with his knuckles. "What was that slashing nonsense in the second period though?" Eli raises his voice and takes a careful step back. "Pretty sure you're useless to your team in the box."

Derek, emerging from the showers, yells an "amen."

Eli's expecting an argument from Alex—that it wasn't intentional, but instead, Alex's expression shutters.

"He deserved it."

And that's Alex being entirely serious.

"Well," Eli says. "I guess it's good you slashed him, then."

Alex's smile returns.

Derek makes a resigned noise and mutters something about children.

It is at this point that the draw of Sweaty Hockey Player apparently becomes too difficult for Hawk to resist, and she, while still technically maintaining her heel, stretches her neck out to shove her nose in Alex's crotch.

It effectively derails the conversation.

"So," Alex says, still laughing a minute later after Eli has chastised Hawk and she's sitting at his feet looking repentant. "Dinner?"

"Dinner," Eli agrees.

"Dinner?" Jeff repeats hopefully.

"Please?" Kuzy asks.

"Sure," Eli says.

"Oh, is Eli cooking?" Rushy calls.

Several more faces turn to look at him expectantly.

Eli glances back at Alex, who shrugs, a little resigned but pleased.

"Dinner at Alex's place!" Eli announces to the room at large. "I'm making lasagna."

23

ALL TOLD, ALEX HOSTS eleven people for the impromptu dinner. Well. More like Eli hosts eleven people. Alex isn't even there for half of the preparation process because Eli doesn't have enough ingredients—or ovens—to cook for that many people all at once. So while Eli makes the first batch of lasagna, he sends Alex to the grocery store with a specific (insultingly specific, really) list of things to purchase. By the time Alex gets back, one lasagna is in the oven, and Asher and his girlfriend, Rushy, Rads and his wife, Kuzy, two rookies, and Jeff and Jo have all arrived and are either playing video games in the living room or watching Eli work his magic in the kitchen. Hawk is cuddling with Kuzy on the couch, and Bells is grumbling angrily from the top of the refrigerator.

When Alex comes in, laden with Eli's reusable grocery bags, Eli is grinning, gesturing with a knife midway through cutting onions, recounting an apparently hilarious story to a small group of onlookers.

He's wearing the forest-green apron Alex bought and left conspicuously folded over the oven handle two weeks before. Alex may not be good at fashion, but the contrast between Eli's skin, the white T-shirt he's wearing, and the deep-green of the apron is nice. Very nice.

Eli looks like he belongs there. And Alex wants him to. He wants this to be normal—excessive grocery lists and reusable canvas produce bags and dinner parties with their friends. He wants to settle a steadying hand on Eli's hip as he delivers more vegetables to the cutting board, kiss Eli's temple before putting the eggs in the refrigerator, and maybe palm his ass when he gets snarky about how long it took Alex to find the twenty-eight "quick" things on Eli's list.

He can't though. Not now, at least.

So he delivers vegetables with a fleeting touch to Eli's shoulder, puts away the eggs as instructed, and pours Eli a glass of cider. Eli likes cider, and they just won a game, and the checkout girl was hardly going to card him.

"Well thank you, Mr. Price," Eli says, accepting the glass. "Derek was just asking how I met you. You want to help me tell that story?"

"I do," Jeff says from the living room, vaulting over the couch.

"Can we not?" Alex says. He knows his face is flushing, but there's nothing he can do about it.

"Sorry, kid," Rads says solemnly. "Seniority."

"I'm your captain."

"You're also underage," he says, eyeing the beer in Alex's hand.

Alex sighs.

"All right, so—" Eli says, scraping the mound of vegetables off the cutting board and into the pot. "I'd just moved into my dorm at the start of the semester, and I was pretty nervous because it was the very first day of practice with the figure team."

By the end of the story, the video game is paused, Jeff and Eli have reenacted several pieces of dialogue, there's been a significant amount of laughter at Alex's expense, and Alex has finished his beer and is considering hiding in the bedroom.

"He has admittedly redeemed himself since," Eli says, grinning up at Alex, and Alex is helpless to do anything but smile back at him.

He feels like it has to be obvious—that there's no way he's not just broadcasting his giant, unwieldy feelings everywhere. But no one calls him on the fact that he clearly has a massive crush on the green-apron-wearing figure skater in his kitchen. The conversation topic changes, and the living room occupants resume their gameplay with friendly threats of violence.

Alex needs to sit down.

It's a nice night, is the thing.

Everyone gets along, and no one says anything cringeworthy, and the food is, obviously, delicious. The only problem is that Eli can't stay since he has homework to finish and ballet class the next morning. And he doesn't even get to kiss Eli goodnight because Jo offers to drop Eli off at his dorm when she and Jeff leave, and it would be weird if he didn't accept. So Alex sleeps alone and eats breakfast alone and is already a little miffed when he drives to practice the following morning.

Things don't improve in the locker room.

Matts is running his mouth to the call-ups again, who are either just as ignorant as he is or too green to talk back to a more senior player, even if they're older than him.

Alex has a headache and newly sharpened skates in his hand. He considers ignoring Matts—he just wants to practice and go home—until he hears Eli's name.

"The fuck did you just say?" Alex snaps.

"Everyone was thinking it, I'm just saying it," Matts says blithely.

"I wasn't thinking it," Asher says quietly from his stall.

"Everyone was thinking what?"

"It was just weird having the kid in the locker room," Matts says, and Alex's stomach goes sour.

"Weird?" He repeats as he's pretty sure if he tries for a full sentence, he'll throw up.

"Look," Matts says. "I know he's your friend or whatever, but just because you're okay with a gay dude staring at your dick doesn't mean the rest of us are."

And Alex.

Has no answer for that.

Well, he does have an answer, but it involves outing himself and a decade of pent-up self-hatred and vitriol and possibly a fist to Matts's stupid fucking face, and he can't—he isn't ready to—

"Stupid," Kuzy says. "Why's Eli look at you when *I'm* in room? I'm have best dick. You?" He makes an unimpressed noise.

That gets a round of laughter, and Matts rolls his eyes.

"Whatever, man," he says and goes back to lacing up his skates as if he hasn't just fucking decimated Alex. As if he doesn't care, or maybe doesn't even know, the effect his offhand comment has had. Because he's right. There probably are several guys on the team thinking the same thing. Guys who love Alex now, but who would never respect him again if he came out. *When* he comes out? Fuck.

He should say something, but his eyes are feeling dangerously hot, and he can't seem to open his mouth.

"Statistically speaking, Matts," Jeff says (and thank god for Jeff, honestly), "it's likely every locker room you've ever been in has had at least one guy in it who's interested in dick. It's unlikely they were ever interested in yours, though, considering the person it's attached to."

That gets a second, louder round of laughter.

"Jeff," Kuzy says despairingly. "No fair. *I'm* funny one."

Alex takes a breath. He needs to get out of his head and be the goddamn captain and say something. But before he can, Rushy says casually as hell:

"Jeff's right. I'm bi, and I've never once looked at your dick, Matts. Or, you know, anyone else's on the team."

The whole locker room goes silent.

Kuzy is the first to recover. "Not looked at mine?" he asks, feigning offense.

Rushy grins. "No, but if this is you giving me permission ... "

"But you have a girlfriend," Asher says.

"Believe me," Rushy answers, "if she knew I had his permission, Kicks would fully support me ogling Kuzy."

"Ogling?" Kuzy asks.

"To 'ogle' is to, like, stare at someone in a sexually appreciative way," Jeff explains.

"Oh," Kuzy says. "Yes. Have permission for ogle."

"No," Asher says. "I mean. How are you bi? You have a girlfriend."

Rushy blinks. "The whole 'bi' thing literally means I like both. Sure, I'm totally in love with Kicks, and hopefully she'll be willing to marry me at some point. But"—he shrugs—"doesn't mean I stopped finding guys attractive."

"Guys like me," Kuzy says, in case they needed reminding.

"Yeah, buddy," Rushy agrees. He keeps taping his stick as if he hasn't just tipped Alex's world on its axis.

"So," Jordie says. "Have you like—" He stalls out, gesturing a little, and Rushy laughs.

"Sure. I mean, I've been with more women than men; it's easier. But I dated a guy in juniors. Hooked up with a few more after I was drafted."

Jordie looks scandalized by this. "When? You were rooming with me."

"Whenever I wanted to. I didn't know how you'd take it, so I didn't tell you. And then I met Kicks, and it didn't matter so much anymore."

"So why say anything?"

"I have the second-highest save percentage in the NHL right now. And Matts is being ignorant."

"What does your save percentage have to do with it?" Asher asks. He really is a sweet, naive, child.

"Because no one is going to say I can't play hockey, now. I've proven myself. So if someone in this locker room decides to go to the press, sure, it'll be hell to deal with, but I won't have to worry about being traded."

"You were worried about being traded before?" Asher asks, horrified, like it's something he never even considered. Like it's not something Alex has been agonizing over for nearly a decade.

"Of course. No GM is going to hang onto an unproven, controversial player. Especially if there are other, valuable players on the team talking about being uncomfortable with them in the locker room." He looks up from his tape roll to glance purposefully at Matts. "Team cohesion is more important than giving some no-name queer rookie a chance to prove himself. I've known that since juniors."

"But that's bullshit," Jordie says.

Rushy shrugs. "That's hockey."

Matts is looking at the floor between his skates.

"Doesn't have to be," Jeff says quietly.

"No, it doesn't," Rads agrees. "But change has to start somewhere." He looks pointedly at Alex, and Alex, finally, manages to find his tongue.

"Thanks for trusting us," he tells Rushy. "I'm sorry you didn't feel comfortable telling us before, and—" He clears his throat. "—as captain, that's my fault."

Alex holds up a hand to stop Rushy's protests. "I know everyone likes to make fun of Jeff's monologues about inclusivity and stuff—"

"Thanks, bro," Jeff mutters.

"But this is exactly his point. We shouldn't let this shit slide anymore. We're a team. And, like, fuck management or whatever politics they've got going on. You—not only you, Rushy, anyone—should never doubt their team has their back. Not for something like this."

It's not eloquent, but it's the best he can do.

Rushy nods.

"Thanks, Cap."

Alex turns to address the rest of the room, arms crossed. "I feel like this goes without saying, but I'm going to say it anyway. Unless Rushy decides to come out publicly at some point, no one talks to the press about this. If the media does somehow get ahold of the information, I'll personally make sure that the person responsible is traded. Understood?"

He gets a lot of nods, but also several people who just—look away.

Alex is already exhausted, and practice hasn't even started yet.

"Let's get out on the ice," he says, more resigned than anything, "before Coach decides to bag skate us."

Practice isn't as bad as he expects it to be, but it's not great either. Jeff isn't out of the boot yet, so he's working with the trainers on PT; his line is clearly feeling his absence. The chemistry on Matts's line is all off too. Asher is more concerned with glaring at Matts than passing to him. Alex is distracted with keeping an eye on Rushy, and Kuzy gets yelled at a couple times for being out of position because he's both glaring at Matts and keeping an eye on Rushy. Rushy, however, performs brilliantly, even gets a helmet-pat from Coach after a drill, where he makes four particularly graceful consecutive saves. The locker room is strangely quiet afterward and empties quickly.

Alex is gratified to see that multiple people—over half the team—stop at Rushy's stall before they leave, and he's smiling, accepting shoulder-slaps and fist bumps.

Alex approaches him last. When it's just them left in the locker room.

"Hey," he says, and then he just ... doesn't know how to continue.

"Hey," Rushy agrees.

"Thank you," Alex says, and—fuck, that's not what he meant to say.

"For?"

Alex just stands there. Who the hell thought making him captain was a good idea? He's a walking disaster. No wonder one of the most-used Tumblr tags to describe him is "dumpster fire child." Which maybe isn't even fair. A burning trash heap would probably handle this *better*.

"Alex?" Rushy says, sounding a little concerned.

"I'm gay," he says because he might as well, and he's just so damn tired. "And I'm starting to think about coming out. But I'm not ready yet. And you were so chill about it. And the guys were—well they're kind of ignorant but—" Rushy laughs. "—for the most part, they were cool. And that's good. So. Thanks."

Rushy looks contemplative but not at all surprised.

"You mean you've been thinking about coming out to the team or coming out publicly?"

It's a little hard to get the word out. "Publicly."

Rushy sucks in a breath.

"Not, like, soon. But within the next couple of years, maybe? Hopefully after a cup win."

"Fair." Rushy leans back on his hands. "You think it'd help if I came out first? A bisexual guy with a girlfriend might be a good, uh, first step for the hockey community."

Alex doesn't understand. "What?"

"I'm just saying. I'd want to talk to my agent and Kicks first but—You're Alexander Price. You coming out will be a much, *much* bigger deal than me coming out. If I can do anything to take some of the pressure off you, I will."

Alex refuses to cry in the practice facility locker room. He clears his throat.

Rushy rubs the back of his neck, flushing a little. "Just say 'thanks, man' and go cuddle with Eli or something. You look kinda rough."

Alex opens his mouth to—he doesn't even know what, deny it maybe?—but Rushy is already shutting him down.

"Don't play, dude. You're ass over elbows for the kid. If you aren't already together, you should be."

"We are," he admits, and that admission, at least, is shockingly easy.

"Good."

Rushy zips his bag and shoulders it, then punches Alex gently in the solar plexus.

"Seriously. Go home. Chill with your boyfriend. Feel free to tell him about me. I trust Eli." He taps the brim of Alex's hat, which should be condescending but somehow doesn't feel that way. "You'll be okay, kid."

Alex shoves his hand away to keep up appearances.

"You're, like, three years older than me."

"Five," Rushy says. "Respect your elders. I've gotta go call my agent, just in case. Probably need to schedule a sitdown with Coach. Does management know about you?"

"No," Alex says faintly. "Not yet."

"Okay, I won't say anything, then. You should probably tell them though. As soon as you're comfortable."

"Yeah," he agrees. "I've been—yeah."

"All right, good talk. See you tomorrow."

Alex walks on autopilot to the parking lot.

He cranks his car. Puts it in gear. Puts it back in park.

Calls Eli.

Eli answers on the third ring. "Hey! You out of practice?"

"Yeah. Are you free this afternoon?"

"I'm actually about to head over to your place now. My afternoon class was cancelled, and I thought I'd film a video before getting to work on a paper."

"Oh. Nice." Alex buckles his seatbelt and puts the car in gear again. "I'm on my way to Pretty Bird, but I can get it to go. Want me to pick up a salad for you too?"

"Please."

"Okay."

Alex takes a breath and reminds himself it's okay to ask for things that he wants. That it's not needy or annoying if it's important to him. It comes out stilted anyway. "Can you stay the night?"

"Was planning to. Is everything okay? You sound off."

"Uh. Something happened at practice, and I just—I'm about to call Anika but ... "

"Hey," Eli says. "Whatever you need, okay?"

"Okay."

"So. What do you need?"

"You. On my couch. Or in my kitchen. Just. With me? I guess. It might be nice if you napped with me. And Hawk. We could all nap together?"

"I dunno; that sounds like a pretty huge imposition, but I guess I can manage it."

"Yeah?"

"Yeah. I'm in the car now, so I'll see you in a little bit, okay?"

"Okay," Alex says, feeling significantly better.

"Oh, but on the salad can you—"

"No croutons, extra avocado, dressing on the side."

"Well of course you already knew that. Why did I even ask?"

"No idea," Alex says seriously.

"Hey," Eli says, "whatever's going on, I've got your back, okay? Unless it's, like, moving a body. Then you should probably call Kuzy."

"What, because he's Russian?"

"No, because he's comically huge. Does he have mafia ties I should be aware of?"

That startles a laugh out of Alex. "Probably. Anyone that nice has to be hiding something."

"True. I'll see you in twenty."

"I bet I can beat you home."

"You're on, Mr. Price. But don't you jostle my salad in your haste."

Alex grins at the windshield. "'Jostle your salad'? Who even says that?"

"Me."

"Clearly."

"Goodbye, Alexander."

"Goodbye, Elijah."

24

BEING WITH ELI IS EASY.

They eat in companionable silence, and then Alex closes the bedroom shades and strips to his boxers and crawls under the duvet cover, and Eli follows him without being asked. Alex is bigger than Eli. Usually he likes that, but right now, he just wants to be held—not that he would admit it, doesn't think he could even begin to ask for it. But Eli seems to know anyway. He arranges them so Alex's head is on his chest and Eli's arms are around his shoulders, and then Bells curls up in the small of his back and Hawk stretches out on top of their feet, and Alex closes his eyes because *yes*.

This is what he needed.

The static hum of anxiety dissipates a little under Eli's careful hands, under the soft drag of his fingers across Alex's skin, the little patterns he draws between the freckles on Alex's shoulders. And surrounded by warm cotton and steady breathing and the hush of gentle afternoon kindness, Alex falls asleep.

When he wakes up, Eli's arms are still loosely around him, but his head has shifted off Eli's chest and onto the bed beside it, so Alex's face is mashed into the side of Eli's ribcage. He's drooling a little. It's great.

He presses his mouth against Eli's skin because it's right there, and he can. And then he bites, gently, because ... well, he wants to.

Eli's formerly slack fingers curl into his hair but don't pull him away. He makes a soft noise that Alex feels a little proud to be responsible for.

"Hey," Alex says, "is it okay if I leave a mark?"

The fingers in his hair tighten. "Knock yourself out."

He takes his time leaving a hickey, then rolls onto his back and shuffles up the bed, grinning.

"Feeling better?" Eli asks, turning on his side to face Alex. He props his head up on one hand, looking a little flustered, opposite palm pressed to the mark Alex just left.

It's a good look.

"Much better," Alex agrees.

"You want to talk about practice?"

And the really, really cool thing is Alex is pretty sure he could say "no," and Eli would drop it.

"Matts was being ignorant and said some stupid shit, and then Rushy came out."

"Rushy is gay?" Eli says, scrambling into a seated position like the situation is urgent. "I thought he was crazy in love with his girlfriend."

"Bi."

"Oh. Right. There I go with binary thinking. Jeff would be appalled." Eli glances toward the door like he's expecting Jeff to barge in right that moment to chastise him. "Wait, you said he came out. On the ice or in the locker room?"

"Locker room. Matts looked pretty embarrassed afterward, so maybe it'll be okay. Most of the guys were cool. I mean, everyone loves Rushy. He's like sunshine in human form."

"He's not coming out publicly, though, right?"

"Not now. He, uh, offered though."

Eli just looks at him.

Alex licks his lips. "I told him about me. After practice. He said if I decide to go public, he'll come out first. As, like, a stepping stone?"

"Bisexual goalie with a steady girlfriend is a lot easier to digest than gay prodigy captain."

"With a boyfriend," Alex agrees. "Yeah. That's what Rushy said. I still can't believe he would do that for me. It would make things easier, probably."

Eli doesn't respond, and Alex glances up at him, then does a little crunch to sit up as well, slinging his elbows around his knees.

"What?" Alex asks.

"Is—are we boyfriends?"

"Oh. Uh. Yes? Do you not—?"

"No, I do. We just hadn't had that conversation yet, so."

"What conversation?"

"The one where we used that word?"

"I said I'd maybe *come out* for you. We had that whole, like, super mature discussion."

"Well, I didn't know! I've never done this before, and we only kissed for the first time, like ... forty-eight hours ago. I'm trying not to be, you know, clingy or whatever."

"Pretty sure I'm the clingy one, and I think it's closer to seventy-two hours now." He reaches for Eli, bottom lip jutted out. "Come here."

"Oh my god, Alex."

Eli leans forward, though, and Alex gently tackles Eli back into a position that might be called "lying." He takes a moment to arrange their untidy pile of limbs, throwing a leg over Eli's hip, cinching their bodies together.

"See?" he says smugly. "I'm the clingy one."

"Literally," Eli says into his neck.

"I refuse to apologize."

"So. Boyfriends."

"Yeah. I mean, I'm serious about this. I want you to be mine. Not in a creepy possessive way."

Eli coughs.

"Okay, maybe a little bit possessive, but I would be yours too. We'd be, uh, each other's?"

Alex really is a walking disaster, but Eli's grinning up at him, so clearly, he didn't fuck that up too badly.

"Yeah. I understand. I'd like that too."

"Good," Alex says, relieved. "So Jeff has some private rink time tonight that he can't use because he's still in the boot. But he wants to try out an ice sled if we're willing to go too. Want to join him and be grossly romantic?"

"I'd love to. I have to finish my government paper first though." Eli makes a face. "Finals are only two weeks away, and I need to start studying this weekend."

Alex winces. "Okay. Do you think we have time to make out for a couple minutes first?"

"I dunno." Eli pretends to look at the nonexistent watch on his wrist. "I'm pretty strapped. No more than five minutes."

Alex nods seriously, reaching for his phone.

"I'll set a timer."

Skating at the rink after official close makes it feel like winter, which is a rare feeling in Houston. Alex isn't sure what it is, but he likes it, the nighttime cold, the dim echoey hallways, the Christmas music over the PA system—left on from family free skate earlier that evening—that Eli and Jeff insist they don't change.

Alex gives Eli "checking lessons" that mostly involve him gently running Eli into the boards and hugging him until one or both of them dissolves into giggles. Eli tries to teach him how to do a basic spin that involves even more falling than the "checking lessons" and about the same amount of muffled laughter.

Jeff despairs of them, but gets pretty good at maneuvering his borrowed sled around and coaxes Eli into showing him pieces of the new routine he's working on for the regional competition in January. Alex's schedule might permit him to attend it, too, if he can get permission to skip a morning practice. He hasn't talked to Coach yet, though. He needs an excuse other than "I want to go watch my boyfriend at a figure skating competition."

They pack up before the Zamboni driver can kick them out at 10:30. Jeff, bemoaning a distinct lack of Jo at his home—she had to take a trip back to Dallas—invites himself over to spend the night with Alex.

It's not unusual. In fact, more often than not, Jeff spends the night in Alex's guest room when Jo is out of town because he's the most extroverted person to ever extrovert and hates being alone. But Jeff still hasn't caught on that Eli and Alex are officially together, even though they've been, Alex thinks, painfully obvious. The last thing he wants is to keep up this are-we-aren't-we thing for the rest of the night when it's one of the few nights he'll have with Eli before they're on the road again. That, and he just really wants to talk to his best friend about his boyfriend, and he can't if his best friend doesn't know about his boyfriend.

"I don't think he's getting it," Alex says when he and Eli are back in the car again. "Which is ridiculous. I'm not sure how much more obvious I can be."

"Well. I guess we need to up our game?" Eli says.

"I'm not sure how to do that aside from, like, straight up making out in front of him."

"That works."

He'd been joking, but ... "Yeah. Okay."

They disobey a few speed limits to make sure they get back to Alex's place before Jeff and have a very unsexy conversation about where they plan to get "caught."

They're still arguing about it when they hear the uneven stride of Jeff's Aircast in the hallway.

They freeze, Eli still gesturing toward the couch, and Alex just ... picks Eli up and puts him on the island.

"Good plan," Eli mutters, cinching his legs around Alex's waist, and by the time Jeff has fumbled the door open, Alex has one hand up the back of Eli's shirt and his tongue shoved into Eli's mouth.

The door clicks shut.

"Oh my god," Jeff says faintly.

And then, with unholy glee: "Oh my god!"

And then, moments later, with concern: "Oh my god."

Alex and Eli dissolve into laughter.

"Do you need a minute?" Alex asks.

He tries to turn and face Jeff, but Eli's legs are still tight around him, and when he looks back at Eli, hands sliding down to cup the thighs bracketing his waist, he gets distracted.

Eli is still laughing and looking at him like—like Alex is something important. Eli licks his bottom lip, tongue followed by his upper teeth. He sits there, biting his lip and looking at Alex, and Alex feels *so much*. And it's stupid. To feel this much this soon. It's stupid and reckless and amazing, and Alex has to swallow down whatever words want to accompany this unexpected emotional upheaval. He didn't think it was possible to feel so vulnerable and indestructible simultaneously.

"No," Jeff says. "I don't need a minute, but I think you might."

Eli collapses into Alex's chest, laughing again, and Alex wraps his arms around him and puts his face in Eli's hair, and it's all very histrionic.

Jeff sighs, then moves to sit at the bar. "Whenever you're ready," he says magnanimously.

Hawk happily leans against his leg, nudging his hand with her nose for pets.

Bells uncurls from her place on the counter to show Jeff her butt, then settles in exactly the same place, this time facing away from him.

This doesn't help Alex, who's trying to stop his slightly hysterical laughter.

"So," he says, still wrapped around Eli. "I have a boyfriend."

"No kidding," Jeff says. "Who?"

Eli lets go of Alex to flip him off.

They separate, a little regretfully, at least on Alex's part, but Alex keeps one arm around Eli as he slides off the counter.

"How long?" Jeff asks.

"Only a couple of days," Eli says.

"Since the night Eli got back," Alex clarifies.

"Not to be that person," Jeff says. "But have you two talked about this? I mean, I'm happy for you, don't get me wrong, but ... "

"Yes," Alex says, maybe a little too sharply. "And I've talked to Anika about it. Twice."

Eli drags his palm from the small of Alex's back to the tight space between his shoulder blades, then back again.

"Sorry," Alex says before Jeff has a chance to respond. "Just. Yes."

"Okay." Jeff spins his phone on the table. "Who knows?"

"You. And Rushy. I told him after practice today, sort of on accident. I want to tell Kuzy too."

"Okay. You planning to come out to the team?"

"Not yet. Eventually though. If things—if I have a reason. I'm talking to my agent tomorrow."

Eli's hand, still moving restlessly up and down his spine, stills.

"Management?" Jeff asks.

"Probably next week once we're back from the roadie."

"That's fast," Eli says quietly.

"They need to be prepared. Just in case."

"Well," Jeff says. "I'm here for you. Both of you. Whatever you need."

"Thanks, man."

"When are you planning to tell Kuzy?"

Alex glances down at Eli. "Uh. You want to invite him over now?"

Kuzy arrives twenty minutes later with pastries from his Russian cafe.

When he sees Eli and Alex on the couch holding hands, however, his face goes dark. "Alex," he says as he puts the bag on the counter. "I need to talk with you. Alone."

Alex and Jeff exchange concerned looks, but Eli ... starts laughing.

Kuzy's expression goes from something like anger to complete bafflement.

He's not the only one.

"Uh. Eli?" Alex says.

"Sorry," he says. "Oh god, I'm sorry. It's—he thinks you're breaking my heart leading me on or something. Dmitri, we're together. Alex and I. We're together."

"Together," he repeats, arms crossed.

"Like. Dating?" Eli says.

"Boyfriends," Alex adds. Because he likes the word.

"They got their heads out of their asses," Jeff supplies, ever helpful.

"You talk?" Kuzy asks Alex, still looking suspicious. "Eli tell you—" He pauses, face squinching up in annoyance. "English worst. You know feelings now? Both?"

"Yeah," Eli says. "We've had a couple talks. We know how each other feels."

"Okay." Kuzy's still frowning at Alex a little, but at least he uncrosses his arms. "Eli's sad, when I'm take him to airport. Because you touch him, sweet for him, always, but not together. I'm see you hold hands, and I'm think I have to—" He gestures between Alex and himself, frowning. "—sit. Talk, uh—sense?"

"To talk some sense into him?" Eli supplies.

"Yes. I think I'm have to talk some sense into him."

"Well," Eli says. "I appreciate the thought, but it's not necessary."

"Good." Kuzy retrieves the pastry bag from the counter and moves to join the three of them, except there's not enough room for four adult men on Alex's couch, especially not when three of them are NHL players, and two of them are over six-foot tall.

It quickly devolves into a wrestling match because, yes, Alex is fully capable of admitting they are all overgrown children. After several minutes of Kuzy chirping them gleefully in Russian and Jeff's occasional yell of "Hey! Watch the leg!" Alex finds himself winded on the floor, looking up at Eli who wisely removed himself from the fray and is now sitting on the loveseat. He's holding the pastry bag on his lap, licking his fingers. He pulls a tiny glazed scone thing out and takes a bite that is definitely judgmental, one eyebrow raised.

Jeff and Kuzy have more or less given up, each sprawled with their heads against opposite couch arms, occasionally kicking weakly at each other. Jeff has the upper hand because Kuzy is trying to be gentle with Jeff's injured leg, while Jeff is using his Aircast like an expensive weapon.

Alex crawls onto the love seat with Eli and eats the scone thing out of his hand, purposely messy, while clambering over his lap and into the space next to him.

"Oh my god," Eli says, wiping his spitty hand on Alex's shirt. "Are you twelve?"

"Twelve inches," Alex says.

"I'm pretty sure that's not true."

"It's not," Kuzy and Jeff say simultaneously.

Alex glowers. "I'm telling Coach to trade y'all."

"Y'ALL?" Jeff repeats gleefully.

Alex hides his face in Eli's neck.

Eli pats his cheek consolingly.

He presses a discreet little kiss to the soft skin at the base of Eli's throat and keeps his mouth there, smiling, because this—this is exactly what he thought he'd never have.

"Hey," Jeff says. "Alex, stop slobbering on Eli and share the goods. Can we turn on the Rangers game?"

Eli tosses the bag to Kuzy, who then instigates another minor war with Jeff, pretending he's not going to share. Eli laughs softly, leaning into Alex, and Alex wraps an arm around his chest, anchoring them more fully together, dropping another kiss to the short, wispy hair—desperately trying to curl but not quite long enough—behind Eli's ear.

"Hey," Alex whispers, and Eli shifts to look back at him, still smiling from Kuzy and Jeff's antics.

"Hey," he agrees.

And it's—

Good.

Perfect.

25

THE WEEK BEFORE FINALS, Alex is gone on a roadie, which is probably a good thing because that means he's not around to distract Eli from studying. It's dead week, so at least Eli doesn't have classes to deal with, but the stress is bad. He's had two seizures in the last ten days. His doctor said it was probably fine because being a college freshman at finals is a lot. Eli's also practicing for a regional competition in January, and he was stupid enough to try to get both of his math requirements out of the way first semester. Statistics isn't so bad, but calculus is trying to kill him.

"I'm going to fail calculus," he tells Alex morosely over FaceTime on night four of the roadie—three nights before the exam. "I'm going to fail and have to take it again next semester, and then I'll fail it again."

He lets his cheek rest on cool granite and ignores the soft laughter coming from his laptop.

He's at Alex's place; the desk in his dorm is too small, and the island in Alex's kitchen is perfect for spreading out his various textbooks and problem set reviews.

Not that it will matter.

Because he's going to fail.

"You're not going to fail. You have a B-plus in the class, and the final is only worth 15 percent. Even if you fail the exam, you'll pass the class. Remember? We did the math yesterday."

That's true. They had.

"Calculus is homophobic," Eli mutters.

"What?" Alex says. "How?"

"I'm gay, and it inconveniences me."

"You're ridiculous, is what you are. Get up."

"Why?"

"Because we're going for a walk."

"We?"

"Yes. I'm going to hang up. We're both going to put our shoes on. And then I'm going to call you back on your phone, and we're going to go for a walk."

"But then I can't see your face," Eli whines.

"When was the last time Hawk went out?"

"Okay. Point. I'll go get my shoes."

Five minutes later, Eli is bundled up against a surprisingly chill wind with Hawk beside him, nose to the ground and happy as they make their way down the sidewalk.

Coming from a small town, it still baffles Eli how wildly alive the city is—even at 10:00 p.m. on a Thursday night.

He waits to cross the street with a dozen other people, some already drunk, and nearly all of them dressed completely inappropriately for the weather. He smiles into his scarf. Well, it's Alex's scarf. It smells like him. It's nice.

"So," Alex says. "The weekend after we get back. I know that'll be right after finals for you, so it's totally okay if you just want to sleep, or whatever. But I was wondering if you want to come to the Breaking the Ice event? Jessica texted me, and they're looking for volunteers who can skate to help out."

"Breaking the Ice," Eli repeats. "What's that?"

"Oh. It's this charity thing the Hell Hounds do a couple times a year? We have kids from the group home and foster system come and skate with a couple guys from the team and staff. Most of them have never been on the ice before, but some of the older ones come to the free camps we host during the summer. It's kind of a mess, but it's fun."

"I'd love to. When is it? Which guys from the team will be there?"

"It's Saturday from ten to one. Little kids for the first hour and half, then the older ones. And I think right now it's me, Kuzy, Rushy, Matts, Jordie, Asher, and Rads. A couple of the vets are going to be there, too, and some of the WAGs. Jo won't be in town but—Oh! You'll get to meet Kicks. She's going to be here for most of Christmas break. She gets in next Wednesday, I think."

"Matts?" Eli says.

Alex sighs, as if maybe he'd been hoping Eli would miss the name squished into the middle of his list.

"He's been cool the last few days. I think Rushy talked to him. They're pretty close, or I thought they were, so maybe—I dunno. It should be fine though. If he gives you any trouble, I'll take care of it. Or Kuzy will, let's be real."

Eli laughs softly. "Kuzy is not allowed to punch Matts in a rink full of children."

"I'll pass that along. Also—" Alex clears his throat. "Did you maybe want to go out? Like on a date. Once you're done with finals obviously."

"A date," Eli says. "Sure?"

"I—I did all this research. And I have this list of places I'd like to take you and things I want to do and—"

"Alex. Yes. I want to go on a date."

"Okay. Good. I just want to do it right, this time."

"What do you mean, 'this time'?"

"I couldn't go all in before. Because it wasn't real. I can now."

"What do you mean, 'all in'?" Eli says suspiciously. "Do I need to set an expense minimum?"

"No, I mean—" Alex huffs out a breath. "You know how you said that back home there was like a set of steps you would take when dating? Dinner. Movies. Truck make outs?"

"Yeah."

"I have a version of that. In my head. And I want to do it right, now that it's real."

"Oh. So like, there's going to be intent now? You're going to *woo* me?"

"Yes," Alex says, sounding a little relieved and completely unaware he's being teased. "Exactly."

"Yeah? You gonna hold my hand in the car and kiss me at my door at the end of the night?"

"Yes?" Alex seems honestly bewildered, as though he hadn't even considered another course of action. "I mean, probably not at your door because, dorm. And there could be people in the hall. But maybe inside your room? If you invited me inside. Or in the car, if you just wanted me to drop you off. Though kissing over a center console might be a little awkward. Or we could go back to my place, and I could kiss you in front of my door because the hallway is private. That's kind of weird, though, since it's my door and not yours. But I'd rather you come home with me anyway so you could spend the night—which, it's fine if you don't want to, but if you do—"

Eli can't handle this.

"I do," he says, and his voice is a little rough—from the cold air, not, like, emotions or anything. He clears his throat. "I will. Want to spend the night. Probably. So we can plan for that."

"Right," Alex says seriously. "Okay, good."

On Sunday night, Eli books his flights home for Christmas. He'll only be there for four days because of competition prep, but it's something. Cody's Christmas plans are similarly condensed due to his game schedule, and they've managed to coordinate their arrivals and departures within an hour of one another. Cody's mom will pick them both up at the airport on the 23rd, and Eli's dad will drop them off on the 27th. Which is good, as neither of them has had time to talk for more than a few minutes for the past several days, and it doesn't seem like that's going to change any time soon. He's not sure who's handling finals worse: him or Cody.

"It is so damn cold here," Cody complains, voice muffled by his scarf. He's called Eli while walking back from the corner store on an olive oil run because apparently roasting something in the middle of the night is more important than continuing to write a final paper due in less than twenty-four hours. "I mean, honestly, it's no wonder I can't get any work done. I think my brain is frozen."

"Well. Running around outside after dark probably isn't helping."

"Shut up. What's the temperature there?"

Eli makes an uncertain noise, checking the weather app. He's been cocooned in a fluffy microfiber blanket on Alex's couch with a dog on one side of him and a cat on the other for the better part of the evening. He is very warm and very cozy and hasn't been outside since Hawk's afternoon walk, and that was before the sun set.

"Uh. Looks like it's forty-six degrees."

"Ugh. Why did I decide to go to school in the freaking frozen tundra? It's barely above freezing."

"I don't think Princeton counts as the 'frozen tundra'. And you could have asked one of the guys to drive you to the store so you didn't have to walk. You can't be the only one awake."

"I tried. Cap pulled rank and said no one was allowed to"—Cody drops his voice into a terrible impression of a French-Canadian accent—"facilitate my procrastination tactics."

"Good man."

"You're supposed to be on my side. And I doubt any of them will have an issue *eating* procrastination roasted brussels sprouts when they're finished. I'm doing a balsamic reduction," he says, pout evident in his tone. "They love that shit."

Eli doesn't even try to muffle his laughter.

"So," Cody sighs. "You going to tell your parents about Alex over Christmas?"

Eli hadn't even thought of that. "No?"

"Why not?"

"We've been together for, like, a week. And he's been on a roadie for most of that week."

"Please. You've been together for longer than that; you just weren't admitting it. And it'll be closer to three weeks by then, even with your flawed counting."

"Still. For my parents, the whole me being gay thing has been ... a concept. Having a boyfriend would make it real. And on top of that, he's not some guy, he's ... "

"Alexander Price."

"Alexander Price," Eli agrees.

"So," Cody says. "Did you finish your history paper?"

"Sort of. I've had some aphasia the past few days, so it's done, but it needs significant editing. I said René Descartes was a 'special think-y boi' because I couldn't remember the word 'philosopher'."

Instead of laughing, as expected, Cody goes quiet.

"Hey," Eli says, "that was funny. I'm funny. Even when my brain is sucking, it provides amusement."

"Have you been getting migraines again, too?" Cody asks, and Eli sighs. Yes, he has, and he never should have brought up the aphasia.

"Yeah. Only two though. And they were short."

"How many seizures have you had this month?

"Three," he says grudgingly since there's no turning back now.

"Have you told Dr. Boss Lady?"

"Yes, I've talked to her, and you *know* that is not her name. She says it's probably not a big deal, and I should be good as soon as finals are over."

"Have you been driving?"

"No, Mom, I've been taking Ubers when I have to go to the library. Any other questions?"

"Dude. Why do you need an Uber to go to the library? You live on campus."

Shit.

Eli freezes, one hand on Bells's back, and glances a little desperately around Alex's apartment as if there's something within reach that will save him.

"Holy shit," Cody yells. "Are you staying at *Alex's* place?"

"It's quiet here!" he yells back. "I don't have to deal with all the bad music and sex noises and horrible shared bathroom. And Alex's kitchen island has space for all of my books, and his blankets are really soft and I have to come by every day to take care of Bells anyway and she'd be *lonely* if I didn't spend the night."

"Holy shit," Cody repeats, breathless with laughter this time.

"I'm hanging up on you."

"That's fine. I'm back anyway. Should I send a housewarming gift since it seems y'all have moved in together? "

"Goodbye, Cody."

"Also, I know you're new to the whole dating thing, but I think cohabitation merits a conversation with your parents. Just FYI."

Eli hangs up on him.

And then promptly answers the phone again because Alex is calling. "Hey."

"Hey," Alex says, and it sounds like he's smiling. How is that a thing that Eli even knows?

"You win?" he asks, just to make sure.

"Of course," Alex says loftily, which is fair. The Hell Hounds are first in their division and second in their conference, and they were playing the *Sabres*.

The fact that Eli can think this with such superiority is a little bewildering. Apparently, he is officially a Hockey Person™ now.

How embarrassing.

"Didn't have time to watch?" Alex says.

"Nope. Finishing a practice problem set and then editing my history paper."

"You finished the paper? Nice!"

"Yeah," Eli agrees and doesn't mention the extensive editing that will be needed. Mamá didn't raise no fool, and Alex would be even worse than Cody. "I also just got finished booking my flights for Christmas. I'll be gone the 23rd through 27th."

Alex sighs, overly loudly and intentionally dramatic. "Ugh. Christmas. At least I can eat one of your frozen meals instead of Chinese this year."

"What?"

"It's tradition," Alex says. "On Christmas, I eat Chinese takeout and watch zombie movies and feel sorry for myself. But this time, I'll have your food to eat. So that's cool."

That. Does not sound cool.

"Alex."

"What? I'm joking. It's not that bad. Seriously, Christmas isn't a big deal for me."

It occurs to Eli that this is something they've yet to talk about. "You don't want to see your family? Doesn't the team have almost a full week off?"

It takes a moment for Alex to answer, but Eli is used to that at this point, so he waits.

"I was an accident. College pregnancy during my mom's wild phase or whatever. I don't think she even knows who my dad is. And my mom and I haven't ever been close. She wasn't, like, shitty or anything. She took care of me. But she got remarried when I was twelve, and I think it was a relief for her when I started billeting at fifteen. She started over with Chad, and now they have two perfect honor-roll kids and a little yappy dog. Chad is a hotshot banker, and mom has dinner on the table when he gets home every night and volunteers at the church when she's not doing PTA stuff. I don't really fit into whatever it is they have going on now."

"Alex," Eli says again.

"I mean, it could be worse. I know some guys whose families were awful, and then they made it to the show, and their parents came crawling back, trying to make amends. But they can never know if their dad is calling them every week because he wants to make up for being an abusive asshole or if he needs more money for his gambling habit. Are they inviting you to Christmas because they want to see you or because they know you'll replace the leaky roof? At least that's not the case here. Mom doesn't need my money. She doesn't need me at all."

And suddenly Eli's eyes are hot and his free hand is tight-knuckled in the blanket wrapped around him and he has never felt such malice toward a person he's never met. No wonder Alex was so fucked up—no wonder he got his first taste of fame and acted out with drunk rancor and sneering interview soundbites. No wonder. He had *no one*. No family. No friends. And the one person he did have abandoned him, though, granted, that wasn't really James's fault. But add in Alex's sexuality and the general hypermasculine, competitive nature of hockey, and it's a miracle he's still so kind underneath the ever-cocky media exterior.

Eli swallows and tries to console himself with the thought that, now, at least, Alex has Jeff. Alex has Kuzy. Alex has Rushy. Alex has him.

Alex has *him*.

Or. Eli has Alex? They have each other.

Maybe it's the realization of that responsibility, maybe it's the fact that Eli doesn't do emotions well, and there are a lot of them happening right now. Regardless, whatever it is, he finds himself saying:

"Come with me. For Christmas, I mean. To Alabama. Come home with me."

26

"YOU DID *WHAT*?"

Cody's voice is just as incredulous as the one in Eli's head—the one that's been second-guessing his impulsive invitation to Alex ever since he offered it fifteen hours before.

He pinches his phone between his ear and his shoulder so he can tuck his frozen fingers into his pockets.

"I don't even know. I wasn't thinking."

"Obviously you weren't *thinking*, what *were* you doing?"

"Navigating feelings of impotent rage?"

"Eli."

"You didn't *hear* him, all right? I don't think Alex has had a good Christmas in years. Maybe ever. And he thinks that's normal. Which is not okay."

"Sure, that's sad, but—"

"He usually gets takeout and watches zombie movies by himself, but he said that at least this year, he could defrost one of my meals from the freezer and eat that instead."

"Oh, Jesus take the wheel," Cody says. "That *is* sad."

"He doesn't have anyone else. His mom just up and got family 2.0 and ... I don't know. I just ... want him to be happy."

"So you're bringing him home with you."

"Yes. Maybe. He said we should talk about it in person but that he'd like to come. I just need to, uh. Call my parents."

And isn't that a horrifying prospect.

"Right," Cody agrees. "So, just to clarify—in the space of ten minutes last night, you went from 'no I'm not going to tell my parents about Alex; that's ridiculous' to 'hey, Mom and Dad, I'm bringing my boyfriend Alex home for Christmas; please feed him and love him forever'."

"Uh. Yeah. That about covers it, yeah."

Cody laughs. "Only you, Eli. I do hope he comes though."

"Yeah?"

"Of course. I want to meet him."

And that. That is something Eli neglected to consider. Cody giggles a little menacingly.

"I need to go rethink my life choices," Eli says.

Eli waits to call home until 5:10 p.m. the following day, which means his mom will be home, but his dad won't be yet. It's the coward's way out, and he is unashamed.

He paces the length of Alex's kitchen while the phone rings.

"Rodríguez residence, how can I help you?"

He exhales. He should have known his sister would answer. "Hey, it's me."

"Oh, hey, Eli. ¿Qué lo wa?"

"Nothing. I need to talk to Mamá."

"Are you in trouble?" she asks suspiciously.

"No."

"MAMÁ, ELI IS ON THE PHONE, AND HE'S IN *TROUBLE*!"

"What the fuck—*shut up*."

"Elijah?"

"Oh. Hi, Mamá."

"Mijo," she says, and she's got her serious voice on. "What have you done?"

"Nothing, Francesca is lying."

"Why are you calling, then? You never call."

The serious voice has now shifted to one of chastisement.

Jesus.

"Are you hurt?" she asks. "Have your seizures been getting worse?"

"No. No, I'm fine. I'm sorry. I've just been busy with finals. I'm pretty sure I got an *A* on my exam this morning though."

"Okay," she says.

It's not okay. He really should call more often.

"I wanted to talk about Christmas," he says.

"What about Christmas? I got your flight itinerary from the email, and I spoke with Cody's mother. Four days isn't very long, but I guess it will do. Abuela arrives next week and is staying until January 16th."

Her tone heavily implies that Eli should be able to similarly accommodate a month-long visit like his retired seventy-five-year-old grandmother.

"That's nice. Listen. I—uh." He takes a fortifying breath. "I wanted to know if it would be okay if I brought someone home with me."

"Brought someone," she repeats flatly. "Home with you. ¿Qué quieres decir?"

"Mi novio."

And for some reason saying it like that makes it even more real.

"Tu *novio*," she repeats loudly, and he can hear Francesca yell in the background: "Shut up, Eli has a *boyfriend*?" with more disbelief than he thinks is really necessary.

"Elijah," his mother says, and, oh no, that's the serious voice again. "¿Tienes novio y no me dijiste nada hasta ahora? ¿Por qué nunca me dices nada? ¿Cómo se llama? ¿Cuánto tiempo llevan juntos?"

"Mamá," he sighs.

"*Elijah*."

"His name is Alex. We've been friends since the start of the semester. We've sort of been dating for months but just made it official last week."

Her silence is judgmental.

"I wanted to wait until we'd been together longer to tell y'all. But he doesn't have any family. He usually spends Christmas eating takeout alone, and he was excited because this year he could eat something from the freezer that I'd made instead."

"Oh," she says. "Oh, that poor child."

Eli does a little fist pump. "I can't leave him alone, Mamá."

She makes a considering noise. "¿Habla Español?"

"Ah. I don't think so."

"Well. Does he skate with you or"—she sounds hopeful—"does he play fútbol?"

Eli coughs on a laugh. "No. He, um, he plays hockey."

"Ugh. Hockey. Debí saberlo. You and your ice. Is he a good boy? Is he sweet to you?"

"Yes. Very."

"Well, okay."

"So. I can bring him?"

"Of course. The boy is not going to eat a frozen meal *alone* on Christmas."

"Thank you. Will you tell Papá?"

"Your father will be fine with it. Though he may not like you sharing a room with your Alex."

"We're not—we're, uh. Not. We're taking things slow. And if Abuela is in the guest room, there won't be anywhere else to put him anyway."

Oh god. He can see the headline now: *Lead scorer in the NHL injured from sleeping on a twenty-five-year-old floral couch.*

"Slow," she repeats skeptically. "Claro."

Francesca yells something in the background, and she sighs.

"Can he pay for his airplane ticket or—"

"Oh, no," Eli says, resisting the urge to laugh hysterically. "Money isn't a problem for him."

"Well, good. Bring your Alex. I'll talk to Papá. We can put the air mattress in your room."

And they'll feel free not to use it.

"Thank you."

Francesca yells again, and his mamá mutters something under her breath about children shortening her life span.

"I need to go deal with your sister and her drama. We should talk again this weekend so we can make food plans with Abuela. Ask your Alex if he wants anything special."

"Okay, will do. Thank you. I love you."

"If you really loved me, you would call more often," she says.

Alex's plane gets delayed twice, and with the dreaded calculus exam looming the following morning at 10:00 a.m., Eli gives up and goes to sleep just past midnight.

He's awoken a few hours later to Hawk leaping off the bed and running out of the room, toenails skittering across the floor as she loses traction moving from rug to concrete. There's a jingle of keys, the sound of bags being dropped on the floor, and then Alex talking softly to Hawk. Shortly afterward, Eli hears the hum of the ice dispenser, the refrigerator opening, and then the distinct and, at this point, distressingly familiar noise of Gatorade being poured over ice.

Alex is a weirdo.

Things go quiet again, and Eli considers getting up, but he's also so tired. Eli is still in the warm blurry space just adjacent to sleep, debating the pros and cons of moving, when the mattress dips next to him, and Alex crawls under the duvet. He's still fully clothed and kind of smelly, but he gathers Eli to him, inelegantly and a little desperate, and then he just—

Exhales.

Long and slow.

"Hey," Alex says into the back of Eli's neck.

His breath smells like Blue Frost Gatorade.

"Hey," Eli agrees.

"I missed you."

It's easier to say out loud since Alex said it first: "I missed you too."

"I should probably shower," Alex murmurs.

"You should definitely shower. And brush your teeth."

"All right, asshole."

Alex doesn't move for several more seconds though. Eli doesn't mind.

Eventually, he does let go of Eli, straightening, and leans over to run his knuckles down Bells's back. Bells responds with a sleepy cat noise—half purr half chirp—that makes Eli's heart do things.

"Sorry I woke you up," Alex murmurs. "I know you've got your big test tomorrow. Go back to sleep, and I'll try to be quiet, okay?"

"Mmkay."

Alex presses a kiss to Eli's temple, then another one to the slope of his cheekbone. Then another next to his mouth. Eli pushes gracelessly at his face, grumbling a little, and he laughs.

"Okay. Okay, sorry. Showering now."

"Mmkay," Eli agrees again and goes back to sleep.

When Eli's alarm goes off at 8:00 a.m., Alex is dead to the world beside him, head half-under one pillow and hugging another one.

Eli stifles a laugh and moves to the living room. His yoga mat is still rolled out on the floor in front of the windows from the day before, and he settles into his routine with only a couple soft groans. He's going to need to visit the chiropractor when finals are over because his neck is seriously pissed off.

Twenty minutes later, he's sitting in cobbler pose—the bottoms of his feet pressed together, thumbs against his ankle bones, Breathing With a Purpose—when Alex stumbles out of the bedroom, arms crossed over his bare chest against the chill. Both cat and dog trail after him, similarly discontent.

Alex squints at Eli for a moment, then moves to sit next to him. "Hey," he says, voice scratchy and unfairly sexy. "Are you okay?"

"Yeah?"

"What are you doing?"

"Uh. Breathing exercises?"

"No, I mean," Alex blushes a little, and Eli doesn't think it will ever get old, how visible it is when Alex is flustered. "That just looks kinda like the shit my therapist makes me do sometimes. Did you have a panic attack? If you did, you should have woken me up. Or. I mean. If that would help. Unless it wouldn't. Uh. Help."

And, oh, that's why Alex's face has been all concerned.

"No, this is just preventative. I've been extra stressed because of finals, so I'm supposed to start my day with breathing and being mindful and relaxing and stuff."

"Oh, okay. Should I leave you alone, or?"

"Nah. I'm pretty much done anyway. Hungry though. Omelets?"

"Yes, please."

They make breakfast in companionable, sleepy silence, with lots of lingering touches and stupid smiles, and then Eli does one last set of practice problems, trying to keep his Mindful Breathing thing going.

"So," he says once his problems are done and his plate is empty. "I talked to my mom last night."

Alex pauses, fork halfway to his mouth. "Okay?"

"You are officially invited to Rodriguez Christmas."

"Oh." He puts his fork down. "Really?"

"Yes? Were you thinking they'd say no?"

"I don't know. Did you tell them about me or just that you were bringing someone?"

"I told her I wanted to bring my boyfriend. Nothing about ... " He gestures to encompass Alex as a whole.

"The NHL thing?"

"The NHL thing," Eli agrees. "By the way, your face was on the bus I took yesterday. It's the one with the red filter where you look all sweaty and intense. I have a picture, remind me to show it to you later."

"Why were you on the bus?"

"I'm not allowed to drive right now, and Ubers were getting expensive, which, judging by the look on your face, I should not have said since now you're going to try to give me money."

Alex closes his partially opened mouth, scowling. "I was not."

Eli rolls his eyes, moving to deposit his plate in the sink. "Sure. Anyway, I don't think anyone in my family will recognize you, but my aunt is the definition of a Facebook Mom, and the last thing we need is her posting a picture of the kids on Christmas morning with you and me cuddling on the couch in the background or something. So. We should probably tell them? Or at least make sure there aren't any social media posts happening with your face in them."

Alex doesn't say anything, and Eli returns to the bar with pursed lips.

"So?" Alex is grinning at him.

"So what?"

"So what do you think we should tell them?"

"Oh, I have no idea. Sorry. Can I think about it?"

"Yes?"

"Okay." Alex is still smiling.

Eli is ... a little unnerved. "Why are you smiling like that? It's weird."

"Are we going to cuddle on the couch on Christmas morning?" Alex asks.

And anyone else might be joking, but Eli is 99 percent sure Alex is not. "Uh. Probably? I mean. I'd like to."

"Cool," Alex says and takes another bite of his omelet. Eli can't decide if he should roll his eyes or be touched. He doesn't get a chance to decide, however, because Hawk gets up from where she's been awkwardly lounging over Alex's feet and moves purposefully over to Eli. She just as purposefully sits down beside him and then headbutts his knee.

So much for the stress-relieving powers of yoga.

Alex's fork scrapes loudly across his plate.

Hawk paws at Eli's shin, whining, and then headbutts him again.

Eli sighs. "Can you pack up all my stuff so we can leave as soon as it's over? And drive me to my exam? I was kind of assuming you were going to anyway, but—"

"No. I mean, yes, of course. Are you—bedroom?" Alex is half standing, his butt hovering uncertainly above the stool.

"Hey," Eli catches Alex's face between his hands. "I'm fine, remember? Hawk and I are just going to go lie down, and if anything bad happens, she'll let you know. Okay?"

"Okay. Is it—can I come with you?"

And that. Is unexpected.

Eli slides his hands down to rest on Alex's shoulders.

"You want to watch me have a seizure?"

The thought of Alex seeing him like that is ... not good.

Which is stupid; it's not like there's anything to be embarrassed about, but—

"It's not that I want to *watch*," Alex says, wincing a little. "But I want to be with you?" He shrugs a little helplessly. "Sorry. Is that weird? That's probably weird."

"No. It's sweet, actually. But I don't know if I'm comfortable with that yet. Can we talk about it later?"

"Yeah. Of course. I'll"—Alex jabs a finger in the direction of Eli's books—"get everything ready so you won't be late."

"Yeah. Cool."

"Cool," Alex agrees.

"Hey," Eli says.

"Yeah?"

"Breathe," Eli reminds him.

"Right."

He kisses him, though Alex doesn't really reciprocate, and retreats to the bedroom to find his bag, Hawk at his heels.

"I'm packing you a lunch," Alex yells a few seconds later from the kitchen. "Do you want blue, red, or yellow Gatorade?"

"Orange," he yells back, just because he knows Alex hates it.

"Heathen," Alex says. "You're getting red."

27

ON THURSDAY AFTERNOON, ALEX stops by CVS for ice cream on the way home.

Eli's last final—the history paper—was due at 1:00 p.m., and Alex can't decide if Eli will be sleeping when he gets home or wanting to celebrate. Maybe wanting to celebrate sleepily? Regardless, he's pretty sure Eli won't want to go anywhere, so. Ice cream.

It occurs to him as he's standing in the cold section however, that despite taking Eli for froyo at least a dozen times, he doesn't know what his favorite flavor is. And just because Eli occasionally sneaks a spoonful of the Ben and Jerry's Cherry Garcia that Alex's grocery delivery service stocks in his freezer, it doesn't mean that's what Eli would choose for himself. Honestly, this is something they should have talked about already at this point in their relationship, and Alex is a little disappointed in himself.

He considers calling Eli to ask, but if Eli is sleeping, he doesn't want to wake him up. And he can't call Cody; Princeton is in the middle of playing a game, and even if he managed to catch Cody between periods, he probably shouldn't be interrupting an NCAA hockey game for ice cream–related inquiries.

In the end, Alex gets four different kinds of frozen yogurt and three kinds of ice cream and carries his armful of plastic bags to the car without shame. He'll invite some of the guys over later, and they'll take care of whatever Eli doesn't want.

When Alex struggles to unlock the door to his condo twenty minutes later, trying to be quiet and failing with his hands full of plastic bags—Eli would probably point out that had Alex remembered the reusable canvas bags in his car, the crinkling would not be an issue—he's a little surprised to hear music.

And then he finally opens the door and gets a good look inside and ...

Well.

Eli sleeping, he was prepared for.

He is not prepared for Eli in his kitchen wearing the Louboutins.

He is, however, prepared to admit it now: They're sex shoes.

Because *holy shit*.

And, god. How stupid had he been to laugh when Eli first showed him the picture of those shoes on his phone. There is nothing weird or embarrassing—or whatever preconceived notions he'd had—about Eli in those shoes.

And it looks like the only thing Eli is wearing apart from the shoes is Alex's All-Star jersey from the year before. It falls to mid-thigh on him, black and red and so incredibly hot that Alex is going to need a moment.

Maybe a couple of moments.

Eli grins, crossing his arms, and hitches one hip against the countertop. "Take a picture. It'll last longer."

"I don't want to take a picture," Alex answers. "I want to stand here and look at you."

"Oh. Well." Eli bites his lip, and that really doesn't help matters. "That's fine too."

Alex hadn't noticed at first as he was a little preoccupied with all the muscular calf and thigh on display, but Eli's hair is different. It's been growing out of a subtle undercut for a while, but now the sides are clipped close to his skull in a sharp, tapered fade, and the curls on top are a little looser than normal, sort of pulled up and wild. Alex is having flashbacks to being fourteen and fantasizing about making out with a guy with a mohawk.

It's a good look, is what he's saying.

Alex would just stand there and keep ogling him, but the ice cream is heavy and cutting off the circulation to his fingers. He moves to set the bags on the counter. “Hi,” he says because he’s a moron.

Eli laughs. “Hi,” he agrees. “Why did you bring half the CVS cold section home with you?”

Alex had been intending to play it cool, but that goes right out the window. “I didn’t know what your favorite ice cream was. And I didn’t want to call to ask in case you were asleep. And Cody is in the middle of a game. So I tried to remember the flavors you’ve gotten before when we—”

And, thank god, Eli kisses him since he probably would have continued talking through his entire thought process.

“It’s mint chocolate chip,” Eli says against his mouth, laughing when Alex does a little fist pump.

“I knew that.”

“You didn’t.”

“I didn’t,” Alex concedes.

He brings one hand up to cup the back of Eli’s head—rubbing his fingers against the grain of newly close-cropped hair at the back of his skull.

“You like it?” Eli asks.

“So much.”

“I was way overdue. I decided to try a new place just around the corner as a reward for getting through finals. Kinda pricy, but worth it, I think.”

Alex kisses him again. Otherwise, he might offer to pay for all of Eli’s haircuts from here on out at any place Eli chooses, regardless of price, except Eli doesn’t like when he does things like that. So Alex lets his hands slide over the wings of Eli’s shoulders, fingers tracing the “Price” on his back, trying not to feel quite so viciously possessive and utterly failing.

In the shoes, Eli is as tall as him, and Alex likes it—them being eye-to-eye.

"Are you cooking anything, uh, time-sensitive?" he asks, glancing at the vegetables on the island.

"Nope. Kuzy and Jeff invited themselves over though. They should be here around 7:00 and"—he smirks a little—"I should probably change before then."

Alex glances at the clock on the oven, toying with one edge of the jersey Eli's wearing, knuckles against bare skin. "You want to make out on the couch for the next twenty minutes then?"

"I believe I do. We should put the ice cream away first though."

"Yeah," Alex agrees, not moving, leaning in to kiss Eli again.

Eli turns his head at the last minute, and Alex whines at him.

"Ice cream. Freezer."

"Right," he says into Eli's neck. "In just a second."

"Alexander."

They have to use their Tetris skills to get everything to fit in the freezer properly as it's already full of Eli's cooking. And then, when they're finally successful, Alex sucks a mark onto the curve of Eli's throat in celebration of their achievement.

Or something.

Alex tugs on the hem of the jersey. "Are you wearing anything under this?" he asks, resisting the urge to check for himself.

"Mr. Price," Eli says, grinning. "What kind of boy do you think I am? Of course. I've got underwear on."

Alex can't decide if he's disappointed or relieved by this information.

"It's your underwear though," Eli says. "If that matters."

Alex makes an aggrieved noise, knocking their foreheads together, and Eli laughs at him.

"Couch?" Eli asks.

"Yes, please."

The Hell Hounds have a home game the following night. Eli doesn't go because he's still recovering from finals and already committed to helping with the Breaking the Ice event the following day. Of the two, Alex would rather Eli be on the ice with him than sitting in the stands watching him play.

Not that both wouldn't be nice.

Regardless, it's a good game—solid play on both sides—but the Hell Hounds win due primarily to Rushy's fantastic goaltending and the second line's offensive play.

Houston and Carolina had made a trade the week before: One of the Hell Hound's veterans and a third-round draft pick for Yevgini Oshepkoff. The Hell Hounds have needed another solid center after losing Mark the year before, and Alex is pretty pleased with the quick chemistry Yevgini—or Oshie as he was quickly dubbed—found in his first practice with them. Clearly, it wasn't a fluke if tonight's game is any indicator, and the team, high on its win, retires to their favorite bar to "properly" welcome Oshie to their ranks.

Alex spends the first half hour talking to him about an assortment of things—apartments, travel, stick curvature, food, cats. Then Kuzy muscles his way between them and engages Oshie in what sounds like an angry conversation in Russian but, judging by their facial expressions, is perfectly friendly. Kuzy had been ecstatic to hear about the trade because he and Oshie played together for a year in the RSL before they were both drafted to NHL teams. Oshie has been staying in one of Kuzy's guest rooms for the past five days, and Alex will be completely unsurprised if it becomes a permanent arrangement.

Alex plans to only have a beer or two before heading home to eat a late dinner—Eli was finishing a cooking video when he left for the arena and whatever he'd made smelled amazing—but one round of shots led to another. The next thing he knows, it's nearly midnight, and he's leaning pretty heavily against Jeff's shoulder, smiling contentedly at the various pockets of his teammates surrounding them. Matts and Rushy are playing a friendly round of pool, while most of the others are playing a less-friendly and increasingly dangerous game of darts. A few of the call-ups are trying desperately to look cool while talking to a group of girls at the bar, and the veterans are holding court in the booth next to them, beers in hand, watching with amusement as Kuzy and Oshie get progressively more exuberant.

"Hey," Asher calls to Kuzy, "another round of shots?"

"As you wish!" he yells back.

Oshie introduced him to the *Princess Bride* a few nights before, and now he won't stop quoting the movie. His new favorite word is "inconceivable."

"Or," Rushy says, laughing, "maybe we should slow down on the shots, eh?"

"Inconceivable!" Kuzy shouts.

There it is.

"We have a good team," Alex says to Jeff.

"We do," Jeff agrees.

"But actually," Alex turns to look at him, to make sure Jeff knows he's serious. "I have a good ... everything, right now. I'm like. Really happy. And shit."

"And shit," Jeff agrees.

"You made it happen though," Alex says because he doesn't think Jeff is getting it. "I was so fucked up before. And then you yelled at me and made me get a therapist. And—"

Alex comes to a sudden, stunning, realization. "You introduced me to Eli."

"Well. Not exactly," Jeff says. "But sure, I'll take credit."

"He never would have come to the Hell Hounds practice if you weren't there. And he'd still be thinking I was a giant douchebag who parks in handicap spots. And I'd probably still *be* a giant douchebag who parks in handicap spots. Oh my god."

"I take it things with Eli are going well?" Jeff asks dryly. It's clearly a diversion, but it works since, of course, things with Eli are going well.

Eli is his favorite person.

"His ass," Alex says somberly, "is a paradox."

"Excuse me?"

"Eli's ass," Alex says, raising his voice a little. "It shouldn't be allowed."

"Eli's ass shouldn't be allowed," Jeff repeats. "Because it's a paradox?"

"Yes."

"I'm sorry; are we really talking about Eli's butt right now? Is that what's happening?"

"Yes."

Jeff glances around, and Alex remembers that his affection for Eli and his butt is supposed to be a secret. They're alone in the booth, though, so it's okay.

"It's okay," Alex says. "No one is listening. I can talk about Eli's butt if I want."

"Fine," Jeff sighs. "Tell me why Eli's ass is a paradox."

"Well," Alex says. "It's just—so big? For someone so lean? But not too big. It's like the perfect handful. Two handfuls. Which is good. Because I've got two hands."

He looks at his hands, considering.

Yes. Good.

"Uh-huh," Jeff says. "Let's get you some water, bud." He pulls on Alex's arm.

Alex pulls back. "I love him." He's still staring at his open palms. "And I know it's too soon for that or whatever, but I do. So much. And it's—I don't know how."

"You don't know how to what?"

"*Love him*," Alex says a little desperately. "Right. The way he deserves."

"I think you'll be able to figure it out."

"He's just—he's so important, Jeff."

"I know, kiddo," he says, and Alex feels like he might actually understand. "I know. Let's get you some water, okay? And then I'll take you home to him."

And that.

That sounds like a great idea.

"Yeah, okay."

Alex wakes up to an empty bed, a mild hangover, and embarrassingly vivid memories of the night before.

He stumbles into the kitchen where Eli is cooking and plants himself, facedown, at the breakfast bar.

"Kill me," he says.

"Nah," Eli says, sliding a Gatorade in front of him. "I've gotten kind of attached to you. Here. You want some sausage? Grease is supposed to be good for hangovers, right?"

He eats his sausage and tries to think of ways he can show Eli he appreciates him without spending money.

He's not very successful.

"I need to book my airfare for Christmas," Alex says later as they're driving to the rink. "Will you get mad if I upgrade you to first class?"

"Yes."

"But I'm asking you beforehand instead of just doing it."

Eli gives him an unimpressed look.

"But I don't want to sit in economy."

"Then don't sit with me and the rest of the peasants. Sit in first class alone."

"But you and your family are going to be hosting Christmas, so I won't have to pay for a hotel, or get a rental car, or food. Getting you home in comfort is, like, the least I can do to repay you."

"Do you really expect me to believe that you haven't already bought me an obscenely expensive gift?"

And. Yeah. Eli has him there.

"Please?" he tries.

"No."

"Fine," Alex sighs. "I guess it's only three hours."

"Good. I'll wave as we pass you to sit with the unwashed masses."

"No. I mean, I'll get a seat with you in economy. It's only three hours. I'll deal."

"You're ridiculous. You realize I'll have the window so Hawk can be in the corner. That means you'd have to sit in a middle seat."

Alex winces. He may not be the biggest hockey player, but he's still broader than the average adult. "No big deal. I'll cuddle with you."

"No, you won't. The last thing we need is someone taking a picture of you plastered all over me on a flight to Alabama."

"I'll pretend to very platonically fall asleep on your shoulder."

"Like that's better?"

He has a point.

Eli sighs before Alex can come up with a response.

"We'd have a lot more privacy in first class, huh?"

"Yes?" Alex glances at Eli and immediately corrects himself because that's Eli's I-might-cave-if-you-present-a-compelling-argument face. "Yes. So much more privacy. We'll have more space, and once the flight starts, they close the curtain thing so no one from the rest of the plane can come through. Which means our bathroom stays a lot cleaner since fewer people are using it. It also means we could probably get away with some cuddling. Definitely some discreet hand-holding under our blankets. Did you know we'll get free blankets in first class?"

Eli laughs, and Alex knows he's won. "Fine. If there are two seats next to each other in first class that are still available, you can upgrade me to sit with you."

Alex leans over the center console, lips puckered, eyes still on the road.

Eli makes a disgusted noise but kisses him anyway.

"Thank you," Alex says, reaching for Eli's hand.

Eli accepts it, lacing their fingers together, and rubs his thumb absently against the cold-chapped skin of Alex's first knuckle. Alex should probably moisturize more. Or get a pair of gloves. Maybe both.

Eli's hands are embarrassingly soft in comparison.

Eli doesn't seem to mind the roughness of his skin though. He isn't even looking at Alex, judgmental about the state of his hands or otherwise. He's half smiling at a woman in the car next to them who's wearing her coat and scarf so her dog can hang his head out the open window—tongue lolling and deliriously happy.

Alex wonders if maybe that's how he feels: Deliriously happy.

Hawk notices the other dog, and Eli laughs, his hand tightening around Alex's, tugging a little as he turns in his seat to talk to her about the "handsome boy" next to them. Alex has to look away before he gets into an accident or says something stupid he can't take back.

It might be easier if Eli didn't smile like that—if his new haircut didn't accentuate the bones in his skull and the slope of soft skin at the nape of his neck.

It seems impossible that everything Eli is can exist in just one person.

And yet.

There he is.

Alex brings their joined hands to his mouth, kissing Eli's knuckles; his chest hurts, and he has to do *something*, and that's the least damning action he can think of.

28

JUSTIN MATTHEWS HAS NEVER been good with kids.

Hell, he wasn't good with kids even when he *was* one.

He was an only child, the youngest by a considerable margin of all his cousins, and the whole hockey thing didn't leave much time or capacity for socializing. He never went to camp unless it was a hockey camp and was homeschooled past the third grade so he could dedicate more time to practicing. Even once he left for Shattuck at fourteen and had freedom away from his parent's stringently enforced schedule, his father's continuing refrain—engrained since mite games—remained: *those boys are not your friends; they're your competition.*

And sure, Matts had friends now. Sort of. But those relationships were built on grown-up things, or at least grown-up hockey-player things, like on-ice chemistry, video games, mutual hatred, alcohol, or some combination therein. He wasn't good at talking to adults about most things outside of those categories, so talking to children certainly wasn't in his wheelhouse. He'd managed okay so far at fan events, taking pictures with gap-toothed preteens, signing jerseys, and tossing pucks over the glass during warm-ups. But he doesn't think he's had a conversation with anyone under the age of ten in over a decade, nor does he particularly want to. So he doesn't know why, exactly, management is so insistent that he be part of the Hell Hounds' Breaking the Ice event.

Well. He does. He knows they're hoping he'll become one of the franchise faces, and god knows, he wants that to happen, too, but while his on-ice production has been good, his off-ice chemistry with the team is admittedly lacking. It seems Alex Price isn't the chill party-boy Matts thought he was and, instead, wants the locker room to be a Safe Space or some shit.

But whatever. If holding some orphan kids' hands and hauling them around the ice for a while is going to get him the contract extension he wants, here he is. Judging by the parking garage, he's pretty sure he's one of the last to arrive, which is confirmed when he pushes his way into the locker room.

"Hey," Asher says as Matts sits in his stall, trying to down the last of his coffee and pull his skates out of his bag at the same time. "You're late."

And Asher had been cool right up until the whole thing with Eli and Rushy. Now the kid is a passive-aggressive asshole.

"He's here, which is the important thing," Rads says. He then raises his voice to address the room at large. "Okay. Overview if this is your first time. The under-tens are getting kitted up right now, and they'll be on the ice in a few minutes. Most of them haven't skated before, and the little ones might end up wanting to be carried. Just go with whatever they're comfortable with. In an hour, we'll clear the ice, take a break, and then the over-tens get their turn. Several of those kids have been coming to our camps, so that will be more hockey-focused rather than skating-focused. And they know what they're doing, *Rushy*."

"Yeah." Rushy laughs. "I learned my lesson last time. I"ll wear my pads for the big kids."

"What happened last time?" Asher asks.

"Got hit in the neck with a slapshot," Jeff murmurs. "He flopped around gasping like a fish for a couple seconds and ended up with a massive bruise. The poor kid thought she'd killed him. I'm surprised you haven't heard this story. We don't like to let him forget the time his career was almost ended by a kid at a philanthropy event."

"Hey," Rushy says. "She was seventeen, and she'd been in the Little Hounds program on scholarship since she was eight. She's playing in *college* this year."

"Which is why he's wearing his pads for the older kids," Rads finishes. "Anyway, these kids are in foster care or group homes. A lot of them have been separated from their siblings, relatives, etcetera, so just be aware. Don't bring up family or Christmas. Cool?"

And that solidifies Matts's decision to talk to them as little as possible.

There are nods all around, and Matts realizes he should be putting on his skates.

"Any questions?"

"Uh," Asher says, looking nervous. "What *should* we talk to them about?"

Some of the guys laugh, but Matts is right there with him.

"Most of them will direct the conversation, but if you get a shy one, just focus on the skating. If they don't want to talk, it's fine. This isn't a therapy session, it's a philanthropy event."

"Could be both," Jordie leans over to whisper to Rushy. "I know shooting pucks at your face always brightens *my* spirits."

"And watching you get all pissy when I block them brightens mine," Rushy agrees.

"See?" Rads says. "You shouldn't have any issue interacting with them. You're all still children yourselves. Let's get out there."

There's a mass exodus for the ice, but Matts still has to lace his skates, and then Rads is sitting down in Asher's vacated stall next to him, which can't be good.

"I know I'm late; sorry."

"It's fine." Rads glances at the door, making sure everyone else has left, then leans forward, bracing his elbows on his knees.

Sometimes it's painfully clear Rads is a dad.

"Eli is here," Rads says, nodding toward Alex's stall where there's a relatively conspicuous figure-skating bag tucked next to the usual pile of stick tape and half-empty Gatorade bottles. "Is that going to be a problem for you?"

"No," Matts says, eyes on his feet.

"When we're done today, he's going to be in the locker room. If that makes you uncomfortable, you can stay on the ice until he's gone."

"It's fine," Matts says, tightening his laces with a little more force than is strictly necessary. "I get it. It's not a problem."

I'm not a problem, he means. But he is. Enough of one that the alternate captain has stayed behind to give him a lecture. Jesus.

"You're a good kid," Rads says. "But Eli is too. I know you and Rushy seem fine, but—"

But Rushy is a six-foot-two hockey player with a girlfriend, and it's easy to pretend that he's straight. They're also friends. Maybe. Which, yeah, is different than Eli, who is fit but small, and a *figure skater*, for god's sake. He's like a living stereotype. But it's not like he has a real problem with the kid.

"Seriously," Matts interrupts. "I get it. I shouldn't have said that shit before, and I won't bring it up again. Okay?" He ties his second pair of laces even though the skate still isn't quite fitting right because this conversation needs to be over. "I swear."

"Okay," Rads says. "Good."

Matts makes a break for the ice. The prospect of two dozen kids under the age of ten is less dire than remaining in the locker room with Rads in dad-mode.

He's got the "I'm not mad, I'm disappointed" vibe down a little too well.

The thing is, skating with a bunch of uncoordinated children isn't that bad. They're bizarrely noncompetitive and super pleased about going in a straight line or completing a circuit of the rink without falling. They mostly talk *at* him rather than expecting him to talk back, which is its own relief. It's nice.

Then Asher points to a kid who's clinging to the boards looking distressingly close to tears and says, "Hey, you got that?" as if Matts is supposed to have any idea how to handle an emotional kindergartener in a puffy camouflage coat.

"Uh, sure," he says and skates over.

"Hi," he says, crouching a little. "My name is Justin. But most of the guys here call me Matts. So I guess either works? What's your name?"

The kid just looks at him, eyes wide and blue and wetlooking. He's wearing a tiny Hell Hounds snapback with Alex's number on it, which is admittedly adorable.

Matts taps the brim of the hat. "Do you, uh, like hockey?"

And the kid bursts into tears.

Shit, shit, shit.

He glances over at the camera guy who—yes—is filming this.

"Oh. Oh, dude, no. Don't cry. What's wrong?"

He goes down to his knees, panicked, one hand rubbing awkwardly at the kid's back. "Hey, come on. Just tell me what's wrong, and I'll fix it, okay? Are you hungry? Do you need to go to the bathroom?"

Wait, no. That's what you check when infants are crying, not kids.

"Do you not *want* to skate?" he tries.

And then, quite suddenly, Matts has an armful of sobbing child and a cold, snotty nose smushed up against his neck.

"I do," the kid gasps out wetly. "I do want to skate. Just not hockey skate. I want to Olympics skate."

"Hockey players go to the Olympics. Oh. You mean figure skate?"

A nod. "With music. And spins."

Matts has no idea how any of that works, but it's an easy enough fix.

"All right. Okay. Hey, what's your name?"

"Jesse."

"Okay, Jesse. They've got figure skates at the rental counter; let's go swap yours, and then we'll find someone who can teach you some spins. Sound good?"

The kid isn't actively crying anymore, just sniffing a little, but he doesn't seem appeased either.

Matts leans back, trying to get a better look at his face.

"Hey. What's up?"

"There aren't any other boys wearing figure skates," Jesse whispers, wiping his nose on the sleeve of his jacket. "And Charlie said only girls can figure skate, even though that's a *lie*."

Matts has to actively suppress a laugh at the sheer malice behind the word "lie."

"Okay, well, Charlie is a di—uh, dummy."

Jesse's face brightens considerably.

"So you should ignore him. Boys can figure skate. Girls can play hockey. There's a guy here who used to be a figure skater when he was a kid—he even won, uh, I think it's called World Juniors? He won a gold medal there before he started playing hockey. And Kicks is a girl, but she plays hockey for Stanford right now."

He points to Kicks, who is demonstrating for a yelling group of onlookers what a cross-check looks like. Rushy, her victim, is possibly cheering the loudest.

Jesse looks a little scared of her, which is fair. People should be.

"Anyway, point is, skate however you want. Gender doesn't matter."

Oh my god. He sounds like Jeff.

"Now, let's go get you the right skates, okay?"

"Okay," Jesse agrees.

He holds Jesse's hand, keeping him upright, and leads him out of the rink and back to the rental desk. Then he helps lace the new skates and holds his hand back.

As they step onto the ice again, the only problem is that Jeff is nowhere to be seen.

"Uh," Matts says, stymied.

It's not like there are multiple players on the team who also have figure skating backgrounds.

Well.

Not on the team, no.

But there is Eli.

Eli, who's currently skating circles around a group of kids who are shrieking with laughter as they try and fail to tag him. He's wearing patterned black leggings that transition seamlessly into black skates and a long-sleeved knit gray shirt-dress thing that flutters around behind him, just out of reach of the kids' flailing hands.

Matts takes a fortifying breath. "Hey," he says, crouching next to Jesse. "Look over there. That's Eli. He's a figure skater, see?"

Jesse's eyes widen. "He's *really* fast," he says. He's not wrong. "And he has cool hair." Matts can't argue with that either.

"You want me to introduce you to him?"

"Yes! Please."

"Okay. Sweet. You wait here. I'll be right back."

Matts doesn't have a chance to think about what he's going to say to Eli, but the fear that Jesse might start crying again if he takes too long is enough to send him off across the ice with intent.

And then, as luck would have it, the pack of kids chasing Eli herd him, as he skates backward to avoid them, directly into Matts's path.

It's a minor collision, and Matts is able to get an arm around Eli's waist to steady him so no one falls down except for a few of the kids. But they're already more or less covered in ice and apparently made of rubber, so that's fine.

"Sorry, sorry," Eli says, laughing as Matts gets him upright again. Except then he turns fully and gets a look at Matts's face and—Eli flinches away from him—a visceral, full-body movement that makes him feel nauseous even though he hasn't done anything wrong.

"Sorry," Eli repeats again, putting some space between them. His voice is entirely devoid of the laughter that formed it a moment before. "My bad."

"No, it was my fault. I, uh, was coming over to ask if—There's a kid over there." He gestures to where said kid is waiting, and Jesse waves helpfully. "He wants to be a figure skater. I got him the right skates, but I was wondering if you could help? I have no idea what to do."

A few of the kids who had been chasing Eli run into his legs, clinging, and he automatically reaches down to steady them, hands drifting over shoulders and heads.

"Sure, yeah. Let me just—"

Kuzy snowplows to a stop beside them, showering the kids clinging to Eli with ice.

They scream appreciatively.

"Eli," Kuzy says. "You good?"

Matts is a little pissed that Kuzy seems to have decided Eli needed rescuing from him or whatever.

"Yeah," Eli says. "Justin was just—"

"Matts," Matts says.

"Matts was just telling me about a future figure skater. I'm going to go teach him a few things. Can you take over, here?"

It seems like they have a brief non-verbal conversation, Eli's hand resting, almost warningly, on Kuzy's comparatively massive forearm. Then Kuzy grins broadly and goads the kids into chasing him instead. Matts leads Eli over to meet Jesse, trying to ignore the fact that several of his teammates are watching him a little too closely for comfort.

The minute they're within reach, Jesse attaches himself to Matts's leg, weirdly shy as Eli introduces himself, and then, when Matts tries to pry Jesse's fingers off the hem of his jacket to hand him off to Eli, the waterworks threaten a return.

"Hey, no," Matts says. "I thought you wanted to learn figure skating. Eli is, like, the best figure skater I know"—and that isn't even a lie—"so what's wrong?"

"I wanna stay with *you*," Jesse says, tears clinging to his eyelashes.

"Okay, all right. I'll stay too, then. Eli can teach us both how to figure skate, okay?" *Oh my god, how do parents ever discipline their children*? Matts is the most massive pushover.

Jesse grins, abruptly tear-free. "Okay."

When Matts looks back up at Eli, relieved, Eli has his bottom lip tucked between his teeth, frowning at him. Not in a bad way, or at least Matts doesn't think it's bad; it's more like Eli is confused.

Eli blinks, expression clearing, and leans forward, hands on knees, to address Jesse. "I dunno," he says, mock serious. "Some hockey players are pretty bad students. I tried to teach Alex how to do a super easy jump the other day and it took him almost an hour to get it right. I bet you'll be a faster learner than Matts; what do you think?"

Jesse looks up at him, considering. "Probably," he agrees and reaches his free hand toward Eli.

Eli accepts it, and he and Matts move slowly forward, tugging Jesse along between them, a little wobbly but surprisingly stable, all things considered.

"Are you friends with Alex Price?" Jesse asks Eli. "He's the captain of the Hell Hounds. We made thank-you cards for him. He paid for all of us at Hyer House to come here special even though we live far away. And he gave us hats. And we get to stay in a hotel tonight and go to a game tomorrow."

That's news to Matts.

He meets Eli's eyes over Jesse's head. Eli looks equally surprised by this information.

"Yes, I'm friends with Alex. He's a good guy, even if he's not very good at figure skating. Luckily," Eli adds conspiratorially, "he's really good at hockey though."

"I saw a bus with his face on it this morning," Jesse says.

"No kidding. Is it the picture that's all red-tinted where he looks super serious?"

"Yeah!"

"Cool. The bus I take to the library sometimes has that same picture on it."

Jesse squints up at Eli, stumbling a little as he's not paying attention to the ice anymore. Matts tightens his grip on Jesse's hand.

"Why do you take the bus?" Jesse asks. "I thought rich people had cars."

"Oh," Eli says. "Well. I can't drive right now. And I'm not a rich person, so."

"You dress fancy like a rich person," Jesse says.

Eli splutters a little. "Thank you? I think. This outfit was a gift."

His eyes cut across the ice to Alex, who's ostensibly teaching a stick-handling drill but spending more time watching Matts than the puck. "Anyway, you're doing well. Do you want to try a spin?"

Completely unsurprisingly, he does.

As do several other kids, it turns out.

They accumulate four girls and one more boy. Twenty minutes later, Matts finds himself carrying a toddler with purple mittens and a pom-pom on her matching hat, having a serious conversation with her about bananas, while Eli takes turns guiding the other kids—one of which is the toddler's older sister—through slow, simple figure skating exercises. Jesse only lets go of Matts's hand when it's his turn to try something, sometimes insisting that Matts accompany him, and it's—fun.

Eli is soft-spoken but encouraging, knowing when to do something stupid or funny to get a frustrated kid to laugh. He seamlessly includes Matts in his jokes like they're a team, even though Matts is mostly a piece of furniture that the kids cling to while watching Eli demonstrate things.

All the kids hug him at the end of their ice time—footage the cameraman is obviously pleased about—then Alex is ushering Eli off the ice with a Gatorade and a power bar, his hand proprietarily on Eli's lower back, his eyes still on Matts.

Matts thinks that will be the end of it, except then Jessica pulls him aside and tells him she loves the dynamic between him and Eli, and can they continue their little impromptu figure-skating camp with some of the older kids as well in the following hour? Which is how Matts finds himself learning a few simple figure skating moves, awkward in his hockey skates. He's one part muscle, helping hold waists and arms for balance while Eli directs movements, and one part comedic entertainment, falling, sometimes intentionally, sometimes not, while he attempts the same tricks. They're a good team, is the thing. More often than not, one of the cameramen glides around their little group of ragtag teens and preteens, taking low shots of moving feet before panning up to grinning faces.

At the end of the second hour, Matts realizes this is probably the longest he's been on the ice without touching a hockey stick in over a decade.

It's also probably the most he's laughed in the same amount of time.

After another round of hugs, the kids are bundled out of the rink by their various guardians, and the team heads for the locker room. Matts realizes, as he's stepping off the ice, that Eli is still over by one of the goals, tossing pucks into a bucket. He's not doing it with much enthusiasm though. In fact, it looks like he's purposely taking as much time as possible, stopping to retie his laces despite the fact that he's about to take his skates off.

He could be waiting for Alex, who's being interviewed on the opposite end of the rink, the only Hound left on the ice, but Matts knows that's probably not the case. He thinks about what Rads said that morning, and the way Eli flinched away from him, and—it sucks. Because Eli is actually pretty cool. And Matts may not be the dick everyone seems to think he is, but he also isn't very good at being nice either.

Fuck.

He doesn't know how to do this shit.

"Hey, Eli!" he yells, arms braced on the glass at either side of the exit. "Come on, you'll want to shower before Kuzy gets in there. He sings."

Eli straightens, lobbing another puck toward the bucket by the goal, looking uncertain, and Matts jerks his head toward the locker room.

"Come on," he repeats.

Eli skates off the ice to join him.

"I don't need a shower. It's fine. I was just"—he gestures a little vaguely behind him—"going to help out here while I wait for Alex to wrap up and change."

"Dude, you are literally covered in ice. Probably also germs since kids have been using you as a jungle gym all day, and it's, like, flu season. You should shower."

He realizes maybe he's coming on too strong with the niceness.

This shit is hard.

"Unless you don't want to," he finishes awkwardly.

"Okay," Eli says slowly, dragging the word out. "Well. A shower might be nice. I still need to grab Hawk though." He nods to where his dog has been patiently watching the morning's proceedings in the stands.

"So grab her, let's go."

Eli considers him for a moment, the same weird pinch from earlier between his eyebrows.

He glances at Alex, still talking to the camera, and then inhales purposefully.

"Okay," he says. "Yeah, all right. Let's go."

29

"SO," ELI SAYS CHEERFULLY when they get in the car. "What the fuck was that?"

"Shared hallucination?" Alex suggests.

"Seems plausible."

Alex starts the engine and heads for the garage entrance, not sure what else to say.

"I mean," Eli continues, "that was the same guy who didn't want me looking at his dick in the locker room a week ago, right?"

"Right."

"And now he's insistent that I shower with him so I avoid contracting the flu? Did Kuzy threaten to kill him or something?"

"I don't think so, but you know he has those mafia connections."

Eli grins. "True."

Alex drums his fingers on the steering wheel. "It seemed like you were getting along well."

"We did, is the weird thing. He was good at following instructions and actually learned some things, I think. And he was ridiculously sweet with the kids. Kind of a pushover but, like, genuinely concerned about them? I heard him asking Rushy if there were any Hell Hounds–funded figure-skating programs for kids like there are hockey camps."

"I don't think there are."

"I wouldn't be surprised if he donates to start one."

Alex exhales, shaking his head. "I'm still leaning toward hallucination."

"Tell me about it."

"I guess I'd rather an aggressively friendly Matts than an ignorant homophobe Matts."

"Same."

Eli orders pizza on the way home. They have an agreement now: Eli orders the food so Alex doesn't have to talk on the phone, and Alex pays for it. Due to the everpresent Houston traffic, the pizza arrives at Alex's condo only shortly after they do. Alex is on the yoga mat stretching out his shoulder with a roller bar when the concierge calls to get permission to send up the delivery guy. Eli answers the phone for him, says "yes," and then Alex gets to watch as Eli moves comfortably around the kitchen, getting utensils from the cabinet and emptying the dishwasher when it turns out there's only one clean plate left. Watching Eli cook in his kitchen is one thing, but this is good too. Eli unerringly distributes measuring spoons and cutlery to their respective drawers, and the fact that he knows where Alex's potato peeler goes feels like it means something.

Alex didn't own a potato peeler before Eli, and Eli is the one who designated its home as second-drawer-from-the-right between the oven and refrigerator, but the point is that Alex likes it.

When the doorbell rings, Eli fishes Alex's wallet out of his coat pocket to locate some cash. Once the pizza is paid for and distributed, Eli brings both their plates to the living room and turns on the Avs-Panthers game. Alex moves to sit with him, and they settle, inside elbows knocking companionably, Eli muttering about the high-sticking bastard on the Panthers who bloodied Alex's lip and nearly took his helmet off six games previously, and Alex—has to take a moment.

This—them—feels natural. Habitual. Like they've been coexisting for years and will for years to come, and it's—God, that would be so good. It's not even a scary thought, that Eli might be it for him. It's only scary that Eli might not feel the same way.

Eli catches him staring and tips his head a little, bemused. "What?"

"Nothing." Alex clears his throat and scoots a little closer. They can't hold hands since they're eating, which is a damn shame. Maybe it's that the novelty hasn't worn off yet, but Alex really likes holding hands.

"So," he says, "I like your hair today."

Eli raises an eyebrow. "It's the same as yesterday. Or, I tried to do it the same anyway. I used the same product the barber did."

Alex had noticed it on the bathroom counter that morning: a little blue bottle that smelled like heaven. "Why'd you change it? Your hair, I mean."

Eli shrugs. "It was getting long, and if people are going to keep taking pictures of me, I need to make sure I look good in them."

"You always look good," Alex says, and it's not even a line.

"You're sweet."

"Also true."

"And humble."

"*Very* true."

Alex's phone rings before Eli has the chance to drag him more thoroughly, and it's his agent so he answers.

"Hey Jamal," he says, setting aside his plate.

"Alex," Jamal says gravely. But then, Jamal says everything gravely. "I've reviewed all your contracts and spoken at length with Jessica Andrews, the head of Hell Hounds PR. I'm sorry it's taken longer than expected, but some of the endorsement deals took a while to go over."

"Oh ... kay? Is there a problem with the endorsements?"

"Not explicitly, but Under Armour, Tag Heuer, and Diesel all have clauses about your eligibility as a representative. If they deem your independent behavior is a contradiction to their values, or if they believe your behavior reflects badly upon their brand, your contract can be terminated."

"And you think if I come out—"

Eli shifts, setting aside his own plate, to look at Alex.

"I don't think any of them would pull their endorsements," Jamal says. "If anything, you coming out will increase the visibility and effectivity of the advertisements that feature you. I just want you to know that there is a *possibility* of repercussions if you become too polarizing a figure."

Alex laughs a little bitterly. "Diesel signed me a month after my second DWI, but it's being gay I have to worry about. Fantastic."

Eli goes very, very still beside him.

"Alex," Jamal says, "I honestly don't think it will be a problem, but if it becomes one, know that there will be dozens of other companies clamoring to sign you—ostensibly as a show of support, but more realistically to capitalize on what will be a significant jump in star status for you. You're the king of the hockey world right now, but it's still a relatively insular world. That won't be the case when you come out."

"Right. Okay. Well, it's not like I need underwear-modeling gigs anyway. I have more money than I know what to do with as it is."

Jamal sighs.

Jamal often sighs when talking to Alex.

"All right," Alex says. "So, you said you talked to Jessica? When is my meeting with management?"

"Monday. 11:00 a.m. You don't play the Flyers until 7:30 p.m., so that should leave plenty of time for your nap."

"Okay, is it all right if I talk to Coach first?"

"Yes, but Jessica has requested that you don't tell anyone else on the team or staff until you've met with management and discussed a trajectory."

"A trajectory," Alex repeats.

"A timeline. We're assuming you'll want to come out in stages—first to the core of the team, then the whole team, then staff that works closely with you, then staff collectively, then other players in the league, and so on. And we'll want to plan each step with contingency strategies in place in case someone goes to the media prematurely."

"Oh. Right. Okay."

"Do you have any other questions?"

Alex has so many questions, but most of them will probably be answered in forty-eight hours.

"No. I guess I'm good. Thanks."

"All right. I'll see you Monday at 11:00."

"Yeah. Bye."

Alex exhales as he hangs up, flopping back against the cushions. "Well. I'm finally telling management. Now I need to tell Coach first so he's not blindsided."

Eli doesn't say anything, and Alex pauses, midreach in retrieving his plate, to glance at him.

Eli looks ... not good.

"What?" Alex says.

"You have DWIs?" he says.

"Oh. Yeah." Alex scratches the back of his head. "One from the night of the draft. One from the night of my first hat trick as a rookie."

"Did you hurt anyone?" Eli asks, barely audible.

"No. I wasn't in accidents or anything. The first was just bad luck—I got pulled over for expired registration. The second was a speed trap. The game was against the Rangers on New Year's Eve, and cops were stopping everyone in the city."

"Okay." Eli licks his lips, still so serious, so wide-eyed that Alex feels unsettled.

"You don't do that anymore though?"

"I mean. I still get drunk sometimes—not nearly as often as I used to, to the same extent. Before, I drank when I was unhappy and just kept drinking until I didn't feel anything anymore. Now, I only drink when I'm celebrating."

Eli's eyebrows go a little pinched, but it's still better than whatever his previous expression was. "You weren't celebrating the night of the draft or your first hat trick?"

"Yeah, no. After the draft, James was MIA, refusing to take my calls, and I was the first-round pick wearing a jersey that should have been his. And the hat trick—I was in the locker room afterward, full of guys I'd only known for a month, holding my phone in my hand and realizing I didn't have anyone to call to share it with. I wasn't in a good place, then."

Eli scoots closer, reaching for his hand, and Alex breathes a little easier. Whatever is going on, if Eli is touching him, he's probably not mad.

"I'm sorry. That sounds terrible."

Alex shrugs. "Things are better now. A lot better."

Eli takes a breath.

The kind of breath that means something.

"You don't drive when you've been drinking now, right?"

"No. No, I haven't. I won't. I know it was irresponsible and stupid."

"Okay."

"Hey." Alex squeezes Eli's hand. "You're freaking me out a little here. Are you all right?"

Eli considers him for a moment, eyes moving between Alex's, then lifts their joined hands and molds Alex's palm to Eli's jaw. He forces his fingers down to press against the line of scar tissue that cups the curve of Eli's left ear.

"A drunk driver did this to me. Almost killed me. You can't ever do that shit again. Not even if you've only had a few drinks, and you're pretty sure you're okay to drive. You have to promise you won't."

And fuck.

Fuck.

"I promise. I swear to god."

He reaches for Eli but pauses, unsure of his welcome, and when Eli folds easily into his arms, it feels a little like mercy.

"I'm so sorry. It was stupid. I know it was stupid. But I haven't since the second DWI. It's been over a year, and I won't—*I won't.*"

"Hey," Eli says, more into his neck than to him. "I believe you; it's okay. I just need to know that you know how serious it is. I would probably be an Olympic prospect right now if a drunk teenager hadn't hit me head-on the night of the homecoming dance."

And Alex thinks he gets what Eli is trying to say—that it was only luck Alex didn't similarly destroy someone else's life.

"Okay," Alex says. "I understand. Never again."

"Okay."

They sit there holding each other until Hawk comes over with her leash in her mouth, looking forlorn.

Eli laughs wetly into Alex's collarbone. "I should take her for a walk. You want to come, or do you need to call your coach?"

Alex had completely forgotten about that in the past few minutes. "Coach," he says.

Eli straightens, framing Alex's face with his hands, and presses a decisive kiss to his mouth. "Good luck. Don't let Bells eat my pizza."

Bells, sitting on the coffee table and eyeing Eli's abandoned plate on the arm of the couch, looks insulted by the insinuation.

"Will do."

He watches Eli collect his boots and coat, Alex's scarf, the keys, and then Alex waves at him like a moron when he slips out the door.

He pulls Bells into his arms and cuddles her to his chest, mostly against her will.

"I was such a disaster," he tells her. "Still am, a little bit."

She blinks solemnly at him in agreement.

"Don't let me fuck this up," he whispers. "Okay?"

She butts her head against his chin.

"Okay, good talk. Should we call Coach now?"

He decides they probably should.

He shifts Bells into his lap, so he has a hand free, and pulls up the contact information for one Coach Robert Sullivan.

"Alex," Coach says after the third ring. "Is everything all right?"

And he abruptly forgets the speech he's spent the last few weeks practicing in his head.

God, he hates making phone calls.

"Uh. Yes? I mean. I'm great. I'm afraid I might be creating some problems for the organization soon though. Which—That sounded more dire than I meant it to."

"Okay," Coach says guardedly.

"Um. I need to miss practice on January 13th."

"Okay?"

"But that isn't actually—"

"Hold on," Coach says, "Jessica is calling."

And then Alex is on call-waiting and debating banging his head against the coffee table, except not having a string of concussions is one of the few things he has going for him right now.

"Why am I like this?" he asks Bells.

She has no idea. The line crackles.

"Alex," Coach says. "Why has Jessica just invited me to a mandatory meeting with management, you, and your agent on Monday morning?"

"Yeah, that's why I was calling. I didn't want you to be, like, blindsided or whatever."

"What does this have to do with you missing practice on the 13th? Are you ... unhappy here?"

And oh god, Coach thinks he's meeting with other teams or something.

"No. No, that's not it at all. I need to miss practice so I can go to the Intercollegiate Figure Skating Championships. Which are January 11th through 13th."

Coach doesn't say anything for a moment.

"I don't understand. Why do you need to go to the college—figure skating thing?"

Alex takes a deep breath. "Because my boyfriend is competing."

"Your boyfriend," Coach repeats. And then, after several seconds of silence, "So many things are making sense now."

"Yeah." Alex stalls out, wishing he could see Coach's face.

"It's Elijah, right? The figure skating kid?"

"Well. He's eighteen, so not really a kid. He's only one year younger than me."

"You're a kid, too, kid. Jesus. All right, give me a second."

Alex pets Bells with a purpose: that purpose being not having a panic attack.

"Okay," Coach says. "Okay. So. I appreciate you telling me ahead of time, and I hope you didn't wait this long because you thought I wouldn't be supportive. I am. And had I known sooner, I—well, that's no excuse, but I could have supported you better, regardless. So, I apologize."

Alex swallows. "Thank you."

"All right. Are you wanting to come out?"

"Not now. But eventually. And I won't—I'm not going to obsess over the time I spend with Eli until then. So if someone figures it out and decides to go public with it ... I figured we should be ready."

"That's smart. I'm assuming we'll talk more at length about this on Monday, but do you need anything from me until then? You have any questions for me?"

"No? Knowing you're supportive is all I need. Oh, and um—" He bites his lip. "Is it okay if I miss practice so I can go to Eli's competition in January?"

Coach sighs at him again. "Yes, Alex."

"Okay."

"You're a good kid," Coach says, which is about as effusive as he gets with overt statements of affection. "It seems like Eli is too. You let me know if you ever need anything, okay? If there's ever anyone who gives you trouble. On or off the team." And no, *that* is probably the most effusive he gets.

"Thanks, Coach."

They hang up, and then, before Alex can even set the phone down, it's ringing again.

He answers without looking. "Hey, Coach. You forget something?"

"Oh. Um. I'm not—hello?" And that.

That is not Coach. He's pretty sure it's—

Alex takes a breath. "James?"

"Yeah," James says quietly and a little uncertain. "Yeah, it's me. Hey, Alex."

30

ALEX IS MORE ASLEEP than awake when Eli pours him into his first-class window seat, tucks a blanket around him, and tells him to take a nap.

Alex doesn't argue.

The last twenty-four hours have been exhausting, both physically and emotionally. Talking to James, short and awkward as the conversation was, had been good but harrowing. And then the next morning, he talked to management and had to listen to them map out the minutiae of his personal life as if he were a problem they had to plan to fix, or maybe not fix but brace for.

Like a natural disaster.

He feels like a natural disaster sometimes, so maybe that's apt. And then they'd lost the last game of the year to shitty calling and, maybe, admittedly, some unwise choices on Alex's part. Yes, he was sent to the box twice, but it wasn't his fault the refs weren't doing their jobs. If Roussel wasn't going to get called for slashing him, what else was he supposed to do but retaliate by tripping him?

Hockey is stupid.

And *then* he'd gotten boarded at the beginning of the third and was out for the rest of the period while they did concussion protocol and made anxious noises about his ribs even though Alex told them he was fine. Maybe he wasn't *fine*, exactly, but he could have played. Honestly. At least he'd gotten one of the trainers to go retrieve Eli from the box so he didn't have to watch his team lose on the shitty TV in the medical room alone.

They got home late, nearly midnight, and Alex couldn't sleep because, yes, his ribs were hurting, and by the time his painkillers kicked in, it was nearly 2:00 a.m. Then Eli was waking him up at 5:00 since they needed to be at the airport by 6:00 for their 7:30 flight. While Alex was feeling arguably better than he had been the night before, it was in the same way that getting hit by a Prius would be arguably better than being hit by a truck.

He's tired.

He's hurting.

He's grumpy.

He listens to his boyfriend and takes a nap.

When he wakes up some indeterminable amount of time later, it's to Eli sitting sideways, back against the armrest, feet in the seat, socked toes tucked under Alex's thigh, a book propped on his bent knees. He's small and bendy like that. He even looks comfortable.

"Hey," Alex says, and his voice rasps.

He swallows and tries not to squint; he knows it's not a good look on him.

"Hey," Eli says, grinning. "How are you feeling?"

"Like a 239-pound defenseman tried to end my life last night."

"Two hundred and thirty-nine is oddly specific."

"I googled his stats while I was waiting on my X-rays."

"Of course you did."

Alex reaches for the Gatorade conveniently waiting for him in the cupholder.

"What time is it?"

"We're about ten minutes out from Huntsville."

So he has ten minutes before he meets Eli's best friend for the first time and, subsequently, Eli's entire family, while sleep-deprived and on narcotics.

"Fantastic."

"Hey. It's okay. We'll just tell everyone you're hurt and you need to rest for most of the afternoon, and you can go upstairs and lie down until dinner. It's going to be fine."

Alex makes a pathetic sound. He feels pathetic, and he knows it will garner him sympathy.

Eli makes a face at him, shifting so his legs are tucked underneath him, and he's leaning into Alex's space. He retrieves a second blanket, drapes it over his own lap, and then Alex feels Eli's fingers nudging his, hidden underneath free airline flannel.

And, well. That's nice.

They hold hands for the rest of the flight.

Alex is able to get off the plane under his own power. Honestly, he's not sure how Eli managed to wrangle both him and Hawk onto the plane to begin with, but obviously, his boyfriend is talented. They take the elevator down to the baggage claim. Then Alex finds himself abruptly abandoned when Eli drops his backpack and Hawk's leash to run full tilt toward a similarly exuberant blond man who Alex can only assume is Cody Griggs.

They embrace like they haven't seen each other in years, and Eli pulls Cody over to meet Alex. The kid is definitely jacked, but he's also weirdly well groomed. No man's eyebrows just *look* like that.

"You play *hockey*?" Alex says, in lieu of hello or some other standard greeting. It's what he's thinking, and apparently, Vicodin takes away his filter.

Cody considers him with one immaculate eyebrow raised and a smirk that can only mean bad things.

"Yep. And probably better than you at the moment."

He can't really argue that.

"That was some hit," Cody continues. "I'm honestly a little surprised you're standing upright on your own right now."

"He wasn't this morning," Eli says, the traitor. "And he's on painkillers."

"I can see that."

"This was a terrible idea," Alex says, and they both laugh at him.

Hawk sidles up to Cody, vibrating with excitement, and he bites his lip, looking down at her.

"Hey, baby girl. Your vest is on right now, but I'll give you so much love in the car, okay?"

Eli gets a reluctant Hawk to heel again, Cody's baggage carousel starts moving, and they head off, arm in arm, to go retrieve his luggage.

Alex elects to sit down.

Twenty minutes and three suitcases later, they exit the terminal to humid air, sunshine, and a blonde woman standing beside a very old, very blue pickup truck. She's shading her eyes with one hand, practically on her tiptoes, scanning the swarm of people coming out of the door and then—

"Cody! Eli! Oh, my boys—"

She hugs them with a fierceness that makes Alex's throat uncomfortably tight and takes each of their faces between her palms to pull their foreheads down into kissing range, then pulls at clothing and despairs over how thin they are.

And then she's moving toward Alex, smiling, giving him perhaps the gentlest hug he's ever received while tutting about the violence of professional sports. So, it seems she knows who he is.

"You'll sit up front with me, of course, sweetheart, and let the boys have the back. I'm afraid the suspension won't be kind to you either way, but at least you'll have a little more padding up front. Come along."

Eventually they're headed off down a bizarrely traffic-less road with the windows open and country music on the radio. Cody's mom tells the story of the truck—a Chevy that she bought with all her savings as a grocery store clerk at nineteen—and how she picked up Cody's father for their first date in it. His vehicle was a motorcycle, and she didn't have a death wish, now did she? Alex finds himself smiling, watching in the rearview mirror as Eli and Cody talk indistinctly to each other, grinning like idiots. Hawk sits mostly on top of Cody, head out the window, ecstatic.

"And well," Cody's mother is saying, "it's always been my baby ever since. Even when my real baby"—she nods to Cody—"came along.

Not that keeping it running hasn't been a job and a half. But that's another story."

Alex focuses his attention back on her, one elbow leaned against the sill of the open window, fingers light against the old, cracked leather of the steering wheel.

"Sounds like an interesting story," he says, "if you want to share it?"

She does.

Eli's house isn't what he's expecting.

In his head, he'd been picturing something out of a western movie. A long driveway with big trees. White siding. Wood beams. A wraparound porch.

The trees are big, but the driveway is a combination of red dirt and gravel, and the house looks far more Victorian than southern, with scalloped woodwork around the peaked attic windows and thin spiraling columns holding up the latticed arch of the roof over the porch. It's big but clearly aging, and it's the exact sort of place some HGTV couple would salivate over buying and renovating while gushing over its "charm".

It's beautiful.

He's about to say so as Cody's mom turns off the engine, but then—

"Are those goats?" he asks. There's a fence line just behind the house, and several little bodies are hurtling toward it, and they're making noises like—

Okay. They're definitely goats.

"Yes," Cody's mom says, and she might be laughing at him. "The Rodriguez family usually has two to four dozen at a time. They're a nice little source of added income. I think a good portion of Eli's skating lessons over the years were paid for with money from goat or sheep sales. Or goat milk soaps—his grandmother sells them at the farmers market in the summers."

The first few goats reach the fence line, screaming—Alex honestly can't describe it as anything but screaming—and Hawk launches herself out of the back of the truck to greet them, shoving her nose through the openings in the fence, low to the ground and wagging so hard Alex is slightly afraid she might do herself an injury.

"Johnny!" Eli yells, jumping down to follow Hawk.

"Hey, baby boy! Michelle! Yuna! Tessa! Ashley! My girls."

Eli follows Hawk to the fence, and some of the goats stand on their back legs, begging for pets. Eli, in his floral Vans and skinny jeans, bends to kiss their noses and coo over them.

Alex may need to adjust his world view a little bit.

"Why do they have people names?" Alex asks, more to himself than anyone else. "Goats shouldn't have people names."

Cody opens the passenger door and offers Alex a hand.

"They're all named after former or current figure skaters. Like Johnny Weir, Michelle Kwan, Yuna Kim, etcetera."

"Oh. Oh my god. Please tell me there's a goat named Jeff Cooper."

"There used to be," Cody says. "But he was kind of a dick once he hit puberty, so they sold him."

"That," Alex says fervently, "is the best Christmas present you could have given me."

"Uh-huh. You gonna get out of the cab, or are you planning to come home with Mama and me?" Cody asks.

Alex takes Cody's hand, cursing under his breath on the way to the ground, and stands there uselessly as Cody gets his suitcase out of the truck bed and carries it toward the house.

"Elijah!" Cody yells. "Stop kissing crusty farm animals and come see to your guest."

Eli glances back at them guiltily, then jogs over to retrieve his own bags, calling Hawk to follow him.

He's extending his arm, ostensibly to help Alex up the porch steps, when the front door opens, and a tall woman in a bright, geometric-patterned dress steps around the screen door and into the light.

"Elijah!"

"Abuela!"

There's a round of hugs between Eli's grandmother, Eli, Cody, and Cody's mom, and then Eli's grandmother is in front of Alex, holding his face between her hands and staring at him like she can see directly into his soul. The fact that she might be a little taller than him only emphasizes his anxiety.

"Uh. Hi," he says. "I'm Alex."

She's pretty, not despite the wrinkles on her face but maybe because of them. She clearly does a lot of smiling.

"Oh, Eli," she says, turning Alex's face to the side, then back to meet her eyes again. "¿Por qué todos mis nietos deben enamorarse de gringos? Ay, al menos él es lindo."

Eli makes an embarrassed noise, with a strangled, "*Okay*, why don't we go inside, now?" that leaves Alex really, really, wishing he knew Spanish.

"It's good to meet you, Alex," she says, patting his cheek. "You call me Abuela, or Aba, like the little ones, okay? Come inside. You look hungry."

She releases him, moving to hold open the door, and Eli wraps himself around Alex's right arm, pressing a laugh briefly into his shoulder before pulling him up the steps.

Cody and his mom leave their bags in the entryway, call their goodbyes with promises to see them soon, and head back for the truck.

"Abuela," Eli says as they progress down a narrow but high-ceilinged hall, "Alex was hurt in his hockey game last night, and we didn't get much sleep. So after we eat something, we're going to go up and rest for a while. Do you know if Mamá has anything big planned tonight?"

"Family dinner," she says, leading them into a kitchen positively exploding with floral wallpaper.

"How much of the family?" he asks guardedly.

She waves a dismissive hand. "Little family, no aunts or cousins."

"Okay, good. You know if Papá will be late tonight?"

She makes a noise that universally means, "who knows" and starts pulling Corning Ware bowls out of the refrigerator. She frowns at Alex as he sits, slowly, at the well-worn table tucked in the half-moon recess off the kitchen. The windows look into a side yard that is bursting with bird feeders and, by consequence, birds. Alex can't remember a time he's seen that many birds in one place before.

"Where are you hurt?" Abuela asks, and it takes Alex a moment to realize she's talking to him.

"Oh. It's nothing. I just have some bruised ribs."

"The whole left side of your back is purple," Eli mutters, spooning things onto two plates. "That's not nothing. Do you want butter on your sweet potato?"

"Yes, please."

Abuela wipes her hands on a dish rag and moves across the room to a bulky leather purse. She returns a moment later to press a small canister of something into Alex's hand.

"Here. Vivaporu."

"Oh, jeez," Eli says, moving to sit beside Alex with their plates. "Not with the vapor rub again. I think science has proven that Vicks cannot, in fact, cure everything."

"Actually," Alex says, "that probably would help. The trainers have, like, a fancier version, but it helps with inflammation, increased blood flow, and helps bruises fade faster. Especially if you add—"

"Salt," Abuela agrees, setting down a canister of Morton on the table. She taps her temple. "I know."

"Thank you."

Eli groans something about encouraging her madness, offering Alex a fork, and Alex accepts it with a grin.

Lunch is leisurely, comprised mostly of Abuela sneaking Hawk food, Eli answering questions about how his first semester is going, and Alex being embarrassingly entranced by the birds outside. He wonders if it's the medication or the fact that he doesn't think he's seen a wild bird—much less dozens of them—this close before.

When they're finished, Eli takes him up a very old, wide staircase with an ornate banister, and into, Alex is delighted to find, Eli's childhood bedroom. The wallpaper here is a deep jewel-toned green that makes him even sleepier than he was before. Eli helps him undress down to boxers and a T-shirt, while Alex gets distracted trying to read the titles of books on the shelves above the desk and looking at the little Lego creations on the top of the long chest of drawers opposite the bed.

"I told James I'd call him back today," Alex says absently, eyes caught again by the birds outside.

"You're in no shape to have that conversation right now," Eli says, hiking up Alex's shirt to smear some vapor rub on his ribs. "I'm sure James saw the game last night and knows you're high as a kite right now. But if you want, I can text him and let him know you'll need another day or two?"

"Yeah," Alex agrees. He pats his ass, forgetting for a moment that he's not wearing pants. "Oh. My phone is in my—"

"Jeans right butt pocket," Eli says. "I know. I'll get it in a minute. Hold still; apparently, I need to rub salt on you now."

Eventually, Eli gets him tucked under the satisfyingly crinkly gray duvet, and Alex is pretty sure he says something about wanting Eli to stay, but he can't be certain because he falls asleep almost immediately.

He wakes up once, briefly, to the sound of a car coming down the gravel driveway, but he's warm and everything smells pleasantly of menthol and Eli is snug up behind him, breathing slow and sweet against the back of his neck, and he drifts right back off again.

The second time he wakes, it's to Eli leaving the bed, followed quickly by Hawk, who shakes, rattling her collar tags. Alex grumbles something about betrayal as he watches Eli get dressed—silhouetted against the window.

"My dad will be home in half an hour or so. I need to go down and say hi to Mamá and help them start the food. You stay here; I'll come get you a little before dinner, okay?"

"No," he says, starting to sit up, "I can get up now. I don't want to be rude."

"What will be rude is if you stare out the window at the birds all of dinner because you have to take another pain pill. And, I mean, if you really need to, that's fine, but the doctor said if you didn't push yourself today, you could switch to Advil tonight. Which is much kinder to your poor addled brain."

Eli finishes tucking his shirt into his jeans and ducks to kiss Alex's forehead.

Alex likes it when he does that.

"So. You rest. And I'll come get you in another two hours."

"Okay," he agrees. "The doctor also said I have to walk around, though, to make sure I don't get fluid in my lungs. So I can't just stay in bed all day."

"I'll take you out around the back forty after dinner if you're feeling up to it. But let's keep the exertion for after you've been grilled by my family. You're my first boyfriend. They're probably going to be ridiculous. You need to be on your game."

And that's more than a little intimidating.

"What's a back forty?" he asks blearily, and Eli grins like he's being cute. He makes a note to google it before dinner. "Kiss my forehead again," he demands, closing his eyes.

Eli laughs at him, but acquiesces.

Two hours and several Advil later, Eli helps Alex put on jeans and a white button-down, Alex's favorite "I'm an adult" brown leather belt, and matching shoes. He holds his hand as they descend the stairs. He continues holding it while he introduces Alex to his Mamá (Alicia)—who has the same wide smile as Abuela and long dreadlocks twisted up into a bun that gives her several more inches in height—his Papá (Joseph)—a lean man, not quite as tall as Alex with horn-rimmed glasses, graying light-brown hair, and a thin tidy mustache—and his sister Francesca—who looks shockingly similar to Eli, only younger and with longer, braided hair. She's wearing a basketball jersey and the kind of superior expression only middle schoolers can truly achieve.

He gets a hug from Alicia, a handshake from Joseph, and a disdainful look from Francesca before they all sit down at the table. Naturally, the first question Eli's mother asks is: "So, how did you two meet?"

Alex glances sideways at Eli, uncertain how to respond; they'd planned to talk about how they were going to handle the whole *Alex's career* situation on the plane, but for some reason, neither of them had remembered that conversation still needed to happen.

"Uh," he says eloquently.

Eli raises a questioning eyebrow, and Alex nods, not exactly sure what he's agreeing to, but he trusts Eli.

"So," Eli says, pressing his palms together. "That's actually something we need to talk to y'all about. And. We'll probably need to tell Tia Rose and the others at Christmas too."

Everyone stops eating except for Francesca.

"Okay," Alicia says slowly. "Mijo, is everything all right?"

"Everything's fine, Mamá. It's—Alex isn't just a hockey player. He's, uh, he's the captain of the Hell Hounds."

"Oh. Captain," Alicia says, still looking confused. "How ... impressive."

"No, I mean, he's the captain of the Houston Hell Hounds. Like. The NHL team."

"Shut up," Francesca says.

"Francesca," Alicia chides.

"NHL," Joseph repeats. "NHL like National Hockey League? How *old* are you?"

"Oh. Uh. Almost twenty?" Alex says.

"No way you're dating a professional athlete; that's not fair," Francesca whines.

"What?" Eli says. "What do you mean it's not fair; that doesn't even—"

"Use the Google," Abuela says to Francesca, handing over her phone. "Type 'Alex Houston Hell Hounds'."

"That might not be a good idea," Alex whispers to Eli, harried.

"Twenty," Eli's dad says thoughtfully. "Well. That's not so bad. A captain at twenty though. That's a lot of responsibility."

"Oh my god," Francesca shrieks. "He *is*, look." Then she's passing around Abuela's phone, and, yes, that's Alex's NHL headshot, which isn't exactly flattering, but it could be worse. Like his draft photo.

Alicia, now holding the phone, looks up at Alex. "You're a professional hockey player?"

"Yes. Ma'am."

"Wait," Francesca says. "How are you gay? Professional hockey players can't be gay."

"*Francesca*," everyone at the table except for Alex shouts.

"Sorry. I'm just saying. That's, like, a big deal. Do we have to keep this a secret?"

"Yeah," Eli says. "Sort of. Alex isn't out yet. Nobody can know he's here or that we're together. So everyone needs to be careful about what they post on Facebook and Instagram and stuff."

Alicia sighs, passing the phone back to Francesca. "I will definitely need to speak with Charlotte and Rose before Christmas, then."

"Oh my god," Francesca says faintly.

"What?" Eli says.

"Alexander Price's estimated net worth," she reads, phone still in hand, "is 3.5 million dollars." She turns her attention to Alex. "You're a millionaire?"

"Uh. I guess? I mean. Yeah."

"And you're dating *Eli*?" she says, disbelief coloring her tone.

"Yes," Alex says, much more assertively, putting down his fork so he can reach for Eli's free hand. "And I'm lucky he's willing to put up with me. I can't—I'm not an easy person to date. And we didn't start dating for a long time, even though we both really liked each other. I wasn't willing to ask him to be a secret. That's not right, and I wish I could tell everyone that we're together, but—"

He's getting a little off track.

"But the fact that he's willing to be with me anyway is um—The best thing. And I'm really happy. And I don't deserve him. So. Yes. I'm dating Eli."

Eli is grinning down at his plate.

Abuela pats Alex approvingly on the shoulder. "Good boy," she says sotto voce.

Alicia clears her throat. "Well. An NHL player. That is ... certainly something. I still want to hear how you met though."

Alex winces a little. "It's not the best story."

"Oh, it is," Eli corrects, squeezing Alex's hand. "So. It was back in August, the day after move in, and I get to the rink for the first-ever morning practice ... "

31

THE FOLLOWING MORNING, ELI wakes up to the familiar, muted sound of birdsong and the shadowy figure of Alex, barefooted and rumpled, sitting on the floor in front of the window.

Hawk is sprawled across his lap, and he's petting her absently, a mug of coffee in his other hand.

Eli stretches, sitting up, and leans over to check his phone.

"Alex," he groans. "We're on vacation. Why are you awake at 7:30 a.m.?"

"Sorry," he says. "I think I threw off my internal clock sleeping so much yesterday. You can stay in bed; I'm good watching the birds."

"You and the stupid birds," Eli says. "I'd rather you come cuddle me."

Alex doesn't need to be told twice.

"How are you feeling?" Eli asks after Alex has slipped back under the duvet and given him a coffee-flavored kiss.

"Good. Surprisingly good. I think the vapor rub healed me."

"It did not."

"It *did*."

They don't go back to sleep, but they do linger in bed for another half hour before putting on jeans and making their way downstairs.

The rest of the day is similarly leisure.

They spend the morning wandering around the property, throwing occasional sticks for Hawk and introducing Alex to all the goats, sheep, chickens, and two grumpy but cute, curly-haired miniature donkeys. Cody comes over a little after 11:00 with a tin of cookies from his mother and stays for lunch, and then he and Eli make a joint video for their YouTube channel while Alex takes a nap upstairs. Well. He doesn't nap, Eli thinks, or at least he isn't napping when Eli goes to collect him a little over an hour later. He's shirtless, doing stretches, head tipped to watch the birds outside. Initially, Eli had thought the bird thing was due to the narcotics, but now he's starting to think Alex just ... likes birds. Which is endearing in a way that he isn't sure how to process.

"There's a sweaty half-naked man on my bedroom floor," Eli muses, leaning in the doorway. "My fifteen-year-old self would be screaming if he could see me now. Or, I guess, if he could see you now."

"You should come kiss me for his sake," Alex says seriously and, well, who is Eli to argue?

"I thought you were supposed to be taking it easy," Eli says, breathless, several minutes and a little bit of light grinding later. He runs a finger down Alex's sweaty neck. "This doesn't look like you're taking it easy."

"I am," Alex says innocently, shifting his hips in a decidedly not innocent way. "It's not my fault Alabama doesn't believe in seasons. Seriously, how is it so hot here? It's December."

"Honey, it's seventy-five degrees. That's not hot. You should know what hot is; you live in Houston."

"Where it is currently a reasonable forty-five degrees," Alex argues. "Because it's December. Also. Honey?"

"Yes?"

"No, I mean, since when do you call me honey?"

And oh. That's embarrassing.

"Sorry."

"No," Alex says, ears pink. "It's fine. I just—I've never, uh—" He pauses, looking thoughtful. "Can I call you things too?"

Eli doesn't laugh as it's clear Alex is self-conscious but powering through anyway. "Things like what?" He resists the urge to tack on a "sweetheart."

Alex opens his mouth. Then he closes it.

His ears go a little bit more red. "Can I think about it?"

"Of course, sweetheart." And, well, Eli has never been good at denying himself.

From the way Alex is looking up at him, it's not a problem.

Eli clears his throat. "So. Abuela wants to go last-minute grocery shopping, and I said you wouldn't mind driving since Papá is out fixing the fence, and Mamá is at the church."

"Sure thing; do I have time to shower?"

"Yeah, no hurry."

Neither one of them move for a moment. When they hear Hawk's toenails clicking up the staircase, Eli reluctantly stands and helps Alex to his feet.

And in the bright afternoon light, damp, and golden, and tousled, and *looking* at him, Alex is—

Something.

Alex shifts, glancing toward the open bathroom door, then back at Eli. He tucks one thumb under the elastic of his shorts and tugs, enough to emphasize the cut *V* of his hips.

"Do you. Uh. Want to join me?" he asks, nodding toward the tub.

Eli's fifteen-year-old self would be having a heart attack right now.

"Yes," he says, then immediately has to backtrack. "But I can't. We can't. Not when Francesca is right next door, and her room shares a door with the bathroom."

"Okay. No pressure. I was only asking. Maybe when we're back in Houston? And we're the only ones at my place?"

"You do have a very serviceable bench in that shower," Eli agrees.

"And I think you said something about wanting to try out my bathtub too."

"I did. I did say that."

Alex makes a little bereft noise and ducks to bite at Eli's neck for a minute before taking an intentional step back, tongue pressed, barely visible, to the swollen curve of his bottom lip.

"Okay." Alex says as if he's trying to convince himself. "Okay. I'm going to shower now. Plan to leave in twenty?"

"Yeah," Eli agrees. "I'll, uh, I'll go let Abuela know."

Someone could probably make a popular reality TV show about grandmothers and altruistic, overly eager NHL players shopping at Walmart together.

Eli can't decide if he's charmed or annoyed.

Shopping with either of them alone is bad enough. If he so much as stops to read the label of a new kind of yogurt, it ends up in the cart. With both of them, however, this turns into a not-so-friendly competition that results in Alex getting his own basket when Abuela refuses to let him pay for anything in the cart she's pushing. Alex fills said basket with things he knows Eli likes, while Abuela sneaks looks into his basket and adds the same products to her cart. Honestly, they're only going to be in town for another forty-eight hours; there's no way Eli is going to drink two liters of sparkling Italian grapefruit soda in that time span.

"Aba," he says finally, exasperated when he catches her trying to subtly fish out the bag of kale chips from Alex's basket while Alex is distracted by a sample pusher.

There'd only been one bag left on the shelf, so she couldn't get a second bag of her own.

"What?" she says innocently.

Alex looks between them, eyebrows raised. "Everything okay?"

"Everything's fine. Did you want to get toothpaste?"

Somehow, they'd both managed to forget theirs, and Eli's parents only stock the house with the blue generic kind. Eli's become spoiled using the fancy Toms shit Alex has, and it seems silly to buy a whole new tube but—

"Oh, yeah. One sec."

"Seriously," Eli says, once Alex is out of earshot. "Sé que no parece, pero en realidad está bastante ansioso por este viaje. Si lo dejo enfocarse en cuidarme, le ayudará a no obsesionarse con otras cosas."

He understands her desire to fuss over him, but letting *Alex* fuss over him is probably the only thing reining in Alex's anxiety right now, and Eli's not about to let his interfering grandmother derail Alex's retail therapy.

"Ah," she says, looking apologetic. "Me preguntaba por qué no estabas haciendo un escándalo," she says. "Bien. Voy a devolver las cosas."

He knew she would understand. She operates the same way, after all. "Gracias."

By the time Alex returns with the toothpaste, Abuela's cart is short a dozen items, and they're talking about the number of people they'll need to feed for Christmas brunch (a lot) and whether they should pick up some eggs in case the chickens have a production rut (probably).

He expects Abuela to switch to English once Alex returns, except she doesn't.

"¿Por qué sigues hablándome en español?" he asks several minutes later after she's enquired about his opinion on mushrooms in Spanish. "Alex no te puede entender."

It doesn't seem that Alex minds them speaking in Spanish, but it's strange she would persist since she usually considers that sort of thing rude if everyone present can't understand.

"Ya sé. Estoy tratando de ayudarte."

But that makes no sense. How is her speaking Spanish *helping* him? It's not like he needs the practice.

"¿Qué quieres decir?"

"Le gusta cuando hablas español. Mira su cara ahora mismo."

Eli glances at Alex and ... okay. Yes, Eli realizes. That's definitely Alex's badly concealed turned-on face. Apparently, he likes it when Eli speaks Spanish.

Interesting.

"¿No lo sabías?" she asks.

"No," he admits, "I didn't know."

"You're welcome," she says.

Dinner is a subdued affair, mostly because they're doing prep work for the next day, but they follow dinner with eggnog and dominoes, which Alex is surprisingly good at, despite having never played before.

Francesca only asks a couple of invasive questions, and his mother only shares a couple of embarrassing baby photos, and his father only makes a couple of vaguely threatening comments.

It's a good night.

Alex does receive a few suspiciously large Amazon packages, which he secrets away with Abuela to wrap in the laundry room and deliver under the tree. But Eli figures his boyfriend being overly generous isn't really something that warrants a fight on Christmas Eve, so he lets it go.

And then it's past 9:00 p.m., and Hawk is yawning where she's half sprawled over his lap. Eli is tucked under Alex's arm, casually leaning into him as Alex tells a story about meeting Cristiano Ronaldo at an Under Armour shoot—Eli's father listens, enraptured, Francesca pretends she's not equally impressed—and it's just—

It's perfect.

There are Christmas carols on, and Abuela is crocheting something and—

He used to dream about this.

About a "someday" in the vague and distant future.

Where someone would love him as much as he loved them.

And that's—Well.

That's definitely what's happening here.

He looks up at Alex, and Alex is looking down at him with a half-smile, eyes crinkled and fond. He's looking at Eli the same way he's been looking at Eli for months, since maybe even before the awkward lurch of a kiss on the living room floor.

And what's worse, Eli knows he's looking at Alex—*has* been looking at Alex—in the same way.

It shouldn't come as a surprise.

He recognizes that, distantly, as he stands.

"You okay?" Alex asks.

"Yeah, I need to—I'm tired. I'm gonna go take a shower."

He knows he's being rude, but he somehow neglected to realize until now that he's in love with Alex.

"I'm in love with Alexander Price," he says to himself in the mirror upstairs a minute later.

And then he says it again, a little breathless, because it's true.

"I'm *in love* with Alexander Price. Fuck."

"Uh. Should I come back later?" Alex asks from the bathroom doorway, and Eli turns to look at Hawk, betrayed. It's her responsibility to let him know if anyone else enters the bedroom.

She is unrepentant.

"So," Eli says since it's not like he has any other options. "I love you. Apparently."

"Okay?"

"I'm—okay? What do you mean 'okay'? This is not okay. This is the opposite of okay."

And that's Alex's hurt face.

"No," Eli says, reaching for him. "I mean—That came out wrong. Sorry. How are you being so calm about this? This is a big deal."

"Because it's not new for me," Alex says. "I've been in love with you for a while."

"A while."

"Yeah."

"All right." Eli takes an intentional breath. "So. We're doing this, then."

"We're doing what?"

"This—we're in love. With each other. That's a thing that's happening."

"Yes," Alex agrees.

"Sorry. This makes things a lot more real, I guess."

"Do you ... not want it to be?"

"No. No, I do. Oh my god, I do. But I thought you'd get tired of me. Or change your mind. And I'd be brokenhearted, and it would be shitty. But you've gone and talked to your agent and management and—Are you really going to come out?"

Alex shrugs. "Yeah. I'm still not ready right *now.* But we're planning for me to tell a few of the core guys after break and the rest of the team at the end of the season—preferably after winning the Cup—so they have the summer to come to terms with it. I'll start telling other people in the organization next season."

"That's soon."

"I know. I don't know how to explain it right. But I was afraid, before. Of what would happen if it got out that I was gay. And I was so preoccupied with that fear it didn't even leave room for me to think about the good things that might come with being out. And then I met you and—"

He takes a breath.

The kind of breath that means he's trying to formulate a sentence he's never said out loud before.

"I was so lonely before you. Except I didn't even realize I was lonely. I thought that was the way I was supposed to be."

Eli's throat is abruptly tight. "Alex."

"So. My point is. There's no going back for me, now."

"Okay," Eli says and sort of throws himself at Alex, and Alex catches him because of course he does.

"Hey," Eli says a minute later, palms pressed to the sides of Alex's neck.

"Hey," Alex agrees, lacing his fingers at the small of Eli's back.

"Te amo," Eli says.

And Alex's face lights up like the fucking sun.

It's not fair.

It's so easy—too easy—for Eli to make Alex smile like that. Eli can't decide if he loves or hates having that ability. He doesn't know if it's one he should be trusted with.

"Yeah?" Alex asks softly and so happy.

"Yeah," Eli says, and he means it.

He means it.

Means it in a big, terrifying, unwieldy way.

Alex grins, ducking to kiss him, and Eli closes his eyes and tries not to be scared.

"Good," Alex says. "I love you too."

Acknowledgements

I SAID IN THE dedication that this was for fan fiction writers. Fic was the first place I ever found stories about LGBTQ+ characters that had happy endings (often written by real-life queer adults!), and for a confused queer middle-schooler absolutely drowning in spiritual guilt, this discovery may very well have changed my life.

So I'd like to acknowledge all the Livejournal and Fanfiction.net and Dreamwidth writers who introduced me to the wonder of writing, the GeoCities and print zine folks that came before them, and the Tumblr and AO3 creators now. I wish I could thank every commenter on every fic I've written and every friend I've made through fandom, but that would take too long. So instead, I'll list a few that have been particularly encouraging in my writing journey: labelleizzy, plagues-and-pansies, thelincyclopedia, vibraphone1o1, beaniebaneenie, parrishsrubberplant, emmalovesdilemas, cesperanza, david_of_oz, emmagrant01, venomwrites, protectorowl, shutupsavannah, nearlydeparted, maybeitstimetoearnmybluebead, a-isoiso, actual-corgi, draskireis, ursamajorstudio, littlewhitedragonlet, aussie-twat, onetwistedmiracle, echrai, sleepanon, pcr-and-glamour, pianosinthewild, glutenwitch, sexydexynurse, springbok7, gnomer-denois, ohdarlingwatson, zzledri, oatdog, sparrowink, sadkazzoosolo, lambbabies and everyone I've forgotten to add or who has changed their username. I like your shoelaces.

Thanks to S. Stein for the series title, David for the wisdom, and Chelsea for the goats.

Thanks to my cover artist (fandom's own) Jick, and my editor who took my love of em dashes and other writing quirks in stride. Thanks to my longest-running fans: my parents and uncle R, my baffled-by-fandom-but-nonetheless-supportive partner, and, of course, Deacon, the best dog in the world.